GOODREADS CHOICE AWARDS FINALIST

———————

"This imaginative yet very real look
into war-torn Syria is a must."
—*BOOKLIST* (starred review)

"*The Map of Salt and Stars* is important and
timely because it shows how interconnected two
supposedly opposing worlds can be.
Our many stories are part of the same larger
tale, part of the same larger map."
—*THE NEW YORK TIMES BOOK REVIEW*

"Every once in a while, a novel comes along
that perfectly aligns with the cultural moment.
The Map of Salt and Stars is that kind of
book. . . . The finest literature tells the one story
that stands in for the many. John Steinbeck
accomplished this with the Joad family in
The Grapes of Wrath, and Joukhadar has
written a novel with a similar weight and
power about Syria's displaced people."
—*THE PROVIDENCE JOURNAL*

"A stunning dual narrative about families,
crossing borders, and finding a new way home
. . . and two unforgettable heroines united by
their bravery and hope."
—SHELF AWARENESS FOR READERS
(starred review)

"VIVID AND URGENT." —THE NEW YORK TIMES BOOK REVIEW

Praise for
The
Map of Salt
and Stars

"In Joukhadar's intoxicating debut, the past and present are brought to life, illuminating how, in exile, neither can exist without the other. With clear, exquisite prose, Joukhadar unspools a brightly imagined tale of family and grief, mapmaking and migration. This important book is a love letter to the vanished—and to what remains."
—Hala Alyan, author of *Salt Houses*

"*The Map of Salt and Stars* is the sweeping, thrillingly ambitious tale of Nour, Rawiya, and their parallel searches for home. In twin narratives that unfold eight hundred years apart, Joukhadar captures the unrelenting courage of those who persist amid the trials of exile. A truly remarkable debut."
—Kirstin Chen, author of *Bury What We Cannot Take* and *Soy Sauce for Beginners*

"In [his] rich and often heartbreaking debut, Syrian American writer Zeyn Joukhadar tries to make whole the broken memory of a nation caused by the deadly conflict in Syria. . . . Joukhadar's vibrant prose brings to life the very real and devastating struggle that many refugees continue to face today."
—Daily Beast

"[An] ambitious debut . . . Joukhadar plunges the Western reader full force into the refugee world with sensual imagery."

— *Kirkus Reviews*, starred review

"Nour's family constantly endures hardship . . . but her young, honest voice adds a softer, coming-of-age perspective to this story of loss, hope, and survival."

— *Booklist*, starred review

"In many ways, *The Map of Salt and Stars* is at once a testament to the brutality of the current Syrian conflict and a reverent ode to ancient Arabian history. . . . *The Map of Salt and Stars* presents an Arab world in full possession of its immense historical and cultural biography, marred by its modern tragedies but not exclusively defined by them."

— *BookPage*

"In [his] debut novel, Joukhadar's jeweled prose sparkles with fanciful images. . . . *The Map of Salt and Stars* is, in sum, a hero's odyssey, a spellbinding geography of family and hope."

— Shelf Awareness

"A haunting, inspiring story, one which remains in this reviewer's mind long after the final pages. Highly recommended."

— *Historical Novels Review*

"Joukhadar's language choices lilt with melancholy, elegy, and images so distinct that the reader can smell, taste and touch the world of [his] creation. . . . The major message of *The Map of Salt and Stars* is that the destruction of a homeland threatens to destroy history, but that history can never die as long as people, like Nour, choose to remember."

— *BookBrowse*

The
Map *of* Salt
and Stars

The
Map *of* Salt
and Stars

———— ✱ ————

Zeyn Joukhadar

ATRIA PAPERBACK

New York   London   Toronto   Sydney   New Delhi

ATRIA
PAPERBACK

An Imprint of Simon & Schuster, Inc.
1230 Avenue of the Americas
New York, NY 10020

First Atria Paperback edition March 2019

ATRIA PAPERBACK and colophon are registered trademarks of Simon & Schuster, Inc.

For information about special discounts for bulk purchases, please contact Simon & Schuster Special Sales at 1-866-506-1949 or business@simonandschuster.com.

The Simon & Schuster Speakers Bureau can bring authors to your live event. For more information or to book an event, contact the Simon & Schuster Speakers Bureau at 1-866-248-3049 or visit our website at www.simonspeakers.com.

Interior design by Kyle Kabel
Map by David Atkinson/Hand Made Maps Ltd.

Manufactured in the United States of America

10   9   8

The Library of Congress has cataloged the Touchstone edition as follows:
Names: Joukhadar, Jennifer Zeynab, author.
Title: The map of salt and stars / Jennifer Zeynab Joukhadar.
Description: First Touchstone hardcover edition. | New York : Touchstone, [2018]
Identifiers: LCCN 2017029991 (print) | LCCN 2017039000 (ebook) | ISBN 9781501169106 (eBook) | ISBN 9781501169038 (hardcover) | ISBN 9781501169052 (softcover)
Subjects: LCSH: Refugee children—Syria—Fiction. | Refugees—Syria—Fiction.
Classification: LCC PS3610.O67925 (ebook) | LCC PS3610.O67925 M36 2018 (print) | DDC 813/.6—dc23
LC record available at https://lccn.loc.gov/2017029991

ISBN 978-1-5011-6903-8
ISBN 978-1-5011-6905-2 (pbk)
ISBN 978-1-5011-6910-6 (ebook)

For the Syrian people,
both in Syria and in diaspora,
and for all refugees

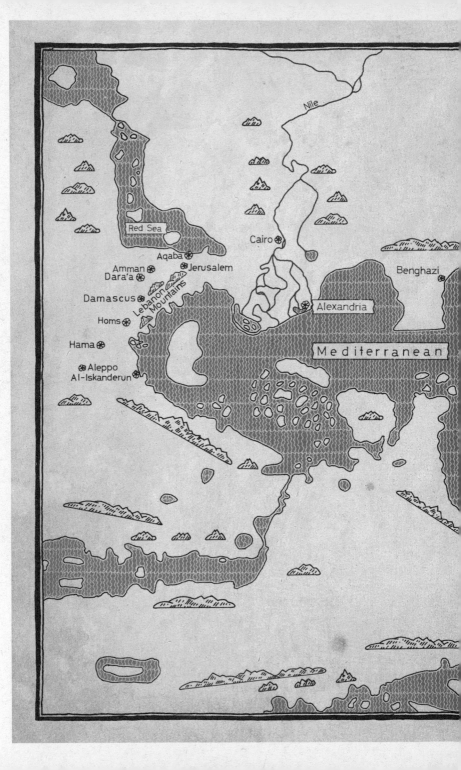

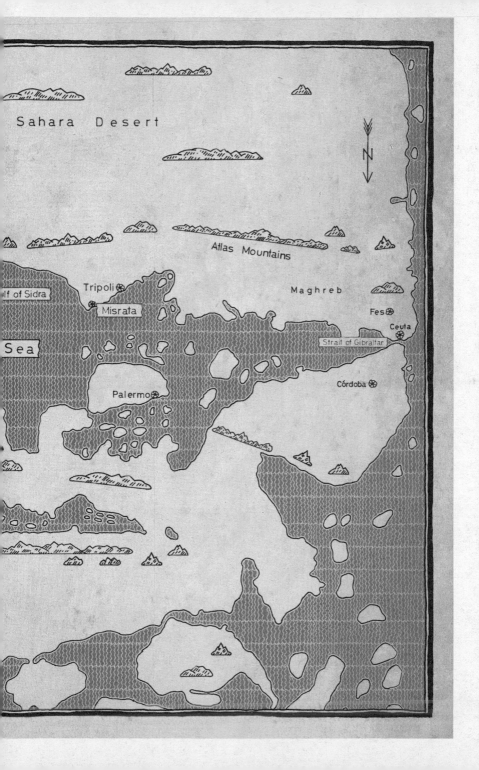

PART I

SYRIA

O
beloved, you are
dying   of a broken heart. The
women wail in the street. The rice is scattered and
the lentils spilt. The good linen is trampled. The wadi runs
with tears. In what language did you tell me that all we
loved was a dream? I don't dream in Arabic anymore—I don't
dream at all. When I close my eyes, I see yours, beloved: two pale
stones in the river. Your arms, the cracked marble of centuries. The stars
your blanket, the hills stepping-stones. We used to move so fast when we
were dreaming. Cup the sea in your navel and wash away my tears. My
tears and yours mingle, beloved. I did not want to sleep, not now, but I
must. Why do we fear death when we should fear falling down? It all
collapses around us—your whispering green, the arc of lightning in
your wrists. The ransomed planets twist away. Is this where
my mother was born, in the curve of your spine? I
bleed; my flesh is teething wings. Until the dawn
when I flee—never will I return, O
beloved—until that morning, wrap your
pale hands around me. Fill my mouth with
the fog of your breath, your heart a
pomegranate seed. O beloved, you
are with me to the end, until the
sea divides, until our broken
memory makes us
whole.

The Earth and the Fig

*

The island of Manhattan's got holes in it, and that's where Baba sleeps. When I said good night to him, the white bundle of him sagged so heavy, the hole they dug for him so deep. And there was a hole in me too, and that's where my voice went. It went into the earth with Baba, deep in the white bone of the earth, and now it's gone. My words sunk down like seeds, my vowels and the red space for stories crushed under my tongue.

I think Mama lost her words too, because instead of talking, her tears watered everything in the apartment. That winter, I found salt everywhere—under the coils of the electric burners, between my shoelaces and the envelopes of bills, on the skins of pomegranates in the gold-trimmed fruit bowl. The phone rang with calls from Syria, and Mama wrestled salt from the cord, fighting to untwist the coils.

Before Baba died, we hardly ever got calls from Syria, just emails. But Mama said in an emergency, you've got to hear a person's voice.

It seemed like the only voice Mama had left spoke in Arabic. Even when the neighbor ladies brought casseroles and white carnations, Mama swallowed her words. How come people only ever have one language for grief?

That winter was the first time I heard Abu Sayeed's honey-yellow voice. Huda and I sat outside the kitchen and listened sometimes, Huda's ash-brown curls crushed against the doorjamb like spooled wool. Huda couldn't see the color of his voice like I could, but we'd both know it was Abu Sayeed calling because Mama's voice would click into place, like every word she'd said in English was only a shadow of itself. Huda figured it out before I did—that Abu Sayeed and Baba were two knots on the same string, a thread Mama was afraid to lose the end of.

Mama told Abu Sayeed what my sisters had been whispering about for weeks—the unopened electricity bills, the maps that wouldn't sell, the last bridge Baba built before he got sick. Abu Sayeed said he knew people at the university in Homs, that he could help Mama sell her maps. He asked, what better place to raise three girls than the land that holds their grandparents?

When Mama showed us our plane tickets to Syria, the O in my name, Nour, was a thin blot of salt. My older sisters, Huda and Zahra, pestered her about the protests in Dara'a, things we had seen on the news. But Mama told them not to be silly, that Dara'a was as far south of Homs as Baltimore was from Manhattan. And Mama would know, because she makes maps for a living. Mama was sure things would calm down, that the reforms the government had promised would allow Syria to hope and shine again. And even though I didn't want to leave, I was excited to meet Abu Sayeed, excited to see Mama smiling again.

I had only ever seen Abu Sayeed in Baba's Polaroids from the seventies, before Baba left Syria. Abu Sayeed had a mustache and an orange shirt then, laughing with someone out of the frame, Baba always just behind him. Baba never called Abu Sayeed his brother, but I knew that's what he was because he was everywhere: eating iftar on Ramadan evenings, playing cards with Sitto, grinning at a café table. Baba's family had taken him in. They had made him their own.

When spring came, the horse chestnut trees bloomed white like fat grains of rock salt under our window. We left the Manhattan apartment and the tear-encrusted pomegranates. The plane's wheels lifted like birds' feet, and I squinted out the window at the narrow stripe of city where I'd lived for twelve whole years and at the hollow green scooped out by Central Park. I looked for Baba. But with the city so far down, I couldn't see the holes anymore.

Mama once said the city was a map of all the people who'd lived and died in it, and Baba said every map was really a story. That's how Baba was. People paid him to design bridges, but he told his stories for free. When Mama painted a map and a compass rose, Baba pointed out invisible sea monsters in the margins.

The winter before Baba went into the earth, he never missed a bedtime story. Some of them were short, like the one about the fig tree that grew in Baba's backyard when he was a little boy in Syria, and some of them were epics so twisting and incredible that I had to wait night after night to hear more. Baba made my favorite one, the story of the mapmaker's apprentice, last two whole months. Mama listened at the door, getting Baba a glass of water when he got hoarse. When he lost his voice, I told the ending. Then the story was ours.

Mama used to say stories were how Baba made sense of things. He had to untangle the world's knots, she said. Now, thirty thousand feet above him, I am trying to untangle the knot he left in me. He said one day I'd tell our story back to him. But my words are wild country, and I don't have a map.

I press my face to the plane window. On the island under us, Manhattan's holes look like lace. I look for the one where Baba is sleeping and try to remember how the story starts. My words tumble through the glass, falling to the earth.

AUGUST IN HOMS is hot and rainless. It's been three months since we moved to Syria, and Mama doesn't leave her tears on the pomegranates anymore. She doesn't leave them anywhere.

Today, like every day, I look for the salt where I left my voice—in the earth. I go out to the fig tree in Mama's garden, standing heavy with fruit just the way I imagined the fig Baba once had in his backyard. I press my nose to the fig's roots and breathe in. I'm belly-down, stone heat in my ribs, my hand up to the knuckles in reddish dirt. I want the fig to carry a story back to Baba on the other side of the ocean. I lean in to whisper, brushing the roots with my upper lip. I taste purple air and oil.

A yellow bird taps the ground, looking for worms. But the sea dried up here a long time ago, if it was ever here at all. Is Baba still lying where we left him, brown and stiff and dry as kindling? If I went back, would I have the big tears I should have had then, or is the sea dried up in me forever?

I rub the smell of water out of the fig's bark. I'll tell Baba our story, and maybe I'll find my way back to that place where my voice went, and Baba and I won't be so alone. I ask the tree to take my story in its roots and send it down where it's dark, where Baba sleeps.

"Make sure he gets it," I say. "Our favorite, about Rawiya and al-Idrisi. The one Baba told me every night. The one where they mapped the world."

But the earth and the fig don't know the story like I do, so I tell it again. I start the way Baba always did: "Everybody knows the story of Rawiya," I whisper. "They just don't know they know it." And then the words come back like they had never left, like it had been me telling the story all along.

Inside, Huda and Mama clank wooden bowls and porcelain. I forgot all about the special dinner for Abu Sayeed tonight. I might not be able to finish the story before Mama calls me in to help, her voice all red edges.

I press my nose to the ground and promise the fig I'll find a way to finish. "No matter where I am," I say, "I'll put my story in the ground and the water. Then it'll get to Baba, and it'll get to you too."

I imagine the vibrations of my voice traveling thousands of miles, cracking through the planet's crust, between the tectonic plates we learned about in science class last winter, burrowing into the dark where everything sleeps, where the world is all colors at once, where nobody dies.

I start again.

*   *   *

EVERYBODY KNOWS THE story of Rawiya. They just don't know they know it.

Once there was and was not a poor widow's daughter named Rawiya whose family was slowly starving. Rawiya's village, Benzú, lay by the sea in Ceuta—a city in modern-day Spain, a tiny district on an African peninsula that sticks into the Strait of Gibraltar.

Rawiya dreamed of seeing the world, but she and her mother could barely afford couscous, even with the money Rawiya's brother, Salim, brought home from his sea voyages. Rawiya tried to be content with her embroidery and her quiet life with her mother, but she was restless. She loved to ride up and down the hills and through the olive grove atop her beloved horse, Bauza, and dream of adventures. She wanted to go out and seek her fortune, to save her mother from a life of eating barley-flour porridge in their plaster house under the stony face of Jebel Musa, watching the shore for her brother's ship.

When she finally decided to leave home at sixteen, all Rawiya had to take with her was her sling. Her father had made it for her when she was a little girl throwing rocks at dragonflies, and she wouldn't leave it behind. She packed it in her leather bag and saddled Bauza by the fig tree next to her mother's house.

Now Rawiya was afraid to tell her mother how long she'd be gone, thinking she might try and stop her. "I'm only going to the market in Fes," Rawiya said, "to sell my embroidery."

But Rawiya's mother frowned and asked her to promise to be careful. The wind came strong off the strait that day, rattling through her mother's scarf and the hem of her skirt.

Rawiya had wrapped a red cloth around her face and neck, hiding her new-cut hair. She told her mother, "I won't stay longer than I have to." She didn't want her mother to know she was thinking of the story she'd heard many times—the story of the legendary mapmaker who came to the market in Fes once a year.

The wind opened and closed Rawiya's scarf like a lung. The painful thought struck her that she did not know how long she would be gone.

Mistaking her daughter's sadness for nerves, Rawiya's mother smiled. She produced a misbaha of wooden beads from her pocket and set it in Rawiya's hands. "My own mother gave me these prayer beads when I was a girl," she said. "God willing, they will comfort you while you are away."

Rawiya hugged her mother fiercely and told her she loved her, trying to commit her smell to memory. Then she climbed into Bauza's saddle, and he clicked his teeth against his bit.

Rawiya's mother smiled at the sea. She had once traveled to Fes, and she hadn't forgotten the journey. She said to her daughter, "Every place you go becomes a part of you."

"But none more so than home." Rawiya meant this more than anything else she'd said. And then Rawiya of Benzú nudged her horse until he turned toward the inland road, past the high peaks and fertile plains of the mountainous Rif where the Berbers lived, toward the Atlas Mountains and the teeming markets of Fes beckoning from the south.

The trade road wound through limestone hills and green plains of barley and almond trees. For ten days, Rawiya and Bauza picked their way along the winding road ground flat by travelers' shoes. Rawiya reminded herself of her plan: to find the legendary mapmaker, Abu Abd Allah Muhammad al-Idrisi. She planned to become his apprentice, pretending to be a merchant's son, and make her fortune. She would give a fake name—Rami, meaning "the one who throws the arrow." A good, strong name, she told herself.

Rawiya and Bauza crossed the green hills that separated the curved elbow of the Rif from the Atlas Mountains. They climbed high slopes topped by cedar forests and cork oak trees where monkeys rustled the branches. They curved down through valleys spread with yellow wildflowers.

The Atlas Mountains were the stronghold of the Almohads, a Berber dynasty seeking to conquer all of the Maghreb, the northern lands of Africa to the west of Egypt. Here, in their lands, every sound made Rawiya uneasy, even the snuffling of wild boar and the echoes of Bauza's hooves on the limestone cliffs. At night, she heard the distant sounds of instruments and singing and found it hard to sleep. She thought of the stories she had heard as a child—tales of a menacing bird big enough to carry off elephants, legends of deadly valleys filled with giant emerald-scaled snakes.

Finally, Rawiya and Bauza came upon a walled city in a valley. Caravans of merchants from the Sahara and from Marrakesh spilled onto the grassy plain dotted by eucalyptus trees. The green rope of the Fes River split the city in two. The folded chins of the High Atlas cast long shadows.

Inside the city gates, Bauza trotted between plaster houses painted shades of rose and saffron, green-crowned minarets, and gilded window arches. Rawiya was dazzled by jade roofs and jacaranda trees blooming the color of purple lightning. In the Medina, merchants sat cross-kneed behind huge baskets of spices and grains. The tapestry of colors caught Rawiya's eye: the frosted indigo of ripe figs, rust-red paprika. Hanging lanterns of wrought metal and colored glass sent tiny petals of light that clung to shadowed alleyways. Children pattered through the streets, smelling of tanned leather and spices.

Rawiya guided Bauza toward the center of the Medina, where she hoped to find the mapmaker. Dust from the streets painted Bauza's hooves. In the heat of the day, the shade of carved stone and mosaic tile felt cool, refreshing. The cries of merchants and spice vendors deafened Rawiya. The air was thick with sweat and oil, the musk of horses and camels and men, the bite of pomegranates, the sugar-song of dates.

Rawiya searched among the merchants and travelers, interrupting sales of spices and perfumes and salt, asking about a man who traveled weighted down by leather-bound scrolls and parchment-paper sketches of the places he'd been, a man who had sailed the Mediterranean. No one knew where to find him.

Rawiya was about to give up when she heard a voice: "I know the person you seek."

She turned and saw a man stooped in front of a camel tied to an olive tree. He sat in a small courtyard off the Medina, his white turban wrapped close around his head, his leather shoes and robe coated in a sheen of travel dust. He beckoned her closer.

"You know the mapmaker?" Rawiya stepped into the courtyard.

"What do you want with him?" The man had a short, dark beard, and his eyes as he studied her were polished obsidian.

Rawiya added up her words. "I am a merchant's son," she said. "I wish to offer my services to the mapmaker. I wish to learn the craft and earn a living."

The man smiled, catlike. "I'll tell you where to find him if you can answer three riddles. Do you accept?"

Rawiya nodded.

"The first riddle," the man said, "is this." And he said:

> Who is the woman who lives forever,
> Who tires never,
> Who has eyes in all places
> and a thousand faces?

"Let me think." Rawiya patted Bauza's neck. Hunger and heat had made her light-headed, and the mention of a woman made her think of her mother. Rawiya wondered what her mother was doing—probably watching the sea for Salim. It had been so long since she'd had Baba to watch the water with her, to walk with her through the olive grove. Rawiya remembered when she was small, how Baba had told her of the sea, that shape-shifting woman who never died—

"The sea," Rawiya cried. "She lives forever, always changing her moods. The sea has a thousand faces."

The man laughed. "Very good." And he continued with the second riddle:

> What is the map you take with you
> everywhere you go—
> the map that guides, sustains you
> through field and sun and snow?

Rawiya frowned. "Who always carries a map? Do you mean a map in your head?" She looked down at her hands, at the delicate veins running the length of her wrist and palm. But then— "The blood makes a kind of map, a net of roads in the body."

The man eyed her. "Well done," he said.

Rawiya shifted from foot to foot, impatient. "The third riddle?"

The man leaned forward:

> What is the most important place on a map?

"That's it?" Rawiya said. "That's not fair!"

But the man only pursed his lips and waited, so she groaned and thought hard.

"Wherever you are," Rawiya said, "at that moment."

The man smiled that cat smile again. "If you knew where you were, why would you need the map?"

Rawiya tugged at the sleeve of her robe. "Home, then. The place you're going."

"But you know that, if you're going there. Is that your final answer?"

Rawiya knitted her brows. She had never even seen a map before. "This riddle has no answer," she said. "You wouldn't use a map unless you didn't know where you were going, unless you'd never been to a place before—" Then it made sense, and Rawiya smiled. "That's it. The most important places on a map are the places you've never been."

The man stood. "Do you have a name, young riddle-solver?"

"My name is—Rami." Rawiya looked back at the Medina. "Will you bring me to the mapmaker? I answered your questions."

The man laughed. "My name is Abu Abd Allah Muhammad al-Idrisi, scholar and mapmaker. I am honored to make your acquaintance."

The blood pounded in Rawiya's chest. "Sir—" She bowed her head, flustered. "I am at your service."

"Then you will sail with me to Sicily within a fortnight," al-Idrisi said, "to the palace of King Roger the Second of Palermo, where a great and honorable task awaits us."

*　*　*

I'VE JUST STARTED telling the story of Rawiya to the fig tree when a blast in the distance shakes the stones under my belly. My guts jump. A low booming comes from some other neighborhood of the city, deep and far away.

It's the third explosion in three days. Since we moved to Homs, I've heard booming like that only a couple of times, and always far off. It's gotten to be like thunder—scary if you thought about it too much, but not something that would hit your house. I've never heard it this close before, not near our neighborhood.

The vibrations fade. I wait for another clap of fear, but it never comes. I pull my fingers from the soil, my thumbs still twitching.

"Nour." It's Mama's voice, warm cedar brown, its edges curled up into red. She's annoyed. "Come in and help me."

I kiss the fig's roots and replace the dirt. "I'll finish the story," I tell it. "I promise I will."

I roll back onto my heels and brush the dirt off my knees. My back is in sunshine, my shoulder blades stiff with heat. It's a different kind of hot here, not like in New York where the humidity makes you lie on the floor in front of the fan. Here it's dry-hot, and the air chaps your lips until they split.

"Nour!"

Mama's voice is so red it's almost white. I tumble toward the door. I dodge the stretched canvas drying by the jamb, the framed maps Mama doesn't have room for in the house. I plunge into the cool dark, my sandals slapping the stone.

Inside, the walls breathe sumac and sigh out the tang of olives. Oil and fat sizzle in a pan, popping up in yellow and black bursts in my ears. The colors of voices and smells tangle in front of me like they're projected on a screen: the peaks and curves of Huda's pink-and-purple laugh, the brick-red ping of a kitchen timer, the green bite of baking yeast.

I kick off my sandals by the front door. In the kitchen, Mama mutters in Arabic and clucks her tongue. I can understand a little but not all of it. New words seem to sprout out of Mama all the time since we moved—turns of phrase, things I've never heard that sound like she's said them all her life.

"Your sisters. Where are they?" Mama's got her hands in a bowl of raw meat and spices, kneading it, giving off a prickly cilantro smell. She's changed her dress slacks for a skirt today, a papery navy thing that swishes against the backs of her knees. She's not wearing an apron, but she hasn't got a single oil stain on her white silk blouse. I don't think I've ever seen her with a speck of oil or a smear of flour on her clothes, not in my whole life.

"How should I know?" I peek up at the counter to see what she's making—sfiha? I hope it's sfiha. I love the spiced lamb and pine nuts, the thin disks of dough crisp with oil.

"Mama." Huda comes in from the pantry, her rose-patterned headscarf streaked with flour, her arms heavy with jars of spices and bundles of herbs from the garden. She sets them down on the counter. "We're out of cumin."

"Again!" Mama throws up her hands, pink with the juice from the lamb. "And lazy Zahra, eh? She's helping me with the pies, or what?"

"Locked in her room, I bet." No one hears me. Zahra's been buried in her phone or holed up in the room she shares with Huda since we moved to Homs. Since Baba died, she's gotten mean, and now we're trapped with her. The little things that kept us going while Baba was sick are gone now—buying candy from the bodega, playing wall ball on the sides of buildings. Mama makes her maps, Zahra plays on her phone, and all I do is wait out these long, scorching days.

Zahra and Huda always talked about Syria like it was home. They knew it long before Manhattan, said it felt more real to them than Lexington Avenue or Eighty-Fifth Street. But this is my first time outside Amreeka—which is what they call it here—and all the Arabic I thought I knew doesn't add up to much. This doesn't feel like home to me.

"Find your sister." Mama's voice is edged with red again, a warning. "Tonight is special. We want everything ready for Abu Sayeed, don't we?"

That melts me, and I slink off to find Zahra. She's not in her and Huda's room. The pink walls sweat in the heat. Zahra's clothes and jewelry are all over her wrinkled comforter and the rug. I pick my way over crumpled jeans and tee shirts and a stray bra. I inspect a bottle of Zahra's perfume on the dresser. The glass bottle is a fat purple gem of a thing, like a see-through plum. I spray some on the back of my hand. It smells like rotten lilacs. I sneeze on Zahra's bra.

I tiptoe back down the hall, through the kitchen, and into the living room. My toes burrow into the red-and-beige Persian rug, upsetting Mama's careful vacuuming. A stereo blasts something that's supposed to be music: red guitar trills, the black splotches of snare drums. Zahra is stretched out on the low couch, tapping at her smartphone, her legs over the floral-printed arm. If Mama saw her with her feet on the cushions, she'd scream.

"Summer twenty-eleven," Zahra drawls through the heat. "I was supposed to graduate next year. Class of 2012. We planned out our road trip to Boston. It should have been the best year ever." She turns her face to the cushions. "Instead I'm here. It's a hundred and fifty degrees. We have no air conditioning and Mama's dumb dinner tonight."

She can't see me boring holes into her back with my eyes. Zahra's just jealous that Huda got to graduate high school before we left New York and she didn't. She doesn't seem to care at all how I feel, that it sucks just as much to lose your friends at twelve as it does at eighteen. I rap her back with my hand. "Your music is dumb, and it's not a hundred and fifty degrees. Mama wants you in the kitchen."

"Like hell." Zahra covers her eyes with her arm. Her black curls hang over the side of the couch, her stubborn eyes half-lidded. The gold bracelet on her wrist makes her look haughty and grown-up, like a rich lady.

"You're supposed to help with the pies." I tug on her arm. "Come on. It's too hot to keep pulling you."

"See, genius?" Zahra lurches up from the couch, taking lazy barefoot steps to shut the stereo off.

"We're out of cumin again." Huda comes in, wiping her hands on a rag. "Want to come?"

"Let's get ice cream." I wrap myself around Huda's waist. Zahra leans back on the arm of the couch.

Huda jerks her thumb toward the kitchen. "There's a bowl of lamb with your name on it," she says to Zahra, "if you don't want to run errands."

Zahra rolls her eyes to the ceiling and follows us out.

Mama calls to us as we pass by. "I want you on your best behavior tonight—all of you." She tilts her chin down, eyeing Zahra. She pushes cilantro into the lamb, breaking the meat apart. "And here—in my pocket." She motions to Huda, holding up her oily hands. "A little extra, in case the price is up again."

Huda sighs and tugs a few coins from the pocket of Mama's skirt. "I'm sure it won't be that much."

"Don't argue." Mama turns back to the lamb. "All the prices have gone up in the last month. Bread, tahina, the cost of life itself. And listen—watch your steps. No crowds, none of this crazy business. You go to the shop and then directly home."

"Mama." Huda picks at dried flour paste on the countertop. "We won't have any part in that."

"Good." Mama glances at Huda. "But today is Friday. It will be worse."

"We'll be careful." Huda leans an elbow against the counter and looks up from under her thick eyebrows, beading with sweat. She shuffles her feet, setting the hem of her gauzy skirt rippling. "Really."

For the last two months, Mama's always told us to avoid crowds. It seems like they pop up everywhere—crowds of boys protesting, people protesting the protests, rumors of fighting between the two. The last few weeks, they've gotten so loud and angry you can hear their singing and megaphones all through the neighborhood. Mama's said for months that being in the wrong place at the wrong time can get you arrested—or worse. But just like in New York, keeping to yourself doesn't always keep trouble from finding you.

I close my eyes and try to think about something else. I take in all the spice smells in the kitchen, so deep I feel the colors in my chest. "Gold and yellow," I say. "Oil dough. I knew it was sfiha."

"That's my Nour, in her world of color." Mama smiles into the lamb, sweat shimmering at her hairline. "Shapes and colors for smells, sounds, and letters. I wish I could see it."

Huda tightens her shoelaces. "They say synesthesia is tied to memory. Photographic memory, you know? Where you can go back and see things in your mind's eye. So your synesthesia is like a superpower, Nour."

Zahra snickers. "More like a mental disorder."

"Stop your tongue." Mama scrubs her hands. "And get going, for heaven's sake. It's nearly five." She shakes the water from her fingers before drying them. "If the power goes out again today, we'll have to eat cold lamb and rice."

Zahra heads for the door. "Good memory, huh? Is that why Nour has to tell Baba's al-Idrisi story a hundred times?"

"Shut up, Zahra." Without waiting for an answer, I slip my sandals back on and open the front door. I swipe the curtain of fig branches out of my face. Dappled shadows shift on Mama's maps. Past our little alley, blue marbles of conversation roll in to us. A car swishes by, its tires making a gray hiss. A breeze rustles white on chestnut leaves.

I walk in the shadow of the building next door, shuffling my feet while I wait for Huda and Zahra to tie their shoes. I want to press my face back into the salty garden dirt, but I poke the corners of Mama's canvases with my toe instead. "Why does she leave all these out here?"

Huda comes out. She glances at the painted maps, stacked to dry like dominoes against the wall. "There are too many to keep them in the house," she says. "They dry faster outside."

"The maps don't sell like they did when we first moved," Zahra says, wiping sweat off the side of her face. "Have you noticed?"

"Nothing is selling," Huda says. She takes my hand. "Yalla. Let's get moving."

"What do you mean, nothing's selling?" I ask. Huda's rose-print hijab blocks the sun. "We buy pistachios and ice cream all the time."

Huda laughs. I've always liked her laugh. It's not like Zahra's, all nose and squeak. Huda's got a nice laugh, pink purple and flicked up at the end. She says, "Ice cream always sells."

The sidewalk stones steam like bread out of the oven, and they scorch the bottoms of my feet through my plastic sandals. I hop from foot to foot, trying not to let Zahra see.

We turn out onto the main street. A few cars and blue buses circle the square, twisting across the lanes. It's Ramadan, and people seem to drive slower, walk slower. After iftar tonight, gray-haired men with full bellies will stroll the streets of the Old City with their hands clasped behind their backs, and the tables outside the cafés will be full of people drinking coffee with cardamom and passing the hoses of narghiles. But for now, the sidewalks are almost empty, even in our mostly Christian neighborhood. Mama always says Christians and Muslims have been living side by side in this city for centuries, that they'll go on borrowing each others' flour and sewing needles for years to come.

Zahra's gold bracelet bounces, throwing ovals of light. She eyes Huda's scarf. "Are you hot?"

Huda side-eyes Zahra. "It doesn't bother me," she says, which is what she's been saying ever since she started wearing her scarf last year, when Baba first got sick. "Aren't you?"

"Maybe I'll wear one when I'm older." I reach up and skim my fingers along the cotton hem. "This one's my favorite, because of the roses."

Huda laughs. "You're too young to worry about that."

"You don't even have your period yet," Zahra says.

"Bleeding isn't what makes you grown-up," I say.

Zahra inspects her fingernails. "Clearly you don't know what it means to be grown-up."

We turn at a brick building. Heat shimmers off the pavement and Zahra's black hair. Down the street, a man sells tea from a silver jug on his back, but he doesn't have any customers. He eases himself down on the steps of an apartment building, swiping sweat from under his hat.

Huda says, "I wear the scarf to remember I belong to God."

I think about our bookshelf in the city, the Qur'an and the Bible next to each other, Mama and Baba swapping notes. Mama used to take us to Mass some Sundays and, on special Fridays, Baba used to take us to jum'ah.

I ask, "But how did you decide?"

"You'll understand one day."

I cross my arms. "When I'm older, right?"

"Not necessarily." Huda takes my hand again, teasing my arms apart. "Just when it's time."

I frown and wonder what that means. I ask, "How old is Abu Sayeed?"

"Why?"

"Isn't tonight his birthday dinner?"

Zahra laughs. "Do you ever pay attention, stupid?"

"It's not her fault," Huda says. "I never told her." She holds her hand against her thigh, her fingers stiff. There's something she doesn't want to say. "Today is the anniversary of when Abu Sayeed lost his son. Mama didn't want him to be alone."

"He had a son?" Somehow I never imagined Abu Sayeed had a family.

"And we're distracting him with food." Zahra kicks a stone and scoffs. She seems almost mad. "We're worried about cumin."

"Abu Sayeed is like us, then." I look down at my plastic sandals, still warm from the sidewalk stones. "He's missing the most important ingredient."

Huda slows. "I never thought of it that way."

The sun simmers the silver roofs of cars.

"We should play the spinning game with him," I say.

"Spinning game?" Zahra smirks. "Speaking of made-up."

Huda checks the street signs before we turn away from the tangle of cars. It's cooler on this street, and the iron gates of the houses are curled into the shapes of birds and the tufts of flower petals. Ladies in crisp dresses water window boxes or fan themselves on the upper balconies. We pass an apartment walk lined with tiny gray-and-white filler stones, and I snatch up a pebble.

Huda catches hold of my hand again and squeezes it. "The spinning game. How do you play?"

I grin and hop in front of her, walking backward and swinging my hands. "You close your eyes and spin around. Then the magic takes you through different levels, and you count to ten while you spin, one spin for each level you pass through. And when you open your eyes, things look the same, but the magic makes them different."

"Levels?" Huda tilts her head toward voices in the distance, the black-orange bark of a car backfiring.

"Levels of existence," I say, throwing open my arms. "There are different layers of realness. Like, underneath this one there's another one, and another one below that. And all kinds of things are going on all the time that we don't even know about, things that won't happen for a million years or things that already happened a long, long time ago." I forget to watch my feet, and I bump into the curb.

"Nour's lost it again," Zahra says.

"So these other realities," Huda says, "are running alongside ours at the same time, like different streams from the same river? Then there's a level where Magellan is still sailing around the world."

"And one where Nour is normal," Zahra says.

"Maybe there's a level where we all have wings," Huda says.

"And a level where you can hear Baba's voice," I say.

The words grab me like my feet have grown roots to the other side of the planet, and I stop in front of the iron gate of an apartment building. Panic weights my ankles, the thought that I'll never hear Baba's stories or his voice ever again. Why should a missing story leave a hole so big when it's just a string of words?

The sun drip-drops along the leaves of a crooked poplar tree. The next block is lined with closed halal markets and shawarma shops, the owners heading home early to break their fasts. No one says anything, not even Zahra. Nobody mentions how Mama and Baba used to live here in the Old City when Huda and Zahra were just babies. Nobody brags that they know all the shops and restaurants, how even Zahra speaks better Arabic than me.

But I feel all those things, the not-homeness of this city, the way nobody hangs blankets from their balconies in New York, the way Central Park had maples instead of date palms, how there are no pizza shops or pretzel carts on the streets here. How Arabic sounds funny in my mouth. How I can't walk to school with my friends anymore or buy gum from Mr. Harcourt at the newspaper stand. How sometimes this city shakes and crumbles in the distance now, how it makes me bite my lip so hard I swallow blood. How home is gone. How, without Baba, I feel like home is gone forever.

Huda's sneakers cast red afternoon shadows. The high-faced buildings yawn up in yellow and white stone. Somewhere, someone pours a cup of water out a window, and the droplets run white and silver into the gutter.

Huda squats on the pavement in front of me, gathering the folds of her skirt between her knees. "Don't cry," she says. She dries my face with a cotton rose at the corner of her hijab.

"I'm not crying, Huppy." I stab my forearm across my face, missing my nose. Huda gathers me in, and I curve into her like a wooden bowl. She's warm, the heat of her red gold like McIntosh apples. I press my face into the soft folds of fabric where her scarf meets the neck of her shirt.

Zahra's laugh is all gravel. "What are you, three? Nobody calls her Huppy anymore."

I scowl at Zahra. "Shut up."

Huda says, "She can call me whatever she wants to."

We walk in silence the rest of the block to the spice shop, and Zahra dodges my eyes. I should have known better: nobody's said much about Baba since the funeral. Baba is the ghost we don't talk about. Sometimes I wonder if Mama and Huda and Zahra want to pretend his sickness never happened, that the cancer never rotted out his liver and his heart. I guess it's like the spinning game: sometimes you'd rather be on any magic level but your own. But I don't want to forget him. I don't want it to be like he was never here at all.

Inside the spice shop, the shelves are crammed with sacks and tins and jars, open bowls of red and yellow powder with tiny handwritten Arabic labels. A man smiles at us from behind the counter, spreading his hands. I stand on my tiptoes and push my fingers toward baskets filled with whole cloves and uncrushed cardamom pods like tiny wooden beads.

Zahra catches Huda's arm, her bracelet swinging.

"I thought of a game," Zahra says in English so I can understand. She smiles in a slow, careful way that comes off cruel somehow. "Why doesn't Nour ask for the cumin?"

Huda darts her eyes to Zahra. "Don't."

"She can practice her Arabic," Zahra says. She smiles with her hand over her mouth.

The man behind the counter waits, scratching the shadow of his incoming beard. I wipe my clammy hands on my shorts. Outside, the tea seller passes by. "Shai," he calls. "Shai."

I think, *Tea*. I know that word. I squint at a pull in a tapestry at the back of the shop, a loose thread of red wool shivering under the fan. I try to remember how to say *I want*.

The man behind the counter asks me a question I don't understand. His voice is all green swoops, the black dots of consonants between them.

"Come on," Huda says, "that's not—"

"Ana . . ." My voice breaks the heat, and everyone goes quiet. I've only gotten out the word *I*. I swallow, digging my nails into my palm, using the pain to stop my nerves. "Ana . . ." My brain pricks and boils, sunbursts of red and pink, and even though I can remember the word for cumin—*al-kamun*—I still can't remember how to say *I want*. I must have said it dozens of times, but with everyone staring at me, my mind goes blank.

The man says, "Shu?" What?

"Ana—al-kamun."

The man is laughing.

"You're cumin?" Zahra belly-laughs.

"Ana ureedu al-kamun." I say it again, louder. "I know how to say it. I do!"

"I know you do," Huda says.

Zahra haggles with the shopkeeper. I press my cheek into my shoulder to keep my eyes from tearing. The coins clink in Huda's palm while she counts them. On the way out, she lets out a low whistle. Over my tangle of frizz, she whispers to Zahra, "Mama was right about the price."

On the way home, Zahra refuses to shut up. "What kind of Syrian are you? You don't even speak Arabic."

Inside, I hear what she really means: that I don't know what it means to be Syrian.

"Stop it," Huda says.

"Oh right," Zahra says, "I forgot. You're not Syrian. You don't even remember our house before we moved to the States. You're American. All you speak is English."

"Zahra!" Huda squeezes her nails into Zahra's arm.

Zahra howls, wrenching her arm away. "It was just a joke. God."

It doesn't feel like a joke. Zahra crosses her arms, her gold bracelet winking on her wrist. I want to rip it off and throw it in the street for a car to flatten.

We walk back through the empty streets of Old Homs, the sun red and long, the shopkeepers ratcheting down their metal blinds. I look around for the exposed roots of a date palm or a patch of clean, bare earth.

We pass the bald ankles of the crooked poplar again. I imagine pressing my fingers into the rough bark, folding my voice into the roots.

Like Two Hands

*

So that was how Rawiya, a poor girl from the village of Benzú in Ceuta on the tip of Africa, came to sail the Mediterranean. She wanted to claim her fortune, to come back and provide for her mother. Her father, who had died when she was a little girl, would have wanted her to. Her brother, Salim, was always gone, sailing the sea with a crew of merchants. His was a hard life, and her mother never knew when his ship would come in, or if it would come at all.

So Rawiya left home as Rami with her father's sling and her mother's misbaha, joining al-Idrisi's expedition to map the whole Mediterranean—which wasn't called the Mediterranean then, but the Bahr ar-Rum, the Roman Sea or the Sea of Byzantium, or sometimes the Bahr ash-Shami, the Sea of Syria. To al-Idrisi, that sea was the gateway to much of the inhabited world.

But Rawiya's world was her mother's plot of land in Benzú, the tiny olive grove and the seashore, the markets of Ceuta, the harbor on Punta Almina. Rawiya had never imagined the world to be so big.

They sailed for more than three weeks before the crew began to murmur that they would soon be nearing Sicily. Heartened by this news, Rawiya stood on the deck of the ship with her cloak around her shoulders. The salt air lifted some of the seasickness that had plagued her for weeks. With a pang, she thought of Bauza belowdecks.

Al-Idrisi joined her, the breeze curling rough fingers through his short beard, his sirwal trousers flapping in the wind. He told her he loved to watch the sea, and the salt spray carved its way through the lines around his eyes, as though he'd done decades of laughing rather than reading. Rawiya wanted to tell him how she had watched the shore as a child, how Salim was somewhere on those waves right now, but she held her tongue. Even now, her mother would be waiting for him—and, she realized with a wave of shame, beginning to worry about her.

"I spent years of my life in towers and libraries, reading and reciting." Al-Idrisi's chest swelled with sea air. "There came a time I didn't want to waste any more years than I already had." He told Rawiya to be careful of words: "Stories are powerful," he said, "but gather too many of the words of others in your heart, and they will drown out your own. Remember that."

Still they could see no land anywhere, only the sea around them, the mast groaning and the sails creaking like the wings of a hundred albatrosses.

"You don't belong in a library," Rawiya said. "You seem at home here, like you were in the mountains and the Medina."

"I once had family who would have agreed with you." Al-Idrisi lowered his eyes to the water and set his elbows on the rail. "The sea has a way of showing us ourselves," he said. "Sometimes I think we came from the water, and it calls us to return. Like one palm reaching for the other."

Rawiya turned back to the carved waves. She had thought the open sea would be flat, like a mirror or a coin. But it had colors and shapes, turning green or black under an approaching storm. Sometimes it was red and purple and silver and white gold. It had sharp edges. It had its tempers, its blue spells, its fits of laughter.

"The sea is a child," Rawiya said, "curious, hungry, and joyful at the same time."

Al-Idrisi said, "The sea takes what shape she will."

And Rawiya thought of her father, the way he used to watch

the shore while he tended the olive grove, the way he used to say the sea changed her shape in the night. She thought of her father's short illness, the way he had slipped irretrievably into the dark like slipping off a ladder in the olive trees. She had never gotten to give him a real good-bye.

Al-Idrisi smiled again, softer this time. "Get some rest," he said, "so you have your strength when we dock at Palermo. There will be much for both of you to learn." For al-Idrisi had brought along a second apprentice, a boy named Bakr, who was seasick and resting belowdecks. "You, Rami," al-Idrisi said, "are the more resilient of my apprentices." And he laughed.

Then al-Idrisi was gone. His laugh bounced off the cargo ropes and the mast. It became Rawiya's father's laugh, all green ripples like sun-scrubbed olive leaves. Over the railing, Rawiya saw her reflection in the surface of the water, her red turban and her boyish face. She didn't recognize herself.

*   *   *

AFTER BABA'S FUNERAL, after the neighbors and my teachers and Baba's friends from work had all left, Mama put away the casseroles and set the carnations in a glass of water. The stems were too long for the glass, so when Mama turned away, Huda picked it up and set the glass by the window, with the heads of the flowers leaning on the cabinet.

Mama didn't notice. It was like she was in a place where nothing could get to her. She moved around the kitchen like the breeze from a fan, flicking on the gas stove and overfilling the teakettle.

While we sat there not saying anything, Mama dotted away the smudges in her makeup and brewed a pot of strong sage tea, the kind that made my friends nauseous, the kind I loved.

The tea tasted like Saturday mornings when Mama would walk with us to the bodega for vegetables and everything smelled like fruit and water. It tasted like fall afternoons when Baba would take me to Central Park and stand down in the empty sprinkler pool to make himself my height while we tossed a ball. It tasted like Baba's bedtime stories.

So I asked Mama for the only one of Baba's stories I was sure she knew. I asked her to tell the story of Rawiya and al-Idrisi.

Mama leaned across the table and curved her eyebrows up above her nose, thinking of how to start. But even though she'd always listened, Mama had never told stories like Baba did. She said, "Many years ago, a brave girl named Rawiya left Ceuta for Fes to seek her fortune."

I said, "But that's not how Baba starts. What about the fig tree and Bauza?"

Mama moved her chair closer to mine and smoothed our woven placemats. "Remember," she said, "even Baba said that no two people tell a story quite the same."

I picked a thread from the weave of my placemat. I didn't want a new version of the story, I wanted Baba's. "I miss the way he told it."

Mama said, "None of us have his voice." She took my hands and stopped my picking. My fingers left a gap in the braided threads, shorn borders.

That night, after I had put on my pajamas and pattered into the kitchen to check on the carnations, I found the first rings of salt on the handle of the teakettle. They made outlines of oceans I had never known before, countries I had never seen.

ON THE WAY home from the spice shop, Zahra begs us to stop at a jewelry store. Down the street, policemen stand grumpy in the heat under a portrait of the president. Shouts echo from somewhere deeper in the neighborhood. Aside from the policemen and Huda and me, the block is empty. I turn away, dangling the jar of cumin in my hand.

"Can't she hurry up?" I kick at pebbles. "Abu Sayeed will be at the house any minute."

"Don't worry," Huda says. "Abu Sayeed lives a street down from the spice shop. If he were on his way, we'd run into him."

I huff and frown. "But what does Zahra need more stuff for, anyway? She's already got that gold bracelet with the stupid patterns."

"You mean the filigree?" Huda shrugs and tightens her shoelaces. "People like different things. Zahra likes to look . . . a certain way."

"But she acts ugly." My shadow on the sidewalk has legs as long as giraffes' necks. They look ridiculous attached to my sandals.

Huda glances into the jewelry shop, then takes my hand. "How about some ice cream?"

We plod across warm stone and concrete toward a tiny ice cream parlor a block away. "Zahra has a lot to figure out," Huda says, "but she's not a bad girl."

"What's there to figure out?" I finger the jar of cumin, watching the windows over the dress shops and the cafés. Women lean out and shake their rugs and curtains, releasing dust. "She's mean now. She's the worst sister ever."

"Don't say that." Huda and I split bread-and-butter around a crack in the sidewalk. Huda raises her arm and lets her wrist curve down to my hand like a dancer's. The breeze fans her skirt behind her like the steel-blue wake of a ship. "Some people take time to find out who they are," she says. "They get pushed around by all these little things, the stuff the world says is important. It's like being blown around in the wind."

I finger the lid of the cumin jar. The powder inside shifts from its own crests and peaks. "That doesn't make it okay to be a jerk."

"No. It doesn't."

A man on a bike passes us. His shadow runs along the wall, flitting over door columns in stripes of black and white. The banner over the ice cream parlor ripples in the heat, and I can just about read the letters. The glass paneling is open to let the heat out. A table and two plastic chairs sit outside, empty.

Inside, towels and framed pictures decorate the walls, and fans tickle our faces with warm air. Every now and then the power gives a little, and the lights dim to brown. The fans stall.

Huda is fasting for Ramadan, so she just orders a cone for me. A man scoops out a chunk of ice cream and shapes it with his hands, rolling it in pistachios and sticking it in a cone wrapped with wax paper. Behind him, a man in a paper hat and tee shirt pounds ice cream with a wooden mallet. He looks up at me when I thank him, noticing my accent.

Outside, the heat attacks my ice cream. I catch the drips with my tongue, holding the cumin in one hand and the cone in the other.

I take a bite out of my ice cream, shivering at the cold. I ask Huda, "How come you're not like that—caught in the wind?"

"I decided there were more important things to me than what the world wants," she says.

"Is that why you put on the scarf after Baba got sick?" Steam escapes my mouth.

Huda hands me a napkin. I run the paper over the creases in my knuckles, sticky with sugar.

"God got me through," she says. "Call him what you want. God in English. Allah in Arabic. The universe. There is a goodness in the world that got me through, that taught me it's important to know who you are. You can get lost." Huda leans over and kisses the top of my head. "You have to listen to your own voice."

A big boom interrupts us, just like the one I heard in the garden. Shards of ceramic tile crumble down from the building's upper floors. I want to think of it like thunder—loud and harmless—but it's too close for that. I flinch and clench my teeth, putting purple dents in Huda's arm with my fingernails.

"What is that?" I pry my sticky fingers out of Huda's skin. "Where is it coming from?"

Huda frowns. "That sounded closer than this morning."

We hurry back to the jewelry store. I finish my ice cream, licking the sugar off my nails. It tastes wooden, like the fear has gone to my taste buds.

Huda leans into the jewelry store and calls for Zahra. I put my palms to the concrete, feeling the last of the vibrations. I think I can feel the foundations of the city still trembling. I wonder how long the buildings can take it. I think back to a rumor I heard Zahra whispering to Huda last week, that the shells came down where the power went out. They didn't know I heard. But I've heard lots of rumors—crowds turning on each other, friends taking sides and picking up guns, people accusing each other of making trouble. But Mama and my sisters and I don't want to make trouble. I just want Mama's maps to sell, and I want Zahra to stop teasing me, and I want to hear Baba's stories again. I think about the price of cumin. I hope the stove and the lights are still running at home. I remember the fans wavering in the ice cream shop.

Zahra tumbles out with Huda, her jeans and her tee shirt sticky with the heat. We turn onto Quwatli Street by the old clock tower and pass the red-and-yellow Kasr ar-Raghdan hotel. Everything is louder here, even the shouting that seems to come from everywhere at once. The ice cream slides around in my stomach.

A cab circles the rotary, blaring Umm Kulthum on the radio, and drowns out the shouting. Umm Kulthum is my favorite, and she always will be. Mama and Baba used to dance to her in our apartment in the city. After Baba got sick, the CD sat in the stereo, crusting over with dust. I used to put the music on, hoping they would dance again. But they didn't.

We skirt the square, heading home under latticed apartment windows and closing shops. This has to be where all the shouting is coming from: a crowd of boys Huda's age gathered around the old clock tower, their voices chalk and chocolate. The crowd bursts with plum shouts like the notes of oboes, the instrument I love most.

I imagine what Mama would say if she were here. The crowds make me want to run, but the three of us stand on the corner, watching. Some of the boys are just old enough that their beards are starting to come in, lopsided and stubbly. Others wear striped polo shirts or button-downs, their jeans whiskered at the thighs and the knees. I look closer and notice a few women moving among them. Arabic fills the air like a flock of startled birds. I wonder who's on what side. I wonder if there are sides at all.

"This is the most intense I've seen it," Huda says.

Zahra shuffles her sneakers like she's getting ready to bolt. She says, "The most in the last two months, definitely."

The shouting pounds and bleats like angry music. I ask, "What are they saying?" No one hears me. Fear presses into me like a thumb. I realize I'm sweating when I smell my deodorant, yellow green like chicken soup. How weird, to smell like deodorant. Isn't that the opposite of its job?

Then Huda puts her hand on my back and guides us away from the noise. We dive down another street. The shouts shrink to black dots, megaphone static. You can still hear them all over the Old City, a thrumming that won't go away, no matter how loud you talk over it.

The alley that leads to our house is crowded with orange light when we come home. We turn in between the buildings, and the sounds finally start to fade. A new map dries outside, leaning on the garden gate. Mama must have gotten impatient with waiting for us to come back and worked on her maps to pass the time. She's always doing something, never still. I look for the shimmer of oil paint, but it's flat. I inspect the gold compass rose, the swoops of Mama's hand-painted Arabic script. The letters make different colors than the English letters do, even the ones I can't sound out. I can read some of them: the blue curve of the *waw*, the burnt-orange *haa*, the sulfur-yellow *ayn*.

Huda opens the gate. In the garden, more framed maps are scattered under the fig tree, drying in the shade. Mama must have moved them to make room for the new ones. The stones steam while the afternoon fades, mixing the scent of chemicals and earth. The low sun turns the yellow walls of our house to brass, falling in slats across the wooden shutters and Mama's hanging window boxes of herbs.

Inside, Mama plunks her brushes in a mug of water, harder than she normally does. Most days I don't think anything of it: Mama is always busy with her maps now, painting the world for professors and people in stiff jackets who come to the house to buy them. But today isn't like other days, because the power's gone out and Mama's set candles in the windows and on the dining table. Every couple of moments I catch myself willing the lights to come on again, hoping they've only flickered out like the lights at the ice cream shop. They don't.

Mama slams a towel in the sink and ruffles her hair when we come in. When she sees me looking at the candles, she forces a smile.

"Where's the turpentine?" Zahra says.

Mama smooths her hair. "Acrylics today."

"They smell a lot better." I make like I'm plugging my nose. Huda pinches my ear. "Ow!"

Mama half closes her eyes like she does when she's enjoying something but she doesn't want you to know she's enjoying it. Huda sets the jar of cumin in the cabinet, and Zahra goes to wash up. I help Mama put away her brushes and wipe off her palette. I feel like I can hear bright Arabic vowels still floating around the room from Mama's clients this morning. When I was little, she only ever used to talk to Baba in Arabic. Now she speaks Arabic to everyone and talks in English only to me. It makes me feel like I don't belong.

"What color is the letter *E*?" Mama asks.

I roll my eyes. The color game again. "Yellow."

"And the letter *A*?"

"Red. It's been red ever since I learned how to read, Mama."

Mama always plays this game with me. She asks me what color is this letter or that number, like she's testing me that they stay the same. Shouldn't she know by now that they do? While I answer her questions, she glances at the map she's been painting and then hangs a white sheet over it.

I make a face. "That makes it look like a dead body."

Mama laughs, which means I'm not in trouble. "I painted something new," she says. "A special map. I painted it one layer after another."

I look at her more closely. "Why would you paint something just to paint over it again?"

"It has to be done that way," Mama says. "Sometimes it's not enough to put something down once. Sometimes it takes more than one try to get it right."

"Like that time Zahra put henna in Huda's hair while she was sleeping." I laugh. "And the next day we had to give her red highlights when it wouldn't come out."

Mama laughs too. "Just because you add to something doesn't mean it was broken. Maybe it just wasn't finished."

Then something inside her cracks, and Mama sits down next to me at the table. She smiles, but she looks stretched and old, like she's tugging the tangles out of a ball of yarn that's buried inside her, like she's searching for something she's dropped in the dark.

"Like the old tales you like," she says, smiling with the good times in her eyes, the times when we had Baba. "You have to weave two stories together to tell them both right." She presses her palms together, then opens them. "Like two hands."

Zahra comes in and opens the cabinet, looking for something. Her gold bracelet glints in the afternoon light. The jar of cumin rests just inside the cabinet door, still warm from Huda's hands, its bronze powder shuddering when Zahra jostles the shelf.

The Lion's Request

*

For another week, the bow of Rawiya's ship sliced the sculpted waves. After a monthlong journey, they came at last to a rocky coastline with palm trees running down to the sea. Rounding the coast with Monte Gallo to their right, they entered a calm bay, where Palermo unfolded below the shadow of the green mountains. Rawiya stood on the deck and listened to the flurry of languages from the dock—Italian, Greek, Arabic, Norman French.

The city of Palermo lay on the northwestern shore of Sicily, a flourishing and cultured island shared by Arabs and Greeks, Christians and Muslims alike. Gold-green palms clustered around white marble churches and dome-capped mosques. To the north of the city stood the limestone peak of Monte Pellegrino, curved like the hump of a whale.

"Welcome," al-Idrisi said as they stepped off the ship, "to Palermo, seat of the Norman king, Roger the Second."

Al-Idrisi's second apprentice, Bakr ibn al-Thurayya, emerged from belowdecks. A lanky, black-haired boy dressed in a rich olive cloak, he was the son of Mahmoud al-Thurayya, a famous merchant whose family name was the Arabic word for the constellation the Greeks called the Pleiades—the Seven Sisters.

Al-Idrisi clapped a hand on Bakr's back. "I met Bakr's father in Córdoba many years before," he said. "I promised to teach Bakr everything I knew."

As al-Idrisi greeted King Roger's servants, Bakr turned to Rawiya. "You're sure to learn much as al-Idrisi's apprentice, Rami," he said. "Did you know he traveled to Anatolia at sixteen? Al-Idrisi comes from a line of nobles and holy men. They say he is descended from the Prophet, peace be upon him."

Rawiya nodded and held her tongue, anxious not to give herself away. But Bakr, who was a curious sort of boy, asked, "Did you come to Fes with a caravan? I came with a company of spice merchants. My father arranged for me to meet al-Idrisi in Fes. He said a few years apprenticing would be good for me."

Rawiya smiled in spite of herself. "I came alone," she said, "on horseback."

"From Ceuta?" Bakr said. "You're lucky you weren't killed by bandits."

Now al-Idrisi, who had been listening to this conversation, gave his catlike smile and said, "I chose Rami for the wit and courage God gave him. Remember that, Bakr. You would do well to borrow some of that nerve yourself."

King Roger's servants met Rawiya, Bakr, and al-Idrisi at the docks and led them to the palace. They passed under cream-colored arches, crowds of palmettos, and the church of St. John of the Hermits with its decorative stonework and red domes in the Arab style. The palace lay not far from the harbor, its windows embellished with carvings of roses and vines, its wooden gates decorated with gold filigree. Servants took their mounts to the stables. Rawiya kissed Bauza good-bye, slipping him some date sugar as he nuzzled her neck.

"So this," Bakr said, "is the horse that brought you safely to Fes."

Rawiya patted Bauza's mane. "I've had him since he was a foal," she said. Bauza was in the prime of his years, with the better part of a decade of good health left in him. "He's a good, strong horse," Rawiya said, "and braver than most."

They marched three abreast into the gilded hall of the Royal Palace of Palermo. Servants in gold and white silk stood at attention beneath the frescoed ceilings. The king came forward, dressed in the riches of his kingdom. His indigo robe was hemmed with red velvet and clasped with gold brooches. His red silk gloves were embroidered with golden eagles, and his red mantle was embroidered with a rearing lion, its muscles detailed with rubies. Its mane and haunches were decorated with rosettes indicating the stars of the constellation Leo, for in those days, people believed that the king was granted his power by the heavens.

"My friend." King Roger clasped al-Idrisi's hands, refusing to let him bow. "You have returned at last." Long ago, King Roger had heard of al-Idrisi's knowledge of mapmaking and his study of the measurement of the earth and had asked him to his court. Since then, al-Idrisi had only left Palermo to find suitable apprentices for the task King Roger had given him.

"Wise king," replied al-Idrisi, "dear friend who has protected me from my enemies. I am at Your Majesty's service. I have returned as I promised—to create for you at last, God willing, a true wonder of mapmaking."

"It is I," said King Roger, "who am at your service."

They left for the king's study, talking of their plans. A servant with hair light as the moon led Rawiya and Bakr out of the hall, across a wide courtyard where birds sang from the balconies.

On the other side of the courtyard, the servant pushed aside a wooden statue, revealing a damp passage. He instructed Rawiya and Bakr to tell no one of the secret door, for it was a hidden tunnel used only by the servants to deliver food to the king's guests.

They passed through the sandy-floored tunnel. The servant opened a door on the other side, and they stepped into the servants' kitchen. Men in white linens bustled about, bowls and pots in their thick arms.

The servant seated them at a wide table, away from the chaos of the kitchens, and presented them with steaming bowls of lentil stew and hard-crusted bread. Fresh winged peas were brought in from the garden and roasted with whole fish and eggplant. Rawiya and Bakr dipped their bread in ricotta and butter drawn from long-necked earthenware vessels. The palace kitchen throbbed with the heat of roasting fat, the burnished scent of eggplant skin, and the glow of orange zest.

After supper, the servant returned with a tray of oblong pastries armored with almond slivers. Rawiya, who had just had the richest meal of her life, took a delicate loop of dough in her hand and asked what it was.

"These delicacies are made from a dough called pasta reale," the servant said. This was a type of almond paste, a Sicilian specialty made by the nuns of Martorana in the convent beside the church of Santa Maria dell'Ammiraglio.

Rawiya bit into her pastry. The warmth of almond and the tang of citrus bloomed on her tongue. She thought with longing of her mother's date cookies and remembered with guilt the barley porridge her mother was probably eating. For the first time, the full weight of having left her behind lay heavy on Rawiya's shoulders. She vowed that one day her mother too would taste this pasta reale—a dough fit for a king.

THAT NIGHT, THE slivered moon held Rawiya's eyelids open. Rising from her bed, she went out into the courtyard and looked up through the pistachio trees at the seven pinpricks of the Pleiades—Thurayya. She thought of Bakr's father. How like the rich, she thought, to name themselves for the stars.

On the other side of the silent courtyard, Rawiya noticed the dark shadow of a door that had been left ajar. Curious, she ducked inside—into utter darkness.

Blinking in the blackness, Rawiya froze at the sound of shuffling coming from farther in the room. She stubbed her toe and whispered curses. When she groped for a candle, she felt rows of something soft and powdery, like folds of animal skin.

She shrank back. Could these be elephants? She had heard tales in the markets, where merchants sold ivory by the tusk and mothers told wild stories to frighten children. She whispered, "I've wandered into the elephant stables."

A low voice said, "No, you are not in the elephant stables, if such things even exist." A man emerged from the dark, silhouetted against a window.

Rawiya approached, embarrassed. "I was lost—"

The man said, "You will always have wakeful companions in this hall."

A torch was lit. Rawiya stood in a vast four-story library, face-to-face with King Roger himself, dressed in a white sleeping gown.

Rawiya scrambled into a bow. "Forgive me, Your Majesty—"

King Roger laughed. "There is no need for apologies. Your master is a dear friend." He explained that he often came to the library at night. He motioned to the shelves of books, their spines polished gold, tawny brown, and russet leather. "Anyone who wants companionship and knowledge will find what they seek here," he said. "We are among friends."

"Pardon me for saying so," Rawiya said, "but isn't it strange for a king to wander his palace at night, reading?"

"Perhaps," King Roger said. "But I love running my fingers along the spines of old friends, poring over volumes of mathematics. I love botany and philosophy, geography and myth. So I wait until all is quiet and the moon is shining, and then I wander as I please."

"Forgive me for interrupting you," Rawiya said.

King Roger waved her apology away. "Come now, my boy," he said, "you are a guest in my house. You may wander these avenues with me whenever you like." He pulled a volume down from the shelf and held it out to her.

Rawiya touched the gilded pages. Ptolemy's *Geography*. "This place must hold the knowledge of all the world," she said.

King Roger smiled. "If your master completes his quest, it will.

This is the task al-Idrisi and I have undertaken: not only to map the Mediterranean, but to create a map of the entire world, a map grander and more accurate than any the world has ever seen."

*   *   *

WE CAN'T EAT until after the sun has gone down because Huda and Abu Sayeed are fasting for Ramadan. The low sun hums in my neck. While we wait for Abu Sayeed, the red shadows get longer. I pick pebbles from in between the fig's roots and choose slices of old granite stiff as floor slats from the rocky soil in the garden. I pull my treasures from my pockets, the ones I collected on our walk to the spice shop for Abu Sayeed—a few domes of pink rock, a shard of turquoise embedded in concrete, small white stones from apartment driveways. Across the alley, our neighbors light candles and check their fuse boxes. I'm glad the buildings block out the shouting from the square.

I think Abu Sayeed has loved every stone he ever saw, even the ones with rough edges, even the ones that get shiny when they're wet but dry dull and disappointing in the sun. Over a summer's worth of afternoons, I've found out Abu Sayeed knows all about stones: boulders, salt crystals, big black slabs with veins of quartz in them, slender pebbles flat as coins. I wonder how much Abu Sayeed knows, and how come. I think back to the time Baba crouched next to me on a wrinkled sheet of rock in Central Park and told me what a glacier was, and I imagine Abu Sayeed telling Baba the same thing.

I hear his voice before I see him.

"Little cloud?"

I spin around, my hands full, my hair swaying like the fig leaves.

Abu Sayeed comes up through the alley. His honey-yellow voice gets louder, laughing and singing in Arabic. The color is brighter and clearer than over the phone. When we first got to Homs three months ago, Abu Sayeed's voice was the only thing that felt familiar.

I run to him when he swings open our iron gate. "Abu Sayeed!"

He steps over canvases and around drying maps, dodging wet paint with the hems of his linen pants. He's changed from the way he looked in Baba's old Polaroids: his mustache has wrapped around his chin and formed a beard, his forehead has wrinkled in the sun, his shoulders have sloped down like he's carried something heavy too long. But Abu Sayeed still has the same web of laugh lines around his gray eyes, and his leathery cheeks are always scooped up into a grin.

He reaches out his hands to me. I meet him between the gate-posts, jostling my treasures in my pockets and my fists. I bounce and shuffle and pull out the stones I've collected, beaming and breathless. "I've got more for our collection."

Abu Sayeed opens the bowls of his palms. I hand him the stones I collected on the dusty streets of the Old City, by the side of the road and behind vegetable shops. I've tried all summer to show him something he hasn't seen before. I haven't managed to stump him yet, not even when I brought him slices of mica in glittering layers, not even when I brought him a chunk of black basalt like porous cheese, not even when I brought him gypsum roses and spears of sandstone, scratchy as Baba's cheeks.

Abu Sayeed knows all the stones by heart. They speak to him, he says. They speak to him, and he tells me their secrets. I don't know if I believe him, but in the pockets of my heart without any words, I want to believe.

Every stone is different. Some stones come from a few towns away, but some are whole continents removed. I once brought Abu Sayeed, not knowing it, a handful of green marble from China, teal lumps of copper from Turkey, thick spears of granite from Africa. Every stone is different and every stone's the same: glittering and ready to whisper its secrets, if I listen.

Today, Abu Sayeed holds my offerings to his eyes and his ears. Zahra and Huda come out and stand close by, waiting, hiding their smiles. Zahra stands barefoot and taps her painted toenails to her ankle, adjusting her phone in the pocket of her jeans.

Abu Sayeed pulls the stories from the stones. He rattles them, and dust comes unsettled from their cracks. He strokes the rough skin of the rock, closing his eyes. Finally, he nods and blinks and closes his fingers around the stones.

"So?" I look up from the treasures in Abu Sayeed's hands. "Did I find it?"

"Not yet, I'm afraid." Abu Sayeed sits down in the garden with his legs crossed under him. "Don't feel bad. I've never seen it either."

I point at a dagger of calcite in his palm. "That's not it?"

Abu Sayeed laughs. "No, little cloud," he says. "You must keep looking."

I draw close to his knees. "You must have seen it. You've seen every stone in the whole world." I can't believe there's a rock on the planet that hasn't gotten warm in Abu Sayeed's palm.

"Ah, but this stone is unique in all the earth." Abu Sayeed motions for us to come close. "The rarest and most precious gem, so incredible it lacks a name."

I frown, trying to look like I'm not convinced, but it only half works. "How do you know it exists if it's got no name?"

"My little cloud," he says, "always the skeptic. Jinn have told men many things they found hard to believe."

Zahra crosses her arms. "Kids' stories."

Abu Sayeed's eyes get round and white. "Oh no, little one. The jinn are as real as you or me. But most of them were sealed in cramped prisons long ago. They wait there to be freed, guarding the knowledge of the ancient world."

"What about the stone?" I ask.

Abu Sayeed laughs and throws up his hands. "Impatient!

"Hundreds of years ago, a group of travelers came upon an old brass bottle stoppered up with lead. When they opened the bottle to polish it, green fog emerged in terrifying shapes—giant birds, lions, serpents. In the center of the fog was a strange man with a face like a thunderbolt. It was a jinni, locked away for centuries. In return for his freedom, the jinni told the travelers of a mysterious stone and charged them with finding it. Though the stone's name had been lost to time, he said, they would know it by its color in the light."

"Its color?" Huda asks.

"In shadow, the stone is purple as ripe beets," Abu Sayeed says. "In sunlight, it glints a searing green, like an emerald."

I can tell by how Huda squints and Zahra sneaks a glance at her phone that they don't believe him. I would never admit it, but I think I would have believed anything he said.

I've been searching street and souq for Abu Sayeed's nameless stone all summer, but I haven't found it. I ask Huda to look for glints of purple and green when we climb to the top of the olive grove outside the city, but she hasn't spotted anything yet. Sometimes she lets me sit on her shoulders, and then I can see everything—Homs below with its satellite dishes and mazes of concrete apartment buildings, the Orontes River west of the city center, and the white-haired Lebanon Mountains far away. Up there, I can see everything but what I'm looking for.

We all go in together when Mama calls us. Abu Sayeed comes to dinner once a week, even though Mama invites him all the time. She says he doesn't come more often because he's lonely in that way that makes a person pace the space between the window and the door. I think Abu Sayeed is the kind of lonely that misses one specific person. Today I wonder: is he lonely for Baba, or his son?

"We made a special dinner," I say when we walk inside. I slip off my sandals so Mama doesn't yell at me for wearing my shoes in the house, and Abu Sayeed does the same. Huda's set the table with our best china, and Mama's set a vase of blue wildflowers in the middle. The power's still out, and the candles are already halfway down. Wax dots Mama's good tablecloth, the white one with the gold embroidery.

"A special dinner?" The skin around Abu Sayeed's eyes crinkles when he smiles.

But I can't say more. I want to say I miss Baba like he misses his son, but I can't. I want to ask if we're both missing Baba, if we're both missing the same person. But the words stay stoppered up inside, too heavy to come out.

A dark-brown boom claps the house. I lift the curtain on the kitchen window, looking for clouds. Three days ago, a tiny speck dashed itself to the ground far off. After the boom, a plume of gray dust came up like ink in a glass of water. I felt scared then, but only in the way you feel when you watch a thunderstorm pass by; as long as it's far away, you aren't afraid of getting struck.

Now I wait for the vibrations to fade. I try to convince myself that it's not what I think, that I'm watching the purple sky through the curtains for rain. But it's not thunder, and no rain comes. I don't smell the cold green of thunderstorms, like we had in the city. I used to stick my head out the window and breathe in over and over, trying to hold it in my nose before it was gone, that clean smell of electricity and water. Today all I smell are green curls of sulfur, the stink of ash.

I wish for the power to come back on, for the lights to flicker to life.

My blood thumps in my shins. I grab an empty glass and go to the tap to fill it for Abu Sayeed. Nothing comes out.

I twist the handle closed, then open again. The pipes hiss and clack, but the tap is dry as slate. I stick my head into the sink and peer up into the spigot. No water. A hundred tiny spiders crawl up the backs of my legs and my shoulders, the feeling that something is wrong.

Mama comes in and sets the sfiha on a wide ceramic serving dish.

"The water isn't working," I tell her. I twist the cold and the hot again to show her what I mean.

She sets the dish down and creases her mouth shut, stomping

over to the fridge. She opens it quick to not let the cold out and shoves a jug of water into my arms. "Don't keep opening it," she warns me, and turns back to the sfiha. "First the power, then the water. I had a feeling it might be like that today. Don't drink too much. That jug is all we have."

I look from Abu Sayeed's glass in my hand to the alley outside the window, the night coming on. I wonder if our neighbors felt the vibrations. "But Mama—"

"But nothing. Fill that glass and sit down already, won't you? You're making me nervous, flitting around like that."

I set the glass on the table and try to lift the jug. It's heavy and slippery with condensation. I set the jug down on the table, trying to get a better grip. A newspaper is hanging off the stack of mail, a big headline and a picture of a city sticking like an arm into the sea. I can make out some of the words in Arabic, the names of Morocco and Spain.

Below the headline is a photo of a man laughing, leaning against a doorjamb. He's got a big round dumpling of a belly and brown pony's eyes. I feel like I've seen him before, but I can't place him. The name under the picture is circled in red ink, too small to read.

"What are you doing over here? Give me that." Mama takes the jug from me, hurrying into the dining room with the dish of sfiha in her other hand. "Yalla, sit and eat with your sisters."

Mama sets down the jug and the dish. She adjusts the candles before sitting down with her napkin in her lap. I push the glass to Abu Sayeed, and Mama fills it.

"I can't apologize enough for the power," Mama says while she pours. Her face is flushed rose. "I don't know what's going on."

"I don't mind." Abu Sayeed waves her away. "The power was out at my house as well."

I think, Abu Sayeed's house too? The spiders crawl up my collarbones.

If Mama is surprised, she doesn't show it. She flaps her fingers at us until we unfold our napkins in our laps. "I have to thank you," she says. "Two professors were here today and bought several maps. They said they were friends of yours."

Abu Sayeed scoots his chair closer to the table, his shoulders sloping even farther down. He smiles. "Your husband, God rest him, was as close to me as my hand to my heart," he says. "I'm happy to help spread the word."

We fill our plates in silence. Behind Abu Sayeed, in the kitchen, the breeze ruffles the pages of the newspaper. The picture of the city by the sea makes me think of Ceuta. I say to Mama, "Is it true Ceuta's got a statue of al-Idrisi?"

"Ah, yes. Ceuta." She settles deeper into her chair, raising her hands to the ceiling. "Paradise on earth, habibti. A pinhole of wonder. Ceuta is where the shores of the Maghreb reach out for Europe."

I say, "And it's where you first talked to Baba." This story I know by heart.

"We were studying at the University of Córdoba," she says, passing the plate of sfiha. "I was in mapmaking, and your father was studying engineering. A group of our friends went on holiday to Ceuta. Your uncle went to live there, you know, years later." Mama darts her eyes away, toward the kitchen, toward the mail pile with the newspaper folded on top.

"Ceuta is a part of Spain," I say, "but it's in Africa, right? Like, on the actual continent of Africa."

"My little cloud," Abu Sayeed says. "A quick learner, as always."

But I can't imagine living between two worlds like that. I've gone so far from New York that sometimes I can't imagine there are so many places out there, so many more than I've seen. They just go on and on, this big wide world, and tiny me, and Baba on the other side of it.

I pick at my rice, studded with pine nuts. "You and Baba saw where Africa meets Europe."

"We and several others." Mama sets her hand against her cheek.

"I had been all over Europe and the Middle East by then, but there was more I wanted to see. Wherever Allah takes you, you always yearn for somewhere else." She stares out at the skin-colored olive branches in the twilight. Then her eyes shift past them, toward the city center, and she doesn't notice Huda handing her the bowl of fattoush. Zahra's not listening, staring at her phone on the tablecloth.

The booming comes, louder than ever, and that green sulfur smell. I stop picking at my sfiha. Mama stares out the window into the just-dark, worry folding her forehead. She doesn't see the fear in my eyes.

From my chair, I can just see out the kitchen window between the curtains. An oily mist hangs over the alley, and I can't tell if it's twilight or dust. It's gotten too dark to tell color. I breathe in through my nose again, desperately wishing for the scent of rain.

Through the Iron Gate

*

After several happy weeks at King Roger's court, Rawiya, Bakr, al-Idrisi, and the expedition bid King Roger good-bye and boarded a ship bound for Asia Minor, where their journey would truly begin. Although Rawiya had to leave Bauza behind in King Roger's stables, the expedition had been outfitted with a dozen servants, horses, and camels, as well as food and water to last several months. They departed from Sicily's northern shore, gazing at the dark strip of the island of Ustica on the horizon. Phoenician peoples had once lived on the island, but its dark grottoes were now empty. Some called Ustica "the black pearl," al-Idrisi said, because of the island's volcanic rock.

The ship turned east and then passed south through the narrow Strait of Messina. Safely beyond the strait's strong currents, they passed by the Calabrian coast unharmed. Sailing southeast, they crossed the Ionian Sea and then the Sea of Crete until they reached the shores of Asia Minor and lowered anchor at the port city of al-Iskanderun.

From the Anatolian coast, the expedition proceeded southeast through the Belen Pass and entered Bilad ash-Sham—the Levant— and the Syrian province of the Seljuq Empire. Below them lay a lush valley, the hillsides green with pines. As they rested, al-Idrisi sketched in a leather-bound book and described the route of their journey. They would wind south through the Syrian province, passing through the cities of Halab, Hama, Homs, and ash-Sham, the lovely City of Jasmine. They would skirt the Crusader County of Tripoli and Kingdom of Jerusalem on the coast and continue west over the Gulf of Aila to Cairo, Alexandria, and the Maghreb beyond. Their goal was to map the lands between Anatolia and King Roger's outposts in Ifriqiya, which lay beyond the Gulf of Sidra and the city of Barneek. From there, a ship would return them to Palermo.

Following the trade routes south and then east, the expedition arrived days later in the city of Halab, called Alep by the Franks, Aleppo in Italian. Halab, nicknamed Al-Baida, "the White," for its pale soil, was an ancient city that stood at the western end of the Silk Road. After resting and recording descriptions of Halab's covered souq, fortified citadel, and Great Mosque, al-Idrisi's expedition continued south across a flat plain into the heart of Bilad ash-Sham, following the Orontes River toward Hama. Each night they stopped at a khan, a roadside castle for housing travelers.

Since they had left Palermo, Rawiya had been getting up before anyone else. The khan was full of travelers, and she was afraid of being caught dressing or being invited to the baths and being discovered. It was hard enough to find an empty room to cut her hair with a stone.

At each khan, she had taken to walking the courtyards, watching the merchants set up their displays of oils and spices, circling the mosques and the fountains. Every khan was essentially the same: a wide, arched entrance, a pair of wrought-iron doors, walls of hewn limestone or basalt. Travelers' leather packs and supplies lined the archways of the summer rooms, and dark passages led to the inner winter rooms. The dusty central courtyards were crammed with money changers, and a square mosque stood in the middle.

One morning, in the last khan on the road to Hama, Rawiya had just risen and prayed when she heard a thud from the central courtyard. Wrapping her turban, she stepped off the expedition's sleeping platform and into the light. At dawn, the khan should have been silent. Rawiya listened to date palms swaying their branches like dervishes in the breeze. What was the thud she had heard?

"You get up so early, Rami." Bakr appeared, yawning. "Even the sun is still asleep."

"I heard a noise," Rawiya said. "Like someone dropping a sack of lentils."

But Bakr only yawned and started to pack his things. Rawiya studied the courtyard again. The upper walk was walled, and she could not see over the heads of the men in dusty sirwal who strode across it, gazing at the coming sun. The sun speckled the horizon green and pink. Around them, merchants unrolled their rugs and hung their wares in the archways. Through the gate of the khan, a breeze drew the scent of water from the Orontes River valley.

Bakr spoke of the merchants he had met in the khan, but Rawiya was only half listening. "The province of Syria is rich with trade," he said. "Nur ad-Din is strict with his market inspectors. The taxes bring in great wealth."

Al-Idrisi came out, stretching, and checked the camels. "I hope you slept well," he said. "We have a long journey ahead of us, and we won't find a khan on the road tonight. No, tonight we push for Hama."

"We won't be setting up camp on the road, will we?" Bakr asked.

Al-Idrisi raised his eyebrows and frowned. "If that isn't acceptable to you, perhaps you should have thought harder about this expedition." Then he smiled, slowly. "But you are young," he said, "and when you see the stars glittering, you will thank me. No, Bakr, not tonight—we will camp soon enough."

This conversation was the first time al-Idrisi had spoken in many days. He was usually deep in thought, buried in his leather-bound book of notes, sketching maps. Only Bakr had sought out the travelers at each khan, hunting after tales. Al-Idrisi had noted all but said nothing, like Rawiya's father had when he had listened to the tales of the Berber travelers when she was young. Looking beyond the gates to the river, Rawiya wondered if the Orontes changed its shape in the night, like the sea.

Shouting erupted above them. "Dead!" a man wailed. "Murdered. Mutilated!"

The proprietor of the khan, a short, heavy man in a striped robe, hurried to the gate. "A body was found," he huffed, "on the upper walk. Dropped by some awful flying beast, the flesh torn out by talons."

Rawiya thought of the thud—like a sack of lentils. She felt afraid and far from home in a way she hadn't before. It had been months since she had watched Bauza scatter the gulls in Benzú with sways of his neck. The pods would be thick on the carob trees this time of year, the figs still green. In the shade of the olive grove, the gliding ibises would cast slivers of shadows.

"Talons, you say?" al-Idrisi asked.

The plain beckoned from beyond the gate, the road to Hama shadeless and exposed.

*　　*　　*

"MAMA?"

The booming is thunder in my bones. The room gets real still, only the beetles twitching at the cracks in the windows. My pulse pops in my wrist. On the table, my knife shakes against my napkin. The lines on Abu Sayeed's forehead are thick and deep as tree roots.

"It must be coming from another neighborhood," Mama says, but she stops eating. She holds her fork in the air, a bite of cucumber salad dripping yogurt sauce. The light falls across the triangle of her nose, as straight as Baba's T-square.

"Are you sure?" Abu Sayeed says something in Arabic. I strain forward to listen, but it's too fast for me to understand. Huda and Zahra look at each other. Now I know for sure that something is wrong.

Zahra's phone buzzes on the table, searching for a signal.

Mama snaps back at Abu Sayeed: "Don't be ridiculous." Her cucumber salad just hangs there, like she's not sure whether to eat it or put it down, like she's not sure which language to use. "We just got here," she says, huffing out the words. "I was born here. I moved my family. Business will be good again. We've been through too much already."

"It would only be for a week, two at most," Abu Sayeed says.

"This will pass." Mama lifts and lowers her fork. She purses her mouth, curling her lips between her teeth like she's trying to trap the words. "We have no part in this. I want to buy bread. I don't want to worry about my girls walking to the market. I keep my head down. I work. I have three children to feed. Where should I go?"

Abu Sayeed dips his head at that, lets his shoulders sag down. Outside, the whumping of a helicopter fills the street, and a cat yowls.

"Eat your dinner." Mama gets up, her long skirt swishing when she dips across the room. Baba used to say Mama was always a lady, that she could run a marathon in high heels and wrestle a lion without ripping her pantyhose.

She stands at the window now, peeling back the yellow curtains, and the helicopter blades pop black and purple over our heads before they move on. Something is happening outside, people starting up cars, babies shrieking. The neighborhood crackles and hums with electricity, like a nest of wires. The fear is a knot in my thighs, my elbows, my thumbs.

Abu Sayeed clears his throat and smiles, but his mouth is crooked, his gray eyes all wrong. He says to me, "Tell me. Why did you say today was special?"

I stare at him, trying to make sense of the words. Somewhere down the alley there are voices, shoes pounding the road. The wind rises, and it pours through the open window, cracking ceiling paint onto Abu Sayeed's plate, dusting his sfiha with gray.

A new sound comes, whirring high as a broken fan. It drowns out everything, even the sounds of car horns and shouting. It reminds me of the day they buried Baba in the earth, the day I lost my voice.

Another boom, closer. The house shakes like a car going over a highway rumble strip, rattling my jaw.

"Why today?" Abu Sayeed is trying to smile, distracting me from the lump in my throat, hot and hard as a coal.

I know I shouldn't tell him, not on a day like this. I know there are some things you can't forget, no matter how long it's been.

Mama stiffens at the window. The beetles rush out and over the windowsill, running on their eyelash-thin legs.

"Get your things," she says, and Huda and Zahra push back their chairs, half-up, half-down, knocking their crumpled napkins and Zahra's phone to the floor.

Mama shakes hard, yanking on the yellow curtains. The rod rattles. "We have to leave. We have to get out now."

I turn back to Abu Sayeed. His smile has slipped, what's left of it locked on like there's not enough time to take it off.

My voice makes sharp yellow triangles. "Because today is the day you lost your son," I say, and something soft cracks open behind Abu Sayeed's eyes.

Mama dives from the window. I don't hear her scream.

It happens fast. That angry high-pitched whirring, like an air conditioner falling from a window or an overstuffed washing machine. A shrieking thrum. Then the weight hits like a slap on my back.

Silence. Red goes black. There aren't any colors anymore.

I CAN'T SEE anything, not even when I blink. My eyes sting like they're full of lemon juice. I want to rub the pain out of my eyes, but I can't move my arms.

Someone coughs, far off. Everything smells bitter yellow. Purple sobs float behind my eyelids. When I crack them open, the room is all gray-black pebbles, like the bottom of a quarry. A tangle of wires pokes through the rubble, revealing shards of mangled plastic screen. Zahra's phone.

The phone jolts me back to dinner, to the last thing I remember: Mama standing at the window.

"Mama?" My mouth tastes acid orange. "Huppy?" I can't hear my voice over the yellow ringing in my ears.

"Nour?"

A hand comes out of the dark. Mama's wedding ring is covered in gray powder. She lifts a slice of wall off me and pulls me up. The pain comes when I move—big red slashes of pain across my eyes, the feel of the skin on my shins peeling off on the stones and glass, my left temple on fire. My elbows bend back, and they throb even when they're bent right again. I gash my bare feet.

"Where's Huda?" I ask. But my voice gets lost in the ringing, and Mama isn't listening to me. She talks to herself, pulling me by the hand toward a moaning sound.

There's no floor now, just piled up tiles and puffs of ripped insulation. Mama's got owl eyes under the dust, her hair gray with it. The dust makes me cough and cough. The coughing makes me panic more than the pain, makes me scared I'll never get another good breath, like the dark will suffocate me.

I scrabble over Mama's hand with both of mine, clinging to her wrist. She bends back, prying me off her, and sets me in a corner lined with crumbled drywall. She mouths words—*Stay here*—but there's no sound.

I count my breaths. A pinky-red spiral loops over my eyes, something that looks like an ambulance siren. I notice it a little at a time: it's the color of one of the neighbors crying somewhere, wailing.

It's so dark I can see the street only because something is smoking, flicking heat on my face. I touch my forehead, and my fingers slip off. My face is slimy, like with sweat, but it's not sweat. The blood sticks to my fingernails.

"Where's Huppy?"

Still Mama doesn't answer. My legs are unsteady, but I waddle over. Mama pulls on a slab of ceiling that's cracked the dining table in two like burnt toast. There's that sniffling, the purple wisps of somebody moaning. I stretch my legs over bricks and crumbs of bricks. Mama yanks up the slab of broken ceiling, and underneath is a torn piece of flowered linen.

"Huppy!" My insides twist up and the pain drops away. Everything shrinks to Huda's rose-patterned scarf and my burning lungs.

I trip on rocks and tile to get to Huda. Mama pulls her up and steadies her, then moves to the cracked table, Huda under her arm. Crying comes from underneath.

Mama tugs on the table with one hand, holding Huda up with the other. She motions to the table, darting her eyes from me to the broken wood. I try to help her, but I only pull and pull. I yank on it, breathing hard and shallow, spiraling into fear. I can't do it. I'm not strong enough to lift anything.

A gray man puts his hand on my shoulder. The powder sits like a beard of fine hairs all over him, sprouting from the bump in his neck and the folds of skin under his eyes. He's a shadow in the cloud of dust that hangs over us.

I know I should be surprised at the gray man, but the pain has faded into numbness, and I can't feel anything. My eyes slip off him, and I focus on the crack in the wood of the table. Through the crack, I study half a porcelain plate smeared with oil and lamb fat. It's the only thing that makes sense.

Mama pulls Zahra out from under the table, and the gray man helps her. They stumble away.

I don't move at first. I stare through the table, like maybe if I keep my eyes on something familiar, everything else will be the same too. But the broken plate doesn't look how I thought it would look; the porcelain isn't smooth the whole way through. It's crumbly and white on the inside, chalky like a broken bone.

The whole world turns red from the screaming down the street. Sirens come from everywhere at once. The city has burst like a blister.

I follow Mama toward the garden, tripping on broken concrete. The neighboring houses look the same as ours. Thick shoulders of metal stick up from the dust. Twisted fences and window shutters poke out like teeth.

All the buildings on our street have been flattened.

When I was real little, Mama took me to play in almost every playground in Manhattan. We went to Central Park a lot, but not just there. We went to Seward Park on the Lower East Side, John Jay Park on the Upper East Side along FDR Drive, Carl Schurz Park along the East River with its bronze statue of Peter Pan, and lots of others besides. Something was bound to get left behind at one of them.

I was only five or six when I lost my favorite doll. It hardly even looked like a doll by then, which was probably why it was so hard for us to find it, because nobody knew what it was. My sitto had made it herself and mailed it to us for my fourth birthday, and since then I'd taken it everywhere with me. It had a funny flat little face like a slice of melon and a paisley dress Sitto had made herself, with Velcro on the back. I had worn off the eyes and the yarn of the hair, hugged off the left side of the mouth, and stroked the little dress into rags. By the time I lost it, it was a lump of brown and pink fabric, but it meant the world to me.

We searched everywhere for my doll, but we never found it, because we couldn't figure out which park we'd left it in. I cried and cried. That was the first time I knew something was really gone for good.

That's how I feel now, looking at our street. This street, like all the streets I saw in Baba's Polaroids, with the same tan buildings, the same black-and-white archways Baba and Abu Sayeed stood under with their orange shirts—this street is really gone.

"Nour—your head—you—"

It's the gray man, speaking through his tangled gray beard. I can't hear what he's saying.

"Abu Sayeed?"

It's him under the gray. I stare at his mouth moving. No sound comes out. He touches the left side of my forehead, and I flinch and screech. The world bursts open at his fingertips, red fireworks of pain.

I scramble back over a pile of brick. I'm in the garden, if you can have a house garden without a house. I lie down on the cold stones with the alley in front of me, trying to cool the fire in my head. I swing my fingers out on either side, then touch my ears. My hair is wet. I bleed everywhere.

Mama hangs Huda over her shoulder and moves slowly toward me. Red spreads down Huda's chest like jellyfish tentacles.

I saw a jellyfish once at the New York Aquarium—a box jelly. I still remember its name: *Chironex fleckeri*, they said. It was small with long white strings. The sign next to the display said its sting could kill you, even though it was only a foot long and its tentacles were floss-thin. I wonder if this is like that. Is pain poisonous?

Mama lays Huda next to me, and our blood mixes like spilled paint. Mama's canvases loom up. Some are ripped, others torn clean out of their frames. They're scattered around the garden, in the alley, and in the branches of the fig. A root has come loose from the dirt, reaching a finger out. I stretch my hand toward it, but I can't grab it. My fingers are too slippery.

Instead, I touch Huda's flowered scarf. Her mouth hangs open, the scarf's hem torn. Her shoulder is a red pulp of meat.

"Wake up, Huppy. Wake up!" I shake Huda, but her head only rolls from side to side on her neck. It's like she's saying no, like the world is too much for her, like she's a jinni who's slept a thousand years in a bottle or a stone. I put my ear to her wrist and don't hear anything. My belly feels like it's scalded with ice. I try her chest. There's a slow rhythm, like music underwater. Her heart is still there.

I lay my face across Huda's collarbone, listening to her breathing. In—a long pause—out. I breathe with her. I think of jellyfish, the way they never really look alive but never look dead. Huda is in that in-between place, even though she's always been strong enough to open all the jars, even though she once won a gold medal in the citywide soccer tournament, even though she's the only one who knew how to fix my bike when I broke the chain.

Minutes pass, and they feel like hours. Zahra stumbles from one corner of the garden to the other, dazed, then wobbles down. Mama finds a shredded towel to press to Huda's shoulder. When Huda's bleeding slows, Mama and Abu Sayeed search the rubble, looking for something. Mama bends down to pick something up. She crouches and rocks back and forth, the length of her navy skirt trapped between her calves and her thighs, letting off little puffs of gray dust. She's got something in her hands—the shard of broken plate. She holds on to that piece of broken plate like it's her rosary or Baba's misbaha. She stares at it, mouthing something. I watch her lips. *The sfiha*, Mama says. *The waste.*

Mama gets up and walks over to the corner of the garden. Her latest map, the one with the layers of acrylic paint, sits drying by the garden gate. The map is unframed and unfinished. The white sheet has blown off, but somehow nothing broke through the canvas. It sits decorated with clumps of dust. Mama fishes out a burlap bag from the wreckage of the kitchen, the kind that held the rice we bought in Chinatown. We use the bags for storing old toys.

Mama takes the map and separates the canvas from its wooden supports. She rolls the canvas up and stuffs it into the burlap, wrapping it tight and tying on a strap to carry the bag. I turn away while she hunts for more things to save: a sooty prayer rug, a couple of pairs of flattened sneakers. She roams the ruins again, shuffling, looking for something she won't leave without. She crouches and scrapes away bits of wall and tile as though she's digging into old leaves. From underneath, she pulls out a dented metal box with its lock melted off. Inside are our passports, including my stiff blue American one, and the Syrian family book where all our names are officially written down. The family book has lost the sheen on its lettering, and its red face is soft and whiskered like old leather. Mama thanks God as she picks up our documents, the only things we have left to prove we're a family.

I press my face into the garden stone. It smells burnt and yellow-green, the color of filth and sick. Zahra's eyes leak tears into smashed figs. Abu Sayeed limps through rubble and charred wood, inspecting the burnt shell of Zahra's phone. He jumps back when he cuts his finger on a broken jar. I smell burnt cumin.

A night breeze flicks up the edges of Huda's hijab. The breeze tugs on a smoldering piece of newspaper from deep in the cut-open house, shredding its ash into the alley. I read the Arabic headline while it burns, translating bits of words: *Morocco. Spain.* That scrap of newspaper photo, the man with the potbelly, his gentle brown eyes laughing. Underneath, the circle of red ink boils and blackens, the name inside it curling into smoke.

Feathers Over the Sun

*

The expedition left the khan and followed the Orontes River south into the wide swamps of al-Ghab plain. In some places, systems of dams and aqueducts sent water to irrigate the surrounding farmland. In others, the water collected in pools where black catfish swam. The coastal mountains lay to the west, and to the east sat Bani-'Ulaym Mountain, with its steep sides and many springs that drained into the valley.

For almost a week, their camels picked their way along the riverbank. Al-Idrisi buried himself in his notes and sketches, copying every detail of the twists and curves of the Orontes River and marking the length of al-Ghab plain. The expedition plodded on to the south until they came out onto the fertile plains surrounding the city of Hama, green and gold with farmland. The breeze swept its fingers through lush grasses and groves of pistachio trees, and in the fields, the old ruts of wheels cut into the red earth. The occasional group of Bedu herded their goats and sheep through the distant groves. The Orontes snaked away before them into the very heart of the city of Hama, where merchant caravans streamed through the gates.

They stopped in Hama for the night. That evening, Rawiya slipped away from her companions. The city wasn't as big as Halab, but having been built along the banks of the Orontes, it was filled with trees and flowers and the clean scent of water.

In the center of the city, Rawiya found the Orontes again and one of Hama's norias, the great wooden waterwheels first built by Byzantine rulers several hundred years before. The noria was connected to an aqueduct that sent water through the whole city. Rawiya listened while the damp wood creaked and wailed in rhythm. It sounded almost like music, she thought. She returned still humming that low note, as though the noria were singing. *Mother,* she thought, the note an ache in her chest, *if only you could hear it.*

The expedition left Hama the next day, following the Orontes toward the city of Homs. When the time came for their morning prayers, they used the river water for wudu to cleanse themselves before praying.

The camels dipped their heads to drink. The long tail of servants stopped behind them, setting out mats and prayer rugs along the sandy riverbank. Three times they washed their hands up to the wrists, their feet up to the ankles, and their faces, passing their wet hands over their hair. When they finished washing, they prepared to find the qibla, the direction of the Kaaba in Mecca, so they would know which way to face while they prayed. To do this, al-Idrisi brought out an astrolabe.

The astrolabe was a flattened silver disk. Its front surface was ticked and carved like the geared face of a clock, delicate as spiders' silk. This carved covering, called the rete, indicated the positions of the sun and dozens of stars when the instrument was correctly aligned with the heavens.

Turning the astrolabe over, al-Idrisi pointed to a chart engraved on the back which listed a number of cities and the corresponding angle of the sun at given times of the year. This was called a qibla map. "Once we find the location nearest us on the chart," he said, "we can use the angle of the sun to find the qibla."

"Those charts have always confused me," Bakr said.

Al-Idrisi twitched up the corner of his mouth, and Rawiya thought she saw him smile. "Perhaps you would like to try, Rami." He handed her the astrolabe.

The astrolabe was just wider than a large pomegranate, still warm from al-Idrisi's pack. Sunlight glinted off the silver face. Rawiya studied the fine-carved points that indicated the stars, noticing the puzzling symbol of an eagle.

Rawiya turned the disk over and squinted at the qibla chart. Never having seen an astrolabe before, she was nervous. She scanned the list of locations. A curve was provided for each of several cities. She knew if she could find the right entry, she could use the curve to figure out the relationship between the location of the sun and the direction of Mecca.

There. She spotted the qibla curve for the location closest to theirs, ash-Sham—Damascus.

"I've got it," she said. Bakr and al-Idrisi crowded to her, following her finger toward the horizon. "If the sun is here, then the qibla must be"—she turned to the south—"there."

Al-Idrisi smiled his catlike smile. "Very good." He dropped the astrolabe into Bakr's palm, and Bakr scrambled to catch it. "See, Bakr, if you spoke less and observed more, you might understand."

The expedition faced south and knelt in prayer. As they finished, they raised their faces toward the rising sun. A great white bird circled them, blocking out the light.

"What a bird!" Bakr cried. "That must be the largest ibis I've ever seen."

But both Rawiya and al-Idrisi knew it was no ibis. Rawiya touched her sling in its leather holster. The sun leaned on the crutch of a mountain, flat as brass. The bird's cream-colored belly cast rippling shadows, his talons flashing. Rawiya's whole body tensed.

"Mount the camels," al-Idrisi cried. "Flee!"

The expedition streamed down the hill past the farm fields toward the shelter of Homs, beyond the elbow of the Orontes. The creature swooped down, larger than any eagle, his wingspan as wide as a ship was long. His white and silver feathers shone like mother-of-pearl. His screech could shatter diamonds.

The beast gained on them, rushing like a wind over their heads, scattering their frightened camels. Rawiya shouted to the terrified servants, urging them on. She tugged out her father's sling and her pouch of sharp stones.

"We'll never make it," Bakr cried.

Al-Idrisi bowed his head to his camel's neck to cut the wind. "Homs lies there before us," he said. "In the city, we will be safe."

The creature's wings swirled dust about their ears. The iron gates lay ahead of them, but the bird was regrouping again, drawing himself up into an arrow, ready to strike. He would soon overtake them outside the gates.

Rawiya pulled back on her camel and turned to face the gigantic bird. She rushed to set a stone in her sling and pull back the strap. Her fingers resisted. Her torn nails nicked the leather and stuck.

"Rami," al-Idrisi cried, pulling back his own camel.

"Turn back," Bakr cried. "You'll be killed."

Rawiya squinted into the wind, holding her breath, waiting for the bird to come into range. She aimed for his eyes.

The creature shrieked, extending his talons, blocking the sun. His rancid breath struck Rawiya's face, stinking of cracked bones and rotting liver.

Rawiya let the stone fly, but the hurricane of wings jolted her aim. The stone hit the beast deep in the feathers of his belly. He screeched and pulled up, diving over the gates of Homs trailing a deep green shadow. Rising, he dropped feathers long and pale as swords and disappeared behind the hills.

Bakr came up beside her. "Wherever did you learn to do *that*?"

Rawiya held up her sling. "I would have hit him in the eyes, but he saw me coming. He threw up wind with his wings." She uncurled her fingers, letting the sling's leather slacken. "A trick my father taught me."

Al-Idrisi stroked his beard, his white turban streaked with dust.

"That is no trick," he said. "A talent like that may prove useful on a road with many dangers. How did you know where to aim?"

"My father told me stories as a child," Rawiya said. "Tales of a selfish, bloodthirsty creature with no love for songs or beautiful things. He kills and steals what he pleases. His whole body is armored with thick feathers, so the beast's only vulnerable spot is his eye."

Bakr shuddered and caught his breath. "What kind of creature is this?"

The sun rose, pomegranate red. "This is the pale terror," Rawiya said. "This is the great white bird the poets call the roc."

*   *   *

THE LIGHTS HAVE gone out. The lights in the apartments, the streetlamps, the traffic signals. The city is darker than I have ever seen it, like the bottom of the ocean. Manhattan was never this dark. Baba used to say Manhattan was more alive at night than during the day.

Mama slides a worn pair of slippers on my feet. I watch her through the curtain of my hair. My head doesn't hurt anymore; my whole body is a numb lump. I rub my elbows, shivering at the first twinge of cold.

"Get up, Nour." Her hands shake my ankles, yanking the slippers higher so they'll stay on. The seams have started to split, melted by heat, and a couple of toes poke out.

Mama pushes matted hair off her cheeks. When she puts her hands on my feet again, her fingers are damp. The salt is back, ringing my ankles.

"It's dark, Mama."

"The power is out." Beetles have chewed on her voice.

The city streets are a maze of twisted concrete and steel skeletons. The thought of getting up and walking makes my fingers tingle and my guts scrunch up. "My stomach hurts," I say. "And I want to lay down."

"Not here, habibti. We're not safe here." Mama touches Huda on the forehead and tosses Zahra a pair of canvas sneakers with the tongues ripped out. Zahra has her head on her knees and won't put them on. Mama scans the wreck of the house one more time for Zahra's smashed phone and curses when she finds it. She counts the coins in the pocket of her skirt. She stuffs a charred wad of bills to the bottom of her burlap bag.

Mama and Abu Sayeed pass Arabic back and forth. I wiggle my toes in my slippers. The stones press against my big toe. Nothing feels real. It feels like the minute before you have to throw up, and you can't think about anything else, just getting through the next five seconds. It feels like that. I wonder if the whole city is flattened out there, and we just don't know it. I wonder how many other places lost power today, how many other blocks are missing their streetlights.

Then I remember what Abu Sayeed said at dinner about the power being out at his house, and the back of my neck hums with fear like a radio snapping to life.

I ask, "What about your house, Abu Sayeed? Is your house still there?"

Abu Sayeed looks at Mama, but no one answers me. All our ears are ringing. Then he goes over to Huda and picks her up in both hands, like a stack of firewood. The knees of his pants are shredded, the linen stained with blood. His legs bow out to the side under Huda's weight, his shoulders straining to stay up. He looks nothing like the smiling man with the mustache from Baba's Polaroids.

Mama pulls Zahra up by the wrist. Abu Sayeed says, "We'll find out."

They cross through the garden gate first—Mama, Zahra, and Abu Sayeed with Huda in his arms. I'm the last to leave the house. The alley in front of me is a cut-open canyon, like somebody took a hot knife to crumbly pastry dough. Behind me, the cracked fig tree trails a branch through a broken window, its trunk smeared with soot and blood. One brown fig hangs ragged, shot through by metal and the sharp splinters of stones. Juice and seeds ooze, splattered on the gate. I touch the latch, and it sticks to my fingers, tugging me back when I pull away.

We leave the garden and the mess of frames and canvas, the paint splatter and the broken dishes. We walk in the dark toward Quwatli Street, but things don't look the same, and even though Abu Sayeed must know where he's going, he seems confused.

Our street isn't the only one that got flattened in our neighborhood. Another street is blocked by walls that came down, collapsed roofs, bricks piled in the road. I don't recognize the shops with their faces crumbled away, the husks of apartment buildings where sofas and bathtubs have been tossed over the curb.

How many Polaroids are there of places that no longer exist?

We turn around, try another way. Everything is gray, that cloud of dust hanging over the road. It's hard to breathe. Zahra whines about her feet. She lags behind, and Mama pulls her. I've got cuts on my toes, but I don't say anything. I watch the dark spot on Huda's shoulder spread, trace the outlines of blood on her chest and Mama's. I think about box jellies.

With all the streetlights out and dust over everything, we grope along the walls on the next block. Dark clouds mixed with smoke cover the moon tonight. Now and then, a car flies around a corner without its lights on, and we dive against the nearest wall. We try to find Quwatli Street, but we end up veering off into a little alley so old and narrow it doesn't have a sidewalk. We go single file.

Abu Sayeed stops and turns around. Huda is limp in his arms. He looks exhausted, like he's carrying an armful of marble. I wonder if his pockets are still full of stones. I wonder if the stones on my dresser burned and cracked when our house came down, whether Zahra's plum-fat perfume bottle exploded like a potato in the microwave. The months it took me to collect all those stones sit in my belly, an indigestible ache.

Abu Sayeed melts into the dark. The only point of light is Huda's flowered headscarf against the collar of his shirt. Her arm hangs, swinging like a chain.

I poke around for Mama's hand, tapping my fingers up her thigh until I find her thumbnail. I hold on tight and burrow my face into her side. She wraps her palm around my ear. She smells like days-old turpentine, that sharp teal smell, and cooking fat.

Mama's hand blocks the loud voices from the next street over, the chalk-gray shouts and pounding footsteps. The burlap bag sways in her other hand, the map's corners peeking out like broad feathers. Through everything, the painted borders of its countries haven't gotten smudged. Acrylic paint dries fast.

"The side street is blocked off," Abu Sayeed says. "Something is happening in the square."

"Happening?" Mama clenches her hand against my hair.

"Where are we going?" Zahra's voice is too loud. "We can't stay out all night. What if it happens again? What if—"

"Hush." Mama's voice is a rough whisper, grainy as concrete.

"We need another route." Abu Sayeed turns slowly from one wall of the alley to the other, like he's looking for a door to open out of the stone, like somebody might send down a fire escape from the sky.

Zahra twists her hands around her wrists, the muscles in her neck stiff as reeds. She hisses, "We have to move, Mama."

"Hush!" Mama's hands flit across her face, her hair, her bag. She's vibrating. "The first week of May," she says, just loud enough that we can hear. "The first week of May, we left." She holds her fist over her mouth, tapping the words back between her lips.

"You can stay with me," Abu Sayeed says. "Just let me think of another way." A stain spreads behind Huda's collarbone like a wing.

A helicopter grazes the rooftops, churning up the hanging dust. When my ankles and the balls of my feet start to shake with the road, everything in me wants to bolt. I hold on to Mama. Blood swells my scalp and my fingertips, like I might pop.

I whisper, "I want to go home."

"Abu Sayeed's house—that's where we'll go. It's not far." But it's like Mama is somewhere else. She says a list of things that haven't happened yet: "We'll get the car. We'll put the girls to sleep. We'll have water. Clean clothes. We'll take Huda to a doctor." She strokes my hair while she talks. In the dark, her eyes and cheeks are just holes. She says, "It will be all right," and then under her breath, she adds, "insha'Allah." God willing.

It's something Baba used to say when he thought nobody was listening to him, when it was quiet enough that I could hear him pray. Like on summer afternoons in the city, when people used to lie on the floors of their apartments and Baba was so tired from fasting during Ramadan that he would lie on the rug and read to me over the sound of traffic. Or on Christmas mornings after we had opened up our presents, before Baba would break the silence with Umm Kulthum, before he and Mama would dance in front of the Christmas tree. Those were the only times quiet enough to hear Baba praying.

"We have to chance the square," Abu Sayeed says.

That's when I notice the black-and-white archway on the building next to us. I close my eyes and run over the route we took this afternoon to get the cumin. Huda took us down this same street. There's no mistaking that archway, the black and white stripes of stone. I can see the photo in my head, the picture I took with my eyes. I imagine the streets we turned down and picture the route like a piece of fabric, running my hands over its twists and turns. A left by the café. Straight past the apartment building with the gray and white stones. A right past the crooked poplar. Then I run over the directions a second time, there and back again. Huda's shortcut. *Abu Sayeed lives a street down from the spice shop.* Huda saying, *They say synesthesia is tied to memory.*

"I know the way," I say.

Mama lets go of me. "To where?"

"I remember this building." I point away down the alley until it disappears around a sharp corner. "One block down, there's a café. You turn right at the crooked poplar—"

"We're in Syria," Zahra says, "not New York. They don't use blocks here."

I try not to raise my voice because people are shouting from the next street over. "I know the way. I remember it."

"You've only been here once." Zahra glances toward the voices.

I stomp my ripped slipper. "Huda could tell you. It's her shortcut. I always remember—right, Mama?"

Mama tightens her fingers on the burlap bag. "Tell Abu Sayeed the way, and let him go first. Don't run off, habibti."

I whisper the turns to Abu Sayeed. We round the corner of the alley and dart across the street, staying close together. Somebody lights a candle in a window. The flame bounces off Abu Sayeed's eyes, bulging with the red branches of veins. The hems of his pants hang from the cuts at the knees, dragging on the ground. I look up and wonder if the moon would be going to bed soon, if I could see it.

We pass the apartment building with the tiny white pebbles and the crooked poplar. What stones have I missed in the dark? The night is too black and dusty to see even the stars over our heads.

It didn't have to be like this. This walk could have been an adventure, an expedition. How many times did Mama tell me how to use an astrolabe, like the old mapmakers? How many times did she show me the rete, how it held all the stars? I think about how much faith people had to have back then to trust the stars would be there when they needed them to, to trust the sky wouldn't fail them.

I watch Huda's arms swing in front of me in the dark. On the next corner, Zahra's golden bracelet catches my eye. I look around at what we have left: Zahra's jewelry, Mama's map. I wait for sharp jealousy to twist in my stomach, but it doesn't come. Huda's fingertips are black with soot. I would give the last thread off my slippers if she would say something.

We come to the spice shop, shut up with a metal curtain. I can tell Abu Sayeed knows where we are because he hurries ahead, his lips apart, words hanging on his tongue. He shifts Huda's weight and whispers, "Bless you, little cloud."

We turn down a side street. Ahead of us, like a minaret in the gray dust, is Abu Sayeed's green car parked on the cobblestones, its lights and alarms going off bright yellow and pink.

For all the afternoons Abu Sayeed has come to our house, we've never been to his. I don't recognize anything. I trip on pebbles I can't see, odd-shaped rocks, bits of brick and concrete. I think again of the stones on the road. Maybe I'm stepping right over Abu Sayeed's mystery stone, the purple and green one, and I don't even know how important it is. Like the bombs that dropped from the sky, not realizing how important the house was they were landing on, not realizing it was ours.

Then Abu Sayeed cries out. We round the corner, past the car. The headlights pop on, then off again. In the flash, we see the rubble of a building, and for a minute I wonder if we've circled around and come back to our own house. But we haven't.

Abu Sayeed walks toward his crumbled roof, the ruins of his kitchen. His feet brush halves of bricks, curling up dust like feathers toward the sky. I wonder how big the bomb was that flattened his house, his street. I wonder if anybody knew it was his.

If I hadn't played in so many parks, would I still have Sitto's doll?

I glance at Mama's burlap bag again, at the map inside. I think to myself how stupid it is that acrylic paints dry so fast. Things change too much. We've always got to fix the maps, repaint the borders of ourselves.

Where the Camel Sleeps

*

In those days, Homs was one of the largest cities in Syria. Lying on a fertile plain and watered by the Orontes, Homs was a place of many gardens, fruit trees, and vineyards. It lay a few days' ride from a Crusader castle called the Krak des Chevaliers, near the border of the Crusader County of Tripoli. But Homs was walled and fortified by the emir Nur ad-Din, and many travelers and merchants gathered in its open markets and strolled its stone-paved streets. Rawiya marveled at the Great Mosque of al-Nuri, one of the largest in all of Syria, and at the tomb of the Muslim general Khalid ibn al-Walid. The city was believed to be a place of protection from snakes and scorpions, a blessed place. In his leather-bound books, al-Idrisi noted the white stone statue of a man on horseback above a scorpion that stood over the gate of the mosque. He explained to Rawiya that he had heard the people of Homs say that if a scorpion stung you, you could be healed by rubbing clay on this statue, dissolving the clay in water, and drinking it. Rawiya was amazed.

They found a khan within the city, adjoined to a mosque, and stayed the night. In the morning, Rawiya woke before dawn, homesick and lonely. Merchants set out their wares in the open markets, selling pine nuts and quince, sumac and oranges, glass beads and silk. Amid the noise, she found herself listening in vain for the familiar lilt of her mother's voice.

Looking around, Rawiya counted her companions. One of them was missing—al-Idrisi.

She wrapped her turban and tied her sling at her side. The khan was quiet, but humming drifted from the second story. She hurried up the stone stairs.

Beyond the khan, the flat gray roofs of stone houses were staggered like stepping-stones. To the west lay the Orontes, its banks scattered with poplars. Beyond the plain, sculpted farmland ringed the hills.

"Awake so early?"

The voice startled Rawiya. Al-Idrisi sat on the low wall, dangling his legs over the two-story drop. He wrote in a leather-bound book in his lap.

"Al-Idrisi—" Rawiya hurried over to him. "Come down before you fall."

"My luck will hold," he said, "and the view won't do me any harm. Come." He patted the stone beside him. "Take in the city before it wakes."

Al-Idrisi's beard was tinged with dust, and the wind lifted stray camel hairs from his turban. Rawiya decided to keep her feet on the ground. She weighed her words and said, "The roc followed us from the khan outside of Hama to the gates of Homs. It worries me. The road to come is exposed."

Al-Idrisi paused, lifted his quill, and then began to scratch away again. "If we ride hard, we can make it to ash-Sham in four days, five at the most."

The laundry lines between the buildings swayed in the wind, and the wooden signs clapped against the stones.

"It's a long way," Rawiya said.

"You must understand," said al-Idrisi, "there are no reliable maps of this region and its routes. This is our task—to create a more complete map than has ever existed before. For now, we follow the accounts of other travelers. Only when we see for ourselves will we know the distance for certain."

"But it's too long a distance," Rawiya said. The wind flapped her sirwal, chafing the embroidered cuffs against her ankles. "If the roc seeks revenge, he will search for us at every roadside khan. He won't let us go without a fight."

Al-Idrisi swung his feet back over the wall and stood, shutting the clasp on his leather-bound book. "It seems your father told you more of this creature than you have said."

Rawiya described sitting on her father's lap as a child, the olives fat on the branch, gray-winged shrikes preening themselves. She spoke of the sun-wrinkled face of an Amazigh trader—a Berber—offering her something tender-skinned, green-purple. A ripe fig. She had taken a bite, gritty and sweet, and the Amazigh man had begun to recite the ancient story of the roc. When Rawiya had told al-Idrisi all of this, she said, "The roc is terrible when angered and will stop at nothing to get revenge on his enemies."

Al-Idrisi tugged at his beard. "Then we hide in plain sight, among the hills and the fields."

Rawiya smiled. "I, for one, will enjoy sleeping under the stars."

LEAVING HOMS, THE expedition followed the trade routes toward ash-Sham, going out of their way to avoid each khan. At night, the servants lit fires, prepared pots of lentils, and warmed round pillars of bread. Al-Idrisi pored over his notes and glanced up at the stars. The green sunset peeled back, revealing the black rind of the sky.

"Tonight we lie content under the dome of the stars," said al-Idrisi, "safe from marauding beasts."

Bakr grumbled as he sat down by the fire. "I would fight a horde of marauding beasts to have a bath like a decent person."

But al-Idrisi only laughed and reclined on his carpet. "Look up, my young friends," he said, "and see the magnificence God's hands have created."

The constellations winked above them. Al-Idrisi told Rawiya and Bakr of the constellations the Bedu and the Arabs had seen long before the Romans and the Greeks.

"The Bedu saw Cassiopeia," he said, "not as a damsel, but as a she-camel. In Ursa Major, they saw not a bear, but three mourning daughters and their father on his funeral bier. In Ursa Minor, they saw two calves turning a gristmill. Where the Romans saw Pegasus, the Bedu saw a great bucket. Instead of Leo Minor, they saw three gazelles running from the great lion." Al-Idrisi clapped his hand to his breast. "Ah, Leo," he said, "the lion. The emblem of King Roger, the lion of Palermo."

Then he pointed out the stars. "The star Vega," he said, "is often seen as a great white eagle. That is, in fact, what the star's name means. An-Nasr al-Waqi—the Falling Eagle."

Rawiya thought about all these different ways of seeing. Standing in the olive grove with her father, she had never known the names of the stars. "And these constellations can be seen as far away as the Maghreb?" she asked.

"Certainly," al-Idrisi said, "and farther. I studied the heavens as a boy in Ceuta, where I was born." And he told them of his family home, an elegant riad on a hill with a blue and white tile fountain in its central courtyard, and of how he had studied in Córdoba before his travels to Europe and Asia Minor. "I hope to return to Ceuta," al-Idrisi said, "once my work for King Roger is finished."

Rawiya and Bakr were surprised. "A man of brilliance like yourself," Bakr said, "must have been impatient to leave Ceuta and travel the world."

But al-Idrisi sat very still with his arm wrapped around his knee and met Bakr's eyes. "Ceuta once held such treasures," al-Idrisi said, "as I would give all my rank and honor to see again."

Bakr blushed and looked away. Rawiya said, "A learned man like you—I thought for sure you came from al-Andalus, across the strait."

Al-Idrisi softened and stoked the fire with a smile. "Never assume anything, Rami," he said. "A man of science must see things as they truly are, not as they appear to be."

The servants put out the fires and retired to their tents. Bakr nodded off. Above them, the camels slept among the stars. Rawiya and al-Idrisi sat for some time, staring up at the stars without speaking, watching the gazelles run.

* * *

ABU SAYEED HANDS Huda to Mama and disappears into the dark, leaving only the crunch of his footsteps in the rubble. He becomes an invisible creature, clawing through brick and cracked plaster, crushing tile like chicken bone.

"Abu Sayeed, where are you going?" I follow him, ripping the toe of my left slipper on stray glass.

"Nour, come here." Mama reaches for my elbow and misses. I trip on the curb, cluttered with shredded pillows and goose down, the metal frame of a belt buckle. The arm of a couch clings to a slice of burnt mattress on the sidewalk.

The streetlights are out. The only light is a string of car alarms going off, some silent, some ruby loud. They blink on and off like the yellow eyes of coyotes.

I saw a coyote once, on West 110th Street. Baba and I were walking past the north end of Central Park. It was December, and the whole sidewalk was ice. The only thawed part was the stone dividing wall between the park and the sidewalk. Baba held my hand while I tiptoed along the top of the wall, crowding up to me when he had to pass a bench. Kids had packed snowballs onto the beige sides of the tenements across the street, and the rails of the fire escapes were stiff canes of ice. I chose my steps, scuffing moss and grime. In the park, the lake was an iced-over hole. Baba's palm was warm on my fingers.

I broke away. I ran ahead a few steps to the end of the wall, and Baba called after me to stop. The park was a black streak on my left, just the stick figures of maple trees.

I jumped off the wall and saw the coyote. It was bigger than a dog, but thinner, and a funny color—gray and gold and brown. The coyote's black nails tapped the sidewalk. All its muscles tensed, hard as vines.

Baba called my name. None of us moved. The coyote stared, its fur stiff as a bristle brush, the tips slick with frost. Its eyes were the color of the amber rings Mama used to wear, the kind she was wearing the day Baba died.

The coyote breathed out mist from the twin teakettles of its nostrils, staring into me.

And then, like a beautiful ghost, it was gone. The coyote trotted back into the underbrush, glazed with ice.

I felt Baba's heat before his hands were on my shoulders. He lifted me clear off the sidewalk. Then we were on a park bench, and I was in Baba's lap. He wrapped me up in his coat like he was afraid to let me out. We rocked back and forth like that for almost an hour, Baba refusing to let me go, me remembering those amber eyes.

"Nour." Mama's calling me. "You're bleeding again."

But I'm not listening. Abu Sayeed is on his knees in the wreckage of his house, his forehead to the smoldering mess. I bounce over the slice of mattress and skate my slippers over flat hunks of ceiling tile, the broken limbs of furniture. I pick my way toward Abu Sayeed's bent back, the worn-down mountains of his shoulders. I never saw him alone in Baba's old pictures, not once.

"Abu Sayeed."

He lifts his face and opens his palms. He rocks his chin up to the sky. He's collected bits of rock and crystals that were probably polished once, but not anymore. They're cracked and coal black. I think I see a chunk of limestone I once gave him, a piece of rose quartz I brought him as a gift. Everything is split apart, and the stones that aren't cracked are coated with grime.

The headlights blink off, on. The car alarms streak the world with red. I want to be wrapped up in Baba's coat again, to feel his warm hands on my back. I picture Abu Sayeed sitting at a café, sharing a plate of mezze with Baba, their arms around each other. I drape myself over Abu Sayeed's shoulders, hugging the back of his neck, hoping the ghosts of safe things seep through.

Abu Sayeed wraps his stones in a handkerchief and stuffs them in his pocket. We walk back to the street. The bumper is dented, but his green car still runs. He shoves stacks of papers and metal cases of tools into the trunk. He says they're geologist's tools.

He starts the car and drives, careful to avoid shattered stone. Zahra is in the front seat, Mama behind her, Huda between us. Abu Sayeed's ripped the hem of his undershirt into a long strip, and Mama wraps it around the knob of Huda's shoulder, trying to stop the bleeding. She looks like she's been splashed with the juice from a can of beets.

The sun starts to come up. We pass the Great Mosque of al-Nuri and turn off onto a narrow alley to avoid Quwatli Street and the square. We loop past the tomb of Khalid ibn al-Walid, where Mama took us sightseeing when we first moved to Homs. I check the gate of the mosque for the statue of a scorpion and a man, but it isn't there. I try and imagine the time that has passed since it was built, the mountains of years that should be heavy enough to crush us.

We drive to the closest hospital, but it's packed with cars and patients. We try another. All the hospitals in our neighborhood are flooded with hurt people. There are no wait times, no estimates. There are only masses of people, stacks of them, long cords of them crusted with brown blood. A boy goes by on a sheet, the doctors carrying the curve of him like a hammock, a tube dripping from his mouth. As he goes by, a doctor glances at Huda's feet on the ground, at Mama and Abu Sayeed holding her up. Outside, the sky and the road rumble like an earthquake settling. The doctor passes us with the boy bleeding in his arms. He says something to Mama in Arabic: *We won't have a place for her tonight.* He leans over and tightens the knot Mama tied in Abu Sayeed's undershirt. Mama and the doctor look at each other with the boy between them. Before he turns away, the doctor says, *She should not wait.*

We get back in the car, and Abu Sayeed steers us out of the city. Mama tears another strip of cloth from Abu Sayeed's undershirt. She doubles it over the knot at Huda's shoulder until the bleeding slows down. She presses another to my left temple, trying to get the blood to clot. I feel cold and sleepy.

We drive past the olive grove on the outskirts of town, the one Huda and I walked through on afternoons when Mama was busy and wanted us out of the house, the one where I sat on Huda's shoulders and looked for Abu Sayeed's nameless stone. We drive away from the Orontes River until the satellite dishes on the rooftops look like tiny ears, past the flat plains of farmland in checkered squares. Beyond that are terraced hills piled up in rings, the far-off outlines of mountains. The river snakes away from us toward Hama in the north, toward the places that used to be swamp before people drained them. Didn't Mama tell me once that they used to call the Orontes Asi, rebel, because it flows from south to north?

"I don't understand why we were shelled." Mama speaks soft like she thinks we're all asleep, like she's afraid to wake us.

Abu Sayeed says nothing at first. The car's tires hum. The engine clacks and complains. "We may never understand," he replies, just as quiet. "In times like these, it's the small people who suffer."

I keep quiet, trying to pretend I didn't hear. Abu Sayeed downshifts, and the car's clacking groan settles into a purr. We drive until I burrow into Mama's neck and start to fall asleep, Huda's arm limp on my knee. I blink my eyes open and shut as we go over a bump. The last thing I see is Mama's amber ring, the one she hasn't worn since Baba died. She holds her hands in front of her and twists the band, catching stray hairs around the stone. I wonder how she found it in the wreck.

THE HOSPITAL IN Damascus is full of moaning and a metal smell like car bumpers. The white tile floor in the waiting room is clean, though, and the brown-and-beige chairs are deep and soft, and I'm too tired to be scared.

Mama goes with Huda and a doctor behind a curtain. Zahra puts her face to the wall and tries to sleep, and I scratch the bandage a nurse has taped over my temple.

Around us, people talk among themselves. While we sit, a family comes in with a baby girl. She must not like the beeping and the doctors hurrying around, because she starts to shriek. Her mama gets up and walks with her around the corner, cooing. The baby's screams die off into a purplish whimper that twists around the waiting-room chairs. I knead the skin on my arms and knees. Fear builds up, hot, knife-edged.

Abu Sayeed squeezes my hand. "No tears, little cloud," he says.

"I'm not crying." I untangle a knot in the hair behind my ear, jerking until it comes out in a clump. It's matted with dried blood that escaped my bandage. Abu Sayeed is still watching me, looking worried. His shoulders are sloped again, like two hills worn down by rain.

I ask him, "Why are you in all of Baba's Polaroids?"

"What?" Abu Sayeed laughs a little. "Your Baba and I were friends when we were boys," he says. "His parents were very kind to me when I lost mine. Your uncle Ma'mun was like my brother in those days, and your grandparents were like a mother and a father to me."

I stop picking at my hair and look up at him. "You lost your parents?"

"When I was very small. After they passed away, I lived with my uncle for a time." He folds his hands in his lap and smiles, soot deepening a dimple in his cheek. "But I like to think that where the world took from me one family, it also gave me another."

"Then you know," I say. "You know what it's like."

"Yes," he says, "I know."

Abu Sayeed and I sit quiet for a minute and listen to the beeping and whirring of the machines. Then Abu Sayeed takes a rough blue stone from his pocket, veined with yellow and white. "Have you ever seen one of these?" he asks.

I shake my head.

"That's because of how rare they are," he says. "This is raw lapis lazuli. Gem cutters have used it to make jewelry for queens, to craft tiles for mosques and palaces. There is no other blue like it in the world." He drops the stone into my palm.

The sharp edges poke at the chubby cup of my hand. Layers of blue and gray wind together in imaginary roads. "I thought jewels were shiny."

"Most precious things," Abu Sayeed says, "don't come out of the earth looking that way." He wraps the stone up in his handkerchief again. "In the earth, even the loveliest gems look rough and worthless. You might see the deepest indigo, but you see dirt too, and salt. But if you are patient, if you polish them with sandpaper and a rag—well, lots of things can become beautiful."

"But what if they're cracked?" I ask him. "What if they're broken?"

Abu Sayeed bends his head down and touches his beard. It's something I've never seen him do before, like he's forgotten that I'm there. Then he looks up at me again and smiles, and I wonder if I imagined it.

"Stones don't have to be whole to be lovely," he says. "Even cracked ones can be polished and set. Small diamonds, if they are clear and well cut, can be more valuable than big ones with impurities. Listen," he says. "Sometimes the smallest stars shine brightest, no?"

But my brain keeps looping back. I'm standing in front of our yellow house, lying in the garden by the fig tree. I try to remember where I left my toys and my bike, like somebody might come and take them while I'm gone. Is somebody sleeping in my burnt-out bed? Are people coming to take our charred blankets and clean everything out and build a new house where ours used to be? I want to walk the olive grove and the hot stones in the garden. I miss home with an angry hunger, even though home is an imaginary place now.

Baba should have seen it before it was gone. Things get lost so fast, so easily. Like dropping an ice cream cone. Like tossing a stone in the Hudson. I wonder if the stories I gave the fig tree are lost too, if Baba ever heard them. Did he feel the tremors when the house came down? Is some part of him tossing and turning in the earth, having bad dreams?

"Last night was too dark for stars," I say.

"No, little cloud." Abu Sayeed lifts my chin with his finger. "If anything, the darker the night, the brighter they shine."

The hospital murmurs, coming awake. Zahra sleeps. Out the window, the horned moon sets, and the North Star winks out.

Bone Island

✳

The road from Homs to ash-Sham began as a pleasant ride through green farmland, yellow fields of grain, and fruit orchards. The expedition passed stands of cypress and pine that became smaller and more sparse as they went along. Eventually the earth became drier, the shady areas where they rested farther apart. Groups of Bedu herded goats and sheep in the hills under the far-off buttes. Mountains rose in the west, blocking the rains from the sea. The pleasant farmland that had blanketed the plains of Homs became an arid steppe as they approached ash-Sham. Rawiya watched the skies during the day, listening for the beating of wings, and slept little each night.

On the third day of their journey, al-Idrisi studied his notes and sketched maps and announced that they should reach ash-Sham the next day. They repacked their supplies in the purple dawn and led their camels past tamarisk trees and low shrubs silhouetted against the gray earth.

Rawiya made out the tiny dot of a figure staggering toward them. The strange man tugged at his haggard beard and his tattered linens. His voice rolled thin across slivers of rock and the parched bed of a wadi. At this time of year, the wadi was dry: these riverbeds only carried water during times of heavy rain. The man's crooked shoes threw up dust. He shook his fists at the sky.

Al-Idrisi lifted his hand, and the whole expedition stopped. He hailed the man, who limped toward them, beating his breast and plucking his beard. Al-Idrisi got down from his camel and went to him, offering him water from his own waterskin and asking why he was so distraught.

"O fate," the man cried, throwing up his hands. "O cruel fate, you have taken my honor and dashed my good name. O divine help, why have you forsaken your servant, Khaldun?"

Al-Idrisi, seeing that the man was half-crazed with thirst, heat, and despair, called for the servants to refresh him. One servant brought a carpet and made the man sit down, while another ran to tear a branch from a nearby tamarisk to fan the man's face. Al-Idrisi himself helped Bakr to prepare the man a small meal of nuts, olives, figs, and bread with oil and thyme.

Rawiya wiped the dust from the man's cheek with a damp cloth to refresh him as he swooned under the blazing sun. Taking the cloth in her hand, she knelt at the man's side and gently buffed the sheen of grime from his skin. As the water cleansed his cheek of dust, Rawiya's cloth revealed the face of a beautiful brown-skinned young man. Rawiya was struck by his beard of black curls, the graceful line of his nose, his dark, thick brows and full lips. As he opened his eyes at the touch of her cloth, she blushed and looked away.

When they had finished eating, it was time for the afternoon prayer. The man knelt beside the expedition and prayed with them, praising God for their hospitality and kindness. Only after he had done this did he clear his throat and speak.

The man, who called himself Khaldun, beat his breast again and raised his arms to the sky. "I was born under an unlucky star," he said. "I was once the foremost of the poets of the emir Nur ad-Din. I sang him songs of great deeds, of heroes and of ancient beasts, and in return, the emir treated me with affection. He provided a large home where my mother and my sister lived, and I myself enjoyed the riches of his court for many years.

"The emir had long fought to unify the Syrian province and defend it from its enemies. He brought many brave men and warriors to his court and often asked me to sing him songs of courageous deeds. But my words were so convincing and my songs so passionate that the emir came to believe that I myself had done these great things.

"Nur ad-Din's favorite story was that of the terrible bird called the roc. The creature had been chased out of these lands many years ago by brave men who drove him from the crags of the mountains and away into the Maghreb. I had heard tales that the roc had settled in a valley of huge serpents where none dared to follow. There the beast was guarded from danger, and he fed on the serpents' flesh.

"But one day, a calamity rolled over the province. The roc returned to claim his ancestral hunting grounds: the city of ash-Sham and all its surrounding country. He terrorized the townspeople, dropping boulders on them from out of the sky, diving down on their flocks and scattering them, carrying off whole sheep in his talons."

The great terror. Rawiya and Bakr looked at each other. Al-Idrisi glanced at them, his lips tight together, his knuckles knit up in his lap.

"By all accounts," Khaldun continued, "this calamity was far worse than before. So the emir, deciding that he must defend the city of ash-Sham against this terror, searched for those who knew of the roc's weaknesses. He sent for me and had me brought into his grand hall. He told me of the wretched creature, and since I had told him countless tales of the first defeat of the roc, he commanded me to kill the beast myself and put an end to the torture of his people." Khaldun tore at his hair and robe. "Why, O Lord?" he cried out. "Why have you burdened your servant?"

Al-Idrisi laid a hand on his arm. "Poet," he said, "continue."

"I told the emir that I was no warrior," Khaldun said, "that I was only a young story-weaver. He would have none of it. He told me I must kill the roc, or else I was a liar and a traitor. He ordered that if I did not kill the roc in forty days, I would be put to death. In the meantime, my mother and sister were put in chains in the palace.

They sit rotting in prison, awaiting the outcome of my quest." Khaldun put his face in his hands and sobbed. "Why," he said, "why have these evil fortunes befallen me?"

"What will you do?" Rawiya asked.

Khaldun motioned to the steppe around them, the silver hills and the scrubby grasses. "I wander the countryside," he said, "seeking the roc to kill me and put an end to my miserable condition. He seeks vengeance on all who enter these lands. "

"Then you won't try to fight him?" Bakr said.

Khaldun laughed. "Have you seen the creature? He can carry five men away in his talons. His legs are wide as palm trunks."

"We saw the beast," said al-Idrisi. "A winged island of bone-white feathers."

Rawiya said, "He attacked our expedition near Homs."

"Homs!" Khaldun put his hand to his breast. "The city of my birth. I have not returned since I entered Nur ad-Din's service." He wept again. "O beautiful city, besieged by calamity from above. I shall not see the curve of your gates until merciful God gives me entrance to the Garden."

Rawiya was moved by his words.

"Your story is sad indeed, poet," al-Idrisi said. "Can we offer no help?"

Khaldun shook his head. "What are a poet's words against the talons of a beast?" he said. "Twenty-five suns of forty are set. What shall I do? I can no more put an end to the roc than I can throw a stone high enough to strike him."

"But perhaps," Rawiya said, "I can."

*   *   *

OUTSIDE THE HOSPITAL windows, Damascus pulses to life. My eyes are still hot and sticky from not sleeping. Mama comes out from behind the curtain. Huda is in surgery.

Abu Sayeed folds his hands. Zahra crosses her arms and snores, propping her forehead against the wall. Who knows where Huda is in this place? It's the first time we've been separated all summer. No matter how hard I try to sleep, I keep jerking awake, feeling like I've forgotten something, like somebody's come and sliced off one of my arms while I wasn't looking.

I pick at the beige padding on my chair, swinging my feet until its legs move from the force of my knees. Red beeps pop all over the hospital. I wonder which IV is Huda's and then wonder whose other monitors I'm hearing. I imagine I can pick out Huda's from the throng, like picking out a single frog in a pond of spring peepers.

When I think I've got Huda's pulse, I press my fingers to my wrist and try to sync my heart to hers, but it doesn't work. All it does is make my fingertips go white and numb until they tingle.

The whole hospital smells like bleach. It reminds me of the time after Baba died, when I had to go with Mama to the funeral home. It smelled like sour apples and Clorox. It was disgusting because the smell of sour apples looks yellow to me, and the smell of Clorox is the color of puke.

Mama brought me in, and we sat down with the director. Huda and Zahra were in school. I was supposed to be home sick with a stomachache, but really I just wanted to come with Mama. I thought maybe if I could see Baba one more time, I would be able to stop missing him.

The director disappeared into a closet and came back out with two cups of black coffee. The main room was all red velvet curtains and deep couches you could get lost in, the curtains so thick they didn't let any light in. It felt like a furniture store without the plastic. I dangled my legs and swung them back and forth. That puke smell clung to everything, the preserved reek of chemicals and waste and tears.

Mama talked to the director until a skinny boy came in, not much older than Huda. The director said, "This is my assistant, Lenny."

We shook hands, his big hand limp and clammy over my small one. Lenny had a few curls of beard hair and a wispy mustache. He smelled like cheese.

I swung my legs some more. Lenny stared at my sneakers. He asked if I wanted some juice. I nodded.

He went to get it, and Mama got up with the director. "Will you be okay?" Mama asked. "I'll be right back. Wait here."

By the time Lenny came back, they had disappeared down a staircase into a dark basement. Lenny handed me a cup of orange juice.

"Where did Mama go?" I asked.

Lenny blinked. "To see your dad's body, probably."

I ran my finger along the wet edge of my paper cup. "You weren't supposed to tell me that, I bet."

Lenny tilted his head to the oily ceiling tiles.

"And I can't see?" I asked.

"You wouldn't want to."

"Why not?"

Lenny didn't answer. I sipped my juice. The pulp and sugar had separated, making a cloudy mess. I took a sour sip and set it on the floor. Then I bolted.

I made it halfway down the steps before Lenny lumbered after me. I couldn't find the light switch, so I followed a green light at the bottom of the stairs. It was really cold down there, like in the freezer section in the supermarket. I stopped on the bottom step, holding tight to the railing. Mama's voice floated around the corner from a room down the hall, clipped and low. The smell was stronger down there, more nauseating, that vomit color smeared on the walls.

Behind me, Lenny clopped down the stairs.

I pounded down the hall and swung the door open. "Mama?"

Mama and the director turned toward me like they weren't sure if they were awake. A body lay on a slab of white plastic, the room lit soft green and egg white. I could see the dry creases around the elbow, the heavy fine-haired thighs, the fleshy pads on the underside of one foot.

"Nour." Fear flashed across Mama's face and coiled around her eyes. "You shouldn't be down here."

I waited for the toes to twitch, for the muscles in the forearm to pop up. No ridges of veins showed through the skin. The arch of the foot was gray, like meat past the sell-by date.

Lenny burst in. I reached up and caught hold of Baba's big toe, curling my first two fingers and my thumb around his toenail. He was cold. I held my breath, that rotted-apple smell thick in my nose.

THE BITE OF antiseptic drifts over my shoulder—that hospital scent. A man in a white coat comes up behind us. He searches for his pockets on the front of his coat, but they're pulled tight by his potbelly. He says something to Mama in Arabic. His voice is gray with spots of pink. Hers is a yellower brown than usual, uneven. Then the doctor walks off, his shoes clipping on the hall tiles.

"Huda is out of surgery," Mama says.

"She is?" I stop counting the beat of the IV monitors, dropping my hand from my wrist. Mama tugs me up and shakes Zahra's shoulder.

We tumble down the hall, through the lobby, and into another wing. Mama hugs the bag with her map and our food in it, jostling scraps of bread and some canned fish we found in the rubble. Abu Sayeed follows. We take an elevator up two floors and turn a corner, then another. My legs hum and shake like they did in the street, my knees stinging with speed.

Mama dives through a door and into a long room full of beds, and there's Huda under a white sheet. My calves shimmy and burn when we stop running, and I try to catch my breath.

Mama and Zahra go inside, but my stomach churns. I stop in the doorway.

Huda's fingers poke out from under the sheet, her palm flecked with dried blood. I can't make out her face, just the squiggles of her pulse and her blood pressure on the monitor. She doesn't look like my sister.

Zahra walks to Huda. Instead of touching her, Zahra tugs on her own fingers, cracking her knuckles. I haven't seen her this quiet in a long time.

Abu Sayeed nudges me between my shoulder blades. At first, I don't move.

"Is she asleep?" I ask.

"I think so," he says.

I walk over to the bed. Huda's arm hangs out from under the sheet, poking between the slats of the bed's railing. I remember her fingers swinging limp in front of Abu Sayeed's knees. The lumpy landscape of her body shudders, then goes coyote-still.

I nestle my fist into the sheet next to Huda's hand, but I don't touch it. I try to remember if Baba looked any different in the funeral home basement. I picture the gray of his skin. Was there a minute or a second that I knew he was dead, a moment when he stopped looking like my baba?

"You can hold her hand," Mama says.

When Baba died, Mama told me it was his time. But it isn't Huda's.

I stare at her fingers, the nails white and ringed with red. Her face is bruised and greenish, like she's out of breath, like she ran all the way home from the olive grove. She wheezes yellow air. Blood splotches up through her bandages, pricking the sheet with cranberry. I'm scared to touch her. I'm scared of making her worse, scared of waking her, scared of her seeing me and forever connecting me with this hospital, with the slippery brown of her own blood. Guilt tunnels in my guts, but I just stand there, staring.

"You can ask anything," Mama says. "Don't be afraid. All you have to do is ask."

From around the corner, another stretcher passes us. The sheet is dotted with red like shredded Gouda rind. The green smell of iron brings me back to the shattered house, the rush of it in my mouth and in my eyelashes.

I pull back my fingers. "She'll make it?"

"She has to rest," Mama says.

Huda's collarbones move up and down, barely visible. Her breath latches, stops, and shudders before starting again. I think to myself, I've seen a dead person before, but I've never seen anybody die. What if death is something that clings to you, like a bad smell?

Abu Sayeed takes my hand in his. "Come on, little cloud," he says. "Let us give her some space."

We can't wait in the recovery ward where Huda is sleeping, so Mama takes us out to a courtyard for guests. It's got a garden and a view of the street past the palms and white jasmine flowers. Ladies stroll down the checkered sidewalk wearing big sunglasses, and phone lines cross in front of concrete parking garages and apartment buildings. A man adjusts a satellite dish on a rooftop. Down the street from the hospital is a big hotel-lined highway that leads to the fountain in the city center, where all the other roads break off like spokes on a wheel. Across the highway, cobblestone bridges with iron railings cross the Barada River.

Mama sits us down on a bench at the back of the garden. She puts her head in her hands. She shakes, the bag at her feet shivering.

I ask, "Are you crying?"

Mama pulls me to her. Abu Sayeed gets up and paces the length of the garden. Zahra walks off to wait inside, in the air conditioning. She runs her fingernails along the wall, her bracelet jangling against the stone. I realize she never bought anything in the jewelry shop before Huda pulled her out.

I brace myself against the bench. "Tell me what's wrong with Huda."

"The shell hurt her when it fell," Mama says. She stops and holds her breath. "When it hit the ground, it broke apart. The metal pieces exploded and became hot, like knives held to the fire. One of them pierced Huda's shoulder."

I already know those knives. I don't want to think about the bomb. I watch Mama's necklace, a piece of blue-and-white ceramic tile fastened with silver cord, sway at her chest. It must be really old, because she's had it my entire life. The blue-and-white porcelain reminds me of the plate she held when the house came down. I realize I'm not sure when it happened, one night ago or two. I should be able to remember something that important.

"So all that metal is still inside her." I make a list in my head of all the things that could get lost inside a person. I picture Huda's bones like islands in red muscle.

"Shway," Mama says—a little. She passes her hand under her eyes, tugging at the skin on her cheekbones. "Shrapnel can be hard to get out."

Shrapnel is a red word. To me, it sounds like metal and anger and being in the wrong place at the wrong time. It sounds like the red and yellow things inside of people, the fear and rage that rot a person out until they rot out somebody else.

"She will rest a few days," Mama says. "Without rest and medicine, it could get infected."

"But she'll be okay when we go home," I say.

That tight-coiled look comes over Mama's face again, the fear in her lips and her forehead. "When we go home," she says, like she isn't sure what the words mean.

"They'll fix our house. Right?" In my head, we drive backward in the car again. The fires burn out, the walls tilt up, and God spreads super glue on the splinters of my bed and on Mama's cracked dinner plates.

Mama wraps her arm around me instead of answering. But I don't want a hug, not now, so I press back against her with my shoulder. Her not answering me is worse than anything she could say. *The first week of May*—isn't that what she said in the alley in Homs?

How can we leave a place I've been waiting to see my whole life? How can we leave twice?

"We can't go anywhere else," I say, my voice high pink. "Unless we go back to New York."

"I don't know yet, habibti." Mama closes her eyes and breathes out, warming my collarbone with her air. "When you're older," she says, "you will understand. You can't bake bread without flour. You can't draw a map of a place you've never been."

That doesn't make any sense. "What about Abu Sayeed?" He has his back to us, shuffling between rows of shrubs and palms. "Where is he going to go?"

"He is family," Mama says. "Baba would never leave a brother behind." Then she remembers to smile. "Do you know why Abu Sayeed is called that?"

I shake my head.

"*Abu* means 'father' in Arabic," she says. "When a man has a son and becomes a father, they call him by his son's name. So he becomes 'Abu' and then his son's name." She studies my face. "Do you understand?"

"But Abu Sayeed doesn't have a son anymore."

Mama strokes the small of my back. "But he did, once. His name was Sayeed."

"What happened to him?"

Abu Sayeed paces. He wears a track in the stones with his leather shoes, his ragged linen pants swaying.

"He had a fight with Abu Sayeed as a young man," Mama says, "and ran away from home." She looks down at her bag, at the dirty carpet that smells like soot and the gold-rimmed map rolled up inside it. "He never came back. They never saw each other again." Mama stares at the garden railing. "He was a geologist."

"Oh." Were the tools in Abu Sayeed's car his or his son's?

"Abu Sayeed used to teach geology at the university in Homs. He taught his son everything he knew. His son could have had a long career; he was brilliant." Mama pulls back from me. "Does this surprise you?"

I follow Abu Sayeed's sloped shoulders with my eyes. One of his pockets sags, and I'm the only one who knows it's heavy with stones.

"I didn't know," I say.

"You didn't know what?"

"That there was somebody else." The leaves cast shadows on us, cooling the top of my head. "Somebody who loved stones as much as Abu Sayeed."

Mama doesn't answer. Abu Sayeed keeps walking, scanning the pebbles on the ground. I wonder if the stones are talking to him. I wonder if they have anything to say he hasn't heard before, words he can hear in his bones.

There Also Is My Heart

*

The following day, the expedition set off with Khaldun for ash-Sham, the City of Jasmine, also known as Dimashq—Damascus. Since Khaldun had no camel, Rawiya offered to let him ride with her. He thanked her, telling her God would reward her generosity. As they rode, Rawiya tried to ignore the heat that spread over her cheeks and under her turban.

Ash-Sham lay in the center of a wide, irrigated plain called the Ghouta. This land was green with fields and orchards and small villages, and it was well known in all the surrounding country for being the closest thing to paradise a person could enjoy. A valley of fruit trees and streams called the Wadi al-Banafsaj, the Valley of Violets, extended for twelve miles from the western gate of ash-Sham.

The city was surrounded by a wall with seven gates. The Barada River came down from the western mountains and flowed east through the city and out into the desert. Khaldun said that between this river and a street called Straight lay the fortified citadel, the Souq al-Hamidiyah, and the Umayyad Mosque with its gold mosaics, enamel tile, and polished marble.

Al-Idrisi listened and noted these things, sketching a map of the Ghouta and the city. But as they neared its walls, the expedition fell silent. Even from far off, they could see the winged beast clinging to the roof of the citadel.

They entered the city before dawn, while the roc slept, and made their way toward the citadel. Ash-Sham was deserted, its people driven off by the roc.

They tied up their camels and began their preparations. The night before, Rawiya had detailed their plan. "I will hide on a rooftop nearby," she had said. "When Khaldun mounts the roc, I will have a full view so I can aim."

"You would have me climb atop the beast's back?" Khaldun had said. "Why would I do something so foolish—and how?"

Rawiya had said, "By distracting him with your song."

Al-Idrisi had smiled his catlike smile. "You have outdone yourself, Rami," he had said. "For it is well known that the roc has but one weakness: the hypnotic notes of song. He cannot resist a lovely voice and immediately falls to sleep." Al-Idrisi had sat back, grinning. "He especially likes tenors."

"Well, Rami." Khaldun had stood and lifted his face. "If a beautiful voice you require, my boy, then as beautiful a voice as you could wish for you shall get. For I am the foremost poet of the court of Nur ad-Din, and I—"

"And al-Idrisi and I?" Bakr asked. "What shall we do?"

"You will wake the roc," Rawiya said.

Bakr grew pale, and so did Khaldun. "The beast will throw Khaldun from his back and send him hurtling to his death."

"Khaldun will lash himself to the roc's back," Rawiya said. "Then he can try to stab at the beast. As the roc descends, I will aim my stone." She wrung her hands. "We will see if it will work."

Now in place, Rawiya crouched on the rooftop with her sling in her hands. The minarets of the Umayyad Mosque gleamed red and violet. Khaldun's black-cloaked figure emerged onto the turret of the citadel. The roc was awake now, clinging to the northern gate. He crushed the keystones at the tops of windows, twisting iron in his talons. The wind carried Khaldun's song as he climbed the turret.

The roc began to drift to sleep, shuddering his wings. Khaldun climbed, his voice never faltering. Al-Idrisi and Bakr huddled in the shadows of the Bab al-Hadid, the Iron Gate, on which the roc sat. Al-Idrisi grasped a horn and Bakr a drum—the only instruments Khaldun had taken with him into the steppe that would be loud enough to wake the roc.

Khaldun took hold of the roc's white feathers and braced his boot on the roc's back. He trilled out a sweet note, but he trembled.

A part of Rawiya feared for him, the part that had been happy she let him share her camel. It had made sense: she was the lightest member of the expedition, and Khaldun's weight would trouble her camel the least. But there had been something in his eyes when he had bowed to her, something small and gentle, like the sea drawing out its breath. It stirred something in her. Rawiya told herself it was only a longing for home, for familiar songs and faces, and quelled her fear by touching her mother's wooden misbaha in her pocket.

The roc shifted in his sleep, swinging his bulk off the gate and draping himself over the walls of the central courtyard. Khaldun panicked and hauled his weight onto the beast's flank. After a moment's hush, the roc settled. Music pattered to the ground, sweet as rose water.

Khaldun pulled himself atop the roc's broad back, mounted himself between the roc's shoulder blades, and sang into his ear. The new sensation set the roc's shoulder muscles rippling. The creature gave a contented sigh and lolled his head over the turret.

Khaldun lashed himself to the creature's shoulders and the base of his wings with al-Idrisi's ropes. Then he signaled to his friends and fell silent.

Seeing this signal, al-Idrisi took up his horn, blaring and shrieking. Bakr pounded awkward time on his drum, his elbows flying. Doves fled from rooftops. Jackals napping in the Ghouta howled and cackled.

The roc twitched. Then he squawked and beat his wings, and his dark eyes flared to life. Khaldun flattened himself against the bird's back and let out a terrified howl. The beast rose, dropping pale feathers on the gate. His shadow roiled across the city, throwing the Souq al-Hamidiyah and the minarets of the Umayyad Mosque into darkness. The roc lifted up into the sky, screeching, searching for the source of the noise.

Khaldun drove his dagger into the roc's back, cutting at his feathers, but could not draw blood. As Rawiya had feared, the roc's only weak spot was his eye.

The roc reached back, snapping his beak. He swooped low over the city, his long tail feathers brushing the dome of the Umayyad Mosque.

Rawiya raised her sling and set a stone in the strap.

The roc thrashed. Khaldun cried out. Feathers skimmed the earth like early snow. Rawiya took aim, squinting against the bright band of the sun.

The roc saw her.

The beast's eyes, yellow as quail yolks, hurtled toward her. It was as though he knew what she had planned, as though he was telling her she could not hide. Rawiya took a deep breath, listening to the crackle and groan of the leather as she stretched the sling.

The beast drew in his wings to dive.

Rawiya let the stone fly.

She had aimed for the roc's right eye. But once again the beast threw up wind with his wings, throwing off her aim. She fought to keep her hand close to true, and the stone hit the roc just above the eye, shattering the bone.

The creature let out a screech that broke every window in the citadel and plummeted to earth. The roc landed in the central courtyard like an earthquake, knocking everyone and everything flat, even the date palms. The beast's great, sharp beak dug into the earthen floor and stuck, his body heavy and still as though dead. Rawiya stopped breathing.

Khaldun.

Rawiya flew down the steps and through the Iron Gate. The roc had landed in the middle of the citadel on the bones of his victims, his face a mess of blood and feathers. The courtyard had become a butcher's floor.

Khaldun, limp and unconscious, slid off the creature's back to the ground. Rawiya rushed to him. The roc had fallen from a great height, and even though the beast had broken Khaldun's fall, he had been stunned senseless and did not move.

His eyes had rolled back in his head, and no breath passed between his lips. Rawiya, her hands trembling, brushed dirt off Khaldun's handsome face and stray tufts of white feathers from his beard. To her own surprise, she began to weep. "Dear poet," she whispered, "I've killed you."

But at her words, Khaldun coughed and, delirious, rasped out a line of poetry: "Wherever there are brave men," he said, "there also is my heart." Then he lost his senses.

"Fascinating." Al-Idrisi entered the courtyard with Bakr and rounded the bird, touching feathers as long as his arm, scratching out notes in his book.

One yellowed eye had broken free of the roc's brow bone where Rawiya had smashed it. Now the eyeball rolled out and wobbled toward her, dull and wide as a large pomegranate. She picked it up. The pupil shrank to a purple-black speck. The fleshy globe began to harden until the eye turned to crystal, perfectly round and smooth. The stone glittered ripe plum, beet purple, fig violet. At the first rays of sunlight, it flashed emerald in her hand.

The roc twitched.

"Back, everyone!" Al-Idrisi and Rawiya carried Khaldun from the courtyard as the wounded roc lifted his head and gnashed at the air. Blood matted the feathers of his one-eyed face. The roc stumbled up, clawed at the stone with his talons, and spread his wings. The beast rose up over the citadel.

"One day," the one-eyed roc cried in a voice like mountains

crumbling, "I will have my revenge." Then he vanished west over the mountains toward the distant Maghreb, toward the lands where the mythic valley of the serpents was rumored to lie.

The emir Nur ad-Din rewarded Khaldun and his friends richly for driving the roc out of ash-Sham. He released Khaldun's mother and sister and gave the expedition silver chalices, purses of gold dinars, gem-crusted statuettes, and embroidered robes of finest silk. He promised them great honor to remain at his court.

But Khaldun begged his forgiveness. "I owe my life to these heroes," he said. "I will follow them wherever they go." And at this pledge, Rawiya was filled with secret joy.

Nur ad-Din agreed to release Khaldun from his service and gifted the expedition an engraved scimitar from his armory. The hilt was solid gold carved in the shape of an eagle, its wings flared, its eye a hundred-faceted ruby.

The next day, the servants loaded the camels with gold and gems. Rawiya checked her sling, frowning when she realized her pouch of sharp stones was empty. Instead, the pouch held a purple-and-green stone split by a dark speck of pupil—the roc's eye.

As the crowd surrounding Nur ad-Din's palace looked on, Khaldun took Rawiya's hand and held it up before the cheering crowd. "This is the hand of Rami," he cried, "who loosed the stone and drove out the beast. As long as I live, I will follow him."

*   *   *

HUDA RESTS IN the hospital five days. Mama, Zahra, and I take turns sharing a cot. Abu Sayeed sleeps propped up in the corner, his chin on his chest. Mama fills out paperwork. When she puts in our address in Homs, I think about where the envelopes of bills will go, now that the house is gone. Can the name of a street on a piece of paper prove that our family was there?

Outside, the summer picks the Barada clean as a bone. When

Abu Sayeed takes me for a walk, the river bottom pokes up like the fin of a whale.

Zahra doesn't want to leave the air conditioning, so Abu Sayeed takes me south of the river to the Souq al-Hamidiyah and the Umayyad Mosque and the old citadel. We walk the Old City of Damascus, tracing the ring of the ancient wall. Most of the gray stones are so ground down they almost disappear into the mortar.

"This wall is falling apart," Abu Sayeed says, crumbling stone between his fingers. I touch it and wonder if there's a level where the old city wall is still strong, where things are still intact.

The day before Huda is discharged, Mama comes with us. She walks with slow steps, wearing a twisted pair of pumps she found in the ruins of the house. Baba was right. She's got no rips in her pantyhose.

Mama shoulders her burlap bag in the heat. Abu Sayeed follows behind us. We walk south, past the river, past the souq. We come out at a long shop-lined street paved with cobblestones, almost too narrow for two lanes of cars. White plaster houses with stone archways sit on either side, their flat roofs decorated with satellite dishes and TV antennas.

"This street is called Straight," Mama says. "Ash-Shari al-Mustaqim. In the time of the Romans, it was near impossible to make a street straight."

I lean out to look one way, then the other. The street runs east to west across the city. We follow the sidewalk, dodging people hurrying by. I want so badly to stop somebody, anybody, and tell them my house burned up, that it fell down, that it exploded. How can life go on like it always did?

"It's the only street mentioned by name in the Bible," Mama says. A beat-up pickup passes us, mumbling over lumps in the cobblestones. "You know the passage, don't you?"

But I don't want to talk about it, so I lie. "I don't remember."

Abu Sayeed says nothing, fingering a stone in his pocket.

"This is the street where Saint Paul stayed, where he fled after Allah blinded him with a flash of light on the road to Damascus," Mama says. "The street where the Lord sent Ananias to give Paul back his sight."

"Why did God blind him?" I asked.

Abu Sayeed says, "Maybe so he could give Paul his eyes."

"That doesn't make sense," I say.

Mama rubs my shoulder and nudges me along, her burlap bag swinging at her side. "You'll understand one day," she said. "When you're older."

I frown. All the way back to the hospital, I remember what Huda would have said: Not when I'm older. Just when it's time.

HUDA IS AWAKE the next morning, but the pain medicine makes her not herself. When she gets discharged, her shoulder is wrapped in bandages, her bad arm in a sling. The doctor tells Huda what to do, how to keep the wound clean, how much medicine to take. No one needs to translate, because after the doctor is gone, Mama clucks and fusses and tells her again in English.

We get in the green car again and drive, passing street vendors selling scarves and oranges, high-rise hotels, and half a dozen churches. Abu Sayeed pulls out onto the M5 highway. Mama says we have to go to Jordan, where there's an American embassy and people who can help us get home again. I hope that means we're going back to Manhattan.

Beyond the Ghouta, flat squares of green turn to orange soil and scrub grass. An old white Mercedes passes us. The green car shimmies, one of the tires lower than the others. I realize this is the closest I've ever come to having a car. We only ever took cabs when we got those big burlap bags of rice from Chinatown.

We're between blue road signs when the car starts to buck, metal rumbling and scraping over road. We pull over. The tires churn dirt.

When we get out, I put my finger in the ground, spiraling through chunks of sand, pebbles, and the dry roots of wild thyme. The soil is orange as muhammara, the dip Mama makes with red peppers and ground-up walnuts. I wonder what Abu Sayeed's son would say the ground is made of: Calcium? Gypsum? Iron?

Abu Sayeed curses and kicks the tires. Wings of steam lift up from under the hood. A quarter mile ahead, there's another blue sign. *Jordan*, it says, an arrow pointing up. I look up at the Q-tips of the clouds.

A blue van pulls up behind us, raking the gravel. A little girl tumbles out and then a tall lady, taller than Mama. The girl runs dirt through her fingers, puts it in her mouth. The lady walks over, her long skirt swaying, and says something in Arabic. I listen. *Broken—your car—we saw your children.*

Mama's hands and the lady's move fast. Mama always talks with her hands. The tall lady's voice is thick as water, ruby purple as pomegranate seeds. Sweat darkens the gauzy linen of her hijab where it meets her forehead and her temples, and it glistens in the spaces between her fingers when she talks.

I walk over to the girl in the dirt. She must be really little, maybe three, because nobody who's been to school puts things in their mouth unless they want to get sick. She smells like she hasn't had a bath in a while. I crinkle my nose at the stinging smell of dirty diaper, the chicken-soup smell of armpits. But I feel bad, because I haven't had a bath in five days either.

"What's your name?"

The little girl doesn't say anything. She wears a pair of fuzzy earmuffs, like something you'd wear in the snow, but it's too hot for that now. Scraggly hair hangs down one side of her head. Her round face is all puffed cheeks and grinning mouth, showing a half-dozen gaps of lost teeth.

Does she know I'm there? I crouch down and pick up a pebble, waiting for her to notice. The girl puts her palms in the dirt again, making paste with her spit. A car blows by us toward the Jordanian border, spinning dust into our eyes.

"Can you hear?" I say. "What's your name?" I try in Arabic: "Shu ismik?"

The little girl spins her head toward me and grins, but she doesn't say anything. The hair on the other side of her head has been shaved off, leaving a velvety layer over her skull. But when I look closer, it's actually an uneven ring around her ear. The hair hasn't been shaved. It's been singed off.

"Can you hear with those on?" I reach for her earmuffs and lift one side. She flings her arms at me, batting me away. The earmuffs fall off. She grabs her other ear, the one facing away from me. There's only pulpy meat where her ear should be, a red mess wrapped in bandages. Her ear has been torn right off, the delicate bone and earlobe ripped from the side of her skull. Tiny nubs of flesh and cartilage poke through the rubbery mass, like strawberry Jell-O capped by a layer of pus. The ring of singed hair extends in a scar down her neck, jagged and pink.

The little girl scrambles for her earmuffs and runs for the tall lady's skirt. I try to think what could have done something like that to the girl, what could have blown a person's ear clear off their head. But then I remember the dining table snapped like stale bread, and I don't want to know.

I turn at a few words in Arabic from behind me. An old man gets out of the van, leaning his weight on the door handle. Abu Sayeed has helped him out of his seat. The old man wears a checked yellow shirt with sleeves to his elbows and tan trousers that are too short for him. When he unfolds himself from the car, his pants sag from his belt, covering up the white linen socks inside his brown loafers.

"He says the girl's name is Rahila," Abu Sayeed says.

"Who says?" I get up and stretch my knees.

Abu Sayeed points to the old man with the crown of his head and then frowns at the dust on my pants and my slippers.

"Are you Rahila's jiddo?" I ask, using the Arabic word for grandfather. The old man looks wrinkled, ancient. His dark hair has a blue-black sheen, the kind you get from dyeing it with henna and indigo. It's combed neatly back, an inch of gray sprouting on either side of the part.

"He doesn't speak any English," Abu Sayeed says. "And I don't think so."

The man says something in fast Arabic, like a deep river. Abu Sayeed translates: "I only had enough bus fare to get to Al-Kiswah. That's where Umm Yusuf found me. She wouldn't let an old man crumble on the side of the road."

When I frown at *Umm Yusuf*, Abu Sayeed leans down. "Rahila's mother also has a son named Yusuf," he says, and I remember how Abu Sayeed got his name, the son he lost.

I sit down in the dirt. "But where are you going?"

Abu Sayeed translates my question. Then the tall lady says something in a storm of Arabic, and Abu Sayeed moves to the back of the van. She gives him something. Abu Sayeed comes back holding a metal leg between two bars of steel, something like a wrench. He calls it a jack. He loosens up the hubcap bolts while the old man answers my question.

"What did he say?" I have to yell over the cars swishing by.

Abu Sayeed gets down on his knees with the jack, frowning up at the belly of the green car. He shouts back a translation. "He used to be a storyteller in a café in Damascus. A hakawati. Then the café was shelled, and he couldn't find work." Abu Sayeed squeezes the jack under the car and fiddles with it. It starts to expand. "He left his home and livelihood."

I perk up. "A storyteller?"

Abu Sayeed translates. The car rises at one corner, like a dog picking up its leg. The old man says something in Arabic to Abu Sayeed, words carving shapes in the wind. He blooms in front of me, his voice a green flower. He looks happy and young, like he'd never grown old at all, like it was only a trick of the light.

Abu Sayeed eases the wheel off and inspects the tire, his nails rimmed with grease. I wait for the old man's answer, watching the curls of his silver beard and his cracked lips.

"Tales of kings and adventurers." Abu Sayeed translates, and the old man smiles. "Salah ad-Din. Sinbad the Voyager. The great love stories, fables that fed my parents and my grandparents."

"Tell me a story," I say.

"I don't tell stories anymore," the old man says through Abu Sayeed, "just the truth of things. I used to love the tales of jinn and the deeds of princes. My heart beat for all that once was—the lovers, the mapmakers, the adventurers." The old man props his weight on the door handle and lowers himself to the dirt, shaking his finger. "Don't forget," he says, and Abu Sayeed looks up while he translates, holding the words back a little, "stories ease the pain of living, not dying. People always think dying is going to hurt. But it does not. It's living that hurts us."

Abu Sayeed kicks at the wheel. "The tire isn't the problem," he says, wiping his hands on his pants. "It's the axle. She won't run a mile more."

We get into Umm Yusuf's blue van. I watch the flat green-and-yellow country pass by. There is so much I've already forgotten that I wonder if I'll remember this. I wonder if something so big could disappear from your head, like opening the door of a moving car and stepping out of it.

We pass crumbs of brick and an old stone railway station, the long-faced windows boarded and barred. The border crossing looms up. First come the cypress trees, then a rounded white curb. Huda is draped half across me, leaning on Zahra, who has her face turned to the cushions. Huda opens her eyes only long enough to smile at me.

We come to a set of white and green archways with wide gates. Policemen stand in the shade, waving us toward the curb. We get out. They ask for our papers. Truck brakes squeal behind us.

Zahra leans against a metal post with her head in her hands. "I'm tired," she sobs. "I just want something to eat. I want a normal bed."

Huda sways, her bandaged arm knocking against her ribs. We wait. Mama and Umm Yusuf talk. The old man sits down on the ground while the policemen check the van.

I tug on Mama's sleeve. She answers me in Arabic, forgetting. "Are they letting us in? When do we go home?"

Mama looks like I bit her. "We can't go home," she says. Umm Yusuf pulls out booklets and papers, pointing to each of us in turn. Mama leans down. She smooths my hair, frizzy from the scratchy headrest. "Remember, habibti, it isn't the place that matters. Your family is here. That has to be enough."

Beyond the archways, the steppe eyes us, a yellow snake pricked with tufts of green. I read the blue signs down the road, half-Arabic and half-English. *Welcome to the Hashemite Kingdom of Jordan.*

Farther on, past the border, the curb is black and white, just like the archways of the shops in Damascus. Stray trucks have taken chunks out of it, like the ruins of the old citadel. The pavement on the other side has a shimmering quality to it, like it's shifting in front of me, as though the world outside of Syria is made of fear and wonder and light.

Something rumbles behind us, on the Syrian side of the border. I turn back and see smoke. A lady behind us says something to her kids in Arabic—*Fireworks. They are only fireworks.*

Even if I didn't know what the rumbling was, my muscles do. My legs tense, telling me to run. While a puff of crumpled smoke fogs the horizon, I feel for the first time how far away we are from Homs, how there really is no going back now. The lady behind me tugs her daughter against her knees and meets my eyes, her face tight with fear. Her son bends his neck to check his phone before stuffing it in his pocket. I can tell by how they stand too far apart that they're leaving room for somebody who isn't there. The world is ripping apart, I think, leaving pain to spread like blood through Huda's bandages.

Farther up, a man waves us through the gates. The old man, the storyteller, gets up. Then there's a flurry of Arabic, and he sits down again. I wonder if he left behind a family of his own, if I could do the same if I had to.

"Why can't he come?" I ask, pointing to the old man. "Why not?"

Zahra hides her face, her right hand dipping into her pocket for the phone that isn't there. Huda's sneaker slips off her foot and drags on the sidewalk. She stumbles. Nobody answers me.

Mama takes my hand and holds on to Huda with the other. Abu Sayeed follows behind us. Umm Yusuf gets back in the blue van, and Rahila puts her palm to the window from her car seat.

"We cross separately," Mama says.

"But the old man—"

He hobbles after us, a slow, measured walk. He ignores the men shouting at him and stops at the border. He leans on the gate after we're through, putting his face to the bars. I realize I never asked him his name.

"He has no family to vouch for him," Mama says.

"Can't we do anything?"

"He doesn't have the proper papers," Mama says, grunting to hold Huda up when she slips. "There is a system. It's complicated."

"It doesn't have to be," I say.

"But it is, whether we like it or not." Abu Sayeed's voice is all black consonants and sour vowels drawn out like oil on concrete. I don't recognize it.

I take another step toward the road beyond the border. I hold my breath, waiting for the moment when Syria and I split apart, realizing that once I cross, there's no way for me to know what will happen to the place I once called home.

Umm Yusuf parks the van by the side of the road up ahead, waiting for us. I look back at the gate as we walk.

The old storyteller presses his forehead to the bars. He reaches out his hand and flattens his palm against them, his fingertips outstretched. He blinks, slowly, and smiles. His combed black hair reflects the sun, his gray roots a feathered crown. His smile becomes a reminder, a picture to fix in my mind forever.

The sun beats hot on the wild thyme. I trip over my feet on the curb. When I turn back again, the storyteller is still watching us, his words still in my head: *It's living that hurts us.*

PART II

JORDAN / EGYPT

Beloved, I
am blind. See,
hands
ones I used
and there is
nothing but
I decay

here, my
before my face — my   crooked hands,   the
to hold you with. We used to feel joy. Now I am blind,
sand in my eyes, beloved. I cannot see your face. I feel
bone. My body is blind and my heart has   gone numb.
like the cut end of a palm branch. Lips basalt   black, the
dry wadi of my spine, skin torn like cloth. I   have
wandered too long under the coin of the sun. I   am a
single ache. I fall down. I long for water, for the
cool ribbon of your hair, but the dunes slice on
before me. I go willingly to my banishment. How often
I think of you and wonder where you are, but you have
turned your face. My mother and my sister cloak
themselves in ashes. Do I mourn your absence, O beloved,
or is it you who mourn mine? I turn my face from that womb
of cypress in the valley and descend. The heavens lie heavy on
my back. My skin burns, dry parchment, stolen voice. Beloved,
you bury me. I will sing for you until the day we walk again in
gardens, until I plunge my face into the green depths and swim up
to where you are. Wait there for me under the navel of the night,
your face pressed like a mirror to the moon.

Hidden Heavens

*

From ash-Sham, the trade roads wandered south through the steppe, curving around the border of the lands occupied by the Franj Crusaders: the southern tip of the County of Tripoli and, beyond that, the Kingdom of Jerusalem over the mountains to the west. The expedition followed the road toward the edge of Nur ad-Din's territory, toward the border with the Fatimid Empire. Patches of shrubby palms and scrub grasses interrupted the steppe, and the occasional group of sheep grazed under stands of cypress or Lebanon cedar.

In those days, the lands were pockmarked by the bloody snarls of disputes between the Seljuqs, the Fatimids, and the Crusaders, but al-Idrisi was unafraid. He checked his notes and guided the expedition to the southeast, away from the trade roads they had been following for nearly a fortnight. He had a particular destination in mind before they turned west toward Cairo and the Maghreb beyond. Rawiya asked him where they were going.

"My boy," al-Idrisi said, "to understand that, you must understand a few other things besides."

As their camels plodded across the yellow steppe, he told Rawiya, Bakr, and Khaldun of his boyhood passion for maps and mathematics. "What I wanted more than anything," he said as he checked the astrolabe, "was to travel and to see the world. That is why I left for Anatolia at sixteen." He laughed. "What a fool. Young and full of adventure, thinking myself invincible. That wondrous journey fixed in my mind the idea of a wide world, full of dangers and beautiful things. I loved that world, in spite of its crushing vastness. I loved it in spite of the terrible weight of its hope."

An oasis with a fortified outpost appeared in the distance. Palms jutted up around the stone dome of a crumbling qasr, a castle. Grooves of abandoned irrigation ditches rimmed the building.

"Deserted," Rawiya said.

"This is Qasr Amra," said al-Idrisi, "once the pleasure-dwelling of Walid the Second, a place of entertainment, songs, and banquets. The caliphs once listened to songs and poetry by the castle's pools. It held a hammam painted with fine frescoes. One day, only the foundation will remain."

But the presence of a bathhouse in such a place perplexed Rawiya. "Why a hammam in the middle of the Badiya?" she asked, motioning to the rocky steppe. "And how?"

Al-Idrisi told them the hammam had probably been supplied by a wadi that filled during the rainy winter months. "An indulgent use of water here in the Badiya," he said. "I have heard stories of deep wells and a complex system for diverting water."

Khaldun stared into the empty pools overgrown with scrub grasses. "Can you imagine it?" he asked. "The caliphs and the poets, the hunting parties, the feasting and song? The performances given here were the pride of their day. Now they are forgotten."

Qasr Amra was built of limestone and basalt, its old walls rubbed smooth by the wind. Inside, cool dark washed over them. The triple-vaulted, domed ceiling curved high above their heads.

Al-Idrisi found a torch, shriveled but intact. Bakr fumbled with his striking flint.

A whoosh of flame burst to life, revealing painted walls. The frescoes were bright as crushed fruit: the sumac-red fur of a bear playing an oud. Sulfur-colored camels laden with blankets. Bathing women with dark hair as glossy as ebony.

Al-Idrisi took them into a tall side chamber. "This is the caldarium," he said, scribbling in his leather-bound book. "In the days when the caliphs used this hammam, the caldarium was the bathhouse's steam room."

A zodiac painting crowned the domed caldarium, the plaster just lifting at its edges. The indigo of Cassiopeia's gown sparkled in the torch glow, and the brilliant turquoise of Sagittarius's bow curved to catch the light. The elegant figures of the constellations spun above them, driven by the wheel of the heavens.

"Only a few have seen these frescoes with their own eyes," al-Idrisi said. "They make up one of the most exquisite examples of a vault of heaven in all the world."

"A vault of heaven?" Rawiya asked.

Al-Idrisi lowered his face from the frescoes. "A dome decorated with a diagram of the stars," he said, "the constellations as you would see them if you were to look down from amid the heavens. The Umayyad caliph must have invited Greek or Byzantine craftsmen to complete it. There is not another to equal it in all the earth."

Rawiya extended her hand toward the crumbling face of an oud player and wondered who had taken refuge here over the years, whether the place might have been looted after it was abandoned. Her fingers hovered over a deep crack in the ravaged stone, like an old scar. It was a noble thing, she thought, to seek beauty in a calloused world.

"The torch won't last much longer," Bakr said. "We should go out while it's still light."

Outside, their camels shuffled their hooves in the dust. Al-Idrisi folded his notes into his leather book and set the clasp, and Rawiya saw a sketch map he had drawn of the Badiya, with south oriented at the top.

Beyond the outer courtyard, the servants waited, circling the camels. The growing winds carried sharp sand, and they pulled their turbans tight. Their faces flushed with torchlight, the expedition stared up at the rising moon.

They readied the camels. Rawiya turned to Khaldun. "My father used to love to look at the stars," she said, "before he died. When he fell ill, he tried once to get out of bed. He took me out past the olive grove at dawn so we could see falling stars sparking." The camels lowed and spat. Rawiya straightened her saddle. "Neither of us knew the names of the constellations, so we used to make up our own. But the skies look different here."

Khaldun helped Rawiya fasten her saddle, the side of his hand brushing hers. Heat crept up her neck. She cleared her throat and pulled away, hoping he hadn't felt the trembling in her fingertips.

A brotherly smile crossed Khaldun's face. "Sometimes," he said, "a picture can only be understood by looking at it upside-down."

Rawiya patted her camel's neck, smiling to herself. "Just like a map."

* * *

AT FIRST, JORDAN is rocky and as flat as the bottom of a foot. But then the road curls west across low hills like crinkled paper. As we wind away from the border toward Amman, everything is yellow earth: ripe-banana earth molded into valleys, knobby amber earth cracked by sun, olive-pinky earth smooth as a spatula. As we drive south, the roads widen, becoming clogged with trucks. We pass small villages, then an oil refinery. A train chug-chugs, far off, past a handful of camels. It never cooled off last night, and even though it isn't muggy here, the day gets hot, and the van's engine rattles. We roll the windows down, watching the heat wisp off the steppe. An endless string of power lines tunnels into the distance.

The buildings get bigger and closer together. Then the hills come, jostling us over their crests. I try and remember what Mama told me once—that Amman was originally built on seven hills, but that it now sprawls across at least nineteen, maybe more. On the edge of the city, the houses are taller, and apartment buildings cluster into the bones of the hillsides. Green comes: sparse grass, linden trees, blue anchusa flowers. Mama stares out the window at the blue flowers and murmurs their Arabic name: "Lisan al-thawr." Bull's tongue.

I stare at minarets and hotels in the distant western neighborhoods of the city, shimmering with glass and new construction. We can't be more than a fifteen-minute drive from there, but here everything is different. The van twists through a sea of brown and white plaster buildings and strips of flat, red-rimmed rooftops. Closing food marts lock up the soda in their mini-fridges and tuck in bunches of bananas hanging by their counters. Lights come on in the square slits of windows. Piles of matchbox houses elbow each other on either side of a potholed street.

From the front seat, Abu Sayeed says, "East Amman."

"Not a single word to strangers," Mama says, "do you hear?" She fidgets with the buttons on her blouse and smooths the burlap bag like it's a purse. Zahra mimics Mama's anxious hands, twisting her gold bracelet. Across the road, an old truck is parked in an empty lot, and kids play soccer in the street. Mama ignores their shouts, smoothing her unwashed hair. Even here, she's a lady. Not a thread of her is frayed.

We pull up to the curb in front of a squatty-faced building in yellowed brick and concrete. The van doors snap open, and we tumble out. A dog barks somewhere, a cone of silver purple. Down the hill, streetlights come on, chasing the orange squeak of a shopkeeper rolling down his metal curtain.

I stumble to a linden tree by the curb, stretching my legs, shaking out my ankles. With my nose to the linden's bark, I smell car exhaust and must and roots.

Mama tugs out her burlap bag. She dusts herself off like she does when she's painting, never getting a speck of paint on her smock. Her fingers bird-twist over her blouse, her hair, her hips. She straightens her pumps even though the uppers are crooked, pulling away from the soles. She helps Huda up from her seat, bending over with her weight.

Abu Sayeed carries out his fistfuls of papers, his case of geologist's tools. Umm Yusuf straightens Rahila's earmuffs, clucking at her wet bandages, and lifts her from her car seat. She coos something in Rahila's good ear, lifting her to her shoulder like Rahila is a delicate piece of papier-mâché. Something about her movements is slow, resigned. When she sees me standing under the tree, she pats my shoulder and leads me up the walk.

We climb the stairs to a little apartment. "My mother and my son are waiting for us," Umm Yusuf says. "They left before we did. Now there will be three generations under one roof again." She smiles, lifting the hem of her skirt as we climb. Her cheeks are full, and her smile is bordered by dimples, but her skin is ashen from lack of sleep.

The stairwell gets narrow as we go up, so I fall behind Umm Yusuf, watching the back of her maroon scarf. Mama climbs up behind me, and that smell is still on her—that burnt smell. The same scent is on me, on my tee shirt and in the hairs that are just sprouting on my arms. The shell must have left sulfur and smoke in us and not just metal. All of us have been soaked in bad memories.

"Mama." I pull her aside. "What happened to Rahila's ear?"

"Don't you have eyes?" Mama snaps at me, her whisper red-edged. For the first time she seems really angry, really afraid. "You saw the shelling. Look at Huda. What do you think happened?" But she must feel bad, because she puts her hand on my shoulder. "Hush, now," she says, and the anger is gone from her voice.

Umm Yusuf unlocks the door. In the apartment, somebody shuffles toward us. Out pops a wobbly pink voice, like how my sitto used to sound on the phone before she died: "Ya Rahila, ya ayni!" The woman behind the door isn't talking to me, but I shiver anyway. Only Sitto used to call me "ya ayni"—my eye—and I haven't heard it since she passed away.

The door swings open, making shadows on the white ceiling tiles. A single bulb hangs in the middle of the room. Faded cushions are lined up along the wall, and a leather-sided trunk in front of them serves for a table. An empty soda can sits on top, a clump of nodding anchusa poking out of the can's rim. For a second that's all I see, the soda can that passes for a vase and the bare trunk for a table. Why didn't I realize you can't just super-glue a dining table back together, a house? How long will it be until we get back the things we lost?

An old lady yanks the door fully open and exchanges cheek kisses with Umm Yusuf, then bends down to gather Rahila in her arms. The lady's thick ankles peek out under a long cotton skirt, her knee-high nylons shimmering along her shins. She speaks in fast Arabic and birdsong vowels. I recognize a few words from the tangle: *I've missed you* and *Where is he?* Umm Yusuf looks around like she was expecting someone else, and the old lady scowls and shoos the air with her gnarled hands.

"Nour." Umm Yusuf bends toward me. "This is Ummi—my mother, Rahila's grandmother. You can call her Sitt Shadid. She's been waiting for us a long time."

Sitt Shadid holds up three crooked fingers and shakes them. "Three month," she says, then opens her hand and waves it around like she's sifting flour. Something in Arabic: *out of days.*

Mama's eyes dance between us. "She means she's waited three months for Umm Yusuf and her daughter to arrive. The time was too long to wait much longer."

Umm Yusuf laughs. "She means if we had taken any longer, she'd be dead."

It's the first joke anybody has told in days, and I'm not sure whether to laugh. I stick out my hand instead. "It's nice to meet you."

Sitt Shadid scoops me up in a bear hug, sweeping me into her round softness. I haven't been hugged, really hugged, in so long. At first I forget what to do, and I stiffen up. I'm afraid that if I don't, the last hug I got from Baba will seep out through my pores and be lost forever. But Sitt Shadid pats and rubs my back, and I relax. I reach across her wide arms, my cheek to her neck. She smells like jasmine flowers and olive soap.

When she lets me go, I scoot over to Huda and grab her around the waist. Huda feels different—thin and angular from not eating, from sleeping all the time. She strokes the back of my neck under my hair, where my bones stick out like a bird's. Her hand jerks and flinches against me, and I know her painkiller is wearing off.

Mama introduces Zahra and Huda in Arabic. Umm Yusuf clicks her tongue. "My son Yusuf was supposed to be here," she says. "I'm sorry, there is simply no controlling him—"

"It's all right," Mama says.

Umm Yusuf shakes her head and moves off toward the tiny kitchen in the corner of the room. "I never should have sent him ahead of us," she says, lifting her hands, "but with Rahila in the hospital, and Ummi not traveling much, I felt at least some of us would get out of harm's way." Umm Yusuf is so tall I'm afraid she'll hit the lightbulb if she doesn't duck, but she passes right under it, grazing the bulb with the top of her scarf. It swings, reflecting light off the window into the dark outside.

We take off our shoes and sit on the cushions while Umm Yusuf and Sitt Shadid fight over who will make dinner. We've come to the apartment just in time to eat the iftar, the dinner you eat during Ramadan after the sun has set.

I sit on a flat pillow on the floor, wriggling my toes toward the anchusa in the soda can. I bite the inside of my cheek. But then Sitt Shadid comes over and sets a hand on the wall, shifting her weight back to sit down. For a second I'm afraid she'll crash into the wall. I try to hold up her weight, but she just rocks back until she drops, and the pillow breaks her fall. When she smiles at me and holds out her palms, I crack a smile too, and it doesn't matter that I can't understand everything she says because I understand that.

We eat tabbouleh with double the parsley and half the usual portion of cracked wheat, and Mama and Umm Yusuf and Abu Sayeed pass stories back and forth in Arabic sprinkled with English. I squint and listen. Zahra picks at her shredded jeans with a sour look on her face. Sitt Shadid sits next to me with Rahila on her knee, and Huda sits on my other side with her good arm around me. She holds her breath when she shifts her weight. I can tell the pain is rushing back into her shoulder. She smiles through it, though, letting Rahila sit in both our laps after we finish eating. Rahila nods off on my collarbone, her earmuffs fuzzy against my neck. She and Huda both smell like the gray green of cumin and iron. Sitt Shadid laughs and rocks back and forth. She sings old songs in Arabic, and Umm Yusuf sings harmony in her ruby-purple voice. Sitt Shadid's notes are warm twirls of cinnamon and beech pink, and the corners of the room hum with them. My eyes droop shut, and my chin drops. I listen until I can't hear the songs anymore, just see their colors, the way the notes plant themselves closer together than they do in Western music. I lift my eyelids just long enough to see Sitt Shadid's cheeks and chin puffy with song, and I feel safe. Then I sleep too.

A FEW HOURS later, Mama wakes us up and shoos us across the hall to get a bath and get ready for bed. Abu Sayeed takes the room next to ours. "We are lucky," Mama says after I dry off. "You must all thank Sitt Shadid when you see her. These rooms were for Umm Yusuf and her children. They gave us two of the three they rented so we don't have to sleep on the street."

"And we can stay?" I ask.

"For now." Mama pulls out the dirty carpet she saved from the house. "Keep your shoes off. The carpet is clean. Soon we'll get something more permanent."

The carpet isn't that clean, but there's no arguing with Mama. While I kick my slippers off, I realize we won't have to sleep outside, that we might have if things had been different. That makes me feel like I love Sitt Shadid a lot, more than I let anybody know. And then the hot sting of shame comes over me, and I wish I had laughed at Sitt Shadid's joke, that I had thanked her one more time in Arabic, that I hadn't hesitated before I hugged the whole round pillar of her.

"Four people in one room?" Zahra folds her arms across her chest, her bare feet sticking out under her ripped jeans.

"Tch," Mama says. "You think we can afford a hotel? What do you want me to do? You think we can just go and get our money from the bank, now that we've left the country?"

"I just figured—"

"Look, here, and see what is left." Mama throws open the flap of the burlap bag, tugging it up from the corner where the torn strap is tied on with a knot. She pulls out a clump of bills and a palmful of coins. A stray US dollar is mixed in with the Syrian ones, and another is buried farther down, leftovers from before the move. "Take it and rent a hotel room," Mama says. "Or would you rather eat tomorrow?"

Zahra sulks and curves her shoulders into her elbows. "I'm sorry."

"You should be." Mama snaps the bag shut. "Didn't you see the children by the road, living in the old fish truck? The urchins in the alleys? Would you like to sleep in the van?"

"We have to make do," Huda says. No one has noticed her sit down under the window, her eyes glassy with pain. It's the first thing Huda has said in days.

In the corner of the room, we find an old blanket, maybe left by somebody who used to live here. We lay down on the carpet with the blanket over us, and it feels so soft and warm that I don't care about the grime or not being in my own bed. Huda gives me her scarf for a pillow. It smells like her sweat. I wonder what Abu Sayeed is sleeping on.

I lie awake for a long time, staring at nothing. The building creaks and groans. I toss back and forth until Zahra elbows me, hard, but I still can't fall asleep. I close my eyes and count my breaths. Outside, traffic whines, making the floor tremble.

I wriggle out from under the blanket. I tiptoe out and knock on Abu Sayeed's door.

He comes out barefoot, his shirt untucked. "Little cloud," he says. "What's wrong?"

I put my finger to my lips. I don't want to wake Mama. I hand Abu Sayeed Huda's scarf so he has a pillow.

He shakes his head. "I can't take this."

"Please."

He disappears into the dark room and comes back with a dirty scrap of fabric. "I have my own," he says, but it looks thin. "Why are you still up?"

I shuffle my feet. "I can't sleep."

"Then let's walk awhile." He shuts the door behind him, and we wander barefoot down the hall. "Sometimes, when sleep does not come," Abu Sayeed says, "I go looking for it."

At the end of the hall is a narrow door. Abu Sayeed and I step out onto a tiny second-floor ledge with an iron railing. The chill of the breeze surprises me after such a hot day. Below us, the sidewalk is empty. The city honks and blinks with life.

"I don't think we should be out here in the cold," he says.

"Can't we stay a minute?" I grab the railing and scan the street down the hill, beyond the rooftops. A bus hisses by, its brake lights brighter than the stars. The constellations shiver.

"I wish I knew all the names of the stars." I sit down, sticking my legs through the railing and swinging them. I tilt my neck back to see the Milky Way. The streetlamps and the bright hotels downtown gray out the sky, leaving just pinpricks of light. I look for the blocks of Ursa Major and the bull, scan the sky for Polaris and Thurayya—the Pleiades. "Did you know the Bedu saw a camel in Cassiopeia? For a long time, that's all anybody saw."

"Is that so?" Abu Sayeed looks skyward. "What else do you know?"

I point out the three mourning daughters, the two calves at the mill, and the gazelles running from the lion. But then I stop talking. I know where the gazelles are running. I know, no matter what the season, that they never stop their sprinting across the sky.

"What else did you find up there?" Abu Sayeed asks.

"I found us," I say. Then I start to cry. "I can't remember Baba's voice. I can't even remember it."

"Little cloud." He kneels next to me on the rough concrete, the night wind making ice out of his fingers. "Of course you do. You don't forget a thing like that."

"It looked like caramels and oak bark," I say. "Those were Baba's colors. But then he died, and they buried his voice. Now I've got the color but not the sound of it. All I've got is a brown streak on the wall." I hiccup and set my forehead on the railing. It makes long dents in my skin. "I should remember. But I don't."

"You didn't forget him," Abu Sayeed says. "You have a picture of your baba in your mind. You just see him differently than other people."

I pull my head back, touching the grooves in my cheek. "I want to be like everybody else."

"No one is like everybody else." Abu Sayeed taps the tips of his fingers to the railing. "All the stars are different, but when you look up, you see them just the same."

I lean over and hug Abu Sayeed, but a cold feeling cuts through the middle of me, like I've lost something I can't get back. My feet dangle through the railing, numb from the wind. Abu Sayeed wraps his arm around my shoulders, smelling of parsley and rock dust.

Beyond the city limits, the steppe is night. I think of Rawiya and al-Idrisi sleeping under the stars. The bulb of a streetlamp erases Leo Minor. I lean toward it without meaning to, separating from Abu Sayeed's warmth like acrylic paint peeling, like a gazelle who knows only how to run.

Stories You Tell Yourself

✳

From Qasr Amra, the expedition returned to the trade road. They continued south toward the Red Sea, toward the end of Bilad ash-Sham and Nur ad-Din's protection. They found themselves on a high plateau with mountains to their west. Al-Idrisi sketched maps and checked his notes. He pointed away over the mountains, where caravans of merchants had described to him a salt-choked inland sea. "South of those dead waters," he said, showing them what he had written, "a great valley runs, the one called Wadi Araba. It runs south as far as the Gulf of Aila, where it empties." No one in the expedition had seen these things themselves, for at the foot of the western mountains lay the forts of the Franj that marked the border of the Kingdom of Jerusalem, and they could go no farther west in safety.

But al-Idrisi lifted his finger to his friends and smiled. "Soon," he said, "we will turn west and cross the Gulf of Aila, which leads to the Red Sea. We will enter the Fatimid Empire, the lands of Egypt and the Nile Delta, and the Maghreb beyond. We will see God's wonders with our own eyes."

Now, news of Nur ad-Din's victory in ash-Sham and the roc's retreat had quickly reached the Kingdom of Jerusalem and the Fatimid Empire. The news had set nerves on edge, for as al-Idrisi himself knew, Fatimid power in Cairo was beginning to weaken.

Corruption and intrigue whispered in every hillside village. Bandits had grown bolder, putting caravans at risk. This only added to the dangers the expedition would have to face before they cleared the Nile Delta and approached the Gulf of Sidra, where King Roger had set up his coastal outposts in Ifriqiya. Until then, al-Idrisi and his friends would have to avoid Franj fortresses, high mountain cliffs, and Fatimid suspicions.

The Fatimids had much to be suspicious about. Nur ad-Din had long hoped to gain a foothold in Cairo. And in those days, the Fatimid Empire feared not only the Kingdom of Jerusalem and Nur ad-Din's new stronghold in ash-Sham, but also Berber forces massing in the west near Barneek and the Gulf of Sidra—the mighty Almohads.

"Why this fighting?" Rawiya asked. "They are all followers of God."

"Look around you," Khaldun said. "In the last several weeks, we have seen the forts of the Franj, provincial quarrels, thirst for gold and water. Refugees expelled from their homes by the invading armies crowd into the cities of Bilad ash-Sham. Ruler plots against ruler. The world is changing."

"But must innocent lives be lost," Rawiya said, "over such thirsts for land and gold? And we are explorers, not spies."

"As any poet knows," Khaldun said, "the story often matters less than the telling."

Rawiya spurred her camel forward. "What is that supposed to mean?"

"Our purpose matters less," al-Idrisi said, snapping his book shut, "than what our enemies believe."

They spoke little that day and the next, brooding on bad luck. The road was long, and the paths that led from the northern plateau through the valleys had not yet been mapped. Al-Idrisi often checked his notes and astrolabe, but they lost the path several times and had to go back the way they came.

The expedition soon entered rocky country. They wound into

a narrow canyon of red cliffs, hoping their path was true. But that afternoon, a sandstorm whipped up from the east, throwing them off the southbound road. Their camels picked their way along the rubble-covered path and clamped their noses shut. Rawiya and her friends wrapped their faces in their turbans. Sand tangled in their eyelashes and filled their mouths with grit. The winds screamed past the cliffs, and the air thickened until they could not see the wind-cut walls.

"We're going the wrong way," Bakr cried. "We've turned around."

"We will be crushed by the winds," al-Idrisi called.

"I see an opening in the rock—" But Rawiya's voice was lost. The storm beat the canyon, the sand grinding at gashes in the walls. The wind yanked up a stone and smacked it into the cliff, and the canyon rang with echoes.

Rawiya groped for her sling. "Give me a stone," she cried. "A coin. Anything."

They could see nothing. Bakr called out, and she followed his voice until she grabbed his camel's reigns. The servants clutched each other, their camels tossing their heads. The canyon walls couldn't be more than a stone's throw away, but they were blind. The sandstorm cut like a dagger.

Bakr, Khaldun, and al-Idrisi emptied their packs. They handed Rawiya Nur ad-Din's dinars, filling her palms. She set the coins in her sling and fired them, waiting to hear the ping of gold on stone.

Nothing.

Rawiya turned in her saddle, firing again. Still nothing. She aimed through the wind, her fingers cramping, the wind driving sand under her nails.

At last, the metal cracked on the canyon wall.

"This way!" Rawiya pushed her camel toward the opening in the rock. The animal picked its way across sharp stones. Feeling their way along the wall, they came to a small cave cut into the rock, enough to shelter their camels and the servants.

Someone shrieked. Rawiya turned back. Bakr's face emerged from the sand, only his eyes peeking out from his turban. "One of the servants' camels caught a hoof on the rock," he shouted. "The animal is all right, but the rider fell." Bakr pulled the injured man out of the wind, limping.

Rawiya led them into the cave, and they laid the man down. "He's broken his shin," she said. "He needs more help than we can give. For now—" She tore a strip of cloth from her cloak and wrapped it around the man's leg, tying it with a strong knot.

They waited for the storm to settle. Though no one said so, they knew they were in danger. The sandstorm had forced them onto a westward road, and they now stood on the border of the Kingdom of Jerusalem—the lands of the Franj Crusaders.

The storm died down near dusk. Rawiya left the cave first, raising her head and a finger to the wind. The rest of the expedition followed, the camels still shaking sand out of the clefts in their hooves.

Only when they turned around did they see it. All around them, cut into the rose-red cliff walls, were majestic dwellings decorated with high pillars, statues, and carvings of flowers. The cliffs on either side had been clawed by wind and time in long stripes. Sand and debris had settled over some of the openings, but others yawned deep into the rock.

"The Nabataean city of Raqmu—Petra. Incredible." Al-Idrisi opened his book and began to sketch and scribble. Rawiya, Bakr, and Khaldun watched over his shoulder. "I had heard stories," he said, his voice rising, "but the paths were never clearly described. I never thought I would see it for myself. Do you understand?" He shook his book in front of him, grinning. "We will map this lost city for the first time."

The expedition followed the canyon paths between the rock dwellings, afraid to speak. By nightfall, they had climbed out of the red mountains. Bedu herders with their flocks hid their faces, watching from a distance.

The expedition emerged from the domed rocks and picked their way down into a sloping valley. Stopping their camels, they shielded their eyes from the setting sun. As the cool of evening gathered, Khaldun clapped his hand to his breast. "This, indeed," he said, "is a gift from God for weary eyes."

A town sat below them, quilted by thick olive groves. Houses dotted the blanket of green, and the streams that ran through the valley churned with mills. Al-Idrisi sketched while they rested, noting the streambeds and the homes nestled against the hillsides. Children watched them, scattered under the trees. If she closed her eyes, Rawiya could almost imagine she was back in Benzú, sitting beside her mother in the shade of the olive grove.

As they entered the village, al-Idrisi called out to a man returning from the grove. "Hail, good sir," he said. "What is the name of this village?"

"Traveling from Nur ad-Din's realm, are you?" The man shielded his eyes.

Thinking fast, Rawiya thought of the Hajj. "We are only pilgrims," she said, "in search of the wonders of God."

Al-Idrisi caught on to her idea. "We lost our way and are in need of a place to spend the night." He motioned to the servant with the broken shin. "One of us is injured."

The man wiped his brow. "I'm surprised to hear you've lost your way. You mean to tell me you haven't seen the new fort, eh? The fort at Wu'eira, north of the valley? I've lived in Wadi Musa all my life. I've seen nothing like it."

Wadi Musa, the Valley of Moses, had been captured several decades ago by Frankish forces. As Rawiya had realized, the expedition had crossed into the Kingdom of Jerusalem without meaning to, passing under the nose of a Crusader outpost.

"We have heard of the generosity of the people of the Valley of Moses," said al-Idrisi with care. "And the Kingdom of Jerusalem is known for its wonders."

There was an uneasy silence. The man studied their camels and al-Idrisi's books and scrolls. "Pilgrims, you say?" The man shook his head and drew close to al-Idrisi's camel. "You are poor liars," he said quietly, "but do not be afraid. I am Halim, and what little prosperity I have I am happy to share. My sons and I never supported the division of these lands. What need do we have of borders drawn in blood across God's creation? Christians and Muslims have tilled the soil of this valley side by side for centuries. We are a generous people, with a love of peace in our hearts. And"—here he motioned to al-Idrisi's books—"I myself am partial to scholars and mapmakers."

Halim led them to a clearing in the olive trees and a small house, where they tied up their camels. Halim and his wife, who could not fit the whole expedition in their tiny kitchen, prepared dozens of steaming bowls of cracked wheat and chickpea fritters. In return, al-Idrisi gave them jeweled bowls and gold dinars from their treasures.

When they had eaten and retired for the night, Rawiya sat awake, looking at the stars. She traced out the camel and the three mourning daughters. How had she never known that the star Vega was named for a falling eagle? The star was even indicated by a bird on the rete of the astrolabe.

Khaldun, who couldn't sleep either, came and sat beside her. "In my experience," he said, "it is a noble person who loves the stars."

Rawiya blushed and said, "The world is so much bigger than I expected."

"And filled with tales." Khaldun tucked his knees into his chest. "But once you've heard too many voices, you start to forget which one is your own."

"I suppose you're right," Rawiya said. "The world is wide, and each of us is so small."

Khaldun eyed the moon. "People think that stories can be walled off, kept outside and separate. They can't. Stories are inside you."

Rawiya turned to look at Khaldun. She felt relaxed, understood—things she had not truly felt since she'd left home. "You are the stories you tell yourself," she found herself saying, as though she and Khaldun had known each other for years, as though it was the most natural thing in the world.

Khaldun nodded. "Certainly." He tossed up a white stone, and it hung suspended between Vega and the horizon before falling to the earth. "If you don't know the tale of where you come from," he said, "the words of others can overwhelm and drown out your own. So, you see, you must keep careful track of the borders of your stories, where your voice ends and another's begins."

The wind rustled the olive leaves, seeming to shake the stars. "Then stories map the soul," Rawiya said, "in the guise of words."

*   *   *

THE NEXT MORNING, Umm Yusuf's son comes back to the apartment when dawn is still a blue fog over the buildings. The door slams across the hall, and I rub my eyes. I throw off the blanket—how am I the only one rolled up in it?—and leave my slippers by the rug.

A throaty voice comes teal and gray under Sitt Shadid's door, a sound stuck deep in the chest. It's the kind of voice that reminds me of the older boys singing songs and throwing up fists in the street in Homs, the angry kind that's all ribs and the wings of shoulder blades. I wonder if all teenage boys are angry like that, if they know anger is a dangerous, unpredictable thing.

I want to coil into the corner and wait until the boy goes away, but I want to make sure Sitt Shadid is okay. I creep out the door and across the hall. The tile in the hallway is a thousand tiny ice cubes on the soles of my feet.

Arguing in Arabic, bursts of a woman's voice pleading like pink violins. I reach the knob and crack the door. The blue anchusa is wilted in the soda can, draping its head over the rim. Sitt Shadid stands with her feet planted, her slippers not on yet, the seam of her knee-highs tight against her toenails. Whoever she's talking to is hidden behind the cracked door. The daylight beats in, lighting up corners that were in shadow last night. Photos taped to the walls flutter over rolled-up sleeping mats and folded blankets. Single cushions line the bare floor. It makes me think of the week one of my friends' families moved to a new apartment, how the place was empty until her parents brought the couch in sideways and reassembled the dining room table. Except there's no U-Haul truck waiting outside here, no box spring to lug in. I think to myself, This is all any of us have.

The person behind the door gives a frustrated sigh. A handful of Arabic words I know come through, like a radio suddenly tuning to a signal: *I need to work, we need to eat.* Sitt Shadid's pink voice: *You'll be caught.* The boy with the teal-gray voice pounds his palm against the wall and says, *You don't understand.*

Sitt Shadid comes back with a hail of angry Arabic, and footsteps storm up to the door. I dive aside and hug the wall. A tall boy huffs out. His gray tee shirt leaves behind a woody smell like sticky evergreens and heat. I hold still, my breath burning in my chest, willing him not to turn. The boy's anger is a knife to me, a weapon. It is the warning sign I should have seen the night the bombs fell on our street. He runs half a fist through his black hair, and I'm so close I can see the pores on the back of his neck. Then he huffs down the stairs, and the door slams below us.

I peek in toward Sitt Shadid. Rahila is asleep on a mat in the corner, her earmuffs rising and falling. Somewhere outside, a dog barks, neon bright in the quiet. If I concentrate, I can just imagine all the things Rahila's family left behind, the brass coffee tray and the children's books and the extra scarves and all the tiny things nobody misses until they aren't there anymore. And I realize that Rahila probably doesn't remember her old house in Syria at all, that pretty soon this will be all she has ever known. Dusty Amman alleys, the broken sewer pipes leaking into the street. The ache of her feet on the bare floor. Wilted anchusa in a soda can.

The fading stars through the warped window whisper to me, *It will happen to you too.* And it's true. Someday I'll have lived out of New York longer than I lived in New York. Someday the summer I lived in Homs will be dozens of summers behind me.

A hard red knot glues itself to my ribs like indigestion, the tangled-up knot of all the things I've loved that will be buried one day, all the things I know I am bound to forget.

Above the apartment, the thrum of a helicopter comes, menacing. The floor trembles under my feet, and I am back in our yellow house in Homs again, the smell of ash in my nose.

I bolt for the stairs.

I tear off down the street. The city is just coming alive, an animal licking its teeth. I breathe hard down the hill, my bare feet thumping pavement. Lights come on in stacks of apartment buildings, and laundry lines shimmy and dance. A mesh of telephone wires chops the air. I rush down toward orange rooftops and the yellow boxes of homes.

I pump my legs, fighting gravity. I twist around a crooked olive tree cut into the sidewalk, tripping around a thick centipede and jumping over a pigeon. Men appear on balconies, drinking coffee or smoking narghiles as they wait for the sky to lighten. Shopkeepers wave delivery trucks into cramped parking spaces. Girls stare at me out latticed windows.

I run through streets I don't recognize. I run up the next ridge and wonder how one city could have devoured nineteen hills. I ignore the sting of tiredness in my calves and wonder if I can run all the way back home, wherever home is now, back to a level of reality where babies don't cry at border crossings and my legs alone could carry me across the ocean. Is there a level I could reach if I ran fast enough, a level where Baba is waiting on the island of Manhattan with his arms open, calling to me from between the coin-operated spyglasses?

I tumble down steps cut into the stony hillside. I zigzag down alleys, past slumped eucalyptus and arrow-necked palms. I run out of breath between three hills, on a side street by a busy intersection. The road is crowded with cars and street vendors, their spices and jewelry piled on long tables. The sidewalks here are so narrow that I have to walk in the street. Cars pass by with their windows down, blaring love songs in English and Arabic. In the distant western section of the city, the round balconies of hotels shimmer, their glass faces yawning.

I'm lost.

I wander, trying to figure out which hill I came from, which neighborhood. But the more I wander, the more lost I get. Nothing looks familiar. No linden tree, no landmarks I know. I keep coming back to the same spot, going in circles. Everything looks different in the daylight than it did in the dark, and even the things I recognize look too much the same. I stop to study the signs, sounding out the letters in Arabic. Across the way, a boy not much older than me stands on the street corner, his feet planted and his shoulders tensed, selling packs of tissues.

Night comes. I shuffle toward the crest of one last hill on my swollen feet, my toenails shredded by asphalt. Car exhaust has turned the hems of my shorts gray, stained my fingers and my knuckles. The scent of roasting freekeh and lamb slice into my hunger.

I sag down under a tree. It's too dark to tell what kind of tree it is, but it smells good, like water and rest, so I lean back on the trunk. My scalp itches against the bark, forcing me to scratch. My whole body is tingling, one long convulsion of emptiness.

I pick a few coin-round leaves from the bottoms of my bare feet. They come away wrinkled with sweat, their softness a relief after the asphalt. Underneath, my soles are split and bleeding, and a tack of white quartz has gashed itself between my toes. I pull it out and brush my blood off its jagged edge. I tuck it in my pocket.

Under red tile roofs, rosy lights come on beneath wooden blinds and curtains. A dog barks silver purple again. Old men with pot-bellies stroll by, hands clasped behind their backs. Ramadan here is no different from Ramadan in Homs: shops closed early, families sharing dates, low tones of relief at the first glass of orange juice after the fast. In the tiny apartment, Umm Yusuf will be stirring lentils and frying sweet onions in oil. The bare floor will be warmed by fourteen feet. The bare walls will be splashed with color from everybody's singing.

"I should have remembered." Tears come hot, but I refuse to let my throat cramp up. I don't want anyone to know I'm crying, not even me. "I should have remembered the way." I thought I was going in the right direction. I always remember, always know how to find my way home. How did I end up so lost?

Rahila will be laughing under her earmuffs right now, fingers clenched around the last scrap of bread. She'll grow up without remembering the time they spent in Syria, thinking that apartment is all the home there ever was.

And what if I never find my way back? What if I live on this street, in this city, for the rest of my life? A broken pipe drips from the cramped apartment building beside me. Is this how people lose themselves, one drop at a time? Memories slide away so quickly—the rooftop garden, the amber-eyed coyote on West 110th, the fig tree in Homs. It would be so easy to forget.

"Nour?"

I wipe my wet chin. A man is silhouetted in the doorway behind me, squinting at my back. He calls my name again in a honey-yellow voice, reminding me of a smiling man in an orange shirt.

"Abu Sayeed!"

I run and press myself into his collarbone, and together we go into the apartment building. A linden leaf peels itself off the sole of my foot. I took myself home without knowing.

"Are you all right?" Abu Sayeed stops outside Sitt Shadid's door and checks my face for scratches. "Your mama nearly died when she found out you were gone."

"I'm okay." The hungry dark gnaws at me, the threat of forgetting. I push open the door to Sitt Shadid's apartment, peering in. The throaty-voiced boy isn't there. The shoes by the door carry the tang of apricots and the must of old walls, familiar smells. But the sound of the pipes dripping follows me into the apartment from the street, and that same rhythmic loneliness curls up inside me like a shadow, a deep wanting.

"Nour, habibti!" Mama rushes to me, surrounding me with hair and warmth. "I was so worried!"

Umm Yusuf hugs me hard too. My sooty fingers stain the hem of her hijab. A circle forms around me, everybody laughing and crying at the same time. Their sounds without words hum in everything, an energy without a language. Sitt Shadid's face runs with tears. She holds up her palms to heaven and thanks God—"Hamdulillah!"—and her voice vibrates the nails in the floorboards.

We eat mujaddara and dates and play backgammon. After we eat the iftar, Sitt Shadid gives me sweet atayef pastries and a stuffed toy, a white bird. I name him Vega. He smells like Sitt Shadid, like jasmine and olive oil.

But as the night goes on, my head starts to itch again—Could tree sap or car exhaust roil my scalp like this?—and I scratch so hard I draw blood. When we go back across the hall, Mama shuts the door and clucks at me. "Why do you scratch your head like that?"

"It itches."

Mama sniffs at the blanket, folded in the corner of our room, and dumps it on the floor. "Zahra," she says. "Get a comb."

While Zahra borrows a comb from Umm Yusuf, I fidget, trying not to scratch. Huda curls up on the carpet, one wrist out, her knuckles resting on the wood. Mama combs out my hair real hard, pulling the skin tight under the bandage on my temple.

"Ow! Don't pull it."

Mama says something under her breath in Arabic.

I make a face, my head burning. "You're not supposed to say that."

But Mama just wipes the comb on her palm and squints at it. Then she combs out Zahra's and Huda's hair. Huda winces and gasps when Mama bangs her shoulder by accident.

"What's going on?" I ask. "Why is nobody saying anything?"

Mama goes across the hall and comes back with electric clippers in her hand. She purses her lips, her fingers tense on the clippers. "Nour," she says, "sit down."

"Why?"

She raises her voice. "Just—sit."

I bend my knees and clunk down on the floor. I stretch my feet on the wood. My toes are tarry burls of dried blood, the arches of my feet stained with grime. The clippers buzz to life behind me.

"Don't cut it," I say.

"Hush." Mama runs her fingers through my hair to part it, lifting a section of thick curls.

"Don't."

The clippers touch the knob of bone at the back of my neck and work their way up. They vibrate my skull and the white quartz in my pocket. We couldn't save any family pictures from the house, so none exist. There are no shots of Baba and me with my dark ringlets. Nothing.

"You have lice," Mama says.

"I don't care." The hair falls on my shoulders in thick strips. I see myself as a boy, my head a lopsided melon. I see Rawiya. "Don't!"

That buzzing, the whine. I shut my eyes. I'm not Rawiya. This isn't an adventure. A yellow wail bubbles out of me.

Mama's hands brush my ears, trembling. "Don't make this harder," she says. I can hear the tears in her voice, firm as a fist.

EVERY DAY AFTER that, Mama goes to the American embassy in downtown Amman and fills out paperwork. We try to make the best of things. I help Sitt Shadid fix up the bare apartment as best we can, plucking fresh anchusa blossoms when we can find them and setting them in a bit of water in the soda can. I try not to think too much about the things we lost—soft rugs under my feet, shelves of my favorite books, stuffed animals and photo albums with pictures of Baba we couldn't find in the rubble.

Outside our window, the neighborhood kids play soccer, and Zahra flirts with Umm Yusuf's son. I stay inside with Huda and my stuffed bird. Even when Umm Yusuf finds me a pair of used sneakers so I don't have to wear my ripped-up slippers anymore, I still won't leave Huda by herself. She sleeps less now and cuts her pain pills in half to make them last.

Mama says she'll get better, that it'll just take time. She tries to get our minds off what she's doing, tries to come home from the embassy every night smiling. But Zahra told me it's not easy to apply for asylum, that there are too many people who don't have anywhere to go and not enough places to put them all. She told me that even though I was born in America, there are no guarantees for people who aren't American citizens, even if they're my mother and sisters. It must be true, because when Mama comes home, I see her out the window by the linden tree, catching her breath before she comes inside. She looks older than she ever did in New York, like she'll cry if she has to put one more smile on. But she does it anyway.

After two weeks of this, Abu Sayeed bursts in one day while Mama is out. His shoulders are sloped with the weight of fasting, and sweat glistens in the gaps in his beard like tiny sequins. "We're taking a trip," he says. "Come."

Propped up by the window, Huda stretches, her bad arm limp in its sling. Just like Rahila's earmuffs, it makes me nauseous to look at it. Their broken places remind me of how contagious pain is, even though I feel awful admitting it.

I shake my head and press it to Vega's wing. "I don't want to."

"Don't be like that." Abu Sayeed walks to the window. Outside, Zahra giggles with the throaty-voiced boy. She spends all her days with him now, twisting her bracelet around her wrist, smiling so much her face should explode. Either she didn't hear the fight he had with Sitt Shadid two weeks ago, or she doesn't care.

"I could use some fresh air," Huda says.

"Come on now, up. Your mama said it would be good for you." Abu Sayeed tugs me up and takes my hand. "No more of this moping. All right?"

When we break out into the sunshine, Huda shields her eyes. Her limbs are just starting to bend, her knees stiff and her shoulders tense. She's like a person waking up after a long sleep.

"Zahra!" Abu Sayeed calls. "I told you once. Bring him or leave him."

The boy blinks. "I'll get Rahila," he says. "She's slept all morning."

We pile into the blue van. Zahra and I sit in the middle row, Huda in the back. Abu Sayeed buckles Rahila into her car seat. The boy sits in front.

"You know, you never even told me your name." I lean forward. The boy doesn't say anything. I drum my fingers on my leg. "Do you even have a name?"

"Nour." Huda pokes me. "You know very well what his name is. His mother is Umm Yusuf."

I cross my arms. "But he never said it to me."

The boy leans back, twisting his lanky shoulders until the tendons in his biceps strain out. His lips are lined with stubble, hardly ever smiling. Under his hard hawk's brow, his face has that stretched-out look teenage boys have, their jaws and bodies all bones.

"Yusuf," he says.

Zahra repeats it so I almost can't hear. She smiles a secret smile to herself and turns her face to the window.

"None of you have been to Jordan," Abu Sayeed says, "so you don't know what you're missing." He rubs his balding forehead, and I touch the shaved vertebrae at the back of my neck. "As a boy, I traveled to Petra, the ancient Nabataean city. I have seen the olive groves of Wadi Musa. According to the tradition, Wadi Musa was the place where Moses struck the rock with his staff, and water flowed from the stone. Did you know that?"

Zahra crosses her arms, jangling her gold bracelet. "Yusuf has been in Jordan three months already."

"But he's never been where we're going," Abu Sayeed says. "I guarantee you that."

We wind through the cramped hillsides of the city, dipping up and down the dry earth. Abu Sayeed turns the radio on, tapping the wheel to American pop music. For the first time, it feels like things are almost normal. Then we pass through the neighborhoods at the eastern edge of Amman, and a cluster of kids walking west stop to stare at us. One of them clutches a pack of tissues to sell, the pockets of his faded sweatpants stuffed with more. In the front seat, Yusuf looks away.

I finger the white quartz in my pocket, and the wind cools my bare scalp. I wonder if the real me is gone forever, shorn off with my hair. I see the storyteller man on the other side of the border crossing, a deep wrinkle like a wadi across his forehead, his rice paper hand on the gate. Something hurts between my ribs.

Beyond the limits of Amman, squatty acacia trees and telephone poles break up the bronze hills. A truck disappears under the shimmer of heat in front of us. Mountains loom. Cliffs of red sandstone rise up, wind-carved, pockmarked like sheets of termite-eaten wood.

An hour outside the city limits, we leave the main road and turn into a fenced-in area. We park next to a silvery saltbush and get out, stepping over loose stones.

"This steppe is the Badiya," Abu Sayeed says. The keys click and chime in his pocket. "It spreads across Jordan, Syria, Iraq, and Saudi Arabia."

Zahra twists her bracelet and waits for Yusuf to get out. Rahila stands next to the van, her hand in her mouth, her eyes wide. A dusty stone and plaster building stands out ahead of us in the steppe. Someone has added white wooden window frames, but they're starting to splinter now. Sand has nibbled at the stones, leaving rough, spongy rock. One building is made up of three smooth domes, several square side rooms, and the dark arch of an entrance.

Abu Sayeed motions for us to follow him. "This," he says, "is one of Jordan's treasures. Qasr Amra. Once it held a palace and bathhouse for a caliph."

We follow the white Reception sign. Abu Sayeed and Huda duck their heads to enter. I follow the swish of Huda's gauzy skirt, the echo of Abu Sayeed's leather soles scuffing across the stone. Red fencing lines the rooms. Blue plaques are hammered into the walls in English and Arabic: No Littering.

Paint has peeled off the walls, leaving splotches of pink plaster. A little decoration is still left—silver sketch lines and purple-gray paint. I make out women's faces, dancing bears, hunters. Empty pools are set into the ground, the tile cracked or missing. Colors cry out under the grime.

"The ceiling was painted once," Abu Sayeed says, and we all look up.

"There are some bright colors up there," Huda says, "or there used to be. Yellow ocher. Cobalt, lapis. What do you think—egg-based tempera?"

"Mama would love this," Zahra says.

"Look." I point up, turning on my toes. "You can see the stars."

Zahra inches up to Yusuf, touching her wrist. "Not well."

But Yusuf doesn't look at her. "They're constellations," he says, his voice low in his chest.

"The stars were painted like people or animals," Abu Sayeed says. "See the plaque here—this is a vault of heaven."

Huda runs her fingers over cracked clay. "It's a map of the sky."

I think to myself, It used to be. Time crumbles everything. I try to picture it like it was once, the paint smooth, the stones polished. People make such beautiful things, I think, even though they destroy so much.

We go out, blinded by the sun. Yusuf waits for everyone else to climb into the van, watching us, flipping a pocketknife open and shut.

I run to Abu Sayeed and pull the white quartz from my pocket, polished clean by the liner.

"I've got something for you." I wait until he holds out his hand, and then I drop the sharp spike of rock into his palm. I don't want to keep it for myself. I want to make something good out of what was bad, something precious out of something small. Like the raw blue stone Abu Sayeed showed me, ugly and humble in the earth.

"I found it," I say, and a little smile butterflies across my face. "On my adventures."

Abu Sayeed grins and folds his fingers over the stone. He tells me, "That's my little cloud."

SITT SHADID BECKONS us inside when we get back to the apartment. She's rubbing Mama's back, which makes me feel good at first, because that's what I like about Sitt Shadid. She always rubs your back, even when you've got nowhere to sit but the bare floor.

But Mama is crying. I hold my breath and run through the possibilities: Amman was shelled while we were away. Somebody died. Mama got stung by a scorpion. But the apartment is still standing, and everybody's here. And even with her crooked pumps still on, it's clear Mama's ankles aren't swollen.

Huda sits down on a cushion, touching her sore shoulder, her sling soaked with sweat. Zahra and Yusuf retreat to the corner by the window, leaning like human curtains toward a breeze they can't feel. It's almost the end of August, and the summer isn't letting up. I would've been starting seventh grade soon. I was looking forward to science class, to filling in maps with the tectonic plates and making my own battery out of a potato. Do they make batteries out of potatoes in Jordan? Will I have to sell tissues instead?

I draw up close to Abu Sayeed, and he puts his arm around my shoulders. Mama and Sitt Shadid shoot Arabic back and forth, and I bounce my knee up and down and listen. As usual, I catch the heads and tails of sentences, a sprinkling of simple words like *go* and *south* and *Egypt*. But then, for the first time, an entire sentence comes through, whole and clear and perfect as a ripe peach. My knee goes still.

We can't stay in Jordan.

The words carry so much weight that it feels like the roof should cave in. I look around to see if anybody else has noticed, but everyone is looking at the floor or off into space. Nobody seems alarmed, but nobody meets my eyes either. They drum their fingers, cough into their fists. I realize they don't know I understand. I realize everybody is pretending, hiding their reactions where they think I can't see.

Mama licks her lips like her Arabic is salt. "I applied for asylum in the States," Mama says, "but the paperwork is slow. They require background checks, fingerprints, screenings, interviews. Even if we complete all these things, it could take several years for us to be resettled—and there are no guarantees."

Zahra whirls away from Yusuf. "We're going to be here years? And what happens if we stay here all that time and we're still not granted asylum?"

"What about school?" I ask. The future spills out in front of me, suffocating hours in this tiny room, time chasing itself like a runaway marble.

Mama breathes out. "I've talked it over with Sitt Shadid. I think we should drive south to find a better place. There is somewhere we can go. A relative of ours. He might help us, if we can get to him." Mama lays her hand on Umm Yusuf's arm. "You are welcome to come with us," she says. "We can figure out the rest."

"We can take the van," Umm Yusuf says.

I bounce up. "What? When are we leaving?"

Mama locks her eyes with mine. Her white blouse is still crisp somehow, and there aren't even any sweat stains under her arms.

But the way the skin under her eyes sags and her chin creases with lines, I can tell she's not sure what to say next.

"Nour, it would be best if—" Mama clears her throat. "For now, we'll keep your hair short."

I frown. "I don't like it."

"It's better if people think . . ." Mama trails off.

"You will look like a boy," Umm Yusuf says. "Understand, it is safer that way. Nour is also a boy's name. Being seen as a boy will protect you from bad people."

"Not that you should be afraid," Mama says.

But isn't there already enough to be afraid of? "I don't want to look like a boy." I wobble to my feet. "I want to look like myself."

"Little cloud." Abu Sayeed rummages in his pocket and brings out my shard of white quartz, holding it out to me, my own words stuck on its edges: *On my adventures*. "What do you say?"

I rub my smooth head. Out the window, the steppe shimmers at the city's fingertips. The farther I go, the bigger the world seems to be, and it always seems easier to leave a place than it is to come back. Did I ever let myself believe it would be easy to get back to the States, as easy as Sitt Shadid giving us the room next to hers?

The light shifts, hitting the anchusa in the can. The caramel color from the soda residue has seeped into its petals, turning it a sickly purple, even though we always say it's blue. Nobody has noticed. It seems like people lose more than they can ever get back—a three-bedroom house, ten inches of hair, a whole color. But nobody ever says it. Does it make it easier to live with loss if you don't name it? Or is that something you do as a mercy for other people?

I drop my hand from the smooth knob at the back of my neck. The linden tree shifts its leaves and blocks the light, and the anchusa turns blue again.

"All right," I say. "I'll do it."

The Season of Salt

*

The expedition set off again the following day. They rounded the curve of the desert, using the astrolabe to guide them, and bent toward the Gulf of Aila, a narrow inlet of the Sea of Qulzum. They had found a winding pass out of the mountains and headed east out of the Kingdom of Jerusalem as quickly as they could, but now they had little choice except to make the five-day journey south through the rocky desert of Wadi Rum toward the eastern shore of the Gulf of Aila. They would cross the Gulf near a town al-Idrisi called Aqabat Aila. Since the Crusader territories stretched south all the way to the Gulf, there was no other way around them. And even though al-Idrisi was thrilled at the dozens of pages of notes he had gathered and the new routes he had charted, Rawiya felt uneasy. Fewer friendly glances were cast their way, and people began to eye their caravan suspiciously. Al-Idrisi had them hide the jeweled saddles and silk robes Nur ad-Din had given them, replacing them with their own worn supplies. He reminded them not to tell anyone they had come from King Roger's court.

"So long as we do not profess our loyalties to Sicily," he said, "we will come out of it all right. But ah," he said, "how the mention of my old friend fills me with sadness." King Roger had taught him many things, he told them. With King Roger, al-Idrisi had marveled at wonders of mathematics and geodesy, the study of the measurement of the earth. He put his hand to his breast. "We must travel far," he said, "before we return to King Roger's court."

They passed between towers of wine-colored rock, and the soil turned to sand. Wild camels kept their distance. Gray desert larks fled as the expedition approached, and blue agama lizards skittered over pebbles.

The sun was unrelenting. Soon the whole party began to wish for the waters of the Gulf of Aila and the Nile River. It was said that the Nile flowed north into Egypt from the mythical Mountains of the Moon.

At last, they came out of the mountains, and the road wandered down toward the Gulf of Aila. Far to the south, farther than they could see, the Gulf emptied into the wide Sea of Qulzum. Rawiya licked her lips and tasted salt, something she had not done since their ship had put in at al-Iskanderun.

A city lay far below, green with palms and pistachio trees — Aqabat Aila. But between the expedition and the city, a cloud of dust seemed to rise out of the rocky hillside to block their way, and their camels stopped, nervous.

Figures appeared in the cloud of dust: riders on horseback, hurrying to meet them. They were dressed in the luxurious fabrics of Cairo, each wearing a wax-white tunic of the finest linen, a white turban, and a patterned robe of pomegranate silk. At each of their wrists, they bore a gold-embroidered tiraz band sewn onto their sleeves — a mark of those favored by the Fatimid caliph.

Al-Idrisi hailed the riders. But they said nothing, only spurring their horses to circle the expedition. The camels groaned and stamped with fear.

The leader of the Fatimid riders stopped and eyed the expedition, his chin lifted in a haughty expression. His fine, dark hair framed a young face, and his hands were soft from a lifetime of pampered wealth. Though he was the youngest of the riders, he bore the most elaborate tiraz, a sign of his accomplishments and his esteem in the Fatimid court.

"I would know your masters," he called out. "Whom do you serve?"

"My companions and I serve God alone," al-Idrisi said, "and no other."

"You refuse to answer, then." The haughty young Fatimid narrowed his eyes, the tails of his turban fluttering at his shoulders. He drew his scimitar, and the sun glinted off its curved blade.

"You question the power of God over a man's soul?" al-Idrisi cried out. His camel stomped and snorted, and al-Idrisi's face burned with a sudden, terrifying rage.

The young rider scowled and sheathed his scimitar. "Caliph az-Zafir has heard tell of spies and traitors entering by this road," he said. "He has ordered us to question all travelers."

Al-Idrisi answered, "We are humble pilgrims, seeking the wonders of God in wadi and mountain." Listening to his words, Rawiya realized for the first time that this was true in its way, for they had seen many wondrous things.

"You must come to the palace in Cairo before you go," the rider said, "and take some rest and refreshment. It is for your own good: Almohad fighters have been spotted to the west of Cairo. A captured Almohad spy admitted to targeting travelers, searching for a mapmaker putting together some precious book of geography." He waved his hand and glanced back at al-Idrisi over his nose. "The roads are not safe these days, it would seem."

Al-Idrisi bowed and said, "I am afraid a long journey awaits us. We must hurry on."

"You will answer our questions and pay your respects to the caliph, or you will not pass." The rider touched the handle of his scimitar. "I am Ibn Hakim. I insist on accompanying you to the palace."

Although he was young, Ibn Hakim was one of the finest warriors in all the Fatimid Empire, and it was said that he was quicker with his scimitar than with his tongue. He had risen up the ranks of the Fatimid court with a mix of flattery and brutality. Tales had spread that he had once cut the arrows of twenty archers with his blade, that he had bested ten men in a duel after they insulted him. Al-Idrisi knew that if he refused Ibn Hakim's request to take them to Cairo, they would be quickly outmatched.

But Rawiya, who had no idea what a dangerous swordsman Ibn Hakim was, inched her hand toward her sling. She nudged open her leather pouch in search of a sharp stone.

She found none. Only the polished smoothness of the roc's eye sat there, the round stone the color of plums and palm leaves. It felt strangely hot, like it held a bolt of lightning. She closed her hand over it.

Heat flashed up Rawiya's jaw, stabbed at the base of her thumbs, and shot down the backs of her knees. *She changes her shape in the night, Sparrowling.* Her father's face appeared around the curve of an olive branch, the morning smell of the sea. *Didn't I tell you?*

Rawiya gasped and snatched her hand back. The roc's eye stone, heavy and hot as a coal, upended the pouch and went tumbling to the ground.

Ibn Hakim's horse reared at the drop of the stone. Ibn Hakim eyed it and, dismounting, bent to pick it up. As soon as he touched it, the skin from his arm to his jaw grew pale and pricked with goose bumps, and he dropped it with a gasp.

"What sorcery is this?" Ibn Hakim said. "My mother's voice is with God. She went to the Garden years ago."

"What is this stone?" al-Idrisi whispered.

Rawiya stammered, her fingers still tingling. "It is nothing but a stone."

But Ibn Hakim was shaken, and any injury to his pride only made him angrier. He drew his scimitar. "This blasphemous sorcery must be destroyed," he said. Raising his blade over his head, he struck the stone.

A great light flashed, and Rawiya, al-Idrisi, and the whole expedition covered their eyes. When they looked back, the stone had been sliced clean in half. One half had exploded upward and lodged in a stony cliff nearby. The other half had been blasted several yards away, wedged in the sand.

Ibn Hakim bent to tap the second half of the stone with his fingers. Sensing nothing, he curled his upper lip into a sneer and lifted it. "Its dark magic has been weakened," he said. "The caliph will examine it himself."

Ibn Hakim turned his horse for the Gulf. The riders flanked the expedition as they approached the port city of Aqabat Aila, trotting hard on their sides. Rawiya glanced back, once, at the rocky outcropping where the other half of the roc's eye stone had landed. It was lodged deep into a crack, partly hidden by a coating of dust and small pebbles, like a shard of emerald sea glass.

It had been late afternoon when the expedition had come into view of the Gulf, and night came on while they were still far from the city. Their captors set up camp on the wide, flat plain that ran along the shore of the Gulf of Aila. The expedition said their evening prayers and ate a small meal of bread and lentils while Ibn Hakim stood guard. His men were alert, keeping watch around them.

But a plan had come to Khaldun while he had knelt in prayer, and now he sprang up. "We must celebrate," he said. "This evening calls for song. Surely you would not mind a verse in praise of the generous Fatimid caliph?"

Ibn Hakim reached into his tunic, pulled out the half of the roc's eye stone that he had taken, and set it on the ground before the fire. Tongues of peacock green flickered in its depths. "Sing, then, poet," he said, smirking.

Khaldun pulled an oud from his pack. He had been a master oud player at Nur ad-Din's court, and the instrument's pear-shaped wooden belly and silk strings were as familiar to him as his own body. Strumming and tuning the oud, Khaldun sat down by the fire. He began to sing a lilting ballad, his voice rolling green as the hills and then surging skyward, like a wadi full of spring flowers.

Then he paused and motioned to his pack, and Bakr tugged out the drum he had beat awkwardly during their battle with the roc. After a moment, Bakr handed the drum to Rawiya.

"I have no gift for music," he said. "If I play, they will have my head."

So Rawiya kept up a rhythm to Khaldun's ballad. At first, Ibn Hakim and his men only glared, their arms crossed over their chests. But as Khaldun's verses became more impassioned, as he thrummed the strings and trilled his voice, Ibn Hakim and his men began to sway and bounce their knees. Soon they were up and dancing, circling the fire and singing along.

When the ballad ended, they collapsed around the flames, grinning and exhausted. Khaldun continued to play his oud: first a song of tragic love that made Ibn Hakim and his men weep, then a lullaby that would have made a camel blink with sleep. Al-Idrisi yawned, and Bakr began to nod. Soon Ibn Hakim and his men, worn out from their dancing and their singing, drifted to sleep around the fire.

Khaldun stopped playing, checking that Ibn Hakim's eyelashes had fallen to his cheeks. Their guards were fast asleep.

Khaldun motioned for Rawiya and the expedition to rise and pack the oud and drum. Rawiya snatched up the remaining half of the roc's eye stone from in front of Ibn Hakim's toes. Then they mounted their camels and sped off into the night, leaving their tents and their captors behind.

"What will we do now?" Bakr huffed when they were out of earshot. "We've left our tents."

"Tonight," al-Idrisi said, "we sleep under the stars."

Bakr lowered his face. "Not again."

"And tomorrow," al-Idrisi continued, "when we come to Aqabat Aila, we will seek out more supplies. Luckily"—he patted the leather pouch that held Nur ad-Din's gold dinars—"monies are in no short supply."

But fear tugged at Rawiya, and she looked back toward the fire where Ibn Hakim's men sat slumped and dreaming. Would they follow?

Soon the fire was only a tiny dot at their backs. The expedition broke for the coast, galloping toward the dark ribbon of the Gulf of Aila.

*   *   *

TWO WEEKS AFTER we arrive, we leave the tiny apartment in east Amman, and it's like we were never there at all. Umm Yusuf packs the cushions in the van, fills the leather trunk with Sitt Shadid's things, and tugs the bare bulb off. We leave only clumps of our dust behind. Mama spends the morning ripping open the tongues of my sneakers and stuffing paper money inside, sewing them up with a double stitch, and I watch her without asking why.

On the way out, Sitt Shadid shakes the water from the soda can and leaves the anchusa flower we picked the day before on the front step. I press my face to the window while we drive off, stretching the imaginary thread between the flower and me until it snaps.

Umm Yusuf drives the van south. She takes Highway 35 until it splits outside the city, and then we follow Highway 15, the one Umm Yusuf calls the Desert Highway. She says it will take us all the way to Aqaba.

"From Aqaba," Mama says from the front seat, "we can get a ferry into Egypt." She musses the baby hairs on her forehead in the sun visor mirror and then claps it shut. "Ya mama, did you know Aqaba used to be called Aila? And al-Idrisi called the Red Sea the Bahr al-Qulzum."

Zahra rolls her eyes. "Mom. Give it a rest, okay, before Nour starts."

I scowl and curve back into the seat. "Like I was even going to say anything."

Out the window, the desert is nothing like I thought it would be. Red sandstone and pebbles, big top-hatted cliffs. The fingers of fallen rocks reach for the road. Telephone poles and power lines are stuck in the hills like toothpicks. Deserts never looked like this in American schoolbooks, where every desert looked like the emptiest stretches of the Sahara.

We drive for three hours before Zahra starts whining about how she has to pee. Since we haven't passed a town in a while and we're the only car around, we stop in a long stretch of rocky hills, and Mama tells us to pee behind a rock if we have to go. Mama stays by the van, unrolling her map on the backseat. She must have saved some old tubes of paint from the house, because she takes them out of her burlap bag and brushes new colors onto the map, yellow and turquoise and salmon pink.

Umm Yusuf and Abu Sayeed help Sitt Shadid get out and stretch her legs. Huda and Rahila stay in the van, fanning themselves. Yusuf bends his knees and rolls his shoulders before pulling out his pocketknife. I hurry in the opposite direction. He makes me nervous.

A quarter mile down the road, the cliffs break open. The land is changing. I can see straight through to the sky here, like looking down a city block in Manhattan. On the horizon, the desert's edges blend red-orange into robin's egg, robin's egg into steel blue, and steel blue into sky without ever stopping.

At least we can see the sky today. Yesterday we couldn't leave Amman because the wind whipped up a bad storm, and everybody nearly snapped, being stuck inside all day while half of us were fasting. There was so much sand in the air, you couldn't even see the clouds. Winds like that must mold the mountains, cut the cliffs, dig up hundreds of years of dust.

I run to the bottom of a tall cliff and squat by the side of the road, away from the van. The breeze tickles my backside, making me look around. But there's nobody here—just me and the red cliffs. It gives me a triumphant little thrill, getting to pee outside for the first time, like I've shrugged off the weight of rules and sadness.

I pull up my shorts and walk up the road a ways so I can look down into the valley ahead. Way out, the Gulf of Aqaba glistens like frog skin, the pinky finger of the Red Sea. When I was little, Mama made me practice my geography by drawing maps. I used to anchor the Middle East around the Red Sea. I wonder if it will really be red or just regular blue, whether real life will match up to the map I've got in my head. But then, Baba used to say a map is only one way of looking at things.

My thoughts snag on Baba like a stray nail in a picnic table. Something about this cliff and this view looks familiar, as though somebody had told me a long time ago to look out for a place like this—to keep an eye out for a rocky cliff to the left and a view of Aqaba in the distance. Baba always painted his landscapes with words, letting Mama take the paintbrush. Now, matching up the world to the picture in my head, it slips into place. Didn't I imagine this view a hundred times?

The winds have peeled thick layers of dust off the cliff. Something greenish is stuck high up, glinting like sea glass.

I scramble up the rock, scraping my knees and my elbows. Stones slip and roll between my legs. There it is, a walnut-sized shard of something. It's a smooth pistachio green, like a bead of knobby glass. I reach for it, stretching my arm.

I can't reach. I burrow my fingernails into the pebbles and sand, scattering the dirt until the green stone starts to wobble. I tear at the ground, ripping up handfuls of scrub grass until it comes free.

The stone tumbles down, bouncing along the hillside, showering the pavement with dust.

I race back down and pick it up. It's bigger than I thought, the size and shape of a plum, and weirdly warm. My fingers send a purple shadow right through the middle of it, but in the sun, it's traffic-light green.

A little thrill goes through me.

I remember Rawiya dropping the stone, Ibn Hakim drawing his scimitar. I inspect the smooth slice on one side, and the skin on my arms draws up into goose bumps. Could time and wind have cut so clean?

There was a time, when I was small and first played the magic spinning game that Baba taught me, that nothing I laid eyes on was less than extraordinary. Now I turn the stone into and out of the sun, and it turns purple—green—purple. I hold my breath and ask myself, is there still space in the world for extraordinary things?

"Nour!"

"Coming." I stuff the stone in my pocket. It sags in my shorts, tugging the waistband down on one side.

Mama stands by the van, her hands on her hips. "You wandered off again, habibti."

"No."

She sighs and motions toward the middle row of seats. "Yalla. In. Now."

In the van, I shift around so nobody notices the stone in my pocket. Abu Sayeed turns around in the driver's seat and smiles at me, but I don't say anything. I'll show him the stone when we get to the water. Abu Sayeed will know for sure what it is. He'll know, like I do, that it's special.

We pass a blue sign with a choice: Aqaba / Ma'an / Wadi Musa. We turn toward Aqaba. Mama hugs her bag tight between her knees, bracing it against the bumps. Zahra and Yusuf roll their windows up, and sweat tingles at my temples and in the small of my back.

I lean forward to Mama. "Put the air on," I say. "Please. It's hot back here."

But Mama isn't listening. Her head is turned out the front passenger window, her chin in one hand, her fingertips resting on her lips. With her other hand, she rubs the corner of the map canvas, stroking it without thinking.

"Mama."

Still nothing. Sweaty and ignored, my eyes bore holes in that corner of canvas. How many months has it been now that Mama has paid more attention to her maps than to me, always preferring to paint instead of talk? It felt like as soon as Baba went into the earth, Mama went back to her facts and her borders, and everybody else went with her. But maybe I'm not ready to let go.

Something mean swishes through me. I hope Mama's acrylic paint smeared before it had a chance to dry. But then I remember that acrylic paint dries fast.

I put my face to the cracked window and swallow dust. I raise my voice almost to a shout. "Why are you so obsessed with maps?"

Mama doesn't realize right away that I'm talking to her. "Obsessed?" She leans back from the front seat. "What obsessed?"

Zahra swats me on the back of the head. "No one wants to hear you."

"You're obsessed," I say. "Like the maps are your kids, not us."

"Don't be ridiculous." Mama bats the dust in the air.

"Is everybody who makes maps crazy like that?"

Mama softens, even though I don't expect her to. "Most of them."

"And engineers—like Baba?"

"Some of them are crazy about maps too."

I frown. "That's not what I meant."

"When I first met him, I thought he was stuck up," Mama says. "Too good to say anything. Imagine: he and his brother were the only other Syrians in my class at Córdoba, and he would not say a word."

"Who?" Huda asks.

"Your father."

"But that's where you met." I lean forward, gripping the back of Abu Sayeed's seat. "Isn't it?"

"Not right away," Mama says. "I talked to his brother."

"His brother?"

"Uncle Ma'mun." Mama straightens her sleeves, fidgeting. "A kindhearted man. He used to write every so often, when you were small. We were friends at university. In those days at Córdoba, he dragged his brother to Ceuta for a day's adventure and me with him.

I hated that painful silence. But even painful things," she says, "are often veined with blessings we can't yet see."

I picture Baba and our yellow house in Homs and think, No, they're not. "So . . ." I drag out the word, waiting. "So you said . . . ?"

"When?"

"To get Baba to talk to you."

Mama rubs a grain of sand out of her eye. "I told him to jump into the strait."

Even Huda leans forward. "You didn't!"

"Ceuta is in Africa, you must remember, although it's part of Spain. So I told him to swim back to Europe, if he was going to be so miserable." Mama laughs. "And he said, 'All these maps of the water and the mountains, and for what?'" Mama's hand snakes up to her neck. She fingers the piece of white-and-blue ceramic on its cord. "He said, 'People don't get lost on the outside. They get lost on the inside. Why are there no maps of that?'" Then Mama drops her hand. "What day is it?"

Huda touches Mama's headrest with her good arm. "The thirtieth. Is it—it's today!"

"How could we have forgotten?" Mama's hands fly to the door handle. "Stop, stop."

Abu Sayeed slams on the brakes. "What is it?"

Huda sets her forehead to the back of Mama's seat. "Eid al-Fitr," she says. "We've forgotten everything."

"We aren't far from Aqaba," Abu Sayeed says. "I'll stop there so we can find a butcher."

We descend into the valley. The desert is rockier here, with buttes and the hunched backs of low mountains. The steel pin of the Gulf of Aqaba lies on the horizon, next to the town people used to call Aila. Mama told me a long time ago that al-Idrisi was one of the first people to call it Aqabat Aila, the name that eventually became Aqaba.

As we come down from the mountains, the road straightens, lined with palm trees. Mama is wild, even though Huda tries to calm her down. She and Baba celebrated Eid al-Fitr marking the end of Ramadan each year, and she says she won't forget it now. My whole life, Mama and Baba celebrated two religions' worth of holidays — Christmas, Eid al-Fitr, Easter. It used to make me wonder whether the most important things we see in God are really in each other.

The road winds between rosy-cheeked apartments, old mosques with chickpea-yellow walls. The sun is already going down when we find a butcher shop. Mama argues with Umm Yusuf in quiet Arabic about who will go and get the lamb. Zahra leans back on the hood of the van next to Yusuf, shaking her head.

"I could use a walk," Huda says. "Nour and I will stretch our legs."

"Take this." Mama takes Huda aside and turns her back to us. She rummages in the burlap bag and pulls out a few coins, pressing them into Huda's palm. She clasps her fingers over Huda's. "Make it last, if you can."

"Come back quickly." Abu Sayeed waits on the sidewalk. "If you don't, I'll come looking for you."

"Okay." Huda and I walk down the hill toward the butcher shop a few blocks down. The tears in the canvas uppers of Huda's sneakers pull and gape with every stride. Our shadows stretch out on their bellies, bouncing with our steps.

"Where are we sleeping?" I ask.

"Tonight? Mama will find a place."

I nod, even though I know Mama only had a few coins left. I twist up my mouth to bite my lip. "Are we refugees?"

Huda looks away at a pair of green-shuttered windows. "Why do you ask?"

"Because I heard Mama say in Arabic that that's what we are," I say. "Lajiat. I asked Umm Yusuf what it meant."

"You're full of surprises, you know that?" Huda lets out her air. "You choose what defines you. Being a refugee doesn't have to."

"But you didn't answer my question." I answer it myself: we must be. And I already know what that means: Nails unhammering themselves. The smell of burning. Torn-up shoes. Newspaper sticking up from the kitchen tiles, a name circled in red.

"I was careful all the time," I say. "I always recycled my juice boxes. I even scraped the bottom of the peanut butter. But it wasn't enough."

"It was nothing you did."

"But—" I stop walking. "How do we do this?"

"By knowing who we are," Huda says. She kneels down in front of me. "Let me tell you something. The doctor said it might not work right anymore." She adjusts her sling. "Even if it does heal."

"The metal in your arm?"

Huda shifts her eyes, like she's looking at something in the distance. "To tell the truth," she says, "it doesn't feel like metal anymore. It feels like a part of my body now. Part of the bone."

We walk again. *Part of the bone*, she said. As though this new bone is slowly changing her, changing the person she used to be.

We spot the skinned goats in the window. The butcher shop is just closing, and a man fiddles with his key in the lock.

"Wait!" Huda runs to catch him, explaining in Arabic that we need lamb to celebrate the Eid. The man jerks his head toward the door and opens it.

"Come on," Huda says. "We might catch the girl who cuts the meat, if we hurry. He says she's washing up."

Inside, the shop smells like blood. Water runs somewhere, whooshing silver white.

Huda rounds the empty meat case. A small lady in a black headscarf is hunched in the back room between racks of goats and chickens, washing her hands in a basin. Popsicle-cold air floods us when we walk in, round billows of translucent blue against my skin.

Huda talks to her in Arabic. The girl listens and then shakes her head.

Huda turns her chin to the side, that clipped, disappointed look. "They just sold out of their lamb," she says. "They're about to close up."

The girl wrings her hands, brushing off something sticky. I reach up and trace her knuckles.

"You haven't been a butcher very long," I say.

They both look at me. Huda asks, "Why not?"

"Because," I say. "Her hands are smooth. If you wash them all the time and touch blood and stuff, they get cracked and dried out. Like Mama with her turpentine."

Huda translates, and the girl laughs. She launches into a string of Arabic. She stutters, clamping her mouth shut. It's like the words are locked inside her, hidden pearls strung along the copper wire of her voice.

"She says her hands will dry out eventually, if she keeps salting meat," Huda says. "She used to play the oboe."

I cover my mouth with my hands like ladies do in the movies. "That's my favorite instrument!"

"She says her father is up in age," Huda says. "They lost their home when their neighborhood was shelled. They lost their business, their grandparents—" The girl says more, but Huda stops translating and looks away.

"So she came here?"

Huda clears her throat. "She brought her father to Aqaba," she says, "and moved in with her cousin. This is the only job she could get." They bat more Arabic back and forth. "She says there is a ferry to Nuweiba tonight, if we can wait. It leaves late, just before midnight."

I pick up one of the girl's hands. I see it right away—the crooked middle and ring fingers, the unnatural twist of the thumb. Something heavy must have crushed her right hand, breaking all the tiny bones. She will never play the oboe again. I look down at my own fingers, wondering if the crumbled brick and the asphalt and the soot have left invisible marks in my bones too.

The girl leans down, the edges of her hijab brushing my face. She sees me studying her hands. For a moment I see myself reflected in her pupils, swallowed by a bottomless blackness. Then she motions for me to follow her to the basin of the sink.

I'm not tall enough to look in. She lifts me from under my armpits, gravity sucking at the bottom of my shoes. The basin is full of blood.

We leave the shop with a few scraps of goat's meat wrapped in brown paper. Huda doesn't say anything, but I catch her wincing and realize we couldn't have afforded lamb. The goat cost all the money Mama gave us.

We walk back toward the van. On our way back up the hill, two older boys block our path. The shorter of the two hangs back, hair matted across his forearms with sweat. The taller boy has his hands in his pockets and a birthmark on his slim jaw in the shape of a dimpled egg, and he might have reminded me of the princes in Baba's stories if he didn't have such a scary look in his eyes. Both the boys wear strange smirks, their eyes half-lidded. Something about their faces makes me pull Huda by the wrist, trying to walk faster. These boys look different from the boys in the square—not angry, but bored, like they're about to steal a couple of sodas from a mini-mart just because they can.

The boys say something in Arabic to Huda, but she ignores them. Under her breath, she says, "Keep walking."

The boys step in front of us. We try to dodge them, but they block the sidewalk. I try to tug Huda past them, but the taller boy grabs Huda in her bad arm. She cries out, and he tries to shut her up.

"Huda!"

They force her into a side street, a little alley. I run after them, kicking at the back of the short boy's knees. He glares at me, whispering angry words I don't catch. His open palms hit me in the chest, and he shoves me down. I hit the pavement hard, skinning my lower back, and the wind is knocked out of me.

Huda shouts for help in two languages.

In some tiny corner of my brain, I know what this is, even though I don't have a word for it. I want to close my eyes. I want to throw up. My whole body is thrumming, like the tips of my fingers will burst open. Under my cheek, the sidewalk stinks of dust and sea salt. It reminds me of winter in New York. Winter was the season of salt.

"Help!"

I follow the boys into the alley where everything is shadow. The tall boy has Huda up against the wall, bending over her so the dim light hits a mole on the back of his neck. The short one grabs at the pleats of Huda's long skirt, lifting them up over the tongues of her sneakers, over her brown calves. He presses himself against her, the buckle of his belt clanking as he struggles to undo it with one hand. Huda kicks and squirms, and the tall boy pushes her skirt up over her knees.

The boys exchange words in Arabic—*Down*. It takes both of them to push her to the ground, and the tall boy gives a shout when Huda yanks out a fistful of his greasy hair. Then he slaps her, and she goes still.

Clank goes the buckle against the asphalt.

Huda rips her head from under the boy's hand. Her scream is weaker, breathless. "Help—"

But no one is coming. I reach into one of my pockets, stuffed with Abu Sayeed's stones. I come up with a chunk of basalt. My hands are shaking, curling clumsily around the rock like the oboe player's crushed hands. I aim the stone, closing one eye, but it sails over the boys' heads.

"Run." Huda thrashes her head and kicks. "Get Mama."

But instead I rush at the boys, clawing at their shirts and reaching for their eyes. I remember what my gym teacher at PS 290 said, when I went to my old public school in the city—that I was small for my age. I jump on the tall one's back, pulling him away from Huda, but the short boy throws me off. The air is rancid with sweat and fear and the blood on my back. Somebody screams a sound that doesn't come from Huda or me, a chest-deep roar that is as red as a severed tongue.

I reach up one more time, digging my nails into the tall boy as he struggles with his zipper. I claw three gashes into the soft skin on his shoulder. He yells and tries to punch me, but I duck. I bite into his arm. He screeches, dropping back against the wall. I jump at him, slicing my teeth into his chest.

I am liquid. I am locked outside myself. I am fire.

Somebody's hands reach over my head, and there is shouting in Arabic. Either I am pulled off the boy or the boy is pulled off me. I collapse across Huda's bare thigh, the both of us still on the ground. The left side of her face is stung with a long welt, and blood and hair are clumped under her fingernails.

I'm still burning. I stare at my fists from somewhere beyond, above the alley. Somebody is screaming again, round and red. I don't hear it. I see it instead: a ruby color, like when I've just woken up and the alarm is only a shape in the air.

Hands touch my shoulders. I throw them off. I curl myself into a ball on top of Huda, sobbing into her flowered hijab, wanting to beat my head against the wall.

"Nour. Nour." My chin is pried up, and Abu Sayeed's face swings into view. "Are you all right?"

"Where are they?" I don't recognize my voice.

Abu Sayeed says, "The sons of dogs are gone," and spits.

Huda pushes her skirt down, avoiding touching her own skin. Abu Sayeed helps her sit up. She wraps her arms around herself and breathes in and out, letting go of air.

I can't. I bottle up my breaths until I feel I'll explode. There are no more words left in me. I am not safe, and I can't keep anybody else safe either. I am not Rawiya. I repeat it over and over: "I'm not. I'm not."

Abu Sayeed leads us back to the van. Mama flits around us, her eyes wide. "Huda, Nour!" She scrapes her hand across my prickly skull and checks Huda's sling. "What happened to you?"

I hug Huda at the waist. "Tell her," I say.

But she doesn't. "We can cross the gulf tonight if we wait," Huda says, her voice tight as a metal box. "The ferry leaves at midnight."

I look up at Huda, but she won't look at me. I wonder if *almost* can cost you as much as *did*, if the real wound is the moment you understand that you can do nothing. I reach up and touch my shaved head, brushing dirt away. Huda tugs the pleats of her skirt down, pressing the folds flat, like it's all she can do not to scream.

The sun goes over the lip of the horizon, and the bronze fades off the water. The Red Sea isn't really red at all, and it's not blue either. It's black as onyx, like the empty spaces between tectonic plates, the holes in Manhattan. Can those empty places ever be filled in? Can you make a map of something that isn't?

I slip my hand into my pocket, feeling for my green-and-purple half-stone. I must have put my hand in the wrong pocket in the alley. I wonder, if I had thrown the weighty half-stone instead, would I have hit the boy square in the eyes?

Nobody speaks. I look at Yusuf, tracing his jaw, the way his hair is cut the same way as the hair of the boy I gashed. That first morning in the apartment in Amman, Yusuf slammed the door hard enough to set the window frames shaking. His gray tee shirt is stained with sweat, smelling like the boy who pulled up Huda's skirt. I turn away. I can't look at him anymore.

The salt breeze pours black water into me. It sinks deep, into a place I can't name, a place I can't chart.

Sea of Blood

✻

The merchant ship landed safely across the Gulf of Aila. Rawiya and her friends led their camels from the ship while the servants brought their packs. They had reached the peninsula called Ard al-Fairouz, the Land of Turquoise, and arrived in a small Bedu camp scattered with goat-hair tents. Dry mountains rose in front of them almost out of the sea, and as soon as they left the shoreline palms behind, the road became uneven and treacherous. They followed a twisting mountain pass between cliffs and fists of rock standing like figures watching them. The cliffs were striped yellow and red at their bases, like someone had scraped their bottom halves with a knife. Where there was no rock, there was only sand. Without water, they were forced to cleanse themselves with dust instead of performing wudu before prayer.

After two days' journey, the mountain pass sloped down onto a sandy plain dotted with hills and acacia trees. Even here, there were few plants and no water. They traveled for a week across the stony red earth, following a caravan road.

The first water they saw was the northern tip of the Gulf of Suez. A cheer went up among the servants, for they knew that within another week they would reach the Nile Delta.

The going was easier and flatter after that, and they were all in a pleasant mood. Soon they saw a thin green line on the horizon.

The desert ended at a line of trees spreading north to south along the Nile River. There at the head of the delta stood the city of Cairo and its neighbor, a center of textiles and porcelain called Fustat.

Rawiya started when they came to Cairo's gates. Huge gashes were cut into the stone as though they had been gouged out by great talons. Khaldun too jolted in his saddle. Each gave the other a questioning look, but they saw nothing else amiss. For now, the skies were clear of stalking shadows.

Dismounting their camels at the gates, the expedition plunged into noise and flowers and music. Tall stone houses rose around them, window frames of carved wood with engraved beams, doors hand-cut in lattices and crescents or flung open to reveal glassware or porcelain plates.

Al-Idrisi led them deeper into the city as they tugged their camels along. They squeezed past merchants, holy men, and women with children. They went single-file along streets lined with palms and filled with oud players and tale-tellers. Rawiya bought a new set of sharp stones for her sling. Bakr admired colorful linen scarves while al-Idrisi hung back, eyeing the crowds.

Bakr held up a scarf in wine red and lapis blue, a pattern of interlocking vines sketched along its length in white. "I never know what my mother will like," he said. He folded it and eyed a second scarf in apricot and peacock blue. "Khaldun, you've seen the ladies at court. Which would you choose?"

Rawiya touched the hem of a beige scarf and blinked away the thought of the one her mother used to wear. "Your mother will love anything you buy for her," she said.

But Bakr snorted a laugh. "You don't know my mother," he said. "My mother is the reason I'm here."

"What, to get away from her?" Khaldun asked.

Bakr laughed. "To prove myself. To prove my worth as a merchant like my father." He studied the scarves again. "My mother is a hard woman to please."

"But she didn't choose this journey," Rawiya said. "You are the one who has to be pleased with it."

But Bakr wasn't listening. He lifted the red-and-blue scarf. "This one, I think."

The vendor wrapped the scarf in clean, plain linen. They pushed onward through the crowds.

"This place," Rawiya said to Khaldun, "is a honeycomb of a city."

"They sing jeweled songs about Cairo for a thousand leagues in all directions," Khaldun said. "The fear in the city now—it's a pity. The fear of spies. Warring factions are looking for an opening after the last caliph's death."

"Death leaves holes," Rawiya said. "That's how it is."

"Holes?" Khaldun tilted his head toward her, a glance so quick Rawiya almost didn't notice.

"Sometimes a person dies," she said, "and leaves a hole too big to fill." She ducked her head to avoid a merchant and his camel. Movement stirred in the crowd behind them, and Rawiya hesitated before she turned back to Khaldun.

"Like the death of a beloved king," he said, "or an imam, or a priest."

"Or a father." Rawiya sidestepped a column of children, bumping into Khaldun to miss them.

He caught her arm, steering them past a crowd of merchants. Rawiya stiffened and blushed at the touch of his hand.

"The bond between father and son is strong," Khaldun said, clapping her on the shoulder. "He is still with you."

"Good fathers never abandon their children," Rawiya said, "not even when they die. All parents, really." The image of her mother came rushing back to her, the thought of the pain her absence had caused. Rawiya said quietly, "Only I wonder if sometimes their children abandon them."

Someone shouted from behind them. Rawiya turned and saw movement in the crowds again—the flash of a pomegranate robe.

"You need not feel guilty for leaving," Khaldun said.

Rawiya slowed down, motioning to her friends. "Someone is following us."

When they turned, a man ducked into a silk shop behind them. Khaldun frowned. "You're right."

The expedition pressed on, passing under the shade of blankets hung over the doorways of shops to protect customers from the sun. Rawiya and her friends turned off into an alley. Banners of colored paper fluttered in the breeze. Stacks of textiles waved their hems, attended by sleepy-looking vendors sitting on cushions, their eyes still sharp.

Behind them, up the zigzagging street, the crowds parted for a group of exhausted but angry men leading their horses. Their leader raised his arm to stop them, and his elaborate gold tiraz flashed in a shaft of sunlight.

"Sir . . ." Rawiya tugged on al-Idrisi's sleeve.

Al-Idrisi turned. "It seems we know more people in Cairo than we thought."

They ran, their camels opening a path for them. They dodged the crowds, diving between shop signs and old men hawking tea and hats, between merchants with monkeys and women with small children. They knocked over vials of spices and jugs of oil and flour, spilling a mess on the street.

They hurtled into a side street, crowded with wrought-iron and brass lamps, their glow flickering. Laundry lines lurched in their wake. They dodged stray cats and men buying lusterware dishes decorated with copper birds and fish.

Rawiya, Khaldun, al-Idrisi, and Bakr darted into a building with its doors open to the breeze. Al-Idrisi sent the servants scattering into the crowd, instructing them to regroup at the city gates.

They had entered a textile factory. Boiling cauldrons of fresh dyes and huge spools of wool, flax, and linen were clustered around the dusty factory floor. On a far wall, a wooden ladder led up to a loft with a window to the street.

"Spies!" Ibn Hakim's voice came shrill behind them. "Traitors to the caliph!" Scimitars hissed out of their sheaths.

Rawiya shoved al-Idrisi behind a stack of wool scraps and ducked behind a pot of indigo dye with Khaldun. Bakr scrambled behind a spool of linen.

Ibn Hakim and his men burst in. "Cowards," Ibn Hakim bellowed. "You have insulted the wrong man. Your treachery will be rewarded with death."

From behind the pot of dye, Khaldun drew his jeweled scimitar, and Rawiya wrapped her fingers around the neck of her sling.

The first guard spotted the toe of Bakr's boot behind the spool of linen and came at him. Rising up from behind the cauldron, Rawiya let a stone fly, hitting the guard in the back of the head. He tripped, pulling down the hem of a linen tunic with him. The whole rack came crashing down on his back. The dye workers, who had hidden themselves, cried out with their hands to their heads.

Al-Idrisi charged the next guard, parrying the man's scimitar away from him. The sword skidded across the floor. Khaldun grabbed it, brandishing both scimitars. He belted out a battle song and came at the remaining guards, spinning with his blades in his hands.

Rawiya hit one of the two guards with a stone. The other surprised Khaldun with a blow to his knees and knocked him down. Al-Idrisi rushed the guard, giving Khaldun a chance to scramble back. Rawiya set another stone in her sling.

But one man was unaccounted for. Ibn Hakim dove at al-Idrisi from behind, his sword drawn.

Rawiya loosed her stone, hitting Ibn Hakim in the hand. His sword clattered away, and he cried out. Al-Idrisi ducked behind a boiling vat of yellow dye.

When al-Idrisi was safely behind her, Rawiya kicked at the vat, sending the boiling dye splashing over Ibn Hakim's men. They screamed and rolled themselves in wool to dry the scalding liquid.

Rawiya, Khaldun, and al-Idrisi started up the wooden ladder to the loft with its single window. Ibn Hakim leapt after them.

Khaldun and al-Idrisi climbed up with Rawiya behind them. As Ibn Hakim reached for the hem of her sirwal, Rawiya grabbed a beam of wood from the loft and shattered it on top of Ibn Hakim's head. He fell to the ground, shaking himself.

Khaldun helped Rawiya up the ladder. But they soon realized that Bakr was still below them, his scimitar locked with the blade of one of the guards. Ibn Hakim marched toward Bakr, pale wrath burning on his face.

"Go," Rawiya said. "Take al-Idrisi to the servants. I'll meet you at the gates."

Khaldun reached for her. "Rami—"

"Go!" Rawiya set another stone in her sling and aimed for the guard. Khaldun grabbed a protesting al-Idrisi and pushed him out the window onto the balcony.

Rawiya's stone hit the guard between the eyes, sending him crashing into a spool of silk. It unwound around him, coating the ground in slippery cloth, and he lost his footing.

Ibn Hakim raised his scimitar. Bakr blocked it.

"Rami!" Bakr cried out. Ibn Hakim shoved Bakr with his blade, and Bakr swung his scimitar. He missed. "I can't best him on my own."

Rawiya leapt down the ladder and charged at Ibn Hakim. She struck him in the small of his back with the butt of her sling, sending him sprawling. He lifted his sword and sliced at her, making her jump back. She hopped over the fallen cauldron and struggled to aim a stone, but she was too slow. Although Ibn Hakim was blind with haughty rage, he was too talented a swordsman for her to escape.

Ibn Hakim's scimitar cut the air above Rawiya's head, aiming for her neck.

Bakr lunged at Ibn Hakim from the side, throwing him off. Ibn Hakim turned toward him, thrusting his blade. He buried his scimitar in Bakr's chest.

"Bakr!"

Bakr collapsed on the factory floor. Rawiya loosed a stone that hit Ibn Hakim hard in the forehead. He dropped to the ground, his eyes rolling back in his head.

Rawiya lifted Bakr into her lap. He coughed blood onto her wrists and her tunic. He reached under his cloak and tugged out a package wrapped neatly in brown linen.

"If you ever get home," he said, "give this to your mother."

"No." Rawiya wiped the blood from his jaw with her sleeve. "We'll get help."

Bakr's tunic was a mess of sticky clots like purple honey. He pressed the package to her chest. "So she knows you didn't abandon her," he said.

A stone's throw away, Ibn Hakim stirred.

*   *   *

THE BENT MOON comes up and the sun goes down, and Abu Sayeed finds a shop still open where we can buy a canister of cooking gas. Umm Yusuf parks the van off a side street near the harbor so we can watch for the ferry. The afternoon heat never wears off, not even in the dark, so I stay away from the gas cylinder.

Umm Yusuf and Sitt Shadid bring out a dented pot and half a bag of rice. The pot sits on top of the canister, on a round bar sort of like we had on our gas stove in the city. Mama cuts the goat's meat into little pieces. Sitt Shadid has some spices she saved in an old jam jar, so she sprinkles them over the meat. That smell fills everything, the smell of fat and oil like we haven't smelled in weeks. My jaw pricks and tingles, making me lick my lips. The tough meat is the only fresh thing we have, and there isn't enough of it to fill everybody's belly. But just the smell of cooking fat and spices beats a meal of plain rice and lentils any day.

While Mama cooks, Abu Sayeed, Umm Yusuf, Sitt Shadid,

and Huda say their prayers, all huddled on our dusty carpet. Zahra hovers nearby, looking unsure. Yusuf kneels by himself, whispering too quietly to be heard.

I don't know how to thank God while my head keeps playing back the boys' fists holding clumps of Huda's skirt. But Baba used to say you should pray the most when you can't see the good in the world. And I know I should say a prayer because, after all, God is God, and today is a day we should thank him.

So I try to remember the prayers Baba used to whisper in our old apartment, and the prayers Mama said when she took me to Mass, and then I add my own because I know that God listens, even if you don't get the words exactly right.

Mama lifts the pot's lid, and the perfume of meat and spices spills out. Each of us takes a little bread in our hands, the flat kind Baba would have called Syrian bread, not pita.

"Make it last," Mama tells us. "We won't be eating meat again for a good while."

But Sitt Shadid only rubs my shoulders and motions for me to eat. "Sahtein, ya ayni," she says with a smile, wishing me two healths.

When our bread runs out, we scoop the meat and rice with our hands. It tastes like laughing and warm blankets and dry socks and bedtime stories. For a little while, I forget about everything else, closing off the dark places that have formed in me like cavities.

I think everybody else must feel the same way, because before long, Sitt Shadid claps her hands and lifts them up, and then she starts to sing. It's a folk song I've never heard before, but Mama seems to remember the tune, if not the words. And then the words don't matter, because pretty soon everybody else is humming or singing too. We all get up and clap around the gas canister and the pot, and then we link our hands and dance. On my left, Abu Sayeed kicks out his feet and slaps his knees through the tears in his linen pants. On my right, even Huda takes hold of her long skirt so it doesn't drag in the dirt when she shuffles her feet to the music. And I know this dance is for everybody at once, and for God, and that even though I probably got my prayers wrong, I hope he still knows we're grateful that we're together, and he's glad.

AFTER WE EAT, we sit in the van at the dock, waiting. The Jordanian flag wags in the dark. That silvery water sound laps at the bumper, and the yellow smell of salt comes through the vents. When I was little and Baba used to tell me stories, the dark used to be full of possibilities. Now it just feels menacing, waiting under the pressure of all the words nobody wants to say.

I jiggle my leg to break the endless string of breaths. Zahra snaps at me to stop. In the front, Mama and Abu Sayeed whisper to each other. Mama clenches her map through the bag, then relaxes her fingers. They think because they're speaking in Arabic that I don't understand them, but I catch words and phrases. Abu Sayeed asks, *When are you going to tell them?* Pieces of Mama's answer float to me in the backseat: *If the wrong person finds out who is waiting—people are kidnapped for less.* Mama adds in English, under her breath, "And I don't want to get their hopes up."

"Mama." She doesn't answer. "Mama."

"Nour." Mama's voice is clipped red again. She folds down the sun visor mirror, using the visor's little light to tug an eyelash out of her eye. Her fingers shake. She tries again.

"When is the ferry coming?"

"I don't know."

The green-and-purple stone is heavy in my shorts. "But is it coming soon?"

"Hayati, I don't know."

"But—"

"Please!" Mama slaps the visor shut and folds her arms around her chest, and in the reflection in the window, I think I see her crying. "We have to wait," Mama says, her voice uneven. "What do you want me to do?"

I don't know. The night is closing in like a hundred invisible hands. I fidget and curl my toes. I start to breathe too fast, too hard. It feels like the van's roof might fall down on me, like the dark might clap shut around me.

"Let me out." I fight with the door handle, but the child lock is on. "Let me out!"

"What's wrong?" Huda releases the child lock and follows me out.

"I'm scared." I bury my face in her skirt. I'm afraid to touch her, as if what those boys tried to do opened a wound that I'm widening.

"It's okay." Huda blankets me with her arms and her scarf. "Huppy is here."

How do I tell her I couldn't save her, that I tried to be brave and I wasn't? How do I get the boys' blood out from under my fingernails, the disgusting smell of their sweat out of my nose? I don't know how to say those things. I don't know how to tell her I'm sorry or ask her how close the boys got to what they wanted before Abu Sayeed chased them away. I don't know how to tell her what I saw in their eyes—that to them, she was only a can of soda to be stolen.

Instead I turn my head and say, "I can't call you Huppy anymore. You're so grown-up now."

"You're wrong." Huda kneels and presses her forehead to mine. "I'll always be your Huppy."

I hold on to her while the breeze passes over us, trying to memorize the feeling of safety in her smell.

After a while, Huda says, "The ferry is slow, but it's cheap, and it will get us to Nuweiba. I bet the drive to Cairo is pretty. Maybe we can see the Sphinx."

"Will we ever be safe again?" My words are so heavy they pop open the night. "Huppy—are there any safe places anymore?"

Huda wraps her arms around my neck. "Ya Nouri," she says, "listen."

She's the only one who calls me Nouri, a word that in Arabic means both *my Nour* and *my light*.

Her voice is hoarse and low, each word delicate. "No one sees the future," she says. "No one knows what's planned. But safety is not about never having bad things happen to you. It's about knowing that the bad things can't separate us from each other. Okay? No matter what happens. Your family still loves you, and you can get through anything if you know that. You're safe with me. With Mama. With God. Nothing can take that away." She runs her thumb across my cheek and offers me the hem of her hijab. "Now dry your tears."

I touch the roses. The linen barely smells like rose water anymore, that smell I love that looks to me like lavender-colored curls. "It's too pretty. I'll ruin it."

"Come on," she says. "I'll wash it on the other side. It's just snot, after all."

She smiles and offers it to me again. This time, I blow.

THE FERRY IS an hour late, and the car deck is filled up with the vehicles of people who have already got tickets. There's no room for the van.

Umm Yusuf mutters and slams the door. We pack up Abu Sayeed's tools and our spare clothes and leave the van behind. We grab our bags and line up along the dock.

It's almost as hot as yesterday afternoon, and it's humid by the water. On nights like this, Baba and I used to lie awake on the rug in the apartment and tell stories. I used to wear my favorite nightgown, the one with satin flowers on it. I wonder what happened to it, if I brought it with me to Amman. But then I remember that all my clothes are torn up in my old room, ripped out of the dresser. I wonder if my nightgown has holes burned in it. I wonder if my sneakers are missing their tongues, hanging from the window glass by their shoelaces.

People crowd up, shuffling their feet across the dark. I stare at a man leaning on a cane. He looks younger than Abu Sayeed. Another family comes up loaded with duffel bags and backpacks, as though they are hauling their lives on their shoulders. The crowds grow, bottlenecking near the entrance, and the conversation drowns out the roar of the waves. Egyptian Arabic is so different from the way Mama talks; the dialect reminds me of the old Arabic movies Mama and Baba used to watch. But some of the kids around us use slang I heard in Homs instead. I start to wonder like I always do: Who are they? Did they come from where we came from? And where are all these people going?

I turn away and swallow thick spit. We haven't got any water, and I'm thirsty from the goat's meat. All this water around, and all of it salt. My stomach tries to drink my spine.

The wind screeches around us, a tight orange voice, and tears through the palm trees like a train. It scratches at the sea until it bleeds white.

We board the ferry at one in the morning, walking up a wooden ramp that bangs wherever you step. The water smacks into the metal hull below my feet. It's got to be at least eighty degrees, but I shiver from my nerves and the height. I know there's no way off a ship except into the water, and I don't know how to swim.

We find a seat on the upper deck near one of the lights, in the wind. As the families board, we crunch in to make room. People press against the railings, holding their purses or their hand luggage. Abu Sayeed sits next to me, Mama on my other side, and Huda and Zahra across from us. Umm Yusuf, Sitt Shadid, and Yusuf cluster close by, Rahila on her mama's lap. I chew on my fingers while the ramp is pulled away from the ferry.

"Are you scared?" Abu Sayeed asks. Sitting next to him makes me feel safe, but then the wind comes at us again, and the big horn goes off on the boat.

I nod, my eyes big, the warm wind tearing them. I've got to be careful, or I'll start crying.

"If it makes you feel better," he says quietly so Mama doesn't hear, "I'm scared too."

"What?" I don't believe him. I study his sloping shoulders, his leathery cheeks bristling with curly beard, his broad hands with their carved knuckles. I can't imagine Abu Sayeed being scared of anything.

He fidgets, curving his shoulders over his lap, and glances around. "I can't swim," he says, as if it's a confession.

"Me either. I was supposed to take lessons at the pool where Baba went, in the city. But we never did it." Heat builds up again behind my eyes. "And he promised."

"I wanted my son to learn," Abu Sayeed says. "I never had the chance to take him. Your baba wanted to go with you. I'm sure of that."

I tug on my sneakers. "Mama told me Sayeed left."

Abu Sayeed rests his hands on his thighs. For the first time since we got on the ferry, his fingers don't move. The ship groans out of the harbor and into the gulf.

"Sayeed wanted something he couldn't find," Abu Sayeed says. "Something I couldn't give him. After his mother died, he wasn't the same. He had to go, he said, to put things behind him. I was angry. I had already lost one, but to lose both? I didn't say good-bye, thinking he would come back. I never saw him again."

The waves snarl against the boat. I think of Baba's Polaroids, how Baba's parents took Abu Sayeed in when he lost his own, how Abu Sayeed's son ran away from the only parent he had left.

I say, "He turned his back on the thing you didn't get to have."

Abu Sayeed lowers his head, studying his fingernails. "I forgave him for that a long time ago," he says.

I rub the green-and-purple half-stone through my pocket. "So you look for stones to hear about your son?"

"Stones can't speak that way," Abu Sayeed says. "But I believe our Maker can speak through them." He interlocks his fingers, and his creased knuckles line up like a chain of brown mountains. "Some prayers go unanswered many years," he says. "The heart knows this."

"But even if God does hear our questions," I say, "what if we can't understand the answers?"

"Sure, some questions have answers we don't understand," Abu Sayeed says. "But you can understand more than you think, if you are willing to wait for the knowing."

"What do you mean, wait for it?" I say. "You mean like with math homework, how some problems make sense after you think about them for a few days?"

Abu Sayeed says, "Sometimes it takes years to understand what Allah wants us to know."

I try to raise an eyebrow, but both go up. "And he just expects us to wait?"

Abu Sayeed smiles. "Little cloud," he says, "that's what faith is."

The boat lumbers into open water where the sea rolls black as the center of a tulip. I wonder what creatures are under us, whispering secrets to each other while our shadow passes.

"Then what do you have in your pockets?" I ask. "I saw you take stones with you when we left. What did you bring?"

Abu Sayeed's smile is sad and crooked. "I brought just one," he says. "A special one." He pulls out his dusty handkerchief and digs inside while the ship jerks. He shows me a flat coin of a pebble the size of a quarter.

"What is that?" It looks good for skipping but not for collecting.

"Sayeed found it when he was your age," he says. "It was the first stone out of the ground when we planted the olive grove. I thought he would bring it with him when he left, but I found it in his things. Out of everything, I thought he would have taken that stone."

"You planted the olive grove outside the city?" I study the stiff brown skin on Abu Sayeed's cheeks and forehead. The sun must have toughened his face while he and Sayeed tilled the olive grove, while he spent his afternoons digging in the fields, teaching the stones' names to his son.

Abu Sayeed turns to the water. "I should have given it back to the earth," he says, "but I didn't have the heart."

The man across from us must have heard part of what we said, because he says something to Abu Sayeed. I catch zeitoun—*olive*. The man leans forward under the lights.

It's the man with the cane, the one who doesn't look old enough for a cane. One of his knees is braced with plaster. The other leg—my stomach churns. Below the knee, his other leg is missing.

Abu Sayeed translates for me. "His family had an olive grove near Halab."

I wonder if he's a bad man. I think of Mama shaving my head. *Just in case.* Huda's brown calves, the clank of a brass buckle on asphalt.

But I try to reason that not everybody can be a bad man, and I want to know why he's only got one leg. So I gather my courage and ask, "What does he do?"

"Used to do," the man says through Abu Sayeed. "That's what you want to know. What I did before this." He holds up the stump of his leg, wrapped in bandages.

"Your leg is gone," I say, and Abu Sayeed hesitates before he translates it.

"I was a footballer," the man says. "A striker. Now—" He stretches his shoulders and coughs with a smirk, which I guess is how he laughs. Abu Sayeed says the rest quietly: "Now I call it a good day if I can walk without pain to the bathroom."

I ask, "Why are you laughing?"

The man shrugs. His Arabic is all brown edges compared to Abu Sayeed's honey-yellow translation. "I left my tears behind when I left my home. It's easier to laugh, since crying doesn't fix a limp. And life continues just the same, doesn't it, even with one leg?"

I don't know what to say to that, so I put my hands in my pockets. I knuckle something hard. A rock.

I pull out the green-and-purple half-stone, cupping my hands so it doesn't bounce over the side. "Look what I found, Abu Sayeed."

I offer it to him. He squints in the green-tinted moonlight, like a thirsty kid with a glass of water.

"It looked green in the sun," I say, "but shadows turn it purple. Just like you said."

Abu Sayeed curls my fingers over my palm, trapping the stone inside.

The ridge of skin between my thumb and my first finger tingles with excitement. Hope stabs through me like a struck match. "Is it what I think it is?" I ask him. "The stone the jinni said to find?"

Abu Sayeed smiles, slowly. "I think inside," he says, "you know the truth."

I stuff the half-stone back in my pocket, and the pitching of the ferry knocks it around. "Is it real or not? I want to know what I'm looking for."

Abu Sayeed pats my hand and smiles, and for the first time, his shoulders seem a little sturdier, his eyes a little less sad. "Maybe if you give it time," he says, "you will know."

I picture Rawiya, hearing her father's voice. *Sparrowling.* What did Baba used to call me? I try and remember his voice: *Ya baba, my sapling. My daughter is as strong as a new palm.* The stone bulges in my pocket. What would I give to hear Baba's voice again?

"And if it's real?" I say. "Do you want to try?"

"Try what?" he asks.

"To talk to your son."

The motor sputters, red and black and angry-sounding. We jolt in our seats. The stench of burning stings yellow and brown in my nose. I grab Mama's arm. Acid sticks to my throat.

The boat rocks and smokes, and Abu Sayeed and the one-legged man grab the railing. Somebody yells a word in Arabic I don't understand, and Mama whispers, "Fire." A cloud passes in front of the moon.

Around us, people panic and shout. Men throw boxes and satchels into the water, grabbing for coils of extra rope and loose bits of wood. People pick up deck chairs with two sets of arms and toss them over the side. They run back and forth, looking for anything they can find. I hear them shouting in Arabic: *Sinking—the weight—we'll all drown.*

My hand is a claw. I can't see land anywhere around us. Water sprays the deck. "Mama?"

"There's a fire," Mama says, biting her lip. "The engine is failing."

My mouth seals itself up, my head heavy, my eyes burning. A man shouts and empties crates into the water. By now I understand him: *We're still too heavy.* Even the one-legged man is up now, limping to the side, helping heave over a suitcase with one hand. The smoke gets thicker, stinging my eyes. I start to cough.

"We're taking on water." Mama and Umm Yusuf heave our extra bag of clothes into the dark, and Abu Sayeed tosses over his geologist's tools. Splashes explode on every side. There's nothing left to throw into the sea. We're still too heavy.

"Abu Sayeed." I catch hold of his sleeve, my eyes watering from the smoke. "What do we do?"

Abu Sayeed tugs me up. Everyone clusters into a knot, pushing back against the wall of bodies. People shove and scream, hauling their luggage over their heads. Mama thumps a yellow life jacket into my hands, and Abu Sayeed helps me fasten it, his hands trembling.

My fingers shake, tugging at the strap. "Where's yours?"

Abu Sayeed shakes his head. "There aren't enough for everyone. The life jackets are for little ones only." Then he darts away toward the railing, dragonfly-quick, and snakes his hands through the smoke. He's a cough in the shadows. "Rafts!"

We follow the sound of his voice. Inflatable life rafts are tied to the side of the ferry, and families pour into them. Next to us, somebody heaves on a rope, and a full raft jerks down into the dark.

"Everybody in." Mama and Abu Sayeed help Sitt Shadid climb in. They nudge Zahra, Huda, Yusuf, Umm Yusuf, and Rahila in after her. Then Mama lifts me up over the edge, putting her foot to the railing.

We both jerk our heads when a rope snaps. The air goes out of all of us in one sharp yelp, and my arms pinwheel in the air. The raft rocks, one corner sagging. Smoke pours up from belowdecks, and the heat makes the rest of the ropes stretch and squeal like an oboe out of tune.

The ferry tips to one side. Wooden benches go flying, slamming into the far railing. The raft bangs against the side of the ferry, bouncing and twisting on its remaining rope.

"It won't hold much longer," Abu Sayeed says. "Go." He helps Mama over the railing with me in her arms, clinging to her neck. We drop to the floor of the raft, Mama's burlap bag swinging.

The ropes twist and groan.

I reach for Abu Sayeed. "In—get in!"

But he turns from the railing, choking on smoke. The life rafts have all been lowered now but ours. They drift on the water under us, somewhere in the far dark. The last passengers plummet into the water and swim for the rafts, leaping from the flames.

I follow Abu Sayeed's eyes. Across the deck is the one-legged man, trapped under one of the overturned benches. His hip is wedged against the deck, and he can't pull himself up with only his arms. Smoke curls around him, and he coughs, reaching toward us.

Abu Sayeed turns back to check the ropes and holds up a finger: *Wait here.*

I panic and grab for the railing, catching my fingernails on the hem of his sleeve. "It's sinking. You have to come back."

"As quick as I can." Then Abu Sayeed smiles. "I didn't tell you," he says, "but I don't need it—an answer from the stone, from Allah. What I needed was you, little cloud. What is most important is already here."

He holds his smile, his shoulders squared and strong. In that moment, he looks like he did in Baba's Polaroids in his orange shirt. Abu Sayeed looks young again.

I reach for him, but he ducks away under the smoke and over to the one-legged man. While Abu Sayeed grunts and rolls the bench off him, flames hiss at the ropes above the raft. The wind jostles us. Abu Sayeed slips back through the smoke, helping the one-legged man over the railing and into the raft. The ropes stretch, licked by flames. Abu Sayeed starts to lift one foot over the rail.

There's a crackling sound and then a loud *snap!* The life raft hangs in the air, and for a second, I'm weightless.

The flames above us rush away into the stars. The deck becomes a stripe of light and heat, as far up as a thunderhead. Everything goes dark. Then the raft smacks into the water, and the waves buck under us. I go flying.

I reach out into the air, sucking in breath, and the sheet of wet dark lunges toward me. Like Rawiya, I had thought the open water would be flat. Instead, it's a hundred churning knives.

But then there's a weight at my ankle, and the water drops away from me. Instead of plunging headfirst into the gulf, my chest bounces against the rubber rim of the raft.

I look back. The one-legged man has me by the foot, his hand the only thing keeping me in. He pulls me back from the waves, bracing his good leg against the rubber wall.

Up above us, Abu Sayeed's face appears through a fog of black smoke, choking and frantic. Mama yells to him that we're okay.

"I can't see you." Abu Sayeed waves smoke out of his eyes. The wind makes froth out of the water, and the waves tower up. The raft starts to drift away from the ferry, tossing and pitching us.

Mama yells, "You have to jump."

Abu Sayeed climbs up on the rail, steadying himself on the edge with his hands. He straightens, coughing. Then he pushes up with his legs and jumps from the ferry. It feels like a whole minute he's in the air, hanging between us and the stars, a big black orb-weaver spider blocking the moon.

But he misses the raft. Abu Sayeed tumbles down into the cold dark, landing with a spray of salt.

"Abu Sayeed!" I cry out. "He can't swim!"

The sea is rough and black. Mama scrambles for a flashlight at the back of the raft, and Umm Yusuf and Yusuf paddle with their hands. We can't see Abu Sayeed. I am desperate, clawing at the raft's rim, screaming into the salt. Abu Sayeed's handkerchief flutters down from the deck, and I snatch it up before it falls into the waves.

"Abu Sayeed!"

I shout and paddle, fighting waves thick as fridges. Mama scans the froth with her flashlight. Green light stabs over the horizon, and I taste my own tears. The one-legged man buries his head in his palms.

Rescue boats come, crisscrossing the waves with their spotlights. Abu Sayeed's hand reaches up toward mine through the green, way down below us, and then his fingers wind away from me into the onyx black, and he's gone.

The Weight of Stones

*

Ibn Hakim began to stir and groan, and the dye workers crept out of their hiding places. Rawiya tried to lift Bakr, but his body was too heavy. She squatted down with her back to him and hoisted him up onto her shoulders, walking bent under his weight.

But Ibn Hakim lay between them and the door of the dye factory. Outside, a small crowd had gathered, murmuring. Rawiya knew she couldn't get Bakr's body up the ladder and out the second-floor window, but she was determined to give him a proper burial.

The only way out was past Ibn Hakim. She grunted under Bakr's weight, stepping carefully toward the door.

Ibn Hakim's hand twitched for his sword, and she jumped back.

But the dye workers, who had seen everything and knew Ibn Hakim to be a cruel and corrupt man, scurried out from behind the dye vats and spools of silk. "We will stall him," one of them said, pushing Rawiya toward the door. "We never much liked Ibn Hakim and his thugs, and we won't help them. Go!"

Rawiya thanked them and ducked out as Ibn Hakim moaned and touched his head. She hurried toward the city gates. Bakr's bulk became heavier and heavier until she thought her bones would break from the weight.

Khaldun and al-Idrisi had already joined the servants and loaded the camels, and everyone sat mounted and ready. When Rawiya arrived, huffing, Khaldun rushed to help her lower Bakr from her back. "Rami, is he . . . ?"

But Rawiya shook her head as shouts grew louder behind them.

Rawiya and Khaldun lashed Bakr's body to his camel, and Rawiya led the animal by the reins. They galloped out through the gates. They fled across the fertile plain of the Nile Delta, following the great river.

For days, they rode hard, stopping to sleep only when it was dark. They made no fires and ate stale bread. Only by the light of early dawn did al-Idrisi scratch away in his leather-bound book, sadly sketching the cone of the Nile Delta, his usual wide and looping script now tight and slipping downward.

On the third day, when they were certain they were not being followed, they laid Bakr down at the river's edge. They washed his body in the Nile as the sun set, massaging its coolness into his beard and his hair.

Al-Idrisi handed the astrolabe to Rawiya. She determined the direction of the qibla, pointing wordlessly to the southeast, so they would know in which direction Bakr's body should be buried. Then they wrapped him in clean linens and buried him beside the blue ribbon of the Nile, lying on his side facing the qibla. Rawiya gripped the astrolabe for a long time afterward, Nile mud under her fingernails. Khaldun gently pried it from her, folding his palms over the backs of her hands.

The whole expedition prayed over the body. Rawiya tugged out her mother's misbaha, counting its wooden beads. Bakr's package wrapped in brown linen lay tucked inside her pack, as heavy as the thought of her own mother's despair. The prayers brought little comfort. Rawiya smeared the last traces of grit and mud over her heart as though a gash might open in her own ribs, as though blood might fill her own lungs. On the opposite bank of the Nile, a crocodile slid one white eyelid shut.

The next day, they broke with the river and headed northwest toward Alexandria. They skirted the city out of fear, for they knew the caliph must have been warned of them. Within two days, they reached the coastal road that connected Alexandria to the Bedu trade hub known to the Romans as Baranis, a seaside city midway between Alexandria and Barneek.

As they left the green behind them, al-Idrisi painted the arrow of the Nile in his book, the bursting-open of the river at Cairo, the shadow of the Pyramids at Giza behind the palms of Fustat. Gradually, his letters grew larger and more even, his *waw* more rounded, his *mim* looping wide.

The red-and-gray steppe plunged down to the sea, bordered to the south by a plateau with steep cliffs. They traveled two weeks, slowed by sharp winds from the south that swept down from the mountains, and their food and supplies ran low. The camels grew restless.

One afternoon, with the port city of Baranis almost in sight, the winds rose from the south and howled against their teeth. Dust poured through the mountain passes like hair through a comb. The winds carried tufts of white down that were too big for an eagle's and, every so often, a pale feather as long as Rawiya's arm.

Battered by the winds and fearing that the roc intended to make good on his promise of revenge, the expedition sought shelter under the cliffs. The roc did not come, but neither did the sandstorm lift. With every break in the dust, the landscape shifted. Whenever they left their shelter, they would find they had gone in circles or had changed direction, heading back toward Alexandria. Then the servants would curse the desert and murmur of jinn, whispering terrified prayers. Many times, Rawiya and her friends sat down and wept from frustration.

Finally, al-Idrisi spotted a group of figures through the curtain of dust. They fought their way there, leading their groaning camels. When the dust fell away, they stood hunched before a group of men on horseback, hiding their faces with their turbans. The winds peeled back, curling around their feet like dried carob pods.

"Hail, friends," al-Idrisi said. "We need food, rest, and water for ourselves and our camels. We are at your service if you can help us."

But instead of returning al-Idrisi's greeting, a man came toward them and unsheathed a pair of daggers. The rest of the men pulled out bows and scimitars, surrounding them with loud shouts. Their horses stamped and circled them. Flags unfurled above them, black-and-white checkers on a red field. Their leader wore a helmet wrapped with embroidered cloth, a scarlet robe, and a brown woolen cloak wrapped over his chest. His horse, black as ink, wore a matching scarlet mantle.

"Stranger," the leader called out, "we heard tell of Fatimid spies in this area. We are commanded to stomp out any threat to the Almohad Empire." He eyed al-Idrisi's saddle and their packs, the servants' new tunics sewn from the traditional striped linen and wool of Cairo.

Al-Idrisi replied, "We have not seen these unsavory characters. We ourselves are humble pilgrims, exploring God's wonders."

But the leader of the Almohad troop, who had seen them approaching from the east, did not believe them. "Liars!" he snarled. "Confess your crimes at once, or it will be worse for you."

"Lies?" al-Idrisi said. "This is God's truth, with not a speck of untruth in it."

But it was no use. Almohad scouts had seen the expedition heading west on the road from Alexandria to Baranis, and the leader was convinced of their treachery. He signaled to his men, who seized hold of their camels and pulled them from their saddles.

The Almohad horsemen ripped open their packs and dug through the satchels of Nur ad-Din's treasure. Ignoring the riches, they tore open al-Idrisi's leather-bound book and his scrolls. It was not treasure they were after, but information.

Rawiya knew right away that it was just as Ibn Hakim had warned them: she and her friends were the travelers the Almohads had been looking for.

Indeed, the Almohad leader, a wizened old general named Mennad, had heard fantastic tales of a band of travelers led by a scholar and mapmaker, a man who was collecting all the knowledge of geography and culture from the Mashriq to the Maghreb. Mennad knew that these travelers must have maps of the Fatimid lands, information he could use to the advantage of his people. Mennad had long been planning an attack to push back the Fatimids, who wanted to regain control of the shores of the Gulf of Sidra and the city of Barneek from the Almohad forces.

The Almohads shouted in triumph when they found al-Idrisi's book of notes and sketch maps. Mennad snatched it up and snapped through its pages.

Now, Mennad was experienced in the ways of war. He had fought many battles and earned long spools of scars down his face, his arms, and his ribs. He had defended his men in battle many times. But Mennad knew that the Fatimid armies were strong, and he needed an advantage. He was a shrewd man.

Mennad tucked al-Idrisi's book into his robe and pulled down his turban. A long, pale scar split his face.

"Now," he said, "you shall pay for your lies. But I expect to have your thanks, spy, before the day is over. I shall not take your life. Instead, for your treachery, you shall fight for the Almohad Empire in the great battle that is to come."

"We will do no such thing," al-Idrisi said, reaching for his scimitar. "Release us."

But the Almohad horsemen snapped up their swords and daggers to al-Idrisi's throat. Surrounded, al-Idrisi lowered his hand.

Mennad curled his mouth into a smirk. "You shall bend to my will as every proud man has done before," he went on. "I am no green shoot, no foolhardy youth. Politics and pride mean nothing to the one who thirsts for truth and freedom. And when I have no further use of these maps and charts"—he smirked—"I will be sure that our enemies cannot use them against us. They will be burned."

Al-Idrisi, knowing that without his maps all their journeys and hardships would be in vain, bent his head and wept.

Mennad and his men led the expedition in a long chain into the desert, posting guards in front, behind, and beside them. The Almohads led them west against the foot of the mountains until they came to a pass that led up to the plateau. The rise was very slow, a natural path over the cliffs. And although Mennad had taken al-Idrisi's notes and maps, al-Idrisi still studied the pass and whispered to himself, calculating the angle of the slope in his head. "If we ever get out of this," he said to Rawiya and Khaldun, "and I am able to complete my work, I will call this place Aqabat as-Salum." The Graded Ascent.

Rawiya whispered to Khaldun, "He has not lost hope."

They traveled for days. Beyond the plateau, the rocky steppe became true desert, a flat yellow stretch of sand like the sole of a foot. Rawiya realized now that no desert was like another. She understood: the desert was alive, a thing with blood and breath, a many-armed creature spreading its fingers.

The Almohads led the expedition to their encampment. There, a scout told Mennad that Fatimid warriors had gathered near the Gulf of Sidra between Ajdabiya and Barneek, less than a day's journey away. In the confusion of the sandstorm, the expedition had wandered farther west than they had thought.

The Almohads shoved Rawiya and Khaldun into one tent and al-Idrisi into another, posting a guard outside. With the book in his possession, Mennad had no further use for Rawiya and her friends except to bolster his forces against the Fatimids—a clash they were not likely to survive.

Rawiya, unable to see any way out of the predicament they were in, strung and restrung her sling, counting her stones for the battle ahead.

"It is a shame," Khaldun said, his head in his hands. "I would have loved to see al-Idrisi's work completed. Instead, our journey comes to this. And Bakr's death was for nothing." He began to cry, crumpling to his knees.

Rawiya laid her hand on his shoulder. "We will find a way out of this. We will get the maps back somehow."

"How will we do that, with only a poet, a scholar, and a young boy?" Khaldun looked away. "I'm sorry," he said. "You have shown great courage, but . . ."

"No," Rawiya said. "I should be apologizing, not you." She tugged the cloth door shut and took a deep breath. Turning to Khaldun, she tried to memorize the kindness in his black eyes, the way the dying light fell across his face. Her feelings for this beautiful man, this gentle poet, had been doomed from the start, Rawiya knew. *I must tell him*, she thought, *though he will never forgive me*.

"If we must die tomorrow," Rawiya said, "you should know that I was not honest when I joined al-Idrisi's expedition. My name is not Rami."

Khaldun's frown softened. "Nobility is not important on the road."

"It's not that," Rawiya said. She untied her turban. Over the last few months, her black hair had grown out in a tangle of curls. "Well? Didn't you wonder why I never grew a beard?"

Khaldun stepped back. "I assumed you were a young boy," he said, "not yet grown."

"My name is Rawiya," she said, "not Rami." She paused, fighting the knot of anxiety in her stomach, and searched his face. "I'm a woman."

Khaldun stood stiff as new leather, hands clenched as though praying. "I always knew you were special," he said, "and I had a fondness for you that sometimes felt like we were more than brothers—" He shook his head, looking lost. "What will we tell al-Idrisi? You lied to him. When he sees the truth . . ."

"Khaldun—"

Khaldun knelt before her and lowered his face. "Whoever you are, I am at your service," he said, "for saving my life and my honor.

I only hope God will grant me the courage and the opportunity to return the favor. Man or woman, I have promised to follow you until the day I die, and I will keep my pledge."

"Khaldun." Rawiya pulled him up. "Don't forget, you saved my life more than once. No one is at anyone's service. Only together will we find a way."

Khaldun returned her nervous smile. "Then what do we do?" he asked. "If tomorrow is our last day of life, what do we do while the moon weeps for us?"

Rawiya touched her hand to her pouch where half of the roc's eye stone sat. That, at least, had not been stolen. Before Ibn Hakim had sliced it clean in half, the stone had shown Rawiya her father's face, his voice. It had let her speak with the dead.

But on this night, Rawiya didn't need its power to see what she wanted to remember: her mother that evening in the olive grove after her father had slipped into darkness, how she had sat Rawiya in her lap, the moon dappling the grass, the smell of the sea all around them. What had her mother said—those words that, ten years later, had made her cut her hair and pack for Fes, words that let her believe in a more beautiful world?

Rawiya closed her eyes and breathed in. "Let me tell you a story."

*   *   *

THE RESCUE BOATS pick us out of the life rafts, and babies shriek like cats. Spray soaks me to the bones. Up in the boat, my teeth chatter, making it impossible for me to keep crying. I stare down into the green and remind myself of what I learned in the raft: no sea is flat.

The flashlight's batteries die. Mama holds on to its metal husk like an extra rib while the sun comes up over the wreck of the ferry. It leans on its side, mostly sunk now. Bigger ships spray the fire with seawater, searching for survivors. Over the side, the sea is alive, churning with limbs. The water holds the dead.

The one-legged man is separated from us on the rescue boat. He coughs and heaves his chest, his chin black. He grips his leg. Only in the light can you see where the fire licked him, the stripes of black on the backs of his hands and his cheeks. The welts where the bench crushed him aren't as obvious, but I can make out the red snakes of bruises where the wood cut into him, the splinters that stuck when Abu Sayeed pulled him free.

Through the crowd of people bringing water to the one-legged man and wrapping him in blankets, I make out the holes in his shirt and the red soccer jersey peeking out from underneath. He sees me but doesn't smile. I stare into him, searching for the glassy look he had under the bench—the look of someone who has locked eyes with their own death. I was right, I guess—staring too long at death can mark a person.

But he only grips his bandaged knee and holds my gaze. People pass between us with water and thermal blankets, but neither of us looks away.

And then the one-legged man nods, like he knows we'll never see each other after this, like he would still hold on to my ankle if he had to do it again.

THE RESCUE BOATS take us to Nuweiba, the first I've seen of Egypt. The police check everybody's identification before we leave the terminal, snarls of bodies wrapped in blankets tugging out soaked passport booklets and visas. Soon we stumble out into the green sun.

The world is orange in that way things are after you've stared at the sea too long. Ships waddle in and out of the harbor. My feet don't work right yet, still making up for shifting waves that aren't there. It feels like riding an invisible skateboard.

I lurch and trip and realize I've been leaking bits of me all this time. The ghost of me is still scattered across the road from Amman to Aqaba. Shreds of me wander the streets of Homs under the shop awnings. I have no voice, no anchor. How can I keep from ripping apart on the wind like dandelion seeds? How can I keep from floating away without Abu Sayeed and his stones to weigh me down?

When we lived in the city, I used to think the black circles of gum stuck to the sidewalk were gravity spots, that they made gravity. I thought somebody put them there to keep us from floating off into outer space. Because why not, right? If we jump too high, do we all just slide off the earth? If the city forgot it was heavy, would the whole thing lift off and crash into the moon?

I seize Mama's hand and scan the sidewalk for stray gum spots. But there aren't any, not the big black ones we had in New York. A startle of fear comes like a stubbed toe in the dark: there is nothing holding me down, nothing between me and the corkboard where God stuck the stars.

We dive away from the crowds outside the ferry terminal. We are a chain of people: Sitt Shadid shuffling her pumps, Umm Yusuf clutching Rahila to her, Zahra holding Yusuf's hand. Since the fire started on the ferry, I don't think she ever let go.

The town of Nuweiba is surrounded by high mountains that come almost out of the water, and the beachfront is scattered with blue fishing boats and straw umbrellas. It looks so wrong today, this oceanfront vacation town, the passing tourists in their sunglasses.

On the street, Mama unrolls her map, shaking it out in case it's wet. But even though we lost all our clothes and my stuffed bird, we still have what was in her burlap bag—her rolled-up map and the dirty rug, a few cans of tuna, half-empty bottles of aspirin and tubes of toothpaste. Umm Yusuf and Mama whisper about where to go, Mama blinking her wet eyelashes.

I watch my feet and breathe. The pictures replay—Abu Sayeed bending his knees, tensing his elbows, his arms and legs wheeling through the smoky air. In my mind, he never hits the water.

I wait for my toes to lift up, wait to feel myself floating off into space.

I drop to my knees. I cling to the concrete with my fingernails. Cubes of basalt and drops of sugar-grainy marble clink in my left pocket. In my right, the green-and-purple half-stone turns, tied up in Abu Sayeed's handkerchief.

I close my eyes. Is his voice waiting for me in there, waiting to call me little cloud?

I hear Huda say, "He saved us."

I open my eyes and see the lines on Huda's palm. She leans down and strokes my face.

"He's the reason we got the life jackets on," Huda says. "He's the reason we got the rafts down before the ship rolled. We would have all drowned without him. He gave us everything."

"Baba saved him." When I raise a hand, the sidewalk leaves dents in my palm. "So he saved us."

Huda nods and turns her face into her palm—that bitter look. The sidewalk bites into my shins. I want to convince myself that this pain is not senseless. I want these pictures of Abu Sayeed to mean something.

Huda wipes her cheek, collecting drops of water under her fingernails. "What are you doing?" she asks.

I look down at my knees on the concrete, at my hand flat on the ground. I say, "Praying."

"Then so am I." Huda pulls a half-empty water bottle from the bag and pours water over her hands. She's performing wudu, washing up before prayer.

It isn't long before everybody notices what Huda is doing, and Sitt Shadid, Umm Yusuf, and Yusuf join in. Sitt Shadid slides off her pumps and unrolls her knee-highs, rubbing water into the cracks on her heels. Yusuf runs his wet hands through his hair. Mama spreads out the dirty carpet on the sidewalk for us. We kneel on it, as many of us as we can fit, with Huda's and my knees sticking off the carpet. The concrete grit eats our shins. Mama crosses herself. Each in our own way, we pray for Abu Sayeed's soul.

But Abu Sayeed was right. Even though God listens, he doesn't always give you answers.

Mama and Umm Yusuf stretch out their palms, accenting words with their chins and their fingertips. In Arabic, I catch Umm Yusuf's words: *We'll head west—Libya—car or bus?*

Mama frowns. *We can't afford a car.*

I stand up, and the sky reaches for the top of my head. Nubs of concrete stick to the dents in my skin. The space between us stretches like an empty hand.

"I wish we never left home," I say. "I wish we'd stayed in Homs. I wish we never came here."

"Have you lost your mind?" Zahra thrusts out her hands. "Home is gone. It's gone forever."

"Things can be fixed," I shoot back. "You don't know."

"It's rubble," Zahra says. "All that's left is rubble. Or don't you know what that is? It's broken dishes, stupid. Drywall. Half a plate. The arms ripped out of stuffed animals. It's black glass and plaster dust."

I hold my breath, trying not to yell. "I'm not stupid."

People on the street begin to stare.

Zahra plants her feet and holds her ground, her torn jeans damp with seawater. "No," she shoots back. "You're delusional. Abu Sayeed is gone. Do you understand that?"

Huda steps between us. "That's enough."

My hands close up into knobby stones, and something in me explodes.

"You're a spoiled brat," I shout. "All you care about is your jewelry and boys. You don't care about your family. You don't care about anything."

Everyone goes quiet, even Zahra.

"Part of me is dead," I say. The sun stings my pockmarked shins. "I never even knew it was alive."

Zahra twists her bracelet. "Why do you think I wear it?" She turns on her heel and walks away.

"What?"

"The bracelet was from Baba," Huda says, lowering her eyes. "It was her seventeenth birthday present."

And then my anger drains away. The bracelet isn't a bracelet to Zahra. It's a gravity spot.

Zahra rounds a corner. I follow her black curls, matted with salt.

"Wait," I call. "I'm sorry. I didn't know." I turn the corner and run smack into her back.

"Look at this." Zahra runs her finger over the wall. A paper is posted over glossy graffiti. "It's a bus schedule west," she says. "There's a bus to Benghazi this afternoon, with a transfer in Cairo."

MAMA, UMM YUSUF, and Sitt Shadid pool their money and share the cost of our bus tickets. Mama chews the inside of her cheek when we pay for them. I can see her doing calculations in her head. She doesn't think I noticed how much she took out, how every expense now is like a plague of locusts chewing holes into the little we have left.

Crowds follow us everywhere we go. People press onto the bus, children sitting in their mother's laps, people crammed into the aisle. The earth seems like it's overflowing with families from every country, not just our own. I see other wars everywhere—in the scar along a lady's chin, or in the bruises on a boy's ankle.

The bus is packed with grimy, tired people, but we can't smell ourselves, not any of us. Families share bread, and the nutty smell of fava beans glides over the seats. I sit between Huda and Mama, careful to lean on Huda's right shoulder. Men talk quietly behind us.

The bus takes us north along the mountains until we hit Taba and turn west. The road is an elbow between cone-shaped hills, striped red and yellow and bleeding sand. We pass shantytowns and acacia trees, places where sand is crusted on the road. Mama says the Sinai Peninsula's got turquoise buried in it, veins of blue-green soaking the rock. She says they used to call it the land of turquoise.

I turn away and think, Abu Sayeed would have loved this.

The tunnel comes quick. I frown at a ship that rises up over the sand, water I can't see. A whole string of ships stretches across the highway, and for a minute, I think we're going to hit them. Then the road dips down under a bridge decorated with a mural with sailboats, mosques, and pyramids. The bus plunges into darkness.

"We're in the Suez Tunnel," Mama says, "under the canal."

The bus chugs down, hugging the wall, and the lights flit past. *Chug-cha-chug-cha-chug.*

I ask, "We're under it?"

Before Mama can answer, we're out of the tunnel again. We see the smog before the city. The Nile Delta is a strip of green from this angle, a tooth pushing north out of a brown jumble of buildings.

"There used to be two cities here," Mama says. "Next to Cairo, there was a city called Fustat. The ruins of ancient temples are still there."

"What happened to the other city?" I ask.

Huda leans against the window and winces, shivering, before she closes her eyes. Her forehead is so hot that it fogs the air-conditioned glass.

Mama folds her hands in her lap, her veins taut and green. "The bigger city ate the smaller one," she says.

WE TUMBLE OUT at Cairo's Turgoman Station. The next bus, the one to Benghazi, isn't for a few hours. The terminal looks more like a mall than a bus station: three floors, glass railings, polished linoleum floor tiles. The brown-red smell of bus brakes sticks to even the smoothest surfaces. The other passengers pour off the bus and scatter into the crowds, away from a bench where we've carved out a pocket of calm in the chaos.

"I need to sit for a minute." Huda shuffles to the bench and lowers herself down, resting her head on her arm. Umm Yusuf sits next to her and flicks her eyes to meet Mama's. Then she looks at me, so quick I almost don't notice. Umm Yusuf has that look grown-ups get when they want to protect you, the look that says: *Don't let her see.*

"I have to stretch my legs," Mama says. "Nour will walk with me."

"I will?"

We leave the terminal together. The heat unfurls over us like a curtain dropping. I blink in the sunshine. Behind us, the sun glare turns the terminal's green and blue glass into daggers of light. A few families wander the plaza, and cars circle the entrance. The sidewalks seem strangely empty, especially now that Ramadan is over. I look back through the glass into the station, thinking I might be able to see straight through into the terminal and catch a glimpse of Huda, but the crowds and the sun glare shimmer in an unbroken mass. I can't see her.

One time, when I was little, I helped Zahra dye Huda's hair. She was asleep, and we snuck up on her. Henna paste is green like ground-up olives, even though it turns your hair red. I helped Zahra paint the henna onto a handful of Huda's hair. It was funny until Huda turned over and the henna got on the couch. Mama grounded Zahra for a week when it stained.

"I didn't mean to stain it," I say.

Mama frowns down at me. "Stain what?"

"The couch. Remember?"

"What makes you think of that?"

We cross the plaza, avoiding the car lanes. I scratch at my shorts plastered to my legs. "I didn't know we would only have it for five years." My torn fingernails catch on my shorts. "I ruined it."

"If anything," Mama says, "it was Zahra who ruined it."

"But if I'd known, I wouldn't have helped." I didn't know how quickly things could change. One minute Huda was laughing, and the next the metal was lodged in her bone. Her skin bled heat through her sleeves the whole ride to Cairo. She never burned up like that before, not even with the flu.

"It wasn't such a terrible stain." Mama turns and follows the crowded sidewalk along the road, fidgeting with a milk-white button on her blouse where the stitching is starting to unravel. "The cushions were already old. They don't last that long, not with three little ones."

"But I didn't know what a nice couch it was." I wipe my nose on my arm, leaving a long wet streak. "I thought we would have it forever."

Women in long dresses and men in short-sleeved button-downs and sandals dart in and out of traffic. Cairo is thick with trucks and bicycles again after the Eid holiday weekend. I watch the drawn-out needle of my shadow as people hurry past. My shadow isn't even as wide as a rack of lamb in the supermarket.

Mama puts her arm around my shoulders as we walk. "Somewhere," she says quietly, "your baba is very proud of you."

"For what?"

"For being brave."

I cross my arms. "If Baba was here," I say, "I wouldn't have to be brave."

"We all have to be brave." Mama squeezes the horn of bone at the end of my shoulder. "This necklace—did I ever tell you?" She lifts the loop over her head and holds the broken piece of ceramic in her hand, the cord snaking between her fingers. Her shadow on the pavement does the same. "When your baba and I were first married, we lived in Ceuta. Did you know that?"

"You mean Rawiya's Ceuta?"

"Just so," Mama says, "although we lived a fair distance from the Moroccan border. We had a small riad near La Puntilla, by the harbor."

We go quiet. Palms and shop-filled alleys line the street. One is crowded with dozens of round hand-wrought lamps, another with scarves the colors of ripe pomegranates and figs, folded like sheets of rubies. Leather bags sit stacked in towers. Concrete apartment buildings cluster toward the cucumber smell of fresh water. One of them is still decorated with the shredded poster of a politician in a pinstripe suit and black tie.

"We had a big garden and a tiled fountain," Mama says. "They said the house used to belong to a nobleman, that it was hundreds of years old. They were just stories, you know, but we chose to believe them. We watched the sea and said one day we would go to America, when the time was right."

"When was it right?"

"Never." Mama laughs and bounces the piece of ceramic in her palm. When was the last time I heard her laugh? "A storm came through the strait one night like a cloud of bats. The winds ripped out the garden and cracked the roof. When the storm fell away, we walked outside and found this."

Mama hands me the necklace. The ceramic is warm and curved a little, a rounded tile painted with blue and white vines. I don't think I've ever seen another round tile like it.

"What is it?"

"All that was left of the fountain tiles. Go on." She nudges me, so I lift the cord over my head and put it on. The warm ceramic taps my belly, swinging with my steps.

"Did you fix the fountain?"

"No." Mama brushes her hair off her shoulders. "We took it as a sign and bought our plane tickets the next day."

"For the city?"

"For Syria first," she says. "It would be a better place, I thought, to have the girls. But it wasn't the same for your father with his brother away, and with Abu Sayeed studying abroad, besides. And even after a decade, that thirst never left him—for distant places, I suppose, the blank parts of his map. So we took Zahra and Huda when they were still small and left Syria for New York."

I picture Mama and Baba holding hands in the airport, watching the eel-bodied planes slip down the runway. I picture the blue pantsuit she used to wear for meetings with people who bought her maps, that crisp white blouse, that boxy pocketbook in black leather.

"I don't get how you can draw a map without the blank parts," I say.

We pass movie posters and vines of graffiti in red and black. On the corner, a riot policeman stands with his hips squared to the street.

"Some people are born knowing they have to fill those places in," Mama says. "They are born with a wound, and they know from the beginning that if they don't find the story that belongs to them, that wound will never heal." Mama pauses and twists her amber ring. She says, "Others take a long time to figure that out."

Old buildings turn their faces toward the sun, their carved wooden window frames and high doors dulled by hundreds of years of heat and wind.

"What about the house in Ceuta?" I ask.

"We sold it to your uncle Ma'mun." Mama laughs again, and I can't believe my luck, the laughing, this necklace. "Gave it, more like. We charged him a quarter of the price."

"So he fixed it?"

Mama frowns and raises her eyebrows, which I guess is a no. "I haven't been back in years," she says. "During our last visit—before you were born—he was still fixing the fountain. It's hard to make something twice, you know, and in just the same way."

"Maybe you can't," I say.

"Maybe not." Mama tilts her head toward the orange sun. "Not exactly."

We turn left and walk until we come to the 26th of July Corridor. The street is a clogged artery of cars and bicycles, men walking by with bread and packages on their heads. We pass a shop I would have called a bodega in Manhattan, stacked high with boxes of packaged foods and rows of soda lined up like toy soldiers.

"Where are we going?"

"I thought you would want to see the Nile," Mama says.

I finger the broken piece of tile. "No. I mean bigger than that. Why are we going all this way? You said somebody is waiting for us, but I don't know where they are."

"Somewhere they can help," Mama says.

But I'm impatient. I want to know what Mama meant when she said *if the wrong person finds out who is waiting* to Abu Sayeed. "Who is they? Who is waiting for us?"

Mama looks off down the street where the palms are waving. "Please understand, habibti, there are some things it is safer for you not to know. And I don't want to get our hopes up."

"Don't you mean my hopes?"

"Yours too."

The water unfolds before us across the street, but I don't register it until we stop walking. We wait to cross the sidewalk opposite the divided highway and watch the Nile turn the color of apricots while the sun gets lower.

"I will tell you this," Mama says. "If we get separated, use the map. You will see what's important, where the road is. We'll end up in the same place."

It sounds like one of Baba's riddles, and the world is too alien and senseless now for riddles. "The map is stupid," I say, folding my arms over the necklace cord. "It hasn't even got any names. I saw."

We cross the street. "It's dangerous to tell the world where you're going all the time," Mama says. "And anyway, you didn't look hard enough."

"Mmph."

And then there's nothing between us and the Nile: muddy, gray green, and wide as the East River. The water is the color of a crocodile's back, rolling and pitching in broad burls and carved ridges. The other side of the river is a blur of yellow concrete buildings, red billboards, and lights coming on in skyscrapers. It almost feels like New York. Almost.

"How many miles do we have to go tonight?"

"In al-Idrisi's time, they used the word *league* more often than mile," Mama says. "Farsakh."

"But it's not al-Idrisi's time," I say, "and I'm not Rawiya. Rawiya never had to ride on a hot bus."

Mama chuckles. "You're more Rawiya than anyone, I think."

The ground hums and vibrates under me when a truck goes by. I squat and run my finger over my own laces, the tongue where Mama ripped open the seams and put money in, thick packs of bills, and sewed it up again. I didn't understand when we were in Amman. Now, far away, the bills make my sneakers heavier. They press me into the pavement. If my shoes are connected to the concrete and the concrete is spread over the earth like batter in a pan, I can send my story through my bones, through my soles, through the streets, into the earth and the river. Can Baba hear my story, our story, through the Nile mud?

"Come on," Mama says. "Let's go."

We start back toward the station. I take Mama's hand. "Baba must have really liked the fountain in Ceuta," I say. "He always liked the one in Central Park. It was like it made him a different person."

Sometimes I used to catch Baba staring into the water, like he was waiting for something to come out and smack into him. I remember the weight in my pocket, the green-and-purple half-stone wrapped in Abu Sayeed's handkerchief. Can I ask him myself?

"Your father was lost when we met," Mama says. "He was looking for himself. But there aren't any maps for that." She smiles and runs a finger over the bridge of my nose. I pull away. "You look so much like him. When I look at you, all I see is him."

"But I'm not him."

"No," Mama says. She pauses and looks away. "I'm sorry."

When I was little, I used to tell myself that if somebody came and took Baba and pretended to be him, I would know the difference because of the color his voice made, that brown streak. I would know it by the color of his smell, the dark-green and gray circles I saw when I breathed into his wrists. But now I think, if the colors were only in me, did I know him at all?

"If Baba didn't have a map of himself," I say, "did I ever see the real him?"

"You know what?" Mama reaches over to touch the necklace. "The most important places on a map are the places we haven't been yet."

"What does that mean?"

"He found the map he was looking for," she says. "It was you."

We trudge toward the bus station's glass face. I ask, "Do you think there's a place in the world where nobody has ever put their feet?"

"I think there are more of them than the other way around," Mama says.

THE ROCKING OF the bus to Libya puts me to sleep again. I drift off on Huda's shoulder to the sound of Yusuf and Sitt Shadid talking in quiet Arabic.

I drift in and out, not remembering what city or country I'm in. I ask myself if we've crossed the border yet, never sure what border I mean.

I don't have dreams anymore, not real ones, not since the bomb fell on our house. The dreams I've got, I don't want to call them dreams. In the dark hours between sleeping and waking, I am screaming and screaming, but nobody hears me, not even myself.

The red zigzags of the bus brakes screech me awake. Is it the same day? It's dark, but not after-dinner dark. More like before-work dark, the kind of dark when the street sweepers are the emperors of the block.

I rub my eyes. Fresh air drifts in through the cracked windows, sharp and yellow with salt.

Mama nudges me. "We're in Benghazi."

I don't hear her at first. "Where are we?"

"Libya," Zahra says into her lap, waiting for people to pass. She doesn't look at me. "On the eastern shore of the Gulf of Sidra."

But Mama whispers a name from the story in my heart, saying, "Barneek."

PART III

LIBYA

This ache has   a thousand
faces, this hunger two   thousand eyes.
Beloved, we are poets, not   warriors, and even the
branches once learned to bend.   And just as every rain
comes from the sea, we are the tongues   and fingers of the Asi,
that river, our bones. Every vein runs with it, every drop of blood a wailing at the
water's edge. Why do our knees bend when we come to the sea? Why does the
arch of every foot become a saber? Will we run forever to arms that will never
hold us, voices that will never speak our names? For every poet knows that the
sea herself has never loved, beloved, and she is thick with our tears. Only the
desert knows what love is. Only the desert opens herself when the rains come,
breathing in our pain, breathing out acacia and tamarisk and flowers. Only the
wadi knows what it is to hold its breath. Only the wadi knows what it is to cry for
joy, saying, yes, there was death here and will be death again one day, and between
the two are laughter and the rhythmic breathing in of generations. How long must
I hold my breath? I am the words on my mother's tongue, I am the dust of stars
inhaled, I am the mother lung, I am the motherland. Does the road to the
loveless sea bend back on itself? I will wear black until the day I die,
beloved. Then your ghost and mine will dance, and the
womb of the wind will breathe us in.
Come and see. The wadi swells
with laughter of exiles
returning.

Sea of Swords and Teeth

*

The next morning, the Almohads woke Rawiya and her friends before dawn. The expedition was outfitted with leather armor, chain mail, and pointed silver helmets. Over their armor, they were forced to wear the red tunics of Almohad warriors. Mennad ordered Rawiya to carry a lance with the red, black, and white Almohad flag at the blunted end. Mennad and his men did not intend to kill her and her friends but to absorb them into their ranks. In the battle to come, the deadly Fatimid army would take care of the rest.

The Almohads did not plunder the expedition's packs for treasure. Mennad was a seasoned and cunning leader, and he had told his men they would be given a share when the battle was over. Even so, the Almohad warriors taunted the expedition's servants, boasting of their luck. And although the remaining half of the roc's eye stone had stayed hidden, Rawiya feared what would happen if Mennad discovered its power to speak with the dead. Where Ibn Hakim had been foolhardy and suspicious of the stone's magic, Mennad would be shrewd enough to see its value, and Rawiya feared the roc's eye stone would allow Mennad to become the most powerful ruler in the Maghreb. So she stuffed the plum-sized half-stone into the folds of her tunic.

The red shield of the sun rose in the east. Mennad stood apart from his men, studying al-Idrisi's notes.

"He keeps the book always at his side," al-Idrisi said. "We cannot steal it."

"We should not have to steal what is rightfully ours," Khaldun said. But he lowered his face, for they all knew that al-Idrisi's book held the knowledge of all the places they had traveled. Without it, they would never complete King Roger's map or their quest.

But Rawiya, who had studied the landscape as the Almohads had led them toward the Gulf of Sidra and Barneek, had other fears. Her father had told her tales of this land and its beasts, and she had not forgotten them.

"There are other dangers we should be wary of," she said to her friends. "Remember the stories of the roc's ancestral hunting grounds, how he returned from ash-Sham to feed in a valley of great snakes?"

Khaldun set his hand on the hilt of his scimitar. "You can't mean here?"

But al-Idrisi had noticed the gashes clawed into Cairo's gates and the downy white feathers on the wind, the way these signs had seemed to follow the expedition from ash-Sham. He recalled that Rawiya had been right once before about the tales of the roc, and he held his tongue.

As they stood brooding on these things, an Almohad guard ran up to Mennad, fear thick in his voice.

"Sir," the guard said, "our scouts killed a beast not far from here, an enormous serpent."

Khaldun met Rawiya's eye. "The enemy of my enemy," he said. And Rawiya nodded, a plan taking shape in her mind.

The Almohads mounted the expedition on horseback and set them among the warrior ranks. Bowmen took their places behind warriors armed with scimitars, spears, and daggers.

The Almohad army marched from the inland desert toward the coast, the expedition captive among them. The steppe became thick with juniper under the shadow of Jebel Akhdar, the wooded mountain to the east of Barneek. The Almohads cheered and sang of pushing the Fatimids back, of sweeping in a thick blade from the steppe to the sea.

The Fatimid army, cloaked in green, rose on the horizon.

Mennad signaled to his men. A great shout went up among their ranks, and they shook their spears and raised their bows. Mennad lifted al-Idrisi's book like a talisman. And Rawiya, who knew how slim their chances were of escaping from the battle with either their lives or al-Idrisi's book, clenched her hands at the reins.

The armies surged forward across the steppe. The Almohad warriors pushed Rawiya, her friends, and the expedition's servants toward the front line, and their ears rang with war cries.

The Almohads' battle-trained horses flew across the steppe, and the warriors' red tunics caught the wind as they went. The wall of Fatimid soldiers towered over them like a green wave, a sea of arrows and sword edges, the sound of their bellows flattening the earth.

But as Rawiya and her friends raised their swords and spears, an echo like a sea wind passed between them. From the north, a third army marched on them, dressed in chain mail and steel, holding high the red-and-gold standard of a lion.

It was King Roger's flag, the royal colors of the Norman Kingdom of Sicily.

The Almohads began to whisper and cry out, saying, "The Sicilian armies have come from the coast." And they cursed their luck.

But Mennad would not retreat. He turned his horse and lifted al-Idrisi's book. "We are the Almohad dynasty," he cried, "and we hold the secrets of the Fatimids' spies in our hands. We fight."

Rawiya saw her opening.

She plunged forward, spinning her lance in her hand, aiming its blade. Her horse sliced through rows of warriors toward the clearing where Mennad stood.

Mennad spotted her. He raised his spear and thrust it toward Rawiya's chest. She dodged, bracing her weight against her horse's flank.

Rawiya aimed her lance for Mennad's tunic. But Mennad, who had earned the scar that split his face from a Fatimid lance, ducked and wrapped his arm around the pole of her weapon. He used his weight to swing the pole of the lance into her side, knocking her off her horse.

Rawiya landed on her chest, the breath clapped out of her, and raised herself up on her palms.

Mennad and his men surrounded her. Swordsmen spun their blades, scimitars flashing, twin daggers drawn. Bowmen notched their arrows.

Mennad threw down Rawiya's lance, and it clattered to the ground.

"Get up and fight, boy." Holding the point of his spear at Rawiya's throat, Mennad said, "Or has your courage fled?"

Khaldun and al-Idrisi cut a path through the steppe toward her, but the tangle of warriors pressed them back.

Rawiya knew she could not defeat Mennad on her own. As she picked up her lance, she reached for the half of the roc's eye stone in the folds of her tunic. If the stone's power was still strong enough, she thought, the dead could whisper to her of Mennad's weaknesses.

Sparrowling—

Just as Rawiya touched the roc's eye stone, the ground rumbled and shook.

From the wooded cliffs, a flash of green streaked down. It was a giant serpent, faster than the strongest horse and ten times as long. The snake lifted its head, hissing, and snapped up Almohad warriors in its jaws.

With a scream, the neat ranks shattered, flooding around the threat.

"The stories are true," Rawiya said. "The roc's ancestral hunting grounds. The valley of the serpents. It exists."

Mennad turned his horse, breaking away from the snake, and clutched al-Idrisi's book to his chest. A group of swordsmen took the distraction to rush at Rawiya and her friends. Khaldun parried with his scimitar, and Rawiya knocked a man from his saddle with the butt of her lance. Grabbing the reins of her horse—for the animal was well trained and had not wandered far—Rawiya swung herself up into the saddle.

The shouts of the Norman army came closer. Blood ran in grooves of dust. Mennad escaped onto the open steppe, flanked by warriors. Rawiya signaled Khaldun and al-Idrisi, blocking an Almohad dagger with the pole of her lance.

Rawiya, Khaldun, and al-Idrisi turned after Mennad and gave chase, screeching like eagles. They burst through his circle of warriors. Mennad raised his spear, al-Idrisi's book tight to his ribs.

The Norman army surged down the cliffs above Barneek. Behind them, both Almohad and Fatimid warriors screamed in terror as another green shape slashed through the armies, tossing men high into the air and swallowing them.

Mennad waited in the clearing, his spear raised, chaos all around him.

"Give us the book," Rawiya called to Mennad. "By right, it is ours."

Mennad's sweat and blood ran down his face. "Then come and take it," he said.

Rawiya raised her lance, and Mennad's warriors lifted their blades.

A shadow passed over them. A white figure glided overhead, blocking the sun.

Al-Idrisi smiled, catlike. "Our doom," he said, shielding his eyes, "or our salvation."

*   *   *

IN BENGHAZI, THE city that used to be called Barneek, the bus rumbles past hairy palmettos and boxy plaster apartments. The city is clumped up against the shore of the Gulf of Sidra, ringed by dry red steppe. Mama says the mountain plateau to the east is called Jebel Akhdar, which means "Green Mountain." Even I know that.

The bus turns right at a big mosque, and the wheels spin out dust and bits of red clay. We pass a park with empty picnic benches and buildings graffitied with flags in red, green, and black. The empty harbor shimmers where Mama says white cruise ships used to dock. The city is the color of dyed eggs, or at least it used to be. Mid-rise office buildings painted pistachio green, pastel blue, cream yellow, and rose are pockmarked by missing chunks of stone. Twisted holes have been blasted through the wrought-iron railings of balconies in flaking shades of peony. On the street, metal shop curtains coated with sage paint have been chipped by bullets.

We stumble out at the terminal and stretch our legs. The hallways are caked in the brown-red stink of brakes. Huda and I clamber off the bus. She stumbles on the steps and almost knocks me down.

I clutch Huda's elbow, even though I know I'm not strong enough to keep her from falling. "Are you okay?"

"I feel a little faint," she says. She wobbles over to a bench and sinks down. Sitt Shadid wraps an arm around her shoulders and says something to Mama—*Too warm*. Umm Yusuf sits on Huda's other side and lets her lean on her shoulder. Mama presses a hand to Huda's forehead.

"Huppy?"

She doesn't answer me. Huda's sneakers don't quite reach the ground. I twist my fingers in her shoelaces, retying one that's come undone. When I look up, Huda's eyes are glassed over like someone who's breathed in too much smoke, like someone trapped under something too heavy to lift. Sitt Shadid fans her, and Huda runs her tongue over her chapped lips.

"What's wrong?" I ask.

"It's just hot out," Mama says.

The rosy brown of Huda's lips has gone ashy, and the thin skin under her eyes has turned gray. I ask, "Are you sure?"

But Mama lays her hand on my head. "You and Zahra," she says, "get some fresh air, and if anyone is open"—she rummages in her bag for a few coins—"buy something to eat." She points her finger at me. "Something we can make last. All right? We have a ways to go, and our family does not beg. Now shoo, both of you."

I don't want to go, but Zahra pulls me out of the terminal. We gulp in sea air. Cars whiz past off the highway, caked in dust up to their door handles. The tires spin tornadoes into the gutter. The sidewalks are littered with what look like bits of iron confetti, but when I pick one up, it's a spent bullet.

I drop the lumpy point of brass, and it clanks to the ground. I wipe soot onto my shorts. I lift my face like a person who's been asleep for a long time and see the city for what it is: the few men walking the streets with their heads down aren't kicking confetti aside. They're wading through the husks of death itself.

"Mama said when the rebels took the city," Zahra says, "they shot off their guns into the air to celebrate."

I shuffle my feet in the clear spaces, trying not to touch the metal with my sneakers, but it can't be done. Every tap of a brass bullet is a brush with a shark.

"What happens when the bullets come down again?" I ask.

To my surprise, Zahra takes my hand. Her bracelet clinks against my wrist. "You'd better not be standing there," she says.

We pass through the pool of scattered bullets and come to a bare stretch of sidewalk. The smell of soot and sulfur gives way to a sea breeze.

I touch the delicate gold of Zahra's bracelet. "I didn't know Baba gave it to you."

"Oh." Zahra lets go of my hand. "Honestly, I forgot I was wearing it."

I kick at dust and tingling jealousy. "I don't have anything left of Baba."

"That's not true," she says.

"You're the one that said the house was gone."

"And whose room was Baba in every night," Zahra snaps, "telling stories? Would you trade that for a bracelet?" Then she rubs the side of her head. "I shouldn't say that," she says. "These past few months, I haven't really been there. Baba's dying . . . it was like I crossed a bridge and couldn't come back."

"I don't want to change."

"But we can't be the same without him." Zahra tugs me down the sidewalk. "Come on. We might never come this way again, you know?"

So we walk. Shop awnings and laundry lines block the sun. Satellite dishes crowd the tops of buildings. Taxis dot the streets. On the balcony of an apartment building, I spot a woman with an easel, delicately stroking watercolors across a canvas. She's painting a cityscape. And I think to myself how many people have created beautiful things here, how many people go on creating beautiful things even when life is full of pain.

"When did he give it to you?" I ask.

"The bracelet? It was my birthday present last year." Zahra cranes her neck to the sun. The wide, hazy horizon shudders in the heat. "After he was gone, I felt like I didn't have anybody. Like I was alone."

What did Mama say? *He found the map he was looking for.* "But I was here the whole time."

Zahra kicks at a stone. "That's where I went wrong."

We come to a walkway by an open stretch of water that leads to even bigger water. Zahra and I sit down on the curb.

"Did you know the Bedu call this place 'Benghazi rabayit al-thayih'?" I roll the sharp edge of a pebble between my forefinger and my thumb. "It means, 'Benghazi raises the lost.' Immigrants have traveled from the western Maghreb, from al-Andalus—people have come from all over to be here."

Zahra crosses her ankles in the froth of dust. "People like us."

A car peels out of a street behind us, and I turn. On the corner, a shop wall has been covered in caricatures and graffiti so thick you can't read the words.

Zahra stretches herself over her knees, widening the tears in her jeans. "You needed me this summer," she says, "but I hid where nobody could follow." Her sneakers are coated with grime, the white rubber on the bottom black with walking. "I'm sad for what you missed," she says. "You should have seen the things Baba showed me when I was little. You should have seen Syria—how it used to be. We used to get fresh green beans and make loubieh bi zeit and rice. We would take out our plates and some folding chairs into the driveway under the chestnut tree. Sitto used to come over, Mama's clients, everybody. That was Syria to me. The green beans, the sagging folding chairs, the oil on people's hands."

I bury my face in my elbow. "Now it's gone."

"But not from us." Zahra rubs her thumb across the back of her hand like she's spreading an invisible oil stain. "The Syria I knew is in me somewhere. And I guess it's in you too, in its own way."

Down the street behind us, two men argue in a dialect I can't understand. I twist my head and lay my cheek on my forearm, and the tiny hairs that have sprouted there this summer are wet. I focus my eyes on Zahra's bracelet. "I wish I knew where."

Zahra says, "Some places are hard to get to."

Dust settles in the holes in her jeans, and she kicks away a spent bullet.

"For what it's worth," she says, "I'm sorry."

ON THE WALK back, Zahra buys dates, apricots, and bread. I smell the brown-red brakes before we see the bus terminal.

Inside, Mama has her hand on Huda's forehead again. Huda tosses her head on Mama's shoulder, her eyelids shut and red. I hold her hand, and it's hot like a pan on the gas stove we had in the city.

"She's running a high fever," Mama says.

I bore holes into Mama's head with my eyes, but she doesn't look at me. Why did she let Zahra and me go, if Huda was sick like this?

Huda crinkles her nose in her sleep. "I left it on the table," she says. When Mama lifts her hand, the shadow of her fingers makes Huda open her eyes. She cracks her lips, and a dried paste of saliva sticks to the corners of her mouth. "The fattoush," Huda says. "I made a whole bowl. Where is it?"

"You were dreaming, little one." Umm Yusuf opens her purse. "Take this." She shakes out two pills from a plastic bottle. It looks similar to Tylenol, so it must be something for fevers. Huda struggles with a bottle of water. Umm Yusuf opens it for her, and Huda drinks.

"Habibti. You feel better?" Mama rubs the small of Huda's back.

"When the medicine kicks in," Umm Yusuf says, "we will see about a car."

"We don't have time." Mama tugs down the sleeves of her blouse, a tiny automatic thing she used to do before clients came over. "On the bus, I overheard the women talking. Even with the National Transitional Council in place, the fighting in Libya has still not stopped. Violence and weapons are spilling over the border into Algeria. There are rumors that Algeria will close its border with Libya soon. We might have a few days, no more. The only way to get through Libya in time is to go over the Gulf of Sidra. We don't have time to go around it."

Yusuf steps toward us, his hands in his pockets, his eyes cast down. "It's over a hundred miles from here to Misrata on the other side of the gulf."

My fear is a cluster of beetles scaling my bones. "I don't want to go on the water again."

"There are no ferries anyway," Zahra says. "Not with the war on."

"There are no passenger ferries." Yusuf leans his elbows on the back of the bench and motions for us to come closer. "But there are aid ferries. They cross the gulf every two or three days. We could sneak you on—"

"Please." Umm Yusuf clutches the bench behind Huda's shoulders. "No more ferries. No more chances."

"And that is exactly my point." Mama tucks a strand of Huda's hair back into her hijab before turning to Umm Yusuf. She launches into Arabic. I watch her mouth moving, and each word lights up like a new bulb. *The fighting spreads like fire around the gulf. Sirte sits between Benghazi and Misrata. It will be under siege within a week.*

Umm Yusuf leans toward Mama from Huda's other side. *We'll drive quickly. We'll avoid the fighting.*

There's no avoiding it, Mama shoots back.

The last time Mama fought with anybody like this was the last two weeks Baba was alive. They did most of their arguing in Arabic, but I knew it was about the chemo. Baba had hurt enough, but Mama wasn't ready to let him go. There are some things you don't need words to say.

I can tell from Umm Yusuf's face that she's not giving in, but Mama is frantic. *The roads are lawless,* she says. I think of the city streets, of the pockmarked buildings, of how the carpets of bullets and shell casings would roll and scatter in a strong wind.

But Umm Yusuf slices her palm out in front of her. *They say aid ferries have been mistaken for rebels,* she says. *The fighting is still fierce from Misrata to Tripoli. You could be rocketed.*

Rocketed?

They both sigh and turn away for a second, their eyes falling to me. In their faces, I can tell they think I haven't understood. They think I don't know what a rocket or a shell can do to wood and metal and stone. They think I can't still see the height of the waves on the Gulf of Aqaba if I close my eyes.

But the top of my head is pulsing, and my fingers are trembling, and in my head I am counting up the broken families I have seen. I am counting the missing fathers and the buried brothers, giving form and breath to those who were left behind, asking myself how many times you can lose everything before you open yourself to nothing.

Mama shakes her head and says, "Where there is no order, people will take advantage."

Umm Yusuf darts her eyes to Sitt Shadid. "I will not take chances."

Zahra tugs on her thumbs again. "How long will we have to stay hidden, if we sneak onto one of these boats?"

"You should arrive in Misrata within a day," Yusuf says. "If you hide among the cargo, you'll have a good chance."

"What do you mean, 'you'?" Zahra seizes his elbow. "You're coming with us."

"Sitti won't cross the water," Yusuf says. Sitt Shadid watches him, squinting at his English. "She won't cross water again in her life. She says it was enough to lose one person. She wants no more death."

Zahra white-knuckles his arm. "Please, I don't— " She tilts her face down, her hair catching on the buttons on her sleeves. "Haven't we lost enough?"

Yusuf looks away, the skin under his eyes red with sleeplessness and salt. "I won't leave Sitti. Don't ask me to."

Huda shivers between Umm Yusuf and Mama, pressing her face into Mama's arm.

"And if they close the borders?" Mama takes hold of Umm Yusuf's shoulder. "If you drive hundreds of miles out of your way and can't go on, what then?"

"The future will unfold as it must." Umm Yusuf takes Mama by the hand and touches her forehead to hers, and Mama's hair clings to the static in the folds of Umm Yusuf's scarf. "Maktoub," she says: It is written. "We have to take our chances."

I only realize I've been holding my breath when I get dizzy. I sit down on the bench near Huda. The choppy waters of the gulf pound against the inside of my skull. Is Abu Sayeed waiting for me in the green?

I touch Huda's scarf. Umm Yusuf's pills must not be working, because the dust on my fingers slicks into a paste with her sweat.

THAT NIGHT, WE camp out behind the ferry depot, hidden by boxes of aid cargo that are supposed to go on the ferry. Mama gives Umm Yusuf a few coins to help them pay for a place to spend the night. Then we say good-bye to Umm Yusuf and her family and wish them luck.

Mama spreads out the dirty rug behind the cargo boxes. She and Huda sleep on it side by side, their bare ankles on the ground. Zahra leans her head back on a box. By the time I spot Yusuf darting back toward us, I'm the only one left awake behind the ferry depot. He arrives as a shadow between buildings, ducking behind boxes and balconies.

"You came back," I say.

"I promised I would help you get on that boat," Yusuf says, "and I will." He sits down next to Zahra, who leans into his warmth without opening her eyes. He stiffens his shoulders and lowers his voice. He's trying not to wake her up.

"I have to apologize." I lower my face and wiggle my feet, my legs bent up crisscross applesauce.

"For what?" Yusuf asks.

"For being wrong about you."

Huda and Mama snore on the dirty rug. The designs are gone, messed up by the fire and the dust and the dirt. It was pretty, years ago, when Sitto gave it as a prayer rug to Mama and it sat in a place of honor in our house.

I rub my scratchy head. I'm not so pretty anymore, either.

"I thought bad things about you," I say to Yusuf. "I thought you were like the other bad men."

"What bad men?"

"The ones that took Huda," I say. "The ones that pulled up her skirt. I kicked and scratched, and I bit one of them and made him bleed. But I wasn't big enough to stop him. He just kept unbuckling his belt." My eyes burn like wet fire, my throat full of acid.

"She never said a thing." Yusuf dries my face with his sleeve. "You and your sisters have been through things no one should have to go through," he says. "You couldn't come through all this bad stuff and be the same."

"Bad stuff?" I sniffle. "It's just stuff."

Yusuf pulls out his pocketknife and does that thing again, the one where he flicks it open and snaps it shut. "We left after my father was killed on the way to work," he says. "He was half a kilometer to the office building, and it was over. The shell came from nowhere."

"It hit him?"

Yusuf flicks the knife open again. "It hit the building across the street. The ground level collapsed. A stone flew across—" He clicks his tongue and taps his temple with his forefinger. "They say he died right away. No pain."

"They always say that." The night creeps up on us, standing the little hairs on my arm on end. "They always say nothing hurt, and it went fast," I say. "But you've seen it, so you know it isn't true."

"People say lots of things to feel better."

I pick at the hard concrete. Huda and Mama toss on the carpet, and two pigeons sitting on a cargo box startle and fly off, cooing. In the distance, a car peels away, and someone fires a machine gun into the night.

"I bet you've been back," I say, "to the street where it happened."

"Before we left, I went," Yusuf says. "I used to walk by that corner on my way home once a week, even though it was out of my way."

"That's funny."

"What's funny?"

"We always go back," I say. "We go back to death-places. It's like somebody dying opens a door, and we have to look in."

"Maybe what isn't there is more important than what is," Yusuf says.

"Maybe."

He snaps his pocketknife shut. "I used to like meeting people and listening to their stories. But now I keep forgetting who I am." He holds out his pocketknife to me. "This was my father's."

I take it. A name used to be hand-carved into the wooden side, but it's been rubbed so much over the years that you can't read it anymore. The knife is warm from Yusuf's hand.

I say, "It's pretty."

"It's yours."

"What?" I can't tell what face Yusuf is making in the dark.

"No one should travel without a pocketknife," he says. "I want you and your family to get where you're going. I want you to be safe."

"Thanks." In my head, I think, Will we ever be safe again? I tuck the pocketknife into my left pocket because the right one is still heavy with the green-and-purple half-stone. "Sometimes I feel like all the people I've ever met are still with me. Like they're right around the corner and they'll pop out any second."

"That sounds nice."

"You know it's not." The sea crinkles like a dryer sheet. "Does it ever stop feeling like the earth is one big nerve? Like everywhere you step, dead people feel it?"

Out in the harbor, the water crunches and pops, gray and black, like a person chewing ice.

"I don't know if it ever stops hurting," Yusuf says.

He pats the space next to him, and I sit by him with my head on his shoulder. We stay like that, Zahra leaning on Yusuf's one side and me leaning on the other, until the pigeons stop cooing. I fall asleep.

I DREAM I'M floating in the Red Sea. I dive down and look for Abu Sayeed. He's somewhere in the kelpy green where I can't find him. I search and search, my eyes burning with salt water, until my chest burns and shudders and I have to come up and take a breath.

I gulp air and start to think that maybe I was wrong, and not just about Yusuf. Maybe I was wrong about Homs and Syria, and about the city too. Maybe home was never where I thought it was.

The water is onyx black. I lie in the dark with the stars over me and the sun edging into green. I remember the olive grove outside Homs, the leaves like green and silver toothpicks. I remember how the fig tree smelled, the purple oil on the roots, the must of bark sweating.

Would things have been different if I had told my story to more than just the earth? If I had told my story on the road, on the bus, in the butcher shop, to the old storyteller man, to the oboe player washing blood off her hands, to the one-legged man who used to play soccer—if I had told my story to them, would I know how to tell it to myself?

And that's when I start thinking about God. I wonder, how is God not torn up about the terrible things in the world? If he or she or they see every single one, then how is God not so sad that he can't watch anymore? If life is one long newsreel, why does she still read the headlines?

Why doesn't God look away?

Mama says God feels everything. But to bear every single awful thing, every scraped knee, every blown-up house? Bad men jerking up a pleated skirt? The clank of a belt buckle on pavement? Drowning with stone-filled pockets? The red screaming of shells? Plastic backpacks under bricks? Leaving without good-byes? Bullets worming into bones? Broken buildings, broken bodies, broken tongues? The awful weight of everything?

Can a sadness be too heavy for God? Maybe God can bear it all, but I don't know if I can. The world is a stone in me, heavy with Baba's voice and the old clock tower and the man selling tea in the street. I want to believe things are supposed to be better, but I don't have the words to say how.

So I picture a big heart under everything, beating under the weight of expecting better. I picture this big heart under the sea, pumping compassion like thick blood, draining anger and hurt.

That heart fills up the water with warmth. It lifts me like a mustard seed in the yawning mouth of a whale. The water bleeds black under me, and God smiles through the cracks in broken things. I am a crumb of porcelain. I am a lost tooth. I am a shard of lapis.

Morning comes. Yusuf watches the dark. I hold on to that hugeness under me, that big kindness. I keep my eyes shut and imagine I am still that small blue stone asleep in the earth, waiting for God to polish the salt from my skin.

The Green Deep

✳

T he white belly of a great bird passed overhead, the flash of its
silver talons menacing. But Rawiya, Khaldun, and al-Idrisi
were surrounded by Mennad and his men, who stood their ground.
They could not run.

Mennad held up al-Idrisi's book of notes and maps. "You will
have to pry it from my hands."

Above them, the great bird glided past, attracted to the battlefield
by the stench of blood.

Mennad ignored it. "With this knowledge of our enemies," he
went on, "their outposts and their trade routes, we will liberate the
Maghreb from the Almoravids and the Normans. Can you imagine
how many years I have waited to see my people rise?" His voice grew
thick with an ancient pain that crossed his face like a shadow. "I
would rather see the book burned than in someone else's hands."

But as he spoke, a rumbling rose from the earth, spitting flakes
of red clay and dust into the air.

"Watch out!" Rawiya pulled on the reins of Khaldun's horse.
A bowl of ground sagged in the spot where he had been standing.
Pebbles slid down into the dent until it yawned into a hole, draining
loose sand and the roots of shrubs. Soon the pit swallowed juniper
bushes and boulders. The gaping hole became a cavern, puffing
steam and hissing.

Mennad's men whispered and shook, gripping their terrified horses' reins.

From the hole squirmed an enormous emerald snake, its body as wide as a palm trunk. Its scales were jeweled mirrors, its eyes amber globes. It reared its head and thrashed from the earth, roiling the sand. It stretched out its pink tongue, wriggling like an eel.

"Don't move," Rawiya whispered.

One of Mennad's men broke from the circle, but the serpent was too fast. It lashed out its head and lifted the screaming man from his saddle, swallowing him whole. Next it moved through what was left of the Almohad ranks, scattering them and searing them with acid venom.

Khaldun cried, "The armies!"

All three armies were retreating. Dozens of giant snakes burst from the ground, and the great white bird dove at them, carrying off warriors and serpents in his talons. The Fatimids and Almohads broke in terror, their horses squealing. The ranks fled in all directions, running for the steppe or Jebel Akhdar. The Normans retreated toward Barneek, where a ship waited.

"We must not lose sight of Roger's army," al-Idrisi said, for he knew if they did not recover his book and board the Norman ship, they would never make it across Almohad territory to the Norman outposts in Ifriqiya.

Now Mennad was a brave warrior, but he was no fool. As the snake laid waste to the Almohad army and drove off his men, Mennad turned his horse and escaped across the steppe, burying al-Idrisi's book in his robe.

Rawiya turned and chased after him, her red tunic unfurling in the wind.

There was a flash of green. A giant snake, its belly a white rope unspooling from the earth, curved in front of Mennad and lunged at him.

Mennad raised his spear against its fangs. It hissed and dripped venom, searing the ground. Pulling back, it leapt again, grazing his arm with a tooth as long as a dagger.

Mennad gave a cry and lurched in his saddle, gripping his wounded arm. The snake coiled around him, offering him no escape.

"Help me," Mennad cried to Rawiya and her friends. "I beg you."

"We will," Rawiya said, "if you give us our property and our freedom. The book is ours."

"You are free, then." Mennad tossed his spear to his good arm. "But the book is mine."

Mennad thrust his spear at the snake, but it bounced off its hard scales. The snake shot out its neck, its jaw gaping. Mennad ducked, but the serpent's bulk knocked him half off his saddle. He wrapped an arm around his horse's neck and swung himself upright, the sleeve of his tunic matted with blood.

"Return what is rightfully ours," Rawiya called out, "and we will gladly help you."

"Don't be a fool," al-Idrisi cried.

But Mennad had spent half a lifetime fighting for his people, and he had spent months searching for this book of Fatimid secrets. He would not give in.

The serpent tightened its length around him and waited to strike, for its prey was almost out of strength.

Mennad lunged with his spear one last time, aiming for the snake's open mouth. But with a spray of venom, the beast clamped its jaw down on the spear and rolled its great neck, crushing the weapon and ripping it from Mennad's hands.

The spray of the snake's acid venom hit Mennad across his face, deepening his ancient scar. He screamed out and slumped over his horse's neck. The serpent hissed and spat out the broken spear, rearing up again.

Mennad, knowing he was defeated, reached into his tunic. "You are free," he said. "I give you my word." And he tossed al-Idrisi his leather book.

As al-Idrisi caught it, the flash of movement caught the serpent's eye. It sprang for Khaldun, who was nearest. He scrambled to block the fangs with his scimitar.

"Khaldun!" Rawiya notched a stone in her sling and released it. It hit the snake on the neck, bouncing off its scales. Rawiya cursed.

The snake pulled back and lunged again, this time toward al-Idrisi.

"Use this." Rawiya tossed him her spear. Al-Idrisi thrust it into the snake's mouth. The serpent screeched, blood dripping from its fangs, and lunged again.

Al-Idrisi blocked the snake with his Almohad shield, then dropped the shield hastily to the ground. The metal sizzled and steamed as the venom burned through it, leaving a gaping hole.

Rawiya had only one stone left in her pouch. Positioning herself in front of her friends, she notched the stone into her sling and squinted against the sun, steadying her breath.

The snake reared at this new threat and opened its jaws.

Rawiya let the stone fly. It hit the serpent in the back of the throat, bursting in a spray of blood. The beast cried out like thunder. The great, thick body hung in the air, its eyes clouding, before it hurtled to the earth. It crashed down, snapping bushes and juniper trees, shaking the ground.

Mennad, who was a man of his word, had watched all this, bleeding in his saddle. Now he raised his hand to Rawiya, Khaldun, and al-Idrisi. His face and palms were scarred with venom and blood.

After a moment, Mennad's horse limped after his men. In the distance, the great snakes chased the last of the Almohad and Fatimid warriors into the steppe.

Al-Idrisi threw down the Almohad spear, the serpent's blood sticky in the sand. "This is not the last I will see of battle, I expect," he said, "though I wish it was."

While they had fought the giant snakes, the Norman forces had been steadily retreating toward Barneek and the shore of the Gulf of Sidra, where the harbor lay. Rawiya signaled to her friends and turned her horse toward the pearl-sized dots of riders in the distance. Al-Idrisi called out to the servants, who followed.

The expedition made for the thin line of King Roger's men, their hooves throwing up red dust, the gulf shimmering violet beyond.

Now Rawiya had seen the great white bird carry off dozens of men in his talons, but still the beast was not satisfied. He had slid over the battlefield, making long passes, searching for something.

In truth, the monstrous bird was not interested in the slightest in Mennad and his men. He had seen the flash of a stone in a sling, and if his memory served him, he knew very well whose sling it was.

As the expedition fled across the steppe, the great bird soared over them. He rolled as he reached them, revealing one side of his face and then the other.

The remaining eye appeared first, pale yellow and bigger than a fist. Then the bird turned, and Rawiya saw the scar. A great gash had sealed itself shut where the other eye should have been, a pink, raw scar devoid of white feathers.

The one-eyed beast beat his wings and lifted up, preparing to dive. And Rawiya's belly filled with dread, remembering how the one-eyed roc had promised revenge on the expedition before he had fled ash-Sham.

"Break apart!" she cried, urging on her horse as the roc dove for them. "He can't chase us all."

So they separated into zigzagging lines, and al-Idrisi broke away from Khaldun and Rawiya. They turned their horses to the right and to the left, dodging the roc's snapping beak.

The shore swung into view, the red steppe tumbling into white sand. The one-eyed roc shrieked at the water. He turned, beating his wings and circling, giving the expedition a temporary rest.

The Normans were preparing to board their ship and raise anchor. But when they saw the expedition's chain mail and Almohad tunics, they shouted and raised their swords. The Norman Sicilians and the

Almohads were bitter enemies, and they would not listen to al-Idrisi's explanations. Soon, the expedition was surrounded.

A Norman came forward carrying the shield of King Roger's court, painted ruby with the symbol of a rearing golden lion. He drew his sword. "Your last words," he said, "before you return to the dust?"

But al-Idrisi pulled his book of notes from his satchel. Using his dagger, he cut away the book's dusty leather wrapping and held its cover high.

The Normans gasped and stepped back. Under the leather wrapping, the cover of al-Idrisi's book was embossed in royal magenta red, a color used only by the Sicilian king himself. It bore King Roger's personal seal, the same one Rawiya had seen on his mantle when he had greeted them in Palermo: a camel and a golden lion, with red rosettes indicating the stars of the constellation Leo, the symbol of King Roger's power. The Normans did not have to read the Arabic inscription to know it was made in the royal workshop, that its bearer was under King Roger's personal protection.

The Norman warrior tipped his chin and touched his forehead. "Sir," he said, "do you bear a message for the king?"

Al-Idrisi lifted his helmet. "Only a message of the wonders of God's hand."

"You are the mapmaker, friend to King Roger!"

"The same," al-Idrisi said. "And my servants—no, no longer my servants or apprentices. These are my friends: Khaldun, the poet of Bilad ash-Sham, and the young warrior Rami." He spoke quickly of their task: to map the lands of Anatolia, Bilad ash-Sham, and the eastern Maghreb. To the west of the Gulf of Sidra, where they stood, lay King Roger's outposts in Ifriqiya, a well-mapped stretch of territory.

Al-Idrisi held up his book, embossed with King Roger's lion. "We have all we need to complete our quest."

The Norman bowed. "The king's servants," he said, "are at your service."

The expedition boarded the ship with the Normans. The one-eyed roc circled back. The great beast rose toward the sun, and the ship listed from the beating of his wings.

The anchor groaned up from the depths, bursting the surface of the sea. The sails swelled, carrying the ship toward open water. The ship was sturdy and fast and ready to sail, for it had brought reinforcements and supplies from Palermo to Ifriqiya several weeks ago. "We were given orders to wait at Barneek," the Norman said, "and to return you and your expedition to Palermo, if we could."

But Rawiya squinted toward the shore. As the one-eyed roc neared the ship, he carried something in his talons: a boulder the size of a camel. He shrieked in anger.

"Turn to starboard," al-Idrisi cried.

The ship heaved to the side. The one-eyed roc soared above them and dropped the stone, missing the ship by inches.

Khaldun gripped the rail, his face a mask of fear. "We will all be dead long before we get to Palermo."

The roc dove away again, retrieving another stone from the shore and beating his wings hard against the weight.

"Port," al-Idrisi cried. "Turn!"

The ship cut the waves as the roc released the stone. The boulder grazed the ship, smashing the railing and narrowly missing the deck. The Norman sailors scattered. The stone dropped into the green deep with a terrific splash, churning the sea and sending everyone sprawling across the deck.

As the one-eyed roc glided past the ship, he caught Rawiya's gaze in his one remaining eye.

Rawiya reached into her pouch of stones—empty. But in the folds of her tunic sat the half-stone of the roc's eye, wrapped in cloth. Rawiya slid her fingers over it. The stone's warmth pulsed in her palm.

*   *   *

WHEN I WAS seven, Baba took me to the carousel in Central Park for the first time. My sitto had just died, and he didn't tell me where we were going; he said it was a surprise.

I remember we stumbled out of the trees, and the music was all sunbursts and pink ribbons and the horses were spinning. It was magic.

We stayed until after dark. We walked around crunching the last of our ice cream cones. It got so dark you couldn't see your hand in front of your nose. Baba said he didn't want to go home yet. Neither did I.

The thought of going home to our apartment where Sitto's old letters were stacked up inside my dresser drawers was unbearable. I couldn't stand thinking she would never write me again, that I would lie on my bed with my legs up the wall, waiting for a phone call that would never come.

So I licked my fingers and ran off the path into the trees. And I stood in the trees real silent, not even breathing, waiting for Baba to come find me. But I was too far in, and I was real small, and I hid real well.

Baba looked and looked for me while I giggled under my breath. But then he stopped looking and went back to the path, and he called my name. I heard him calling for a long time. Then he came out half a block down under a streetlight, and he put his face in his hands and cried and cried. He bent over and poured tears out like a broken water fountain while I stood there in the bushes.

And I don't know why, but I didn't move or run out. I knew I should have, that Baba was upset, that he was scared he had lost me. But I just stood there. I think part of me wanted to stay like that, under the upside-down basket of the dark, lodged in the stickers and the beer cans and the dead leaves, feeling small and scared and sacred at the same time. There was something about seeing Baba with his head in his hands, something new. It was a side of him I hadn't ever seen. He wasn't my baba anymore. He was just a person, lost and bent over like everybody else.

And then there was a moment I remembered where I was, only I couldn't see my hands or my feet. I had become the dark and the bushes, and my body had evaporated. The me I knew had disappeared. And for a minute, I liked it.

I feel like that now, watching the sun come up over Benghazi with my back to the harbor where the night hangs, waiting to see my arms and my legs. Huda and Mama sleep rabbit-curled on the carpet. Zahra and I are each glued to half of Yusuf's ribs, his knife in my one pocket and the half-stone in the other.

Yusuf untangles himself while it's still dark, after the sky has turned gray but before the sun drinks up the stars. Zahra lays her forehead on his belly, gripping his elbows. He pulls away with a disk of wet on his gray shirt like the center of him is leaking out through his belly button.

"I can't explain in English," he says.

Zahra's palms slip out of his hands. "Me either."

I watch Yusuf slink away from the harbor and disappear down the street, turning the corner where a construction crew is just arriving to work. Zahra's shadow shudders on the cargo boxes.

"That game," Zahra says to me, "with the levels."

"Yeah?"

"Are there levels under this one?" Her fingers trail on the pavement. "Are there levels with real things, happy things? Or is it broken all the way through?"

The light hits my outstretched legs, my worn sneakers, my knobby knees. Was there a time things were different? Did I ever really lie on my bed at home with my legs up the wall?

I breathe in and taste yellow pinpricks of salt. "I'm not sure."

The workers come for the ferry while the day is still new, one man opening up the gangplank, another drinking his coffee. They walk along the length of the dock, checking cargo crates and whistling.

Zahra shakes Mama awake and touches Huda's arm, but Huda doesn't move. Sticky red stains the carpet under her cheek.

"Huda?" Mama's voice is rough like sugar marble, her blouse heavy with the chicken-soup smell of her sweat. She draws out her vowels like a grief song: "Habibti?"

But Huda doesn't respond. When Mama touches her forehead, she pulls her hand back like she's been burned. In the light, Huda's face is pulled thin, like all the juice has drained out of her. Her wrists are wishbones, her ribs raised stripes through her shirt. How did nobody know the fever would eat her up inside?

"She won't wake up." Zahra raises her voice, and Mama clutches her arm. We freeze. The ferry workers walk by, then pass out of earshot.

I start to panic. "Mama," I whisper. "What's happening?"

"Her fever is very high." Mama looks frantic, lost. She lapses into Arabic, her hands fluttering over Huda's face. "There must be an infection, something in the wound. Ya Rabb," she whispers. Oh Lord.

Chocolate-brown and gray voices skitter along the harbor. They belong to men. I peek out from behind the crates. Two men in what pass for uniforms stroll toward us, their guns slung over their backs like bookbags. They don't look like policemen, with their nervy eyes and their scuffed cargo pants, but I guess they must be. I remember Zahra's story about the rebels shooting off their guns into the air.

"Shit," Zahra says. And she never curses in front of Mama, not ever.

"Don't curse." Mama turns to me, and her face is a map of fear.

"Mama?"

"Here." Mama takes out the plastic shopping bag, the one we bought the apricots in yesterday. She slips the map inside and ties the bag shut, making a sort of bubble. Then she slips the bubble into the burlap bag. "Waterproof," she says and smiles. She puts the strap of the bag around my chest, like a makeshift backpack.

I look up at her. "What are you doing?"

"Don't lose it," she says. "The last of the food is in there, and a little money. And the map." She takes me by both hands, and her eyes blaze in mine. "Don't you dare forget, habibti. Use the map. Remember what's important."

"But you're going with us."

"No." Mama presses my two hands together between both of hers. "Your sister needs a hospital."

"But the hospitals are overcrowded with the fighting," Zahra whispers. "Yusuf said they're running out of supplies, that there aren't enough doctors—"

"Listen to me." Mama puts a hand on my cheek and the other on Zahra's forearm. "Get down behind these crates when you go," she says. "Run straight to the boat. Hide below deck. Do you hear?"

Zahra grips her fingers. "Mama, you can't leave us."

"We can't take chances." Mama's voice is sharp. "Algeria will close its border with Libya any day now. Get out. I'll find you."

Something between us lifts up and breaks, something soft and old like a breath held a long time. Mama smiles. The blue-and-white tile is hot on my chest. Mama's eyes are dark brown with little flecks of amber in them, a calmness underneath. I wonder why I never saw it before. I wonder if it's the last time I'll ever see it.

The two men pass us by, fingering their guns.

"But Mama—" I scramble to my feet, tripping over a stray shell casing. "How will we find you?"

"The map, habibti." Mama squeezes my arm and keeps her voice low. "Use the map."

We hold our breath. The men pause in front of the crates, shifting from foot to foot. One of them uses the rubber sole of his boot to scratch his ankle. We can't see much, just the hems of their pant legs.

I shut my eyes. Time stops, air stops.

Then there's the *shck*, *shck* of a lighter and the sizzle of a cigarette. One of the men laughs, and their feet shuffle away again. We let out our breath as they pass by us, talking, leaving the sweet smell of cigarette smoke stuck to the hairs in my nose.

Mama strains to lift Huda up, unbending her knees.

"Yalla," she whispers. "Go."

Mama darts down the street from behind the cargo crates with Huda in her arms. And for a second, the world just hangs there, suspended. Mama's papery skirt flutters behind her, the navy one she was wearing at dinner with Abu Sayeed the night the house fell down. I freeze the picture in my mind: Mama carrying Huda, her crooked pumps clicking, the bare studs in the heels striking the cobblestones. Her woody perfume hanging in the air.

Zahra takes me by the hand, and we duck behind the boxes and skirt toward the boat. The men don't turn, just take another drag on their cigarettes. I look back as Mama and Huda swing out of view, the line of her calf and the heel of her pump vanishing around the corner.

Zahra squeezes my arm so hard it hurts. We tiptoe up the ramp and scurry across the deck, then duck down a set of steps into the dark, away from the ferry workers' voices.

We end up in the hold of the ferry, the ceiling low over our heads, the space stacked with boxes. We jam ourselves into a three-foot square as far back as we can and hunch down between crates. The only shard of dawn light comes from a crack in the floorboards of the deck. I take off my makeshift backpack, the burlap rough in my hands.

We don't talk. The boat groans. The workers shout. The crates squeak. The floor shifts. Every sound is a footstep on the stairs leading into the hold. Every voice belongs to someone who's looking for us, someone who might steal a couple of sodas from a mini-mart if no one was looking.

It seems like forever until the ramp snaps back. The ferry lurches toward the big water, blowing its horn. I open the burlap backpack and unroll Mama's map, and my tears and snot crinkle the corners.

I wish Huda were with us, wish I could hear her call out to me: Ya Nouri! I wish for Baba. Abu Sayeed. Mama. I tuck a hand into my pocket and bump into Yusuf's pocketknife, grimy, still wet with last night's chill. Did I ever wish for a big brother?

Mama's words rattle in my head: *Don't you dare forget.*

Mama's map is thick with acrylic paint, like it's an actual thing, a sculpture, a mold. It's as heavy as two or three canvases, full of colors instead of names, little blocks of paint. I study Mama's brushstrokes under the single shaft of light.

Zahra crawls over to me in the dark. Things jostle up and down, the waves cradling us. Light shuffles down with dust.

"I've never seen a map like that," she says.

"Me either." I stare at the map until the colors blur. A thin slice of light stabs them. I run my hands over the borders of the colors. I feel an utter sort of sadness, like holding on to the frayed end of a rope.

I turn the map from side to side, then upside down like al-Idrisi did with his. I hold south at the top. A row of colors sits above each country, each sea and ocean, each desert.

It's the color game.

"My colors." A tingle starts at the base of my spine and climbs up, each bone a knot. "It's a code. Mama coded the map with my colors."

Each square of color reads like a letter, just like Mama used to quiz me about: brown for H, red for S. Something drops into place like jiggling a key in a locked door: the game she used to play, why she had to ask for my colors to get it right, why she made it seem so important.

Zahra crumples her eyebrows. "What are you talking about?"

"Mama used my colors," I say. "See here? It says HOMS—brown, white, black, red."

"It doesn't say *Homs*. There's no label there."

I point out the squares of color for the name—a brown square for H, then a white one for O, black for M, and red—the letter S is red.

"So all the colors are letters," I say. "They all mean something." But then I squint at the coast of North Africa. "Something is wrong."

"What, did she get one of the names wrong?"

"No. One of them is missing."

Above us, the world bursts with sounds: the thudding of rope hitting the deck, the slapping of sailcloth.

"Mama put all the cities on the map," I say in a whisper. "All the cities from the story."

Zahra rubs her forehead. "Slow down."

"Rawiya and al-Idrisi. All the cities they went to are here." I call out their names, translating from my colors. "Homs and Damascus and Aqabat Aila and Cairo and Barneek—that's what they used to call Benghazi."

Zahra waves her hand in front of her face like she's clearing smoke. "But what's missing?"

I squint at the borders on the map. Each country is painted in a different blob of color. Some are thicker and some thin, like certain countries have an extra layer of paint on top.

I say, "Ceuta is gone."

"Ceuta?" Zahra squints through the dark. "So what?"

"So, all the other cities from the story are here. See?" I tap the canvas. "Ceuta is the only city that isn't labeled."

Zahra broods in the dark. "But Ceuta?"

"Ceuta is where al-Idrisi was born. It's where Mama first talked to Baba, where she told him to jump into the strait. Ceuta is where Uncle Ma'mun bought the house."

Remember what's important.

And I play it all back: Mama gripping the blue-and-white tile on the necklace. Uncle Ma'mun fixing the fountain. *He was looking for himself, but there aren't any maps for that.* The newspaper burning, the name circled in red. The potbellied man laughing in his doorway. The kind, familiar eyes.

"He's the one in the newspaper," I whisper. "It was Uncle Ma'mun."

"What newspaper?"

I grab Zahra's hands. "That's where we have to go. Mama was taking us to Uncle Ma'mun."

Zahra stops breathing. "Wait. Where are we going?"

The ferry rolls. The knife of light falls across my face.

"We're going to Ceuta."

Blood and Water

✳

In those days, it was well known that the roc, though he was the most powerful and deadly of all beasts, was also a trickster and a cunning liar. With his keen eyesight, he saw everything: the pinprick of each hair on every head, the paws of every cat, the buzzing wings of every insect. The roc had used this power to spread chaos through all the lands he inhabited.

And he never forgot a face.

The roc circled the ship. The beating of his wings grew to a roar, and the sky grew dark with his shadow. He watched the expedition and the crew with his one remaining eye, his breath stinking with blood.

"Have you forgotten?" the roc said, his voice like mountains crumbling. "Have the treacherous sons of men forgotten my promise? I swore to you once that I would have my revenge. I have come to collect it."

The crew whispered and drew their swords. The roc glided past the bow of the ship and passed along its starboard side.

"We have no business with you," Rawiya called out.

"You!" The roc's huge shadow drifted over them, as wide as an island. "It is I who have business with you, stone thrower," he said. "And I would know who dares attack the lord of the wind and the stone."

"I am the one who threw the stone in ash-Sham," Rawiya said.

"I am the poet's friend, the mapmaker's apprentice. I am the one who put out the eye of the great white eagle of Bilad ash-Sham."

The roc twisted his wings and rolled onto his back as easily as if he were floating on water, showing the crew the long scar on his face. "Look upon me, then, stone thrower," he said, "and prepare for death. Poet friend indeed!" The roc spat. "Tell your poet, if he lives, that I hear all, see all, know all. I remember him—him and his band of troublemakers."

The roc beat his wings and rose for a final pass. "No more words," he said. "I have come to destroy you and leave you for the waves to devour."

The roc turned and thundered down on them. He swept over the bow of the ship like a great wind, overturning crates of cargo. The expedition's servants and the terrified Normans scattered, but the roc was too fast. He crushed men in his talons and dropped them into the sea.

Rawiya fumbled with her sling, but the roc's eyes were sharp. He knocked her down with the wind from his wings and closed his claws around her. Rawiya struggled and beat her fists against his talons, but his hard scales were impossible to break.

The roc lifted her into the air and dropped her.

Rawiya crashed onto the wooden deck. She saw blackness, then bursts of light. Shock came before the pain: a stabbing, searing agony in her ribs.

Khaldun, in his panic, cried out: "Rawiya!"

Hearing this, al-Idrisi narrowed his eyes. "Who is Rawiya?"

Rawiya forced herself up on one elbow and grabbed the ropes tied around the mast. Hauling herself to her knees, she spat blood on the deck. "I am Rawiya," she said. Her arm shaking with effort, she pulled off her turban and shook out her black curls. She tossed the ends of the red cloth over her shoulders, and the wind and the sun filled it with light, like a sail. "I am the daughter of a poor farmer from the village of Benzú, in the district of Ceuta."

The roc circled the mast, his bulk casting shadows over the deck. Al-Idrisi shot his eyes from Rawiya to Khaldun. "You knew of this?"

"Not until yesterday." Khaldun lowered his eyes.

Al-Idrisi studied Rawiya's hair and her smooth face. "I assumed you were young," he said, "not yet grown into a man, but this—"

"Forgive me." Rawiya struggled to her feet. The Almohad chain mail had protected her from the roc's sharp talons, but the fall had crushed three ribs. She fought for breath, touching her side. Her fingers came away sticky with blood. "I joined your expedition to seek my fortune so I could return and feed my family. My mother is a widow, sir. By now, she probably thinks I'm dead. You already know of my father's death."

"A woman?" Al-Idrisi held out his hands. "You, whom I trusted," he said, "whom I trained. You lied to me?"

And the roc, who had heard all of this, rumbled a laugh from above. "Lying stone thrower," he said, "deceitful daughter of men. My revenge will be more delicious than I imagined."

The roc dove again, his talons grazing the deck. Rawiya and her friends flattened themselves to the boards. Rawiya ground her teeth against the pain and reached for a coil of rope near the foot of the mast.

With a burst of effort, she flung the rope across the roc's path, and it caught his talons. He jerked back, stuck, and twisted himself free. He slid low over the sea and rose again.

"I'm sorry," Rawiya called to al-Idrisi, clinging to the mast. "I did what I had to. I wanted to see the world. You showed me its wonders—rivers, stars, deserts." She lifted her chin. "You once said I had courage, heart. That same heart still beats. The body that cradles it is no large matter."

Khaldun, crouching across from her with his scimitar drawn, said to al-Idrisi, "We live in strange days, but that changes nothing. Rawiya has proven herself a cunning warrior. She has saved us more than once."

Al-Idrisi watched the roc's shadow grow. "Never did I think," he said, "that such a dear friend would deceive me this way."

Rawiya pulled out her sling again and fitted her half of the roc's eye stone into its leather strap. It was too big, wider than any stone she had used before. She remembered her training, her father's hands guiding hers, and the stone grew warm in her hand.

The roc dove for them again, his wings tight against his body. Thinking the roc meant to pierce the sails and disable the ship, Rawiya searched for the beast's lone eye, but he kept his head raised.

Instead, the roc stretched out his talons and grasped the ship's bow. Using his wings to stay airborne, he rocked the ship forward, sending the crew sprawling along its length. Then he let it snap back, sending crates rolling and men crashing into each other.

Rawiya fell and dropped her stone, red pain shooting through her chest. The half of the roc's eye stone rolled away across the deck.

The roc crowed his triumph and dove. With a crunch, his talons cut into the wooden deck on either side of Rawiya. The roc's weight pushed the ship deeper into the water, spilling spray over the sides. Rawiya clawed at the talons, but the roc held her fast and began to crush her in his grip.

"What do you think of me now, daughter of men?" the roc said. "I have shown you my true power and strength. Behold, puny one! Have I not given you a dazzling show of my magnificence and beauty?"

"Truly, O roc," Rawiya gasped, "you are both magnificent and beautiful."

"Truly I am. And now, stone thrower," the roc said, "I will give you your death."

"But there is something, O great roc, that you don't know." Rawiya struggled against his talons. "Your power is not as great as you pretend."

"What?" The beast beat his wings, blasting the crew flat. "You are nothing to me. I am all-seeing, all-hearing, all-knowing."

"Rawiya!" Across the deck, al-Idrisi had caught the roc's eye stone.

He held it up, his hands pressed around it as if in prayer. The roc turned his head toward al-Idrisi and snapped his beak.

Al-Idrisi called out to Rawiya, "I was wrong to judge your secret. Though I never told you, I had a wife and daughter in Ceuta. They drowned in the strait, crossing from Ceuta to al-Andalus. You have all the courage and the strength I would have wished for my daughter. Nothing can change that." He tossed the roc's eye stone to Rawiya, and she strained to catch it. Al-Idrisi smiled his catlike smile, but his eyes were afraid. "You and only you, Lady Rawiya," he said, "can save us."

And in one swift motion, as the roc dug his talons deeper into the ship's wood, Rawiya steadied her breath and set the half-stone in her sling. O *Creator of the wonders of the world*, she prayed, *of this stone and this creature. If the dead can hear, then ask Bakr to give me his eyes. Let his hands and yours steady mine.*

Rawiya struggled for breath against the roc's iron grip and saw herself reflected in his one remaining eye.

"You say you are all-knowing, O roc, but you are wrong," she said. "Only God knows everything."

She released the roc's eye stone from her sling, and it flashed green in the sun. Fired from close range, it burst the roc's remaining eye and pierced soft flesh. Blood exploded from his brow. With a garbled cry, the blind roc lifted his talons from the deck, his wings twisting. The ship bobbed up from the water, freed of his weight, and his lifeless body rolled off the ship. The beast fell into the sea, his great wings spread, blood streaked across his white-whiskered head.

The crew scrambled as the ship listed and bobbed, rocking violently from end to end. The bloated white body of the roc crashed into the green, releasing huge waves. The roc slowly sank, creamy feathers wet with seawater, his beak poking above the whitecaps. Then his blind face slipped below the marbled sea.

As the last pale feathers sank, al-Idrisi cried, "Lady Rawiya has saved us."

The crew cheered. Khaldun knelt beside Rawiya lying on the deck, his hair matted to his face by sweat and salt and tears.

"You." Rawiya touched his cheek. "You once said we are the stories we tell ourselves, that we can be drowned out by other people's voices." She kissed his fingers. "I love you. Whatever happens, that, at least, will not be drowned out."

And Khaldun bowed his head to their hands. "Your story, my lady, could never be unsung. I will follow you wherever the road leads."

As Khaldun helped Rawiya to her feet, al-Idrisi drew his scimitar. Taking it in both hands, he bowed his head and knelt. He offered the blade to Rawiya, saying, "Forgive me."

"There is no need," Rawiya said, holding her ribs. "We have both given up our secrets, both lost something precious. I have only done my duty for my friends."

But soon the whole crew followed. The Norman sailors went silent and knelt on the deck. Soon the ship was an unbroken carpet of bowed heads.

"We owe you our lives, Lady Rawiya," al-Idrisi said. "God has made you a brave warrior, a daughter of the mountains and the desert. He has guarded your steps." Al-Idrisi lifted Nur ad-Din's jeweled scimitar. "I beg you to accept my blade."

"I can't take from you the blade that saved your life," Rawiya said.

"Our expedition succeeded because of you," al-Idrisi said. "You are the one who saved us." He bowed his head. "If Bakr were here, he would say the same."

So Rawiya lifted the jeweled scimitar, the carved eagle at its hilt crusted with pearls and rubies. The blade reflected the sea and its white-feathered prize.

As the ship's crew turned toward Palermo, they erupted again in cheers.

*   *   *

IT'S BEEN HOURS below the deck of the ferry, the sun arcing by overhead, dipping toward the horizon. I can only tell because the light from the crack above has turned reddish. Every few minutes we hold our breath when someone walks over us on the deck, and my belly knots up with wondering how long it will be until someone comes down the stairs into the cargo hold, how long it will be until someone notices two stowaway girls traveling alone.

We sit without talking for a long time while I roll up the map and stuff it back into Mama's plastic bag. I tie it shut, making the same airtight bubble Mama did, and return it to the burlap backpack.

"I used to think Mama's maps and facts were easier to understand than Baba's stories," Zahra says. She rocks back and forth, her knees to her chest. "He used to tell all these stories, and I used to get angry because he never said what he meant. But even a map doesn't tell you everything. How are we supposed to find our uncle once we get to Ceuta?"

"I don't know." I let my shoulders sag, and my necklace clinks against the metal floor.

"And how do we get from Misrata to Ceuta without Mama?"

The ship and the gulf groan like a seagull crying.

"Do you think they'll be okay?" I whisper. "Can they fix Huda's arm again?"

Zahra bites her nails, jangling her bracelet. "I don't know how much they can fix anymore."

Footsteps on the stairs ring out in the half dark, and Zahra and I seize up. Someone is coming, jingling keys in his pocket. For a moment, I hear instead the clang of a brass belt buckle.

We scramble farther back into our little square, but the light hits our faces. Voices tap the crates. Zahra and I squeeze ourselves between boxes, scraping our knees against metal and splintered wood so we don't bang them. We hold our breath.

A man walks by, the heels of his shoes drumming on the metal floor of the hold, reading off a list in Arabic.

There isn't enough room for both of us to stand up all the way, but not enough to sit down either. I brace myself between two steel containers, putting my weight on my knees, hoping the metal doesn't dent and boom like a cymbal.

My calves start to burn.

The voices stop, feet shuffling. Somebody taps the crates. Zahra breathes out, her air hot on my nose, and fills her lungs again as slow as she can. My thoughts get tangled. I imagine in spite of myself how Huda must have felt before the bad men pulled her into the alley, whether she knew before I did what it was they wanted. Did she sense what would happen before it happened? Did she expect to feel their calloused hands on her thighs? Did she know how heavy they would be when they pinned her to the asphalt?

I jerk and tingle when something skitters across the tops of my feet. The legs are stiff and sharp with claws—a crab's legs or a lizard's. I press my eyes shut, but a high whine dribbles from my chest. I think about what I would do if these men pull Zahra and me from our hiding place: which is better, clawing or biting?

My breaths come high and shallow. The crab or lizard scampers away behind the crates. I force myself to stay still.

We used to have a red-tailed hawk that roosted somewhere up by the chimneys at the top of our building in New York. Baba told me how rare it was, that there were only a few breeding pairs in the city, that sometimes birds like to live near humans because they get more food that way. I remember walking down to the subway with Baba while he explained it, staring down the yawning tunnels and wondering if God was on the other side, watching the rats run between the tracks, realizing the city was more animal than human.

But the dark below the ferry's deck has more people in it than anything else, and I've learned already that people are more dangerous than animals, more dangerous than anything else in the world. I keep my eyes closed while the ferry workers start to move again, muttering, shoving crates back into place with their shoulders and the sides of their shoes.

One man calls out in Arabic, crouching down just past the crack where Zahra and I are hiding. *We have a leak*, he calls. When he stands up again, he bangs his head on the corner of a crate and curses.

Until the man mentions the leak, I don't notice the steady pattering of water on the crown of my bristly head. Now I feel it, cold, smelling like wood and motor oil. Where the water touches me, my skin feels like an open wound. I think of Huda's bandages, black smears of blood, the edges of the linen yellow with pus. Didn't Mama say it could get infected? Can a person live with a new bone like that, a bone made of metal and fire, and still be the same person?

I shiver against the metal containers. The tiny space feels like a coffin. In the dark space behind my eyes, I see Huda in the hospital bed, death clinging to her like a bad smell.

The feel of death is strong below the deck of the ferry, and it clings to everything. I thought after the hospital we had left that feeling behind, and I thought the same thing again after Abu Sayeed chased the bad men away from Huda in the alley, after I drew blood.

Now I realize that feeling only followed us. The bad men grabbed Huda without knowing anything about her, without knowing her like I did, how she was more than brown calves, more than screams, more than the body crumpled under them. I am angry they didn't know her, that they thought they were entitled to her belly and her legs, that Zahra and I are here in this dark under the deck, that we've lost everything except each other.

And while the ship rolls, I start to think that maybe death is in us all along, that it doesn't stick to us at all. Maybe it just seems like death clings to us when we notice it inside us for the first time. Maybe, like Mama said, we are all born with a wound that needs fixing.

My calves vibrate and twitch. I watch the red-and-purple light above us, listening for the brown-and-gray voices. The sun is almost down.

I reach for my burlap backpack, where the map is stuffed in its plastic bag, but I don't feel anything. I dig my nails into my palms when I realize the backpack has rolled out from between my feet. It's sitting out in the open, on the floor of the cargo hold.

I wait, biting my lip, hoping nobody has noticed the bag. I count the seconds. I can't see my arms or my legs. I only know I exist by the splinters in my thumbs and the backs of my knees that shake like jelly from holding one position. My heartbeat is the only part of me that feels brave.

One of the ferry workers lets out a bored whistle, that high song-bird whistle I used to hear in Central Park.

When we still lived in Manhattan, there came a day that the red-tailed hawk stopped coming to our window. I didn't see it preening anymore, couldn't watch it looking down on Eighty-Fifth Street with that cold stare, like something else used to be there and the city had grown over it. That hawk glared down at the city like something important was missing.

I found the hawk a few weeks later in the rooftop garden. The stars were coming out over the buildings, and I almost didn't notice the feathers. The hawk had buried itself in the moss, digging its beak into the dirt like it was trying to bore through the earth. One last airborne dive.

I remember thinking maybe it had just lain down to rest. It had one wing over its eyes, like a person napping in a bright room. Its feathers were a perfect marbling of brown and red, the wind ruffling them.

I picked the hawk up, gently, listening for a heartbeat. It was still a little warm, its wings stiff as paper. But I heard nothing.

Before I buried it properly, I wanted it to feel the wind one last time. So I took the hawk and walked to the edge of the rooftop, and the breeze tugged my curls over the edge. The hawk's glassy eye reflected the lights coming on in the other high-rises, the taillights of taxis passing below. Clumps of dirt stuck to its curved beak and its rigid brow bone. Is this why they bury people, to help them kiss the earth?

At last, the voices fade. Palms smack wood and bang metal as they go, until the workers mount the stairs and shouts pop brown and red on the deck.

I breathe again.

As soon as I think the ferry workers are gone, I dive out and grab the backpack. I put it on, making sure the strap is snug.

There's a bang. Voices shout loud above us. The floorboards pucker and creak. I flatten my back against the crates, hoping if somebody bursts down the stairs, they'll think I'm a shadow.

An eerie silence comes over the ferry, and that's when I hear it. A high whine fills the air, a thrumming like the night the house fell down. It builds into a screech, and Zahra reaches out of the crack toward me.

The ferry rolls like an empty barrel. I go flying, my shoulder hitting a crate. I cry out. Deep in the ship, something groans and cracks. My ears ring.

I scramble and try to crawl back between the crates. "Zahra—"

The ferry tilts back again, the spray smashing its sides. I brace myself on a box, catching my backpack on its corner. Through the gray speckles of white noise, the ferry shrieks red like an animal in pain.

"Something's hit us." I can't hear my shouts over the scream of snapping wood and the yelling on the deck.

Wood splinters above us like bones breaking. Sound and spray rush in, and the cargo hold fills with a roar.

I'm underwater before I know it, the shock of cold bruising my ears, blocking any other feeling. Everything is liquid. My skin is blue, my eyes, my ankles, my scalp. I am swallowed by sapphires, my shoulder blades sliced by frosted knives. I am crushed by every shade of blue I have ever seen: Ultramarine. Lapis. Navy. Night.

The Ribbon of Good-bye

*

When at last the Norman ship docked in the harbor at Palermo, Rawiya was glad to see the limestone hump of Monte Pellegrino, the white marble churches clustered against stucco houses, and the red-domed mosques. The expedition had been away for more than a year, and a royal welcoming party was waiting at the dock to greet them.

As they passed through the streets, musicians accompanied them on the oud and the horn, and al-Idrisi led Bakr's riderless camel as a sign of honor. The camel's hump was draped with Bakr's rich olive cloak, its fabric embroidered with the stars of the Pleiades.

While the expedition brought al-Idrisi's books, maps, and sketches into the palace workshop, Rawiya insisted on following King Roger's servants to the stables. Bauza stood in a stall, his head bowed, looking thin and forlorn. Not for the first time, Rawiya was reminded that she had brought Bauza far from their home in Benzú, and that she was not the only one missing home.

The servants apologized, saying Bauza had eaten less and less the longer Rawiya had been away. They said he had even refused sugar cubes and brushings.

But when he saw Rawiya, Bauza whinnied and reared, stamping in his stall. When she came close, he wrapped his neck around her shoulders and nuzzled her. Rawiya buried her face in Bauza's mane and wept, saying, "You don't know how I missed you, old friend."

THOUGH THEIR HOMECOMING was a happy one, it was days until they saw King Roger, who had fallen ill just before they had arrived. The king was bedridden and could not take visitors. But al-Idrisi's return seemed to give the ailing king some strength, and soon he was sitting up in bed, eagerly listening to the tales of al-Idrisi's adventures until late into the night.

For months, al-Idrisi worked from dawn to dusk, and Rawiya and Khaldun served as his chief witnesses in creating a final map of their journeys. This was to be the most accurate map of the inhabited world that had ever been made, a collaboration on a grand scale and the culmination of the long journey they had taken. They prepared too for the most difficult of all the tasks King Roger had set before them: to create a planisphere, a two-dimensional representation of the curved surface of the earth with all its cities and rivers and seas, inscribing these features upon a disk of solid silver. Such a thing had never been created before, and the task was daunting. Still Rawiya and Khaldun found joy in their work transcribing al-Idrisi's sketched maps, never leaving each other's side as they brushed cinnabar or indigo pigment onto parchment paper, blushing with a smile whenever their elbows touched.

While al-Idrisi made his way to King Roger's quarters each night with stacks of the king's favorite books on geography and mathematics, Rawiya stayed up reading the notes al-Idrisi had amassed in the years before their adventure. Al-Idrisi had collected testimonies of merchants from the far corners of the world, tales of sailors who had set off across the Sea of Darkness and barely returned with their lives, descriptions of distant cities and strange beasts. There were more pages than Rawiya could ever read, for al-Idrisi had been gathering these accounts in preparation for King Roger's task for more than a decade.

But as the month of Shawwal dawned and al-Idrisi pressed toward completing his work, King Roger's health began to fail again. Fits of coughing and numbness plagued him. Chest pains confined him to his bed for weeks.

Time passed this way until early one morning, in the last days of Shawwal, when a messenger knocked at Rawiya's door.

Rawiya ducked through arched doorways, past hand-carved railings and vaulted, frescoed ceilings. She crossed the inner courtyard with its stacked balconies and found al-Idrisi and Khaldun in the royal workshop, bent over al-Idrisi's drawing board. As Rawiya entered, Khaldun looked up, and the wisp of a smile crossed his face before he blushed and lowered his eyes again to his work.

"Is it true?" Rawiya asked, approaching her friends. "Is it finished?"

"My task has been fifteen years in the making," al-Idrisi said. "Fifteen years of research, of careful planning"—he lifted his face to Rawiya and Khaldun—"and, of course, the long months of our journey."

"Can it be, after all this time," Rawiya said, "that our journey is over?"

"Somehow it is," al-Idrisi said, "and now here we are in the month of Shawwal. I will never, as long as I live, forget the month of Shawwal."

"This is beautiful." Rawiya stepped to the drawing board that held the finished map, admiring the curves of rivers, the blue lapis of the sea.

"You have not seen a thing. Come." Al-Idrisi turned to a thick book on the workshop table, bound with leather and lettered in gold. He opened the pages, revealing his delicate script and large, detailed maps.

"Is this an atlas?" Khaldun brushed his fingers against the book's velvet spine.

"It was Roger's request," al-Idrisi said. "The book separates the map into seven regions of the world, or climates, each of which is broken up into ten sections. The book contains maps of each of these sections as well as detailed descriptions of them all. There are seventy maps altogether, each with a detailed account of its mountains, rivers, towns, trade, and weather—a comprehensive study of the inhabited world as has never been drawn up before." Al-Idrisi smiled. "One need no longer travel thousands of leagues to reach distant lands," he said. "In these pages, you hold the world itself in your hands."

Rawiya turned to the first map and followed the green rivers with her eyes, lingering on the jeweled twists of mountains in bright yellow, ruby, and purple.

"I had no idea," she said. Turning to the opening passages of the book, she read from al-Idrisi's delicate hand: " 'The earth is round, like a sphere . . .' Marvelous."

Al-Idrisi stepped away from the table, rubbing his back. He had grown hunched in the months after their journey, the weight of years pressing on his shoulders. He looked like he had grown suddenly old, like the journey itself had preserved his youth and now, at last, the years had caught up with him.

"You have done it," she said.

Al-Idrisi gave his catlike smile. "The greatest of my accomplishments is the one I have yet to show you."

Rawiya and Khaldun followed him from the room. "The workers transferred everything to the silver?" Rawiya asked.

"Everything. Roger will be pleased that we have accomplished what he asked for those long years ago." But al-Idrisi looked away as he said it.

Both Rawiya and Khaldun knew very well that al-Idrisi had hurried to complete his work so that his benefactor and longtime friend would live to see the fruits of their labor. Rawiya was sure the only thing keeping King Roger alive was the completion of his and al-Idrisi's life's work: the map, the book, and the silver planisphere.

Al-Idrisi led them down a long hallway to a workroom where royal engravers had been toiling for months to transfer al-Idrisi's map of mountains, seas, rivers, coasts, and towns to a great piece of silver.

Al-Idrisi swept into the room with his palms open, his white turban and sirwal flashing in the candlelight. He asked, "Is the work complete?"

An engraver looked up from polishing the huge silver disk. Speaking in low tones to his fellow workers, he rose from his task and bowed to al-Idrisi. "We have finished the engraving. The polishing is just now complete—to your specifications, of course."

The planisphere gleamed in the flickering workroom candles. "An exquisite work of craftsmanship," Khaldun said.

"It is." Al-Idrisi circled the planisphere, his hands clasped behind his back. He dismissed the engravers, who took their leave with a bow.

"I knew of the world map," Rawiya said. "I knew of the book and its seventy sectional maps, and I knew that you had commissioned a translation into Latin. Those things would have been wondrous enough. No one has ever seen the world in its wholeness or mapped such distant places. But this is . . ."

"Quite extraordinary, yes," al-Idrisi said. "Roger ordered a disk of pure silver to be created, as large as possible." Al-Idrisi ran his fingers over the cracks of the routes and rivers, the glittering letters. "It weighs four hundred Roman pounds and is made of solid silver. We were efficient, so only a third of Roger's silver was used. The planisphere bears all seven climates, the shorelines, rivers, everything. Distances are accurate to the last league. So rich a treasure has never belonged to any king, not in all the world.

"Once work began on the planisphere," he went on, "I wrote the book to match it and the map. That was Roger's wish." A shadow passed over al-Idrisi's face. "His vision was perfect."

Rawiya and Khaldun exchanged glances. "This illness surprised us all," Rawiya said.

Al-Idrisi straightened his garments and lifted his face with a firm smile. "Nothing could keep the lion of Palermo confined to his bed for more than a few weeks."

"Whatever happens," Rawiya said, "you have done more than King Roger could ever have expected. You have made a wonder in his name."

"Let us go and see my old friend. I will have the planisphere brought to his bedside." Al-Idrisi clapped his hands, and the workers returned. They picked up the planisphere and set it on a rolling pallet, breathing hard even after this short exertion. Though the planisphere could be lifted—with difficulty—by several people, it was far too heavy to be carried any distance by hand, even by three or four men.

"Surely," al-Idrisi said, leading the procession toward King Roger's quarters, "the sight of the completed planisphere will lift his spirits and bring him back to health."

"God willing," Rawiya said, and Khaldun nodded, but neither of them dared to believe it.

King Roger was sleeping when they came in, his breaths rattling.

"My friend and king," al-Idrisi said. He kissed Roger's hand.

The king's eyes opened slowly, cracking at their corners, yellow-white pus running along the wrinkles in his face. He smiled and reached to take al-Idrisi's hand.

"My friend," he rumbled, and coughed. "My oldest and dearest of friends." He clapped his other hand over al-Idrisi's. "It has been a long time."

"Only a few days," al-Idrisi said. "I had to oversee the work we set out to do so long ago."

King Roger laughed, a good-natured but rasping laugh, his chest full of water. "Fifteen years," he said, "by my count. But no matter, if the task is at last complete."

The workers wheeled the silver planisphere into the room and set it beside the bed.

"The map and book are both complete," al-Idrisi said. "I have been calling it *The Book of Roger*, though I leave the final title to Your Majesty's discretion. Now this last part of our work, the silver planisphere, is also finished." He bowed his head. "It has all been done in your name, my friend."

King Roger struggled to sit up in bed. "This beautiful thing," he rasped, "this glorious object. Wonderful." He coughed again, and a servant slipped a pillow under his shoulders. King Roger waved the man away. "This old lion will not live to see two such wonders."

"These fifteen years of labor," al-Idrisi said, "have returned their due. Your guidance, your teachings, and your generosity were not for nothing. But as you know, I did not do it alone." Al-Idrisi motioned for Rawiya and Khaldun, and they approached and bowed. "This moment belongs as much to my companions as it does to me."

"I commend them for what they have done." King Roger dipped his head to his chest, coughing. A servant handed him a cloth to hold over his mouth. "Excuse me," he said. "I cannot bow anymore. But I would bow to you if I could. This is my life's work, my heart's desire. You accompanied my friend and led this project to completion at his side. For your efforts, I thank you deeply. You will be handsomely rewarded."

At the movement of King Roger's hand, servants came forward with chests of gold, carved signets of ruby, hundred-faceted emeralds, flaming opals, and daggers with pearl hilts. Al-Idrisi was given the remainder of the silver that had been set aside for the planisphere in addition to these other riches.

"My lord," Rawiya gasped, "you are too generous with your servants. For a poor widow's daughter to see such kindness—it is too much, Your Majesty."

"Ah, Lady Rawiya, whom I once took for a young boy with much to learn." King Roger smiled through his pain. "You once walked with me through the library among the spines of old friends. I see now that you were stronger and braver than ever I knew. Your courage saved the expedition more than once, from what I have heard. You have accomplished great and honorable deeds. Yes," he said, lifting his eye to the three of them, "it is fitting that my treasures should be shared with my greatest friends."

"If I have been half the friend to you that you have been to me," al-Idrisi said, "then I have accomplished something of value in this life."

KING ROGER PASSED away that night, his last breath rising to the constellation of the lion as the moon set. Al-Idrisi was at his bedside. His friend's favorite book lay in his lap, and he held King Roger's heavy hand to his forehead.

Al-Idrisi's tears speckled the leather cover of Ptolemy's *Geography*, pale as stars.

King Roger II of Sicily was buried in Palermo in a tomb of red porphyry, a prized purple-red stone, dressed in his royal finery and wearing a pearl crown. After the funeral, al-Idrisi, Rawiya, and Khaldun sat in front of the silver planisphere in the palace library for days, as silent as the workers who left them to their grim watch. The planisphere, the wonder of the world, the culmination of a glorious collaboration between the greatest Muslim scholar of his time and a wise Norman-Sicilian king, could not save the friend al-Idrisi had so dearly loved. Its mountains and seas would never glint in King Roger's eye again.

As the stars bore silent witness to their grief, Khaldun took Rawiya's hand in his. There in the candlelight, Rawiya thought to herself that sometimes, no matter how hard you try to delay it, you have to say good-bye. Some things happen the only way they can happen, the way they have been set out to. Maktoub, she thought: It is written. And God knows all, while we know not.

* * *

I SPIT WATER. Yellow salt sticks to my teeth. My eyes burn. I thrash, breathing in stinging blue, and break the surface. It's red-dark, the part of the night that's still day, when the sun bends around the horizon and bleeds. The moon has gotten fat again, a round eye.

Black sounds roll like marbles in my throat. The water smacks my face. I'm pushed up by something buoyant under me, and the sea bucks like a carousel horse. I try to call out, but all I get out are garbled gasps. Fear roils up into my mouth.

My hand hits something harder than seaweed, hard enough to bruise my knuckles. A rock. I reach out for it, my eyes still stinging. It's sharp, but I cling to it anyway. Barnacles cut my shins and collarbones.

I rub my eyes, and the water pushes me sideways. Shouts burst from a shore I can't see. My ear scrapes the rocks.

A sneaker pops out of the water, and it isn't mine. I grab for it and miss. I get it on the second try, catching the laces. The white fabric is tinted green, the canvas dotted with sea lice.

"Zahra." Am I saying it or screaming? The water churns. I can't help wondering if it's full of bodies, if Abu Sayeed's hand will come up from the deep. How many times can something that's taken reappear before it's put to rest? How many times can I see Baba's toe on other people's feet, his flesh in the kelp under the almost-moonlight?

The water's hand strikes my back, harder than granite. The wave knocks my head against the rocks, and I taste metal and salt.

The current pulls me under. I open my mouth, not wanting to swallow but not able to do anything else, and the sea stings the insides of my nostrils and burns all the way down my throat.

I open my eyes underwater, clawing for the rock. The water isn't as murky as back in New York, but all I can see are bubbles and red, and for a terrifying second, I don't know which way is up. I tumble with my feet above my head, my hands invisible behind the wall of wet light.

I expect myself to panic. I expect the fact that I'm alone to punch me, but it doesn't. Instead a small voice comes from far away, telling me calmly that no one is coming to help.

But then the wave shoves me forward, and something tugs me up. My knees hit the rock, and I burst up into the light. I cough and spit, my eyes tearing against the sting. Salt for salt.

I can't focus my eyes right away. Through the blur, I make out boards lapping the shore. Corners of broken crates ride the surf, bits of metal and twisted rudder. Far off, people shout, tossing ropes to the bobbing heads of the ferry workers. The ferry sinks with a hole blown in its hull, the kind of jagged gash that only a shell or a rocket could make.

Something waterlogged chafes against my shoulders, and that's how I realize I'm still wearing my burlap backpack. Some air must still be in the shopping bag around the map. The air that lifted me up was Mama's.

Something hits my leg. I let go of the rocks and turn, my backpack banging into the stones. The sea is the color of soda through green glass, turquoise and silver and brown-purple. The sea is a many-colored thing.

Something white rises toward me like a broad sand dollar, the water glassy between us. It's a mirror of the moon. It's a face.

Just below the surface is a greenish disk of skin and fig-blue lips. Tiny bubbles dribble up from the mouth and press against the cellophane water. The water is so much warmer than at the beach in Rockaway.

"Zahra." Someone is saying it with my voice box but not my voice. I reach for Zahra's face, tugging it back above water. I see just the edge of the root-brown rings of her irises, their amber flecks like Mama's. Her hair runs over her lips, tangling in her eyelashes as she struggles. Zahra slips under the skin of green again, another beautiful ghost.

The moon moans, rising, and for a moment I am back in Egypt. Would the Red Sea look red in this light? And how long will it take

Abu Sayeed to settle to the bottom? When the wet season comes and the wadi fills with water, will the rain wash our tongues?

The waves lap at us, twirling our legs, and the stones click like teeth. Water fills the cracks in the rocks. *Different streams from the same river.*

Is any of this real?

I force myself to grab the rock with one hand and Zahra's sleeve with the other. That, at least, I can reach.

She sags back on a wave, her head rolling like raw egg, the back of her scalp bouncing against sharp rock. I don't see the blood until the sea pushes us together, lifting us up and scraping us on the rock, where we hang like linen.

The rising moon ducks behind a red cloud and out again. Zahra's ripped sleeve uncurls like a white ribbon of kelp. I touch Zahra's forehead. Red blooms in my palm, bright poppy.

I blink away the stinging water. Behind my eyelids, I see blood on crushed ceiling tiles. Blood under a bandage. Blood in the sink. Blood on the seaweed.

"Zahra." I try to call her name, but I can't. Shouts come from farther down the beach, surrounding the wreckage of the aid ferry like the bones of a beached whale. In the red light, the scorch marks shimmer like streaks of soot above a fireplace. I don't need the sound of gunshots from the shore to tell me that it was a rocket that left these marks: these are the same streaks that tore through the garden tiles in Homs, lines of ash as if an angel ran his fingers along the bow of the boat. What was it Umm Yusuf said to Mama in Benghazi—that aid ferries might be mistaken for rebels?

I knead the moon painted like Zahra's face. Blood mists the water.

"Up, Zahra." I shake her at the shoulders. "Come on."

Zahra reaches up to touch my face. A swell shoves us. The water rips things from my pockets, bits of quartz and mica I collected. Abu Sayeed's handkerchief slips thick and wet into the surf. The water spreads it, a ten-fingered hand.

I grab the handkerchief from the water and stuff it back in my pocket, where it wraps itself around the half-stone. Yusuf's pocket-knife weighs down the other side of my shorts, pressing on my thigh.

I pull Zahra from the water with my fingernails, slicing red into her skin. The water bears her weight until we climb the rocks. The moon glints off Zahra's wet bracelet like a flat coin.

We peel ourselves from the tide. We are the stones in Abu Say-eed's pockets.

AFTER I SAW Baba's body under the green light in the funeral home, I let go of his big toe and ran past Lenny and up the stairs. I burst through the red-velvet waiting room with its closed curtains. I felt white-hot, a molten star.

I threw open the front door of the funeral home and threw up in the parking lot. I hadn't eaten in two days, so I puked until I dry heaved, spitting up water and orange pulp. My guts wrung themselves like wet laundry.

When I heard Mama coming, I ran. I ran around the back of the building and through an abandoned lot that was all dirt. I darted through iron gates, through people's tiny gardens that were just bare earth, past bodegas and newspaper stands. I passed the man selling honey-roasted nuts from his little cart and shop windows with ads of people drinking juice and bubble tea.

I ran until I came to the edge of the park, three blocks away. There was the fountain Baba had stared into when he used to let go of my hand. There was the break in the stone wall where the coyote had trotted out with its amber eyes. There was the spot just down the path where I had run from Baba and hid in the bushes, where he had crumpled and cried.

It was late winter then, and the lake was still thawing. I waited to see if Baba's ghost would walk out from around the corner, but he didn't. I was alone.

I waited and waited until Mama put her hand on my shoulder and led me home. I kept looking back to see if the magic would work, if wishes meant anything past the age of eleven. I told myself if I could have waited just a little longer, maybe things would have been different.

But they aren't.

AFTER SUNSET, WE crawl from the rocks and steal away from the wreck of the aid ferry. Shouts of celebration ring out as trucks squeal their tires and backfire into the night. Zahra scans the curve of the shoreline and the street signs, and that's how we figure out the ferry made it to Misrata's harbor before it was rocketed. We had arrived.

We stumble in short bursts through the city, avoiding spurts of gunfire and patrolling military trucks. We both jump when we come across the burnt husks of shops, bullet holes in street signs, corners missing from apartment buildings. Misrata, like Benghazi, is bleeding brick and spent bullets. I wonder how many families have watched their homes crumble. I wonder if even Umm Yusuf knew how bad the fighting was, if anybody knew it would feel so familiar.

Zahra and I curl up in an alley behind an abandoned truck, but we don't sleep. We shiver through the night until the sun comes up and dries our clothes. Then we start to come back to life, cracking the damp out of our knuckles and stretching our legs.

Zahra checks the map in its plastic bag, buried in my burlap backpack—still dry. Inside, the burlap smells like salt mixed with Mama's perfume. I picture the air escaping from the shopping bag and wonder if there's more hope in the world than I can see.

Zahra picks through the last of our money, wet as used tissues. The sky is red again, and the city shuffles in windows and lights cigarettes in doorways.

"We have to hurry," Zahra says, pulling me to my feet. "Do it for Mama. Do it for Huda."

She tugs me by my wrist down the street. We wander half a mile until we come to a market where fruit sellers are setting up their boxes. Zahra buys me sticky dates and fingers the money in her pocket when she thinks no one is looking.

We pass a stall with the radio on, fast-talking in Arabic in a dialect too different for me to understand. Zahra stops cold.

"What?"

She hushes me. She stands rigid, listening, and tightens her grip on my fingers.

"You're hurting me," I whine.

"We're too late," she whispers. "Algeria closed its border with Libya this morning."

I crush the meat of a date in my hand. "What?"

Zahra curses again, and Mama isn't there to tell her not to. She takes me aside into the shadows behind a stall selling apricots. "We can't get across," she whispers. "The border with Algeria is closed."

"If we can't get out, we can go back for Mama," I say.

But Zahra shakes her head, pressing her mouth and her eyes shut like she's still bleeding on the inside. The fear in her eyes reminds me of Mama's, the way she doesn't want me to see it even though I do. The cut on her forehead has hardened into a black scab, and I guess mine looks just as ugly.

"Remember what Mama told us about the map," Zahra says. "She told us to meet her in Ceuta. We have to get there now, no matter what."

"How can we get there if we can't cross? You said there's no way out."

Zahra bites her lip. "There's a way," she says. Then she looks down at me with concern. "Whatever happens," she says, "don't say anything. Your English will give us away."

We step back into the sun. The day is getting hot already, and women stroll the market in long, colorful dresses in floral prints. Zahra buys a handful of apricots from a lady in the market and asks her a question in Arabic.

I don't know all the words, but the tone in Zahra's voice tells me what she's asking for, and that she's willing to pay for it. I look away from a row of gypsum roses in a neighboring stall and tug on Zahra's sleeve. "Don't."

Zahra ignores me. The lady leans over and says something. I can translate the simple words: *Don't do this.*

Why not?

You have a young boy. The lady frowns at me, and I can tell she thinks I'm Zahra's son. *The danger is too great.*

But Zahra keeps talking until the lady gives in. She points to another stall where a man scowls into a basket of oranges.

We walk down, and Zahra talks to him in halting sentences. He doesn't smile. He calls another man over, his voice flat and cold.

"I don't like this," I whisper.

But Zahra ignores me again. "Leave it to me," she says.

When the man's friend comes, he and Zahra talk. She tells him I'm her little brother, that our parents are waiting for us in Ceuta. I watch his eyes, the way they wander up and down, the way they linger too long on the folds of her tee shirt and the rips in her jeans.

The man shakes his head. *I can't take you to Ceuta, but I can get you to Algiers. You can travel from there to Ceuta.* His accent and his dialect are different than Mama's or Zahra's, but I can understand most of what he says. I try to figure out in my head how far Algiers is from Ceuta.

Zahra asks, *How much?*

The man eyes her and names a sum. *American dollars or Euros,* he says.

Zahra argues with him, but she has nothing to bargain with. She empties her pockets, everything we have left except what's sewn into the tongues of my sneakers.

When she pulls out the last of Mama's dollar bills, my heart stumbles in its rhythm. I haven't seen American dollars in so long that they look too obvious, too dangerous to carry around—like pulling out your passport in a crowd.

The man snatches up the dollars and counts them. He asks for more.

Zahra offers him her wrist. The man fingers her gold bracelet, brushing his fingers against the moles on her skin.

"What are you doing?" I whisper.

She slaps my hand away and hisses back: "No English."

Zahra slips the bracelet from her wrist and hands it to the man. He jerks his thumb toward a pickup truck.

A little while later, the man drives us and another family to a rickety old house three hours away, outside what Zahra thinks is Tripoli. The door creaks on its hinges, and inside, the tiny house smells like urine and rot. I feel a mix of shame and dread I don't have a word for, a lump inside me screaming that this was a mistake.

The man lets us in with a few short words and shuts the door. We sit in the dark a few minutes, not moving. A boy about my age and an old man—his grandfather?—claim mats on the floor, and we do the same. No one speaks.

"He said we'll get moving in a few days," Zahra says after a while. "The smugglers will take us by truck across the desert to Algeria, maybe Morocco if they can find people willing to pay. We can try to cross into Ceuta from there." She roams the oil stains on the peeling walls with her eyes.

I ask, "But how?"

"I don't know."

I sit with my knees crossed and hang my hands in my lap. "I'm glad you're not one of those people."

"What people?"

"The ones who never really listen," I say. "The ones who give you that big smile when they're just waiting for their turn to speak. The ones who are always blown around in the wind. Thanks for not being like that."

"Not anymore."

We don't say anything for a while. I run my fingers over the nails where people have hung clothes and rags. Behind the fabric are words written on the wall in pen and marker, some in Arabic, others in French or English.

The world changes its shape in the night, one says.

Zahra laughs quietly. "I still have the key," she says. "To the house in Homs."

"You do?"

"Sure." Zahra pulls her eyes from the graffiti on the wall and tugs out the thin silver key from her pocket, its engraved numbers chipped and corroded with salt. "Imagine," she says. "No door. No house. Just a key."

A truck starts outside. Across the room, the old man passes the boy my age a stub of crayon from his pocket. The boy takes off his shirt, revealing a ladder of bones up his back and down his chest. The skin is pulled tight on his brown cheeks, and his black hair hangs in his face while he turns the shirt inside out, pressing his crayon to the tag.

I ask him, "What are you doing?"

The boy looks up at me, shaking the hair out of his eyes. His jeans are too big for him, and his knees bulge like oversized doorknobs. He lowers his eyes when he answers me, fidgeting with the black collar of the striped tee shirt in his hands. For a minute, I realize I forgot to use Arabic, and I open my mouth to try again.

"I put my name on the tag," the boy says quietly in English, his accent different from Mama's. "My name and my grandfather's name and who I am. In case they can't tell who we are from our bodies."

He says it so calmly. I stutter back, "Who you are? You mean your name?"

"No. I mean the story of my life, where I was born and things." The boy holds out the crayon to me. "You want to write too?"

I take the crayon from him, my hand unsteady. I tug open Mama's bag and write my name and Zahra's on the inside of the burlap.

Then I pause. Where should I say I'm from, Manhattan or Homs? And what can you say about your life in five crayon words?

The boy and his grandfather wait, staring out the milky window.

While I think, I lay my head back against the wall. I read another line, scrawled on the wall in pen by someone else who must have passed this way: *We aren't on any map.*

PART IV

ALGERIA / MOROCCO

My name is a song I sing myself to
remind me of my mother's voice. My name
does not bend to   your tongue, does not stop at your borders. My
name is not a flight risk. I sing my name to remind me of a time
when our language was in our blood, a time when our mothers were in
our hair, a time when vowels came from the same deep place as laughter and
the pit of thirst was not so wide. O beloved, I walk the gauntlet of life barefoot and
bound, clawing at the hills for the voice I left in the house where my mother and her own
were born. I gather words like stones to feed my children. They thirst for words that sound
like the shape of their eyes. Where, O beloved, where will I find such words? I need a word
that smells like the wood of my mother's oud, a word that looks like the sun callousing my
father's hands. I need a word that beats like footsteps on the night, a word that bleeds water
when you cut it with a knife. I need a word my daughters can't pronounce, a word narrow enough
for God to enter it. There was a time words made things whole, beloved, a time I bled the name you
gave me. There was a time God and my mother lived in my name, a time I braided
my name into my hair like a vine. I know that a fig is not a fruit but a flower
grown inwards and I am starving for my name, starving to feed to my
children the things they've forgotten, starving to find the words to say
that home was a green place once and will be again. O beloved,
there will come a day I step into the foam of this white mourning
shroud and trample it. I will press your palm to mine and your skin
will be my own. Let us break for that distant shore, each of
us toward where the other waits. O beloved, you
are the only place where we can sing with
our mothers' tongues. In your
eyes, words hang ripe
as fruit.

Bare Earth

*

After King Roger's death, any peasant in Palermo could tell that his heir, William, was not the man his father was. The Sicilian barons spread rumors that he was not fit to rule. They whispered against him, calling him bad and wicked.

But William was impressed by the work al-Idrisi had done for his father, and he promised to reward him generously if he would stay at his court and write another book of geography for him. Because young William was King Roger's son, al-Idrisi stayed. He asked Rawiya and Khaldun to remain in King William's court to assist him with his work, saying he could not do it without them. And Rawiya, who treasured her friends in her heart, agreed to stay for a time.

As word spread that the Sicilian noblemen were plotting against King William's rule, Rawiya became nervous. She and Khaldun told al-Idrisi of their fears, but he waved them away. Al-Idrisi would not leave King Roger's son in his time of need. King Roger had created a haven of equality and learning, he said, and King William would continue his father's legacy.

But it was not to be.

SIX YEARS AFTER King Roger's death, Rawiya and Khaldun met in a secluded corner of the court gardens by night, surrounded by jasmine flowers and almond trees. Here they could talk freely as they could not by day, safe from the frowns and gossip of the court. Over the last several years of peace, they had been inseparable, walking the palace halls, the gardens, or the streets of Palermo. Speculations of their relationship had become widespread. The only other place they could be alone, free to laugh and talk as they pleased, was in the palace workshop as they bent over their notes and the sketches of maps they produced for al-Idrisi, who relied on Rawiya and Khaldun while he worked and wrote in King William's court. They had been given titles of court scholars. Rawiya and Khaldun worked side by side in the workshop day after day, and it was there that they had shared their first shy kiss several months before, their fingers stained with ink.

On this particular night, Rawiya and Khaldun grasped each other's hands as the conversation took a different, more nostalgic turn. "The trees are full and green again," Rawiya said, "and soon the fields and orchards will be in fruit. Six times the olive harvest has come and gone since we returned to Palermo, and still my mother will walk the olive grove and the shore waiting for my return. I was a young girl when I left home," she said, "but I am grown now. It is time I made plans to return home." For Rawiya and Khaldun were both nearing twenty-five years of age and beginning to feel restless to put down roots.

Khaldun looked down at their hands. "I know," he said. "You must go to your mother. She will want to know you are safe."

Rawiya touched her forehead to Khaldun's. "But I don't want to leave you."

Khaldun pulled back and looked into Rawiya's eyes. "I want your home to be my home," he said. "Wherever you go, I will go. That was my promise." He kissed her hands. "I love you, Rawiya. If you will have me, I will follow you to the ends of the earth. If you will have me, I will be your husband."

But no sooner had he said this than a loud shout went up from the courtyard, and Rawiya and Khaldun sprang to their feet. From the palace came the crash of breaking glass, the crack of clubs on marble. Alarmed, they hurried through the gardens toward the courtyard, keeping their heads low, hidden by the branches. Brash voices and the crackle of torches rose from the courtyard.

Rawiya and Khaldun huddled close together, dismayed at the scene before them. Rebels had taken the palace. The rumors of unrest had been true; the barons had stirred up an armed rebellion against King William.

"We have to find al-Idrisi and get out of here," Khaldun whispered.

"The library—that's where he will be." Rawiya touched al-Idrisi's jeweled scimitar, which she had worn with pride these last six years. She knew al-Idrisi would never leave without *The Book of Roger*.

They fled across the gardens toward the library. "It's been six years," Khaldun said, "and his heart is still between those pages."

"He isn't the first to seek peace among his books instead of sleeping." Anger seeped into Rawiya's voice. "This never would have happened under King Roger. A wise king would have—"

"But we have to deal with things as they are," Khaldun said. "We had many peaceful years. We should be grateful."

Rawiya flattened herself against a tree at the sound of voices, and her fingertips brushed Khaldun's. "We had more than most," she whispered.

They entered the open passageway that led to the library. Through the arches across the balconies, they could see men lifting statuettes and hacking out frescoes and tiling, setting fire to tapestries and velvet cushions.

The library was empty, and all the candles were out. There was one other place al-Idrisi would almost certainly be. Rawiya and Khaldun made for the workshop, where a single candle burned.

In his workshop, al-Idrisi was hunched over the silver planisphere in his white scholar's robes. He cursed and wept, struggling to lift the planisphere onto a wheeled pallet, but it was too heavy for one man to lift alone.

Down the hall, rebels shouted as they ransacked the library, hacking at the bookshelves, setting fire to rare texts.

"There's no time," Rawiya said. "We have to leave it."

"No." Al-Idrisi set the planisphere down, rubbing his fingers. "The planisphere is all I have left of Roger."

"You have the book and the map," Rawiya said. "Let that be enough. The rebels will want the planisphere for the silver. It's too dangerous to take."

"Please." Al-Idrisi bowed his head, his beard as white as his turban. Even after years of travels had taken their toll, Rawiya had never seen him look so old. "We can manage it together."

Rawiya circled the silver disk. It weighed more than two men. "All right," she said. "Help me."

Khaldun moved beside the planisphere, and al-Idrisi positioned himself at the head of their six hands. Together, the three of them hauled the planisphere onto the pallet, grunting with the weight.

The doors burst open. Men tore through the workshop, overturning the tables and the drawing board, brandishing daggers and clubs.

"Go," Khaldun called out, parrying a blade with his scimitar. He threw the man off him and blocked a club that came swinging down. His attackers shrieked and kicked at him.

"Khaldun!" Rawiya cried.

Khaldun blocked their weapons and spun, sending one man's dagger to the ground and its owner clutching his wrist. "Go. Now!"

Rawiya pulled al-Idrisi toward the door. More fighters forced their way into the workshop, pushing Khaldun into a corner with the planisphere, his back to the window. One of them set fire to the curtains, and the flames spread across the wooden beams of the workshop ceiling.

Khaldun never saw the arrow that hissed through the window from the courtyard.

Rawiya shrieked.

The arrow tore through Khaldun's robe, spattering blood on the workshop floor. As his attackers cheered, Khaldun lifted his eyes to Rawiya.

Go, he mouthed.

The flames licked at his shoulders, melting the window frame. Go.

Rawiya pulled al-Idrisi from the room, tugging him across the courtyard toward the secret servants' tunnel she had seen when she had first arrived. She led al-Idrisi through the sandy tunnel in the dark, and the brick over their heads shook with dozens of footsteps.

The tunnel had once led to the servants' kitchen, but no more. Rawiya blinked in the moonlight. They stood in an open courtyard filled with rubble, the remains of bent copper pots and shattered pottery at their feet. The ceiling had fallen in; the paneling was charred, the tile smashed.

Rawiya and al-Idrisi picked their way through cracked porcelain and blackened brick and escaped through the servants' entrance. They fled into the night through the palace gardens, over trampled grass and burnt palm fronds. They hid under the palmettos, watching the palace rumble and burn.

Al-Idrisi lowered himself to his knees and prayed, his head in his hands, *The Book of Roger* a heavy outline in his robe.

Rawiya pressed her hand to her chest, feeling for the shrunken muscle of her heart. It thudded open and shut, only blood where words had once been.

*   *   *

THE FIRST DAY passes slowly, and the day after that. Before we know it, we've been staying in the smugglers' house for a week, waiting for the smugglers to gather a big-enough group to make the trip across the desert and the Algerian border. They don't let us go outside to stretch our legs, so young parents pace the room from end to end, and kids press their faces to the windows. Flies buzz in the corners of the ceiling. In the evenings, the smuggler men toss us loaves of bread and shout at us to wait another day. I open my mouth to ask Zahra if we should go back, then remember what Mama said about the fighting around the Gulf: *The roads are lawless*. At night, we hear men's voices, and I pretend to sleep.

The last night, one of the smuggler men comes into the creaking house and shuffles between the sleeping families. He walks like he's looking for someone, scanning each of our bodies. I tremble against Zahra and squeeze my eyes shut.

He stops over us. The floorboards groan. The man breathes heavy and snorts, tapping something wooden against the wall.

Cold dread spreads from my toes to my scalp, prickling me with fear. I hold my breath. The distance between us seems like nothing. He hangs over us in the dark.

But the smuggler man moves on, and I breathe out. He kicks one of the young fathers, who moans.

The smuggler man speaks in Arabic, loud enough to wake the other families, but no one moves.

You, he says. *Get up.* He kicks the man again. *Your family didn't pay.*

The father stumbles up from his wife and shuffles toward the wall. *What do you want me to give?* he shoots back. *I have nothing. I told you, they will send the money.*

The wet crack of a club hitting flesh makes the whole room twitch. The father cries out. The smuggler pushes him toward the door, still protesting.

I have nothing, he shouts. *I gave you everything I had.*

The door slams shut. Around us, people let out their air, uncoiling tensed necks. Outside the window, hard wood claps against muscle. The father shouts and begs. Coins tinkle in the dirt. My heart slams against my lungs, and I bury my face in Zahra's belly.

Her breaths are heavy and uneven, warming the back of my neck. She whispers, "You didn't understand any of that. Right?"

Fear runs tense through Zahra's voice like air through an oboe reed. It's something Mama would have said, something she used to ask me after the doctors spoke to Baba in the hospital.

I open my mouth, thinking how to tell Zahra what I heard. The door bangs shut as the father limps back into the house, and Zahra flinches at each of his steps.

"No," I whisper back. "I didn't."

The next day, a dozen people pile into the back of the smugglers' truck, sitting on sacks and boxes. The truck bed is piled high with luggage and rolled blankets fastened with duct tape. Packages hang over the wooden sides of the truck on ropes, making it look like a shaggy dog with tiny legs. People sit on top of their bags, shoulder to shoulder, and the ones sitting on the edge of the truck bed sit with sticks wedged between their legs to keep them from tumbling off if they fall asleep.

"Go. Go!" The smuggler men clap their hands to make us move faster. They toss us water bottles and tell us to make them last.

Zahra and I climb on, stuffed next to the boy my age and his grandfather. People jostle as the engine starts.

The city shrinks to a beetle on the horizon. The rocky ground turns to sand. Shrubs and grasses disappear. The uneven road throws up clouds of dust.

The boy my age gives his water bottle to his grandfather, who rubs his bushy white eyebrows and the papery skin under his eyes. The boy pulls a bulging sock from his pocket and slips out a plastic medicine bottle. He hands a pill to his grandfather, who swallows it with a sip of water.

He notices me staring. The boy says in quiet English, "It's for his heart."

"Oh." We bounce up and down, sweat jiggling free of our chins.

I consider my words in Arabic, but my nerves fail me, and I respond in English. "I'm Nour. This is my sister, Zahra."

"I'm Esmat."

I ask, "Why do you hide the pills?"

"They cost a lot of money," Esmat says. "I didn't want them to be stolen." He stares at his hands. "Do you like football? I liked to play at home, with my friends."

"My sister Huda played before we left," I say. I can feel the Arabic translations behind the English words, as though my brain has become two interlocking gears. "Where we lived, they called it soccer. She was the best, the captain of her school team."

"That's amazing," Esmat says.

The sun swings its head across the sky. Esmat wags his legs over the side of the truck, kicking at imaginary soccer balls.

"Someday," he says, "I hope your sister can play again."

IN THE AFTERNOON, we stop so people can jump off to pee. Some of them ask for water. The smuggler man curses and pushes them, throwing water bottles at the others until they get back on the truck. He tells us we won't get our money back if we're left behind.

The road winds between rocky buttes and reddish hills, then flattens out into a wide sandy expanse dotted with gray-green tufts of hardy grass. Now and then we pass camels sitting with their legs bent under them, and sometimes, far off, tiny figures watch us.

As we near the border with Algeria, the dunes of the Sahara rise up to the west—cliffs of sand, rippling crests and ridges and mountains of honey-colored sand. The truck rambles on, bouncing and complaining.

As the sun sinks, Esmat gives his grandfather the last of his water. "He has to keep drinking," he says.

At sunset, we take another pee break, and the driver threatens to make us take pills to stop us from peeing. *No water from now on*, he shouts.

Next to us, Esmat shifts between piles of packages, restless. He shakes the last few drops of water from his empty bottle. His grandfather looks glassy-eyed and weak, and his hands tremble.

Esmat hops off the back of the truck and approaches one of the smuggler men, who is stretching his legs. *My grandfather*, Esmat says in Arabic. *He needs water.*

But the smuggler man shouts at him. He pulls a stick out of the truck and hits Esmat hard enough to make him scream. He strikes him on his back, his wrists, his temples. Red welts rise out of the skin on his shoulder blades. I bury my face in Zahra's lap and cry out with each crack of the stick, and even though I can't see them, each welt feels like it stings my own skin.

THAT NIGHT, ESMAT is lying with his head on his grandfather's lap, in and out of sleep, when the truck stops in a scrubby field. The smuggler man who beat Esmat slams the truck door and stomps back to us, telling us to get off.

We stand in the field, shivering. He tells us to start walking, that we're crossing the border into Algeria on foot. He tells us not to make a sound, cocking his finger to his head and pretending to pull the trigger.

Border guards shoot first, he says, *and ask questions later.*

Pregnant women and parents with little kids struggle to keep up. Zahra carries a little boy while his mother hangs nearby, her nose and cheeks badly sunburned and a baby in her arms. Esmat walks next to us, holding his grandfather's hand. Esmat's face and neck are so swollen I almost can't recognize him. As we walk, I wonder if we look like a family. Can people become glued to each other as easily as they get peeled away?

In the dark, our breaths are the wings of a dozen locusts beating.

Then come the pops of bullets.

The shots rip the night at the seams. We dive and run. The little boy jerks and bolts from Zahra's arms. The families scatter, and Esmat and his grandfather lose each other in the chaos.

Zahra grabs my hand, and I hook my arm around Esmat's elbow. We run from the road, ducking under the moon.

The popping gets louder. The smugglers' truck starts in the distance. I trip over something that pulls and sticks in my shins—a roll of barbed wire on the ground, stretching into the night. Algeria.

There's a heavy tug from Esmat's arm, and he slips away. I break from Zahra's hand and turn. In the dark behind us, Esmat's head is silhouetted on the ground, the red welts the smuggler man made on the back of his neck exposed to the night.

"Esmat," I whisper, "we've got to run."

He's too heavy for me to lift. Far off in the dark, border guards' flashlights sweep the ground. Just as my eyes adjust to the dark, the bright pool of a flashlight blinds me and the pops of gunshots come again. I throw myself to the ground and lose Esmat in the dark.

"Come on." Zahra pulls me away from the circle of light, and we run and run until the popping stops. We don't look back.

When we catch our breath, Zahra and I are alone. I look back over the dunes toward the road, but I can't see anything, not Esmat's body, not his grandfather, not the border. Cold has come like I haven't felt since the city, painting my legs with goose bumps. The little pimples are sticky with blood.

Zahra touches the cuts on my shins and the smears of blood on my hands. "The wire?" she asks, thinking all the blood is my own.

I nod. Zahra's jaw is gashed too, caked with blood brown and thick as pan drippings. It's the kind of ugly cut that never heals right, the kind that leaves a long finger of nubby flesh.

I squat down and cover my bumpy knees with my arms. The moon licks the half inch of hair on my head. I blink and see Esmat's frozen face, like he is just about to cry.

"I bet I know what the man would say, if he were here."

Zahra stares back toward Libya. "What would he say?" she asks.

" 'No money back.' "

THE SUN IS a torch. During the day, the rock and sand go from ice to coals under our feet. We plod over dunes, searching for the road. We both know that, if we find it, only one direction is open to us. Even if we brought our identification back to the Libyan border, that border is already shut. We can't go back.

My legs turn to brick. My palms ooze sweat. Zahra and I pass my water bottle back and forth until we drain it. I imagine the half-sweet taste of bread. I imagine the blue rush of cold tap water hitting my tongue. I try to remember the color of ice cream's taste.

The nights are long winters, and we spend them huddled up under the dirty carpet. We eat the last of our dates and tuna fish. The cans pucker and dry out. For the first time, I say a prayer to thank the smuggler man for the extra water bottles he gave us when we got on the truck, the ones Zahra and I have been saving.

We wear holes through the bottoms of our shoes with walking, our muscles cramping up and our backs aching. I wonder if the heat is making the paint melt on Mama's map. Even my skull feels heavy, my burlap backpack and my pockets full.

"Maybe we would have been there by now," Zahra says after a few days, "if things hadn't gone wrong."

Above us, the clouds whip and run, beckoning the coming wet season.

I kick at stray pebbles and see Esmat's face in the patterns in the sand. I say, "I bet the man never meant to get us there."

Zahra wipes sweat off her face and neck, and it drips from her wrist. "The twisted son of a bitch. We were nothing but money to him."

I scratch old blood from my cuticles. "Mama wouldn't want you to curse."

Heat ripples off the ground, buckling the horizon. I wonder if anybody made it back to the truck. I wonder if there is somebody out there who loves the smuggler man, if anybody loves all the mean, unlovable people in the world. I wonder if bad men are good sometimes, when we aren't looking.

And then I wonder: if they find Esmat's body, will they read the words he wrote in crayon on his shirt?

My scalp crawls with fire, the heat painting my vision red. Sweat beads up between my eyebrow hairs and sticks to my lashes. My blood is thick, the stories in me boiled to mush. The words in me, the ones I don't say, have gravity in them. All those unsaid words are like iron gravity spots. I am weighed down by the sticky residue of feeling them, crushed by the heaviness of hope, wondering if my heart is only tubing.

I stop walking. Zahra shuffles on a few steps in the heat until she notices.

I say, "It's September."

"It's probably halfway through September by now," Zahra says. "So what?"

"If Mama were here," I say, "we'd be safe. We'd have someplace to sleep. We wouldn't have to do this."

"What do you want from me?" Zahra says. "If you want to find Mama, we have to walk."

She reaches for my hand, but I rip it away.

"We have to keep moving," she says, and the desperation in her voice bursts into ruby like a hot coal, as red as the welts on Esmat's ribs.

"What's the point?" I shout. "Mama and Huda and Yusuf and Sitt Shadid and Umm Yusuf and Rahila are gone. They're drowned, or shot, or dead, just like Abu Sayeed. Just like Esmat. Just like Baba."

My last word shreds itself on the heat rising from the dunes. In the distance, thunder rocks the sky.

It's the first time I've said it out loud. Something about the world changes the moment I say it, like none of the bad things were quite real until they left my mouth. Like until I gave death words, it didn't actually exist.

Is the world nothing more than a collection of senseless hurts waiting to happen, one long cut waiting to bleed?

Zahra kneels in front of me and says, "We have to keep going."

I sniffle and wipe at my face, but my cheeks are dry. "My feet hurt."

Zahra blinks sand out of her eyelashes like gold eye shadow. She says, "I know." She reaches for my face. "It's okay if you cry."

"I'm not crying." I hiccup, but no tears come. "I can't."

"You're dehydrated." Zahra hands me her water bottle, sloshing the last few drops.

I push it away. "You need it."

"You finished yours this morning."

I take the bottle and drink, and my dry throat makes me cough. Zahra tugs the burlap backpack from me. I notice three olive tan lines in the spots where her bracelet used to hang.

"You sold it," I say. "Baba's bracelet."

"There are more important things than bracelets," Zahra says.

I study her face and the gash along her jaw. Either one of the smuggler men cuffed her in the dark, or she must have sliced herself on the barbed wire. Either way, Zahra will have the scar for the rest of her life. Just like me, she's marked.

I say to Zahra, "Let's just rest."

The thunder ripples across the dunes again, louder this time. Rain spits from the sky in thin bursts. Zahra and I flatten ourselves on the ground. We open our mouths to drink, trying to catch the drizzle on our tongues.

It's not enough, but we don't care. We let the night come over us as the last drops of passing rain fall, torture and pure joy at the same time.

Mama was right. Sometimes pain comes with its own sorts of blessings.

THAT NIGHT, A man walks out of the dark with ten thousand stars at his back.

I see him silhouetted against the purple sky when I wake up shivering, the sand beneath us gone cold. The Milky Way above us is a gash of light. Zahra is still asleep next to me, the muscles in her forearms and her shoulders twitching from thirst. The man takes a few steps toward me, and I realize someone has found us.

I get up, rubbing my eyes, and stumble toward him. As the moon casts its glow over his face, he squints at me under thick eyebrows and calls out a few words I don't understand.

"Who are you?" I call back.

The man answers me, but still I can't understand him. I look back at Zahra, still asleep several yards behind me, and fear takes over. I remember the smuggler man standing over us in the house, the electric terror of being watched, of being alone. *We aren't on any map.*

The man speaks again, slower this time, putting his hand to his chest. "Amazigh."

I repeat the word. "Amazigh?"

The man nods. I try to think back to what Mama told me about the people who live in parts of Algeria and Morocco, the people history books call the Berbers. But Mama told me that, like most people, the name history gave them isn't what they call themselves.

The stars hang low over our heads. Out here, the sky is brighter than the constellations on the ceiling at Grand Central. Everyone, no matter what language they speak, has a name for the stars. I focus on their light, fighting back the fear, and find the only words that come.

I point up at the camel in Cassiopeia. "My favorite."

Zahra stirs behind me, groggy and weak from the day's heat. The man looks confused at my English and speaks again in words I don't understand. Fear bubbles up in red and yellow, the colors of panic. I remember the words I forgot in the spice shop in Homs—Zahra can't help me now.

But the man tries again, speaking more slowly, and his eyes are as young and patient as Abu Sayeed's in Baba's Polaroids.

I lift my hand and point at the sky. What did Mama say the word for camel was, the one Rawiya used?

"An-naqah." And then I think he might not know what I'm pointing at, so I add another Arabic word Mama taught me, the word for stars. "An-nujum."

I stare at the man. He seems unsure, waiting for me to say something else. I point up at the sky again, wondering if I've got it wrong, shivering from the cold. Did Rawiya ever doubt herself so much?

I say, "An-naqah fi an-nujum."

The man waves someone over. Shapes come out of the night—a lady and a girl Zahra's age, leading three camels. They talk to each other in a language I've never heard before.

Behind me, Zahra pops awake. "What's going on?" she hisses.

I study the man's face, knowing my Arabic is only basic, like a little kid's. Can this be a bad man, if he loves the stars? I wonder if the smuggler man followed Esmat's eyes, pointed at the sky.

I try one last time: "Ohebbu an-naqah fi an-nujum." *I love the camel in the stars.* I open my palm to the velvet night and start to lose hope. I must have gotten something wrong.

But my words make the man's eyes crinkle up, and he starts to chuckle. He leans his head back and laughs with relief and understanding, a long, tinkling laugh like the sky blowing diamonds from its hand. He points up at the stars and smiles. "An-naqah fi an-nujum," he says, like he has never been surer of anything.

Relief floods my belly—he does speak Arabic. I try something else. "Ingliziya? English?"

The lady behind him melts out of the dark. "Arabic, French. A little English." She smiles. "Come?"

The lady and the man lift us up and set us on their camels. Before long, we are moving across the dunes, the camels picking their way over crests of cold sand. The lady keeps quiet, riding ahead of us with Zahra. The man gives me water, and every now and then, he looks up and points at a constellation I once picked out with Mama or Abu Sayeed, but he gives them new names. He calls the Pleiades by a name I've never heard, and the lady falls back and translates for me into English: *the daughters of the night.*

I listen to them talk in a language I've never heard before. I don't have to understand everything. The blue-violet voices wind around me, protecting me from my fear. I am covered with a thick rind of safety, like an orange.

The night gets thin as an old raincoat. Toward dawn, we ride in silence, and everybody's heart beats so loud. I listen to the white space. All I hear is breath, like we are all one organ, a single lung.

Two Things at the Same Time

*

Hidden under the palmettos, Rawiya and al-Idrisi watched the palace burning.

Al-Idrisi's face was streaked with the ash of palms and linen. He patted the book and map in his robe without focusing his eyes on the flames. "How could they turn on Roger's son this way?" he said.

"Because he wasn't King Roger," Rawiya said. "People take advantage when power changes hands." She waved at the night, toward the Maghreb in the distance, over the rim of the island and beyond the sea. "Look at Cairo. Look at the Fatimid Empire." In the last few months, word had reached Sicily through the merchants of the fall of the Fatimids, until even the servants had whispered of it. The words bitter in her mouth, Rawiya said, "Those caught in between are the ones who get hurt."

Al-Idrisi turned his head. "We left him. Khaldun and the planisphere are as good as lost. I have been a coward."

"I loved him more than anyone," Rawiya said, slamming her fist into the palmetto's bark. "I wanted to spend my life with him. Don't you think I would have done more, if I could?"

Al-Idrisi clutched the book in his robe. "But to lose so good a man . . ."

Rawiya looked back at the palace, lit up against the stars. The smell of salt mixed with smoke, tart sulfur. Ash turned to black paste on her cheeks.

"Wait for me," she said.

Rawiya darted across the palace gardens and back through the ruined kitchen, through the servants' tunnel, until she skidded to a halt at the end of the brick archway that led into the courtyard.

Voices and shadows roamed the palace, dragging away furniture, paintings, and jewelry. One man passed the entrance to the tunnel with a torch. Rawiya stepped back into the shadows, holding her breath. The courtyard was ablaze with crashing, tearing, snapping flames.

The vandals were burning books.

"You." Rawiya stepped out from the tunnel with her sling in her hand. "What do you think you're doing?"

One of the men tossed down a thick leather-bound book, hand-lettered with gold ink. Rawiya glanced at the cover. It was Ptolemy's *Geography*.

"Is this a joke?" the man snapped. He set his foot on the book, grinding it into the stones. "William's day is over. You should have run like a dog while you had the chance."

Rawiya waved at the book. "I want to know what you're doing with that."

The man smirked. "Maybe I'll burn it."

"Pick it up, then," she said.

The man reached for it.

Before anyone could stop her, Rawiya notched a stone to her sling and fired it, stinging the man in the hand. He fell to the ground, howling.

His friends charged her, dropping frames and cushions and pieces of cut glass. She fired six stones, one after another, gashing her attackers' shins and bruising their bellies until they dropped to the ground.

The man whose hand she had stung ran at her, using a broken

chair leg as a club. Rawiya stuffed her sling into the band of her sirwal and pulled out al-Idrisi's jeweled scimitar, blocking his blow. She staggered back with its force.

The man grinned at her over their crossed weapons. "This is a joke after all," he said. He pressed harder, forcing her back. "A woman with a sword? Has William gone so soft that he leaves women to protect the palace? A woman." He spat. "You are no warrior."

"I am a woman and a warrior," Rawiya said, her blade cutting into his club. "If you think I can't be both, you've been lied to."

She heaved her weight forward, slicing the club clean in half. The man stumbled back and fell. His friends rose, rubbing their sore limbs, and charged again. Rawiya parried their daggers and clubs, shoving men aside with the force of her blade. She dove through their ranks, making for the workshop.

The narrow room was full of smoke. She coughed, blinded. "Khaldun?"

There was no answer.

Rawiya choked on smoke and pulled her head back. Blows came from behind her, and she lifted her sword to block them. She rolled aside against the wall, calling out, "Khaldun!"

"Your friend was lost to the fire," her first attacker called out. He sat on the ground, rubbing his hand and his shin. "Nothing is left of him."

Rawiya ran at him. He surged to his feet and stabbed at her with a dagger, making her jump back. Rawiya lunged away, grabbing Ptolemy's *Geography* as she went. The rest of the men surrounded her, pushing her back toward the servants' tunnel.

With the book in her hand, Rawiya couldn't put her full strength behind her blows, and she stumbled. A man kicked her, and she flew backward through the archway of the servants' tunnel and into the dark.

They began to beat the tunnel entrance with their clubs, knocking down bricks. Ten of them beat the walls at once while Rawiya shook sparks from her eyes, getting to her knees. The walls began to crack. Stone crumbled across the entrance.

Rawiya pushed herself back as stones fell around her knees and ankles. She crawled away from the entrance just as the archway collapsed, leaving no opening.

"Khaldun," Rawiya whispered. "My home."

She stumbled back to the ruined kitchen and across the palace garden, clutching the book she had rescued, the book King Roger had once offered her.

Rawiya crossed to the burnt palmetto where she had left al-Idrisi. She found him weeping with his head in his lap, his white turban shuddering.

*   *   *

TOWARD DAWN, WE climb a high dune and look down on a narrow rocky plain scattered with tamarisk trees. A square tent draped with goat hair rugs and colorful blankets leans against one of the tree's roots, shaded from the rising sun by its bushy leaves. An older boy watches us from a distance, shooing brown goats and two lean sheep. A lamb totters toward us, braying. Dogs chase each other behind the tent, barking at jackals slinking away with the dark.

Normally we don't move at night, the lady says to Zahra in accented Arabic, *but the dogs smelled you.*

She helps Zahra down from the camel, and her daughter sets me on the ground. They shoo us inside the tent and make us sit down. The floor is covered with wool rugs woven in orange diamonds and green starbursts, laid with their edges overlapping each other. The man, who must be the lady's husband, comes in and brings us a silver pot of tea. He holds his arm high up and pours the tea in a thin stream into glasses. After going hungry all this time, I feel the sugar sticking to the hairs in my nose.

The lady comes in and sits down, adjusting her floral-print dress and embroidered scarf. The tea is sweet and hot, and the mint smells a clean, pale blue. The lady says a few words. I recognize *bismillah*—in the name of God.

The lady waits for us to speak.

I bow my head and thank her in Arabic—"Shukran." Then I ask in English, "You speak four languages?"

She smiles. "My French and Arabic are from my school days. The English is from the market. We make kilims." She motions to the rugs on the floor.

"I'm Nour," I say. "This is my sister, Zahra."

The lady tips her head and smiles again, crinkling the sun wrinkles around her eyes. "Itto."

Zahra launches into Arabic, explaining what has happened to us and how we're trying to get to Morocco, then Ceuta, where our uncle lives. *We need to get to Sabta*, Zahra says, using the Arabic work for Ceuta. *We were separated from our mother and sister. We traveled for days.*

Itto translates for her husband, who gets up and goes out. I hear him talking to his son and daughter outside.

Itto frowns. *They were supposed to take you to Algiers, and from there through Morocco to Sabta?*

Yes.

The Moroccan border into Spain is not easy to cross.

I know.

Itto glances at me. *This is your brother?*

Zahra looks over at me and then back to Itto. *She's my sister.* She explains about the lice, and I look away.

This is better. Itto pours us another three glasses of tea. *She made us laugh with her stars. She is a sweet child.*

She is. Zahra looks down into the steam. Itto's daughter comes in with clay dishes of hot couscous topped with spices and almonds. I look from Zahra to Itto, but Zahra doesn't look at me. Like always, she thinks I haven't understood.

Our words come out in Arabic at the same time. Zahra speaks to Itto for me, saying, *My sister only speaks a little Arabic.*

I say, *Thank you.*

Zahra and Itto turn to look at me, and Itto smiles.

In Arabic, Itto says, "There is a place—Ouargla. Fruit is grown there and packed on trucks for sale. Some of the trucks are bound for Ceuta."

ITTO AND HER family take us west on their camels, driving the goats and sheep with them. I think we travel for a week, but I lose track of time. We eat and sleep in their tent and help them herd their flock. The desert becomes familiar, a face decorated with the arched noses of rocks, the lips of dunes, the hairlines of green patches dotted with eucalyptus.

Itto shares her water with us and teaches me words in Arabic and Shawiya and French. At night, she and her daughter mend fabric, and when the light is gone, they tell stories. I listen to their laughter and to the camels shuffling and swaying. The dogs bay at jackals under the moon.

One day, I twist my neck to look at Itto, sitting behind me on her camel. I talk to her in Arabic. My baby sentences have gotten easier, the words coming to me when I reach for them.

"You never asked where we're from," I say.

She squints past the dunes. "You told me you were from Syria."

"Zahra was born in Homs. Mama and Baba lived there a long time. But I was born in New York, in the United States."

"New York?" Itto looks down at me. "You may be American, but you are still Syrian."

I rub the camel's coarse hair with my palms. "How?"

"A person can be two things at the same time," Itto says. "The land where your parents were born will always be in you. Words survive. Borders are nothing to words and blood."

I think of the storyteller man behind the Jordanian border gate. Our camels' hooves sink into the sand. If I put my ear to the ground, could I hear him breathing?

"There was a time others came to claim our country," Itto says. "We couldn't speak our language or name our children what we wanted. But we held to what our mothers loved. Our heritage. Our stories. They call us Berber, from 'barbarian.' But Amazigh means 'free man.' Did you know this? No one can take our freedom from us. No one can take our land or our names from our hearts."

Heat warps the horizon, making things that are close look far away, and things that are far away look close. Did Baba ever feel that way about Syria, I wonder, when he looked out across the East River, past Brooklyn? Mama said Uncle Ma'mun was a different kind of person, somebody who saw life as an adventure. Did Baba and his brother miss things differently too, so that Baba was mourning the same place Uncle Ma'mun kept tucked in his shirt pocket? I think of Yusuf and Sitt Shadid and think maybe there are parts of yourself you never stop missing, once you realize you've lost them.

"I think my baba tried to keep Syria inside him," I say, "but it was too big to hold on to."

"That is why we had to hold on to the old words," Itto says, "until our mothers' voices sprang from our mouths." She squints out at the horizon, as though the land itself holds layers of reality I can't even see. And I realize how little I know of Itto's pain and her ancestors', how every story is more complicated than it seems, even the story of the Imazighen and the Normans who separated them from the land that bore them. If a language or a story or a map can be used to give people a voice or to take it away, only our own words can guide us home.

"Then home is here." I sketch out a circle in the air that holds all of us, the people and the camels and the goats. Then I point at my heart and at my own tongue. "Home is this," I say. "No one can take it from us."

"No one." Itto raises her arm. "There—Ouargla."

At first, the city is just a cluster of trees in the distance. The roads are washed over with sand, only visible because they are flatter than everything else. Itto's husband stops outside the town, and the goats and sheep cluster around him, a lamb in his arms. He raises his arm, watching us go.

The city of Ouargla rises up, rippled and white in the heat glare. Trucks pass, blowing a sheet of sand off the blacktop, revealing yellow lines. The rocky sand turns to stretches of shrubs.

The first buildings appear, tan plaster. The streets narrow. The city is built around an oasis, a thin bowl of shallow water surrounded by palm trees and wading ibises. Groves of palms and fruit trees ring the bowl. The sound of traffic, of leaves rustling, of birds calling—it's all so loud I can't bear it, not after the quiet of the Sahara.

Itto takes us into the market in the city center. Her son and daughter set out their woven rugs for sale. Then Itto takes Zahra and me aside and points beyond the market to a row of trucks parked behind a squat building. Itto nods her head toward the trucks. "Fruit trucks," she whispers. "Probably bound for Algiers or Ceuta."

"Probably?" Zahra bites her lips.

"Or Fes."

I sniff, burning the cracked edges of my nostrils. Something smells rotted and sweet, a brassy, greenish smell. The open backs of the trucks are gaping holes into darkness.

"You will be closer there than here," Itto says. She raises her hands to the heavens. "It is dangerous. God brings peace."

At nightfall, Itto steals us away to the trucks. Outside the building, a man smokes a cigarette with his back turned.

We peek around the bumper. The trucks are loaded with crates, each crate slapped with a green and yellow label. A row down the middle of the back of each truck, between the crates, leads into blank dark. A cold mist of steam wafts out.

"It's like hell," I whisper to Zahra in English.

"These are refrigerated trucks." Zahra ducks her head inside, then glances back at the man with the cigarette. Its red tip blazes and sparks when he breathes in. "It can't be much above freezing in there."

"Go." Itto looks from Zahra's face to mine. "They're finished loading. They will close it soon."

"Wait." I fumble in my pocket and tug out Abu Sayeed's handkerchief, stitched with diamonds. After all this time, it still smells like home. I hold the handkerchief out to Itto.

She hesitates. "This is for me?"

I nudge my hand into hers, and she takes the handkerchief. "For everything," I say. "It's from somebody else. Somebody who would want to thank you too."

Itto clasps her arms around me one last time. "When you find your mother," she whispers, "don't let go."

We clamber onto the truck hitch and into the back. When I turn around, Itto has already sprinted back to her children in the dark, ducking into the shadows between buildings. She reappears down the street. It's too far to tell if she's smiling, but she raises one arm and points at the stars. Then she's gone.

Zahra and I pick our way between the crates. We bump into something that cracks open, thudding a soft glob onto the floor.

"Ew," Zahra whispers. "What is that?"

I try to avoid it, but I step in it anyway. "It's squishy."

"A crate must have broken open." Zahra sniffs the air. "Oranges, maybe."

"I smell bananas. Pomegranates?" The acid-green smell of smashed, overripe fruit is overpowering. Some of it must have rotted.

We settle into the back of the truck, looking for a tight spot. I try not to think of the hold of the aid ferry.

"Itto and her family saved our lives," Zahra whispers.

"I knew they would help us."

"Yeah?"

The tang of oranges and dates fills up my nose when I breathe in. We crouch down between the crates, cramped and shivering. Goose bumps scrape my palms when I rub my elbows.

"Because," I whisper, "nobody can love the stars and hurt people. They just can't."

The crushed fruit between our toes is like a cool gelatin bath. It seeps into the holes in our shoes and stings our blisters like wet fire. Seeds and pulp stick to our ankles and the laces of Zahra's sneakers.

I shiver, blowing on my fingers, and wonder how long I can stand the cold before my skin starts to harden and burn.

Zahra whispers, "I guess you're right."

Underneath

∗

Though she ached in her bones for what she had lost, Rawiya didn't chance the palace again. She and al-Idrisi hid under the palmettos, and flecks of soot streaked al-Idrisi's white robe with gray. Rawiya picked them off, blackening her fingers. The stubborn sun refused to rise between Monte Pellegrino and the green fields beyond the city. The flames burned on. They covered their faces.

"Khaldun survived the roc," Rawiya said. "He survived the desert storms. He survived the Fatimids and the Almohads—just to be murdered in his adopted home."

"Khaldun pledged his life to protect you," al-Idrisi said.

Rawiya said, "I would have given my own to stop him."

"He wanted you to live."

"Then he was a fool." Rawiya spat, and her saliva was gray with ash, her mouth bitter with it.

Al-Idrisi looked up at her, his eyes ringed red. "We have to deal with things as they are."

Rawiya laughed in spite of herself. "That's just what Khaldun said. That we had our years of peace. That we should be grateful."

Al-Idrisi tugged his book and his map from his robe. He brushed sooty cobwebs from the book's cover. "These are all we have left," he said.

Rawiya pulled Ptolemy's *Geography* from her robe. "And this."

"The *Jugrafiya*!" Al-Idrisi set his things on the ground and took Ptolemy's book. "Roger and I read and reread these words. I learned much of what I know of mapmaking from Ptolemy."

Rawiya bent and picked up al-Idrisi's book, the one he had prepared for King Roger. She studied the lettering. "This doesn't say *al-Kitab ar-Rujari*." *The Book of Roger.*

"Roger wouldn't let me name the book for him," al-Idrisi said. "No, officially this is *Kitab Nuzhat al-Mushtaq fi Ikhtiraq al-Afaq*." *The Book of Pleasant Journeys into Faraway Lands.* Al-Idrisi laughed. "Only I call it *The Book of Roger*."

"Then we both will," Rawiya said.

At that moment, a weak whinnying reached their ears. Rawiya held her breath, thinking rebels on horseback had found them. But from out of the darkness came a horse with its neck bowed, and Bauza stumbled into the clearing under the palms where Rawiya and al-Idrisi stood.

"Bauza!" Rawiya rushed to him, stroking his singed mane. Bauza nuzzled her neck, his breathing labored with exertion.

"He must have escaped the stables before they burned," al-Idrisi said.

Rawiya laid her head against Bauza's cheek, and he nibbled at her fingers. She laughed in spite of herself. "I don't have any sugar for you tonight, boy," she whispered, "but you'll have some soon. I promise you that."

Across the gardens, a shadow moved, and with it came the smell of burning. The figure curled into itself, then slumped down between two charred date palms. Ash puffed from its back as the body hit the ground. Behind it, something large and smeared with soot rolled to a stop at the base of one of the palms' trunks.

Rawiya tied Bauza to one of the palms and crept toward the two shadows. Neither moved. The hems of the cloths draped over them were torn into a burnt fringe, and as Rawiya and al-Idrisi approached, they saw that one of them was a man covered by his cloak.

Rawiya circled the man on the ground. His hood covered his head and his face, and his hands were charred and bloody. She kept a pace away, holding her distance, but he didn't move. Al-Idrisi watched the rubble of the servants' kitchen for other intruders, but no one had followed.

Taking a breath, Rawiya swept back the man's hood.

"Khaldun!" She threw herself down next to him, wrapping her arms around his shoulders, kissing the top of his head.

He coughed. "You always seem to find me out of sorts," he said.

Rawiya touched his chest, then pulled back when her fingers found the shaft of an arrow buried in his shoulder. "You need a doctor," she said. "We have to stop your bleeding—"

But Khaldun grasped the arrow, grimacing. "I must have sung a song God liked," he said. Turning on his side, he showed Rawiya the other end of the arrow sticking out from his back. "Straight through," he said. "A clean wound." And he was right, for the arrow had not pierced his heart, and the shaft itself had stopped the bleeding.

"Why did you stay in the workshop?" Rawiya brushed ash from Khaldun's beard. She brought his fingers to her cheek and smelled iron and bitter burnt flesh. "What good is a book or a map if you are lost?"

Khaldun said, "I made a pledge I wanted to keep."

"You are a fool," she said. "You are a kind and lionhearted fool, and I love you for it."

Khaldun touched her face, smiling through his mask of pain. "That has a sort of poetry to it," he said.

And Rawiya kissed his forehead and his lips, the arrow between them.

"You didn't lose as much as you thought," Khaldun said, pulling away from her. He pointed to the linen-covered lump behind him. The linen was a serving cloth from the ruined servants' kitchen, stained with soot and the dust of broken tile.

Al-Idrisi pulled back the cloth and sank to his knees. A wide disk of silver gleamed on a pallet in the moonlight.

Zeyn Joukhadar

"The planisphere," al-Idrisi said.

"The difficult part was leaving the workshop." Khaldun told them how the arrow had struck him down, how his weight had pulled a tapestry from the wall, tangling him up in the cloth. His attackers had set fire to the workshop, the library, and the tapestry, trying to burn him alive. He had taken the tapestry and thrown it, catching his attackers in the burning cloth instead.

"I pushed them out of the workshop with the flaming fabric," Khaldun said, "and left the tapestry to burn out on the stone." He lifted his hands. The top layer of skin had been scorched away, revealing red flesh and pus.

Rawiya tore a strip of cloth from her cloak and wrapped his one hand. Al-Idrisi wrapped the other in his white turban.

"They will heal," she said.

"In time, and with scars," al-Idrisi said. "But it is a small price to pay for your life."

Khaldun went on to tell how he, badly burned and hiding his face to look like a looter, had pulled the pallet from the workshop. He had escaped through the servants' tunnel after seeing Rawiya and al-Idrisi duck through. Exhausted and weighted down by the planisphere, he had collapsed in the palace garden, hidden under the leaves and darkness.

"Then you were already gone," Rawiya said. "You had escaped by the time I came back for you."

Khaldun blinked away the thick paste of ash on his eyelashes. "You came back for me?"

Rawiya bent her forehead to his, dotting her face with soot. "You are the only home I have. I left home once, years ago. I am through with leaving." She kissed his ashen lips. "Yes, I will marry you, Khaldun," she said. "I will marry you."

In reply, Khaldun raised his good arm to her hair and kissed her, lifting his burnt fingertips to the sky.

"You have done more for me than I ever could have asked," al-Idrisi said. "The looters would have melted down my life's work, destroyed everything. Yet I would give it a thousand times over to have you both survive—you, who are like the children God has given back to me." Al-Idrisi bent to kiss the top of Khaldun's head, and his eyelashes left damp scratches in the soot on Khaldun's face. "Bless you."

But all three of them knew that the danger was not over. The silver planisphere, as wide across as a man was tall, was impossible to hide. The metal alone was worth thousands of dirhams. Al-Idrisi's prized device was no longer safe on the island of Sicily, and neither were Rawiya or her friends. As long as they remained, they would be targets.

Together, they decided to take the planisphere to a safe and secret place and to tell no one of its location. For a hiding place, al-Idrisi selected Ustica, the abandoned island of charred rock northwest of the Sicilian coast they had passed at the start of their journey. They would hide the planisphere in one of Ustica's deep grottoes, where it would be protected by the tides and the volcanic rock of the island known as "the black pearl."

"There the planisphere will remain," al-Idrisi said, "guarded forever, safe from selfish hands."

Above them, the great lion and the gazelles ran the gauntlet of the stars.

"And what of us?" Rawiya asked. "Our quest is done, our peaceful years in Palermo over. Someone waits for me across the sea, someone who has been waiting a long time for my return."

Al-Idrisi smiled and raised his face to the heavens. "It is time I return home myself," he said, "to the place where God knit me up in my mother's womb. After all, I have been under way for almost twenty years." He laughed and rose. "Come," he said. "I still have friends among the merchants. Surely one can find us a doctor and a ship that will take us to Ustica and into the west."

"To Ceuta, then," Rawiya said.

Al-Idrisi smiled, his eyes young again. "To Ceuta."

*   *   *

THE REAR DOOR of the truck shuts with a bang. We're left in the dark, sticky sweet and freezing cold. Then the truck shudders to life, the engine popping and backfiring, and we rumble away.

The cold seems to take on a life of its own when the truck starts. Cold air circulates around our feet and our bare legs, cutting and stinging us. The vents might as well be pumping out frozen knives. I finger Mama's piece of blue-and-white ceramic tile on its cord around my neck. It's held my body heat, and I use it to warm my fingers.

"Do you think we're headed in the right direction?" Zahra whispers. "Could they have made a mistake?"

"Maybe Itto read a sign off the building," I say, "or the truck." I pause, and fear sticks to my legs with the smashed fruit. "Itto wasn't wrong. She couldn't be."

We lean on the crates, crouching until our calves go numb. We make no sound, afraid every time the truck stalls or stops that someone has heard us whispering. It's darker than the closet in our New York apartment where I used to play hide-and-seek. It's darker than the beach at Rockaway when we watched the shooting stars, darker than the bushes in Central Park.

The only reason I still know I'm there is because it's too cold not to notice my goose bumps. The cold air swirls across our shins and the backs of our necks, chapping and burning them. Each new blast seems colder than the last, making us wrap our arms around our ribs and burrow into ourselves. The dark is a frozen vice that crushes the delicate bones in my wrists and my ankles until I think they will snap. Zahra and I shiver so hard we bump into each other and into the crates of fruit, cracking our jaws and our elbows on the wood.

It's too cold to fall asleep, but we soon lose control of our numb knees. We bounce and crash to the wooden floor when the truck goes over a hill. We slide in the fruit we crushed, and grainy seeds embed themselves in the hems of my shorts. Pulp fills my sneakers.

We lean on each other, shivering our arms and chins together hard enough to bruise. I get hard cold, aching cold, stinging cold. The tips of my fingers pulse, blood pricking them. Our bodies get rigid, our fingernails stony, our skin like glass. My whole body screams fire. If a crate falls on me, will I shatter?

"How many miles is it to Ceuta?" I whisper to Zahra so the driver doesn't hear.

"Five hundred, maybe, or a thousand."

I brace myself against Zahra, my jaws grinding with spasms. "How much longer?" My words are grit and ice. I don't want to freeze to death. "We'll get there fast, right? Right?"

Zahra pauses before saying, "It depends how much the truck is carrying."

After that, we don't talk anymore.

The truck stops and starts, climbs hills and slides down sharp valleys. Our teeth chatter until our jaws lock up. I go numb. My skin becomes a thick gray blanket, and I start to get sleepy and warm.

That first sensation of warmth is what tells me we really could die in here. It tells me Mama might have sent us out of Libya for nothing. It tells me we might get all the way to Ceuta just for them to find our blue-frosted bodies in the back of this fruit truck.

I read in a book once that freezing to death isn't a bad way to go, that right before you die you feel warm instead of cold. But I don't want to die. I thump my numb fingers against my bristly head, trying to stay awake. The sheen of sweat that once coated my hand flakes away, hardened into tiny crystals of white frost. And then my arms won't lift my hands anymore, so I sag down into Zahra and close my eyes.

If you die in your sleep, do you still dream?

The truck bounces to a stop.

The door slides open and heat pours into the back of the truck. The pain of warmth sweeps over us in waves. We mewl like cats, our skin unbroken sheets of flame.

Somebody shouts in Arabic: "A crate broke."

Then there are more words in Spanish. It reminds me of kindergarten in the city, the way our Spanish teacher came once a week to read picture books while we sat crisscross-applesauce on the rug. Spanish!

"Ceuta," I whisper, loud enough to knock Zahra against a crate of oranges. "We're in Ceuta."

A man climbs into the back of the truck and sees us. He freezes. The cold has locked our teeth together—we can't move or yell. I raise my arm to my ribs, my limp hand frozen into a fist.

Then the man is gone. Three border guards with guns climb up between the crates in his place. They haul us out of the truck and into the searing light. I wrap my arm through the strap of my burlap backpack, holding it in my elbow as tight as I can.

They put us in a van. Zahra and I collapse, my shoulder on her chest, her chin on the top of my head. Compared to the icy truck, the plastic seats are so hot they burn.

Out the back window, everything is green. Hills roll into the sea. A tall silver fence curves away from us into the elbow of low mountains. Square plaster houses with red tile roofs cluster up the sides of the hills and down into the valleys. In the distance, the city snakes down toward the Strait of Gibraltar, thinning to a narrow strip of land near the harbor before widening into the Península de Almina. A low mountain—Monte Hacho, the mountain Mama told me used to be called Abyla—stands watch over the strait like a whale's bent back. Fig and carob trees rise up, white poplars, dwarf pines. Thick stands of aloe shrink between the homes and roads.

I haven't seen so much green in weeks. My brain screams with it.

We come to houses in yellow, beige, rose, and white. The buildings sport satellite dishes, laundry lines, and weathervanes. Palms and orange trees line the streets. After the unbroken desert, I notice the hints of people everywhere: traffic signs. Streetlights. Fences and balconies. Garbage bins.

The van makes a turn. We wander down a hill and curve away from the houses. I press my face to the window. We head for a blank clearing on the edge of the city, lined by a high fence of wire mesh. Beyond the gate are dozens of boxy concrete bunkhouses.

"No." I grab Zahra's sleeve. "We came all this way. They can't put us in a camp." I try and get the driver's attention, behind the partition. "We have to get to my uncle. Nuestro tío. Tío."

But he can't hear me. Zahra slumps down, and I bury my face in her collarbone. We pass the tan concrete and drive through the red-and-white metal gate, past the mesh fence. The van brakes hard. I stare at my hands, clenching and unclenching them, and the muscles burn as feeling comes back.

Out the back window, the gates close.

They let us out of the van, and a policeman takes us into the camp. There are two levels, one upstairs that looks like offices and, on the ground, those matchbox bunkhouses. People stand outside, tapping at phones or chasing kids. Laundry dries everywhere, on fences and bushes and benches. A lady Mama's age strolls around handing out cigarettes to people who ask for them. She counts them, chatting in Spanish.

Another lady with short silver hair thanks the policeman and takes us upstairs. The room is crowded with metal filing cabinets, the desk cluttered with manila folders. In here, it's quiet, and the smells are different: the gray smell of cloth seat cushions, the green of metal. Stale perfume. Soap.

The lady gives us bottled water and takes down our names. She says we're in the CETI, the Centro de Estancia Temporal de Inmigrantes. It's where they keep refugees and migrants, she says.

"We've got to find our uncle Ma'mun," I tell her. I say it in English and Arabic and Spanish, searching her face.

But all she does is take down his name. "You will have to wait here until he comes for you," she says in Spanish.

"But what will happen to us?" I ask.

The lady softens. "You will have to wait for a decision on your case," she says. "You might be moved to a detention center, but here you can come and go as you please. You will stay in a shared room, with a bed to yourself. You'll find the showers nearby, when you'd like to get washed up. You can take Spanish classes."

Spanish classes? The thought hits me that this place is for processing people who have nowhere else to go, that people stay here a long time.

I turn to Zahra, mouthing the words in English: *We can't stay*.

The lady hands me an extra water bottle. "If you need help," she says, "talk to one of the madres—the women who do the rounds."

I ask, "What day is it?"

She blinks, stopping to think as she hands Zahra a green CETI card. "The first of October."

We are taken to a room with ten cots. I claim one, and Zahra takes the one next to me. She spreads out Mama's prayer rug between our beds, against the wall. It feels like saying a prayer.

Other families have decorated the walls around their beds, hung their laundry on the windowsills as if this is their home.

Who will come for us?

I think of the first idea of eternity I ever had. I had asked Baba about heaven and what it was like, and he said it went on forever. And I asked, What's forever?

At the time, we were standing in the bank at East Eighty-Sixth Street and York Avenue, and Baba was waiting to deposit a check. It felt like we had been waiting a long time, even though we probably weren't.

Baba said, Forever never stops.

So I imagined going into the bank and waiting all that time, and then leaving—only to come back in and do it all again. And again. And again.

And that, I figured, was forever.

THAT NIGHT, AFTER we eat spaghetti in the canteen, I rip off my broken sneakers. I throw them down and slump over my cot. Pigeons peck and waddle outside, and children chase them. Security guards stroll by the window, their belts and badges jangling. The little gray noises of the room make me nervous, the other families rustling and whispering like at the smugglers' house. There seem to be so many families in the world with no place to go, so many people tired of hurting but with no place to sleep.

Mama's burlap bag lies heavy in my lap, crinkled dry by desert air, still crusted with salt. If I strain my neck at the window, I can see past the walls of the CETI to the nose of Gibraltar. I imagine yellow daisies by the beach.

I open my burlap bag and try not to remember Mama's hands on it, tying the strap to make a backpack. I take out Mama's plastic shopping bag, the one I retied with the map inside. I unroll the limp canvas. The water didn't get in, so I must have tied the plastic tight.

I trace my finger backward along our route, back through Morocco, over the Sahara through Algeria, under Tunisia to Misrata. I skip the bowl of the Gulf of Sidra to Benghazi. I drag my fingernail along the sea to Alexandria, then Cairo. I rewind through Jordan to the hills of Amman where I got lost. Farther north, I pass the border crossing, then Damascus and the street called Straight. My finger stops in Homs.

I bore holes into the map with my eyes. I am the hawk who expected green where Manhattan was. I am the sea's onyx black, the dark hole through the middle of me. Without Mama, without Baba, without Huda.

It's living that hurts us.

"She said to follow the map, but it didn't work," I say to myself while Zahra sleeps. "We came all this way to be trapped behind a fence."

I take my fingernail and scratch out the color code for HOMS: brown square, white square, black, and red. I scratch it out and move on to the thick layer of green paint covering the whole of Syria, the layer that seems too fat and thick to belong there.

My hurt is a glob of red, slabs of bad colors throbbing inside me like a swollen kidney.

I scratch out whole sections of Syria, erasing Homs and the countryside. Maybe then the map will match how I feel, the way Baba felt: like I've lost a whole city in the pit of me, a whole country whose air I used to breathe.

I scratch until my fingernail hits ink.

Something is written underneath the paint—Arabic letters. I recognize the swooping *waw*, the sharp *kaaf*. It's Mama's handwriting, and I can read it.

After all this time, I can read Arabic at last.

I start at the first line, cracking my tongue on the consonants. "O beloved—" I sound out each syllable, translating from the Arabic. "O beloved, you are dying of a broken heart."

"What is that?" Zahra comes awake, rubbing her eyes.

"It was never just a map." I show Zahra Mama's words. "We've been running with ghosts."

I scratch at other countries, places we passed, places Mama pulled out her paints and colored inside the lines. More poems peek out from under thick paint.

Jordan and Egypt: *Beloved, I am blind.*

When we passed through Libya: *This ache has a thousand faces, this hunger two thousand eyes.*

I scratch out places Mama must have dreamed of seeing with us: Algeria. Morocco. Ceuta.

My name is a song I sing myself to remind me of my mother's voice.

Zahra slides out of bed. "She talks about everything that happened," she says. "The sad things. All the things she wished for."

We were carrying the weight of everything this whole time. "The words were on our backs," I say. I scan the map, picking at other borders. "It's a map of us."

Zahra says, "And all those cryptic stories our parents used to tell—Mama was right. The map was important."

I clench my hands at the corners of the map. "Then why isn't she here to see it?"

"Don't you get it?" Zahra says. "This isn't just a map of where we were going. It's a map of where we came from."

A bulb sparks on outside the window. The acrylic sucks up the dull yellow light. The glare blotches out the poem Mama wrote for Syria. For the first time in years, I think of something Mama told me when I was little: that when you make a map, you don't just paint the world the way it is. You paint your own.

I say, "It's a map of all the awful things that happened."

"But we're still here."

Anger spasms in my guts, the cramping ache of all my words that were buried with Baba, the words I can't get back. "But Mama's not here," I say, raising my voice, my own words straining orange and ruby with rage. "Huppy's not here. They never even got out of Libya. They're not coming, Zahra. I wish Mama's map sank with the boat and Mama were here instead. I want my family back."

"I know it's not enough," Zahra says. "Nothing can be how it was. But we did what we had to do." She touches her face as though she's trying to smooth away the scabby scar down her jaw, an automatic movement like something Mama would have done. "Maybe we're marked," she says, "but we made it."

I lower my eyes to the missing city on Mama's map. "Poems aren't enough."

"I know." Zahra takes my face in her hands. Dust has collected in the cracks in her lips and over the bruised, delicate skin under her eyes. She draws us together, so close I can see tracks in the dust. In the dark, she has been crying. "But as long as you're alive," she says, "you have a voice. You're the one who has to hear it."

The cramping in my belly gets worse, a full, aching sensation. I say, "I don't know what happens next."

"We keep going," Zahra says. "We can still look for Uncle Ma'mun."

I run my hands over the bag. I carried our memories all this way, the story of what happened to us. It was heavy on my shoulder this whole time, but I didn't fall down.

I lift my hands and touch my back, the wings of my shoulder blades. I'm still in one piece, but my body isn't the same as when I left Syria. It's not the same as when I left New York. My skin is different, the patterns of my goose bumps, the cliffs of my ribs. I've got longer legs. I've got carved-out bones.

I press my hands to my face. I am someone I don't recognize. My nose is a sharp hill, my lips thicker. These miles have carved me. Time has a sculptor's hands. You don't even notice them.

The pain in my belly grows, a dull speck of heat. I press my hands into skin and muscle, wanting to scoop out the red pulp of myself. My neck is a narrow highway. My sternum is as hard as crab shell. I think about putting my hand into my pocket where I keep the half-stone. Is there magic left in the world? If I touch that stone, could I hear Baba's voice again? Or is he more in my bones than the earth?

My hand brushes the cord around my neck. Mama's shard of blue-and-white tile warms the skin under my shirt. I've rounded the tile by rubbing, smoothing out the sharpness of memory.

The fountain.

"I know where we have to go." I grasp the tile and pull the necklace out for Zahra to see. "I know how to find Uncle Ma'mun."

But Zahra looks down. "Nour—you're bleeding."

I look down. My shorts are stained red-brown between my legs, a dark, sticky blotch.

I say the first thing I think of: "I guess you were right."

"Right about what?"

"About being grown-up." I tap my chest. My heart, that lopsided muscle, clenches and sighs. "You bleed."

PART V

CEUTA

                    I
            returned at
daybreak. I passed the
    avenue where we used to
        walk when we were young
            and lovely, the streets we
            roamed restless under the horn   of the
                moon. The world was young,   then, and more
                lovely than we knew how to hold.   Once,   everything we knew
            we thought we'd have forever. Your   finger-   tips, the blood
            pulsing in my neck, that warm space on   the rug my   grandmother
            wove for us. I am tracing the borders of her hands. Cold   oceans of time have
            changed what I once loved, but is my skin not a rope? Is my   blood not an
        ocean? Is my bone not a mast? Are our tears not the same   breach, a dirge
            for all we know and love? Are they not the same tide,
                the same salt? The broad white albatross of
                    longing sweeps over me. I carry the
                        memory of borders in
                    my   skin.

Homecoming

*

From the Strait of Gibraltar, Ceuta was a dark, narrow strip of land on the horizon.

The ship groaned around Punta Almina and entered the Bay of Ceuta, where the harbor lay. It had been a month since they left Palermo. Al-Idrisi clapped his hand to his breast at the sight of Mount Abyla, which overlooked the harbor. The city stretched out thin and white before them, the houses shining in the afternoon light.

Al-Idrisi leaned on the rail, swallowing sea air. It had been more than two decades since he had crossed this stretch of water in the opposite direction, headed away from home.

"At last," he said, "I return."

Beyond the peninsula lay rolling fields and olive groves, the rising mountains Rawiya knew from her childhood. The hills would be painted with eucalyptus and pine and the dots of mud-plaster houses. One of them, nestled in the tiny coastal village of Benzú, was the house she had been born in. Beyond that, the desert stretched its fingers to the south, and Ifriqiya watched the sun drown its fire in the sea.

They stepped off the ship, leading their horses. Rawiya stroked Bauza's neck. "Is everything here?" she asked. "The books, the maps? Your research and notes?"

Al-Idrisi smiled. "O Lady Rawiya, always with an eye to detail."

He rubbed his bent back and his silver chin, studying the bags and tapping each one. "Yes," he said at last, "everything is here."

"And what of your family?" Rawiya asked. "Where will you go?"

"I cannot rightly say," al-Idrisi said. "My parents are long dead. The family home may remain. I, however, am the last of my line."

They led the horses past rows of white, yellow, and rose-colored homes and stands of eucalyptus and orange trees. Ships appeared between the harbor and the Rock of Gibraltar, their sails white and full as feathers. Hills rose green before them, and they trudged upward.

It was autumn, and the heat had broken. The sky threatened rain, swollen with gray-faced storm clouds. They crested a hill and stood at the side of the road, resting their horses. Ceuta surged with merchants crossing the peninsula. The road narrowed to a thin strip, a rocky neck of land not wider than fifty men laid head to toe. Dusty travelers scrambled for shelter before the rain, and here and there, women shooed their children toward home. The setting sun turned the western clouds pink over the Sea of Darkness.

"I once heard of a group of brothers, intrepid adventurers who set out to cross those waters," al-Idrisi said, pointing west. "They came back raving of fantastic creatures, strange islands, sheep with bitter meat, and a sea of foggy, foul-smelling waters. A storm turned them back, and they were returned to the Maghreb by way of an uncharted island. No one has yet succeeded in crossing the Sea of Darkness. Someday, I am sure. As with everything, someday we will see what lies beyond."

They dropped into a valley and began to climb again. The homes grew larger and more elegant, and the noise of the city fell away. They passed stately gardens thick with palms not unlike the ones in the palace garden at Palermo, the ones Rawiya and al-Idrisi had hidden under while the palace burned. Remembering the bitter taste of palm ash, Rawiya slipped her hand into Khaldun's.

They led their horses up a winding path toward a large estate. "Just as I left it," al-Idrisi said at the gates, "if a bit dusty at the windows."

They entered the riad's gardens as it began to rain, ducking under the lazy branches of white poplars. A fountain stood, empty and unused, in a central courtyard. Rainwater pooled inside, rippling over blue-and-white tiles.

They dismounted. Behind them, the Rock of Gibraltar lined up perfectly with the cobblestone street.

Al-Idrisi pushed open the front door, blowing dust and cobwebs from the engraved wood. Within the house, all was quiet. The floor tiles echoed under their footsteps. The walls sighed with years. Al-Idrisi curled his hand around a thick layer of dust on a long table, and gray stuck to the side of his palm.

Rawiya drifted to the corners of the rooms where decorative caligraphy and textiles hung. Wooden boxes inlaid with mother-of-pearl lined a single shelf.

She opened one. It creaked open at its hinges, revealing a string of thirty-three lapis lazuli prayer beads with a silver tassel.

"My mother's misbaha." Al-Idrisi slipped the prayer beads from the box and shut the lid. "I wanted to take them with me when I left, but I knew we would face dangers and bandits."

He pulled a second string of beads from his pocket, dull tan husks strung on a cord. "Olive seeds," he said. "These are more economical. They were a gift from my mother before I traveled to Anatolia." His hand cast a long shadow over the couches, the table, the wall.

Rawiya steadied her trembling hands and fingered her own prayer beads in her pocket, the wooden misbaha her mother had given her when she had first left home more than seven years before. Even the familiar scent of the air called to mind her mother's face now. Outside in the courtyard, shearwaters and petrels whistled and preened themselves in the rain.

"I don't think I've seen a home so lovely in all my life," Rawiya said.

Al-Idrisi laughed. "You've seen Roger's palace and Nur ad-Din's. Someday this dusty house will be rubble. They will build again on this hill, but my home will be long gone. How could my modest treasures be more lasting, more lovely than those of emirs and kings?"

"Wealth is no substitute for belonging." Rawiya bowed her head, closing her fingers around the misbaha in her pocket. "Excuse me," she said. "There is something I have to do."

Al-Idrisi looked away down empty corridors toward jewel-crusted windows, their red velvet curtains dulled by age. His eyes roamed the wooden doors engraved with Qur'anic calligraphy, now warped by sea air.

"If I had someone to come home to," al-Idrisi said quietly, "I would go too." He gently shut the box he held, releasing loops of dust and cobwebs. "I will await your return."

RAWIYA AND KHALDUN mounted their horses and descended the hill. The rain stopped, the thunderheads lumbering off over the cliffs of Jebel Musa. Bauza flicked his mane and swung his neck, breaking up clouds of sparrows. It was as though being back in Ceuta again had returned some of his youth to him. Though it had finally come to pass that Bauza had grown old while Rawiya was still young, she took comfort in the thought that he would soon be, at long last, home.

They rode out along the coastal road toward red-tinged Gibraltar until night had nearly fallen. The rocky coast yielded to mountains of red clay and pines hugged by low clouds. Everything was hushed.

Colorful houses in the distance marked the approach to the village of Benzú. Rawiya sat back in her saddle and ran her fingers over the thirty-three wooden beads of her mother's misbaha. The closer she drew to her mother's house, the more deeply sadness and guilt burrowed into the center of her.

"My mother has had no news of me for years," Rawiya said. "She must think I am dead. Why did I lie to her about my trip to the market in Fes? I should have told her of my plans. I never knew so much would happen, that my journey would take me so far away for so long."

"You were still a child," Khaldun said. "You are grown now, a warrior. Everything has changed."

Rawiya patted Bauza's neck. He picked up his pace as they approached the familiar hill that led to her mother's house. Breathing deep of the salt air, Rawiya gave Khaldun a sly grin. "Not everything."

She laughed and urged Bauza on. Though he had grown old in the years they had spent in Palermo, he had more strength left in him than some foals. "Yalla, dear friend," she whispered in his ear. "Let's run this hill one last time."

Bauza raced down the familiar road, pounding the earth with his hooves. Khaldun followed her, laughing. They galloped into the village nestled at the foot of the mountains until Bauza came to a stop in front of a tiny stone and plaster house, its front walk shaded by a fig tree.

Rawiya lowered herself from the saddle, feeding Bauza a bit of date sugar from her pocket. The village houses faced Gibraltar, looking out over the olive grove. She gazed up at the first stars appearing and then out at the bay, empty of ships.

Khaldun dismounted and tied his horse to the fig tree. "Is this the place?" When Rawiya said nothing, he came over to her. "What's wrong?"

"I tried to do only good." A sea breeze ruffled her red turban and billowed her sirwal. "But it leaves so much mending to be done."

"We rarely know," Khaldun said, "when we try to do good, if the outcomes of our actions will actually be good." He laughed to himself. "Perhaps God plans it that way, to teach us that the planning is best left to him."

The first constellations waggled their heads like shy children. Rawiya patted Bauza's neck. "The calves are still turning the gristmill," she said.

Khaldun lifted his hand. "And whatever men do, they will go on turning it, and always, always, the broken world goes on."

"We should go in." Rawiya glanced at the red tile roof, the gnarled fig. She let out her breath. "It's so strange to see things the same. My mother once visited Fes as a child, when my grandfather sold olives in the market. She never forgot." She ran her fingers over the cracked wooden door. "She understood more than I knew."

Khaldun laid a hand on her arm. "Knock," he said. "Knock and return home."

And so Rawiya of the desert and the stars laid her hand on the wood and rapped at the door.

Nothing.

Rawiya frowned. No candles shone in the inner rooms. The door was locked, and for a moment, terror gripped Rawiya that the house had been abandoned. "My God, do you think . . . ?"

Khaldun walked behind the house, searching for light. They passed low words between them, both reluctant to say aloud what might have befallen Rawiya's mother in the intervening years. But Rawiya stalked back to the road, for she knew that if her mother were still alive, there was only one place she would go each evening, when sorrow and loneliness became unbearable.

Rawiya took off at a run for the olive grove. Khaldun flew after her, stumbling and throwing up dust.

She reached it first, panting. The moon hung low and fat as a turnip. The breeze carried the rustling hiss of waves. Rawiya crossed between the olive trees, darting glances through the branches. All was empty.

She came out of the grove onto the rocky shore where she had stood many times with her father. This was the place she had stood after his death, waiting for her brother's ship to come in. Her feet shuffled pebbles from their nooks, clicking seashells into stones. As she squinted down the beach, her toes nudged seaweed.

A dark figure near the surf stiffened at the sound of stones moving.

The figure turned, clutching a scarf around its neck. The shape of a woman emerged from the night, moonlight damp on her shoulders. The years that had come between them fell away, and it was as though not a day had passed since Rawiya had bid farewell to her mother that day the wind came strong off the strait.

"Mama?"

Rawiya's widowed mother, bent and white-haired, began to run. She dashed across the rocks, her arms outstretched.

Rawiya rushed toward her mother's wide grin. The waves drowned out their voices until they were almost upon each other.

"Rawiya!"

Her mother's face seared itself into shock and joy and wonder. She opened her arms wide, and Rawiya fell into them like deep water, warm and full and breathless.

"I thought I would never see you again," Rawiya said.

Her mother stroked away the tears on her daughter's cheek with her thumb and smiled. "I never gave up hope."

Rawiya kissed both her mother's cheeks and the top of her head. "It is late," she said. "You should be at home. Were you waiting for Salim? The ships were in the harbor hours ago."

"I was waiting for you." Her mother touched her face with both hands. "They told me you had been kidnapped, sold to brigands, killed. They told me you had run away. I never believed a word."

"I promised you I would come home." Rawiya pulled back and opened the leather bag slung around her chest. She tugged out Bakr's red-and-blue silk scarf and pressed it into her mother's hands. "A gift from someone who wanted to be here," she said. "Someone who would want you to know I never abandoned you."

They walked back through the olive grove, and Rawiya told her mother of her companions and her journey: Palermo, Bilad ash-Sham, Cairo, the battle at Barneek.

As they came to the road, they met Khaldun coming toward them. He called, "Did you find her?"

Rawiya's mother gathered her long skirt in her fist and hurried across the ten-pace distance between them. She wrapped her arms around Khaldun. "Poet," she said, "tonight you are a guest in my house. Tonight, you are family."

Rawiya's mother pushed open the door, and the hinges creaked and wobbled. And though she had promised to tell Rawiya everything, Rawiya held her breath. The bite of salt had invaded the house, and the sharp smell of the sea had settled on the tile and the curtains. The scent conjured Rawiya's brother, Salim, and even though she knew he must have perished at sea long ago—why else would her mother have given up waiting for him at the shore, and waited for Rawiya's return instead?—it felt as though Salim was still in the house, the salt smell of his rough hands coating everything.

Rawiya's mother lit a candle, and they shook off the chill. The bedrooms were full of shadows. As Rawiya took off her cloak, her mother called out into the darkness: "Come out," she said. "Come and see the wonders God's hands have worked!"

From the bedroom, a bent figure shuffled out, aided by a walking stick. His beard had turned an early gray, and his face was gaunt, but Rawiya would have known him anywhere.

"Salim!" She ran to her brother, hugging him around his ribs. Salim hugged her to him with one arm, balancing himself with his walking stick, for he had been injured at sea and ended his career as a sailor a year before. Salim kissed his sister's cheek. For several long minutes, neither of them could get out a single word, so heavy with joy was their weeping.

Rawiya's mother sat them down and brewed a pot of mint tea. She brought out the best food she had: fine flour and a fat jug of oil, fresh bonito wrapped in linen. The fish's scales glimmered, its gills red.

While her mother cooked, Rawiya spoke of her journeys with al-Idrisi, of their meeting in the market, of visiting King Roger's palace in Palermo, of the defeat of the roc, of how she and her friends had fought their way through giant snakes and three armies to retrieve al-Idrisi's book from the Almohad general, Mennad. She touched the spot where the roc had cracked her ribs, the skin over her heart that had healed into a crooked scar.

When she had finished her tale, Rawiya and Khaldun hauled a chest full of gems and coins from their luggage and set it on the floor. It was Rawiya's share of Nur ad-Din's treasure.

"I have no use for it now," Rawiya said. "It is better that it goes to you."

Salim, who had never seen such wealth in all his life, touched the top of the chest with his walking stick. The chest was inlaid with hundreds of jewels. "This chest alone could feed us for the rest of our lives," he said.

"And you will never have to take to the sea again," Rawiya said, and she embraced him.

Rawiya's mother set before them steaming clay bowls of couscous and pomegranate seeds and broad dishes filled with pastel de bonito, a fish pie Rawiya had been raised on. Tonight was a night of celebration, and Rawiya's mother had prepared the best she had.

When they were all seated, Rawiya cleared her throat and spoke again. "The poets say God rains riches on us even in the wasteland," she said, "and they speak truth. No king could make me any richer." She reached over and caught Khaldun's hand. "We wish to be wed here, where I was born."

Her mother bowed her head. "My child," she said, "you have been blessed with great honor and returned to me. How can I tell God the depths of my joy?"

At her words, Rawiya wept, for she knew how painfully her mother had missed her. "I promise I will never leave you that way again," Rawiya said. "I would have never left that way had I known—"

Rawiya's mother waved her words away. "What does that matter to me now," she said, "when God has given me back my lost child?" High above the house, the last of the gulls rode the sea wind toward their night roosts, calling at the moon. Rawiya's mother grasped both

Rawiya's and Khaldun's hands. "My daughter is called mapmaker's apprentice, brave warrior, roc slayer. Throughout the village of Benzú and the city of Ceuta, you will be known as an enemy of tyrants for years to come. If this is the one you love—the poet-warrior Khaldun of Bilad ash-Sham—no other match for you could be so brave and noble. We have been richly blessed."

"They say the desert is barren and blank as a person's palm," Rawiya said. "But the desert, like a difficult year, is alive with blessings." She kissed her mother's fingers. "I found more there than I was looking for. I found myself."

*   *   *

ZAHRA AND I go to the showers to wash my shorts until the blood comes out. It's almost morning. The madres patrol the CETI, and the lady who finds us gives me a box of pads. I scrub the brown smudge with a hunk of soap and cold water, and my fingernails collect pink foam. The pulsing ache in my belly makes me feel powerful and strong.

I sit down on my cot and swing my legs. "I know what we have to do. I know what we're looking for."

"All you have is a guess, and you can't search a whole city on a guess." Zahra takes Yusuf's pocketknife and begins to cut, pulling the last of our money from the tongues of my sneakers. "This isn't a game. It's not like Uncle Ma'mun's house is on the map with an X-marks-the-spot."

I roll up Mama's prayer rug and pack it with the map. I say, "Guessing is better than nothing."

Zahra moves toward the door without looking up. "I'm not leaving things up to chance anymore."

I spring up with my backpack and follow her out past the other bunkhouses, the empty plaza. Outside, the morning is gray like old chocolate, and the wind drags warmth from the south.

"You stay here while I go to the city offices," Zahra says. "Maybe they can tell me Uncle Ma'mun's address. Someone must know him."

"Why won't you listen to me?" I grab her wrist, then her hand. Her bony knuckles bruise the last of the baby fat in my palms. "I know what to do."

She twists to face me, trying to pull herself free, but I won't let go. Fifteen paces ahead of us, a long-jowled man pulls a key ring from his pocket and unlocks the CETI gate.

"Let me go," she says.

We plant our feet and curl our bodies, leaning in and back in an awkward tug-of-war. Zahra fights to extricate herself from my grip. As we scuffle, one of the madres saunters over and watches us. She carries a wary look on her face, her eyes still half-lidded with sleep, her pocket bulging with a box of cigarettes.

"I'm telling you I know," I say.

Zahra pushes my hands, ringing her wrist with her own fingers like a cuff. "Do you know what would have happened to us if they hadn't opened that truck?" she whispers. "Do you have any idea?"

I lock my knuckles against Zahra's, the damp salt of her sweat oiling my hands. The humid morning strokes the red-and-white blisters on my legs, the cold's fingerprints. Zahra stares me down, slipping my hands off her wrist like invisible bracelets. Her scar ripples her jaw like a bruise on the skin of an olive, the same way these blisters will leave pale opals of scar tissue on my shins. I think to myself, life draws blood and leaves its jewelry in our skin.

Just like Mama's, the veins in Zahra's bloodshot eyes are a road-map of fear.

"You can't go without me," I say. I plant my feet and clamp my hand down on Zahra's arm. I tug her toward me, away from the gate.

"Let go." She wrestles with me. We shuffle dust with our sneakers. "Let go!"

"Hey!" The madre intervenes, pulling us apart. "What is going on here?"

Zahra moves off at a clip toward the gate.

"My sister wants to leave me here by myself," I say.

It doesn't work. "If she has something to do," the madre says, "we will watch you."

The madre keeps a firm grip on my shoulder. I watch Zahra's shoulders disappear beyond the CETI entrance.

"Your sister will be back," the madre says.

I say, "You don't know that."

The madre studies me, then laughs. "The small ones always have the biggest mouths on them." She thumbs the box of cigarettes in her pocket.

"I'm going after her." I start for the gate, shifting my backpack. "She needs my help."

"Hey, now. Oye!" The madre grabs the strap of my backpack. "Little girls don't leave the CETI by themselves. Breakfast is at eight. Until then, you can watch television in the canteen."

Between my legs, the pad is a heavy, scratchy lump. Fine hairs dust the madre's upper lip, the kind that started appearing on mine in the last few weeks. I scratch my belly through the waistband of my shorts and know that I will never wear a belt with a metal buckle again.

I say, "I'm not a little girl."

The madre shifts her weight and puts her hands on her hips. "Come upstairs with me, then."

I follow the madre into one of the offices. She opens her desk, takes out a few pieces of hard candy, and drops them in my hand.

"Go on," she says. "They're sweet."

The tail of my nerves flicks against my ribs. I am too hungry to say no, so I unwrap a candy and pop it in my mouth. But I haven't had a hard candy in so long that instead of sucking on it, I chew. The madre laughs.

"We were away so long," I say with my mouth full. "We didn't always have food."

"Pobrecita," the madre says, and under her unimpressed air, I can tell she really does feel sorry for me. "All that is over. You will have three meals every day, and tomorrow the bus will come and take the children to school. You are here now, safe."

"But I have to go," I say. "I have to find my uncle who lives in Ceuta—"

I see a curl of teal and pops of gray when a voice rises to the window from the courtyard below. I turn my face to the window, following the colors. The teal and gray belong to a throaty voice I can't forget. Below the window, by the CETI gate, it spills out from a lanky boy's ribs and shoulder blades.

"Yusuf!" I run to the window. I struggle to yank it open, but it's locked. I bang on the glass. "Yusuf!"

His black locks bob toward the CETI entrance as he nods hello to one of the guards. Then he passes by and lets his shoulders slump, his hands in his pockets. He's still wearing the same gray tee shirt he had on when I watched him slip away down a Benghazi street.

I bolt for the door and clang down the steps. I'm halfway down by the time the madre calls for security. The policemen come running, blocking the bottom of the stairs.

I turn around and run back up, breezing past the madre.

"Oye," she calls. "Don't run! Do you hear?"

A guard grabs for me. I dodge to one side, slamming my thigh into the side of the bunkhouse wall. Something snaps and cracks in my pocket, but I don't have time to look to see what it is.

The opposite set of stairs is swarmed with security guards. The windows fill with the curious faces of other CETI families. In the courtyard, people playing soccer stop and look up.

I run along the railing on the upper level, looking for another way down. I come to a spot where a couple of laundry lines are tied from the railing to a balcony below. Below me is a flat bunkhouse roof.

The madre and the security guards huff toward me. Above their heads, a gray-and-black bird leaps from a rooftop into the air, its tiny toes curling.

Where is Zahra now, drifting through the world that swallowed my family and marked us all?

I grab the railing and haul myself over. The metal is cool as a river bottom. Taking hold of the laundry line, I fling myself off.

It holds my weight at first. Halfway to the bunkhouse, the line buckles. I reach out with both arms and grab the roof. I pull myself up, scraping my elbows on the concrete.

On the ground, the guards rush down the stairs toward me. The men have spread a carpet in the courtyard for morning prayers. As the guards run by, the kneeling men look up at me, silent and confused.

I run to the opposite edge of the roof. The bunkhouse comes right to the green fence that marks the edge of the CETI. Beyond is the side of a hill with scattered bushes and pine trees. It looks close enough that I could jump, with a little luck and a running start.

Below me, between the fence and the hill, is a sharp drop. A canyon has been sliced into the cliff to make room for the CETI wall, leaving an open gash. The drop is about six feet wide and more than twenty feet deep.

"Stop!" The madre jogs toward me.

I back up a few steps.

"Come down," the madre shouts. "Wait until your sister comes. Climb down from there."

I bend my knees, and heat fills my blistered calves.

I get a running start and jump from the roof, over the fence and the wide drop. I hang in the air, my legs flailing, my arms stretched out to catch the hillside. Sunlight tangles in the half inch of my hair, my scars stretching.

It's the opposite of being in the dark bushes. Electricity pummels every bone in my body. I throb with heat. I am alive.

I land hard, my backpack slamming into my shoulder blades. I slide a few feet down the hill before I catch hold of the roots of a pine tree. I scramble up, scraping my nails in the dirt, scattering orange pine needles.

I run for the forest, leaving the shouting behind.

I jog out to the road that leads away from the CETI entrance. I don't know how far down I am or where I've popped out, but I push on. My worn sneakers pound the pavement, the asphalt burning calluses on the bottom of my feet. I am surrounded by pine forest. I listen for that teal-gray voice, for any voice. I hear nothing.

I stop to catch my breath. I call out, "Yusuf?"

White birds call from the shore, crossing the strait.

I've lost him.

I zigzag from one side of the path to the other, peering into the forest. I climb into the forked elbow of a tree to get a better look down the road, but I can't reach the high branches.

I cup my hands to my mouth and yell. "Yusuf!"

My voice echoes between the pine trunks.

I sit down in the middle of the road and put my head between my knees. Dead pine needles stick to my shorts and glue themselves between my shoelaces.

I reach into my pocket and feel shards of wood, slicing my finger on naked metal. I hiss and wince and pull out the pieces of Yusuf's broken pocketknife. When I slammed into the bunkhouse wall, the impact must have cracked apart the wood and steel. My finger bleeds.

Tears come hot in my throat. If I had been faster, if I had been smarter, if I had been bigger—I felt so big hanging in the air. Why do I feel so small?

Footsteps crunch the asphalt behind me. I turn, bracing a hand on the pavement.

"Nour?"

A teal-gray voice. A gray tee shirt. A three-week beard.

"Yusuf!"

I get up and run. I crash into Yusuf in the middle of the road, the pines dropping their needles in the breeze, salt thick in the air.

I bury my face in his tee shirt. His heart thuds in his stomach. "I thought I dreamed you," I say. The blade of Yusuf's pocketknife bites into my palm. "I thought no one remembered us."

Yusuf wraps an elbow around my shoulders and bends to press his cheek to my ear. "Then we have to remember each other," he says.

"But you came all the way here," I say. "How?"

"There was too much fighting in Libya," Yusuf says. "Did we come all that way to hear the shots in our sleep again? So we kept on. The sea journey was too dangerous, but we could still continue west. It was Spain for us. Ceuta was the only place."

"I have to find my uncle Ma'mun," I say. "Mama said he lives here, or he used to."

"Ummi, Sitti, and Rahila are at the CETI canteen," he says, then pauses. "And your sisters?"

I wring heat out of my face with the back of my hand. "Zahra is in town. Huda—"

He takes my hand. "One thing at a time," he says. "Let's find Zahra."

We walk until the forest pulls back from the road, and the city sprawls out below us. The harbor curls away like an open hand. The buildings are matchboxes of white, yellow, and pink. Seagulls coast over our heads. The salt sticks to my hair and puffs it, making tight rings of curls.

Far down the ribbon of road, a figure trudges toward the city, jeans ripped at the hems, sneaker soles black with walking.

"Zahra!"

We tumble down the hill, shouting. Zahra turns. When she sees us, she presses her hands to her face and then holds them out in front of her, like she's trying to catch something God is dropping in her hands.

Yusuf and I run into her, grabbing each other around the shoulders and the waist, laughing. We collapse together on the side of the road, our arms and legs tangled, knit up by joy.

"How did you get here?" She looks at me twice before she sees me. "I told you to stay in the CETI."

Yusuf holds Zahra tight by her forearms. They kneel, facing each other, the tops of their heads level with my shoulders. "We crossed the border three nights ago, a group of us," Yusuf says. "Sitti and Rahila went in the trunks of cars, one after the other, but Ummi and I were turned away. We were desperate. We took a rowboat into the harbor." His eyes shift toward the strait before he blinks. "I applied for asylum for all of us."

Zahra grins, the kind of stupefied grin that could equally lead to laughing or to tears. Under her eyes, the sea boils.

"Do you know what this means?" Yusuf draws her forehead toward his, as though what he's trying to say can leap through his skin into her bones. "I am staying. If your family can apply for asylum, if you can stay too—"

Her knees still scuffing the grass, Zahra wraps her arms around Yusuf and kisses him. And then she pulls me in and kisses the top of my head where my hair, just long enough now to form tiny curls, has been rubbed with dirt. The air between us is sharp with salt and sweat.

The three of us pull apart and stand. We look down toward the city with its clusters of homes like pearls and olive seeds and red clay.

"What do we do now?" Zahra asks.

I lift the tile at the end of my necklace and pull out the freed blade of Yusuf's pocketknife. I slice the silver cord. The round, broken piece of blue-and-white tile drops into my hand.

"We find Uncle Ma'mun."

WE DIP DOWN to the peninsula from the forest toward the stucco and plaster buildings. We curve around bicycles, down palm-lined streets and narrow alleys. We can see the beach from almost every-where, the shoreline with its stones like cut glass. We pass the white balconies of hotels. We pass parking meters and latticed fences. We pass rose gardens.

We search the city through the afternoon and into evening, but we don't find a house with a fountain in blue-and-white tile.

At the top of one hill, we watch the sun start down. I sit under an orange tree, my legs splayed out on the sidewalk, and stare down the bowl of the sun. The broken tile digs into my hand. Where are Mama and Huda tonight? Did someone bury them the way Rawiya and her friends buried Bakr? I know God heard them both the same at the end, that he loved them both equally even though their prayers were different. I wonder if whoever buried them knew it.

Out here, the sounds of the city seem farther off. The street bends away from us. Behind us, up the hill, are bigger, older houses, the kind with walled courtyards and gardens and elegant tile roofs. I glance at them over my shoulder. All I see is our house in Homs that Zahra still has the key to, our own broken roof.

Zahra and Yusuf sit down next to me, facing the sea. Ancient poplars stretch their arms between the buildings, like the city grew up around them when they weren't looking. In the east, the night is coming from Syria. Somewhere, Itto is guiding her camel into the dark.

Yusuf leans over to me. "I love your sister very much," he says. "I want us to be a family."

I lift my face from the cobblestones. "I'd like that." I pull out the remaining pieces of his pocketknife. "I'm sorry," I say. "I took it across the desert in the fruit truck, and it got pulp on it. And then I ran into a wall before I jumped, and it got broken in my pocket."

Yusuf holds the two pieces of wood and the bent blade in his hands, studying the splinters and the tarnished steel. He fits the pieces back together, tucking the metal back between the wood, until the pocketknife is a pocketknife again. He opens his palm, feeling the heft of the mended knife as though being broken isn't something that destroys you.

He smiles. "Fruit pulp is nothing," he says.

Down the hill, the sea is marbled with whitecaps. Zahra leans out and picks up a pebble from the curb. "Did you know where the Arabic name for Ceuta comes from?" she says.

I shake my head.

"In Arabic, Ceuta is Sabta," she says. "It comes from the Latin *septum*, meaning seven."

"Why?"

"Because the city is built on seven hills." Zahra tosses the pebble in the gutter.

"I never knew that." I think of the seven sisters of the Pleiades and shift my legs under me so I can see farther down. The cobblestones melt into each other in the distance. Through the night haze, the Rock of Gibraltar lifts its chin, lining up perfectly with the street.

"I know this." I stand up, my belly humming with heat. "I've seen this view before."

"That's not funny," Zahra says.

"No, I know this hill," I say. "This is the hill from the story, the one al-Idrisi's house was built on. He said they would build here again. They did."

I run in the opposite direction, away from the sun, toward the houses on the hill. I pass gardens and palmettos, terraced roofs with satellite dishes, arched windows and iron fences. I run until my chest burns.

I turn a corner and brace my hands on my knees to catch my breath. Zahra and Yusuf run up behind me. I scan the lots, big houses with many-windowed faces.

There, in front of me, is a three-gabled house of pink stone. Facing the street is a wrought-iron fence twisted into flowers and long-tailed birds. Between the gate and the house is a garden with a fountain.

"I see it!"

Zahra scrambles up the hill. "See what?"

"I see the fountain." I run to the gate. "Lift me up."

Yusuf picks me up under my armpits, and I get a foothold on the gate. I swing my legs over and jump down into the garden. The sun is just dropping into the sea behind me, making long shadows.

A cracked old fountain, the water drained, sits in front of the big house with its carved wooden door. Palm trees and ferns rustle. Pigeons settle in for the night, cooing soft blue and purple.

I walk up to the basin. I peer through a side window of the house, into a courtyard, but nobody comes. I set my hands on the rim.

There, in the center of the old fountain, is an empty space. The tiles are mostly square, forming a delicate design of flowers and vines in blue and white. But in the center is a space for a circular tile that's still missing. Only rough grout is left.

I hop into the fountain. I reach out with my broken piece of tile and set it into the empty space in the center.

Except for a sliver missing on the left side, it fits perfectly.

I whisper, "This is the place."

"Nour?" Zahra and Yusuf wait on the curb, glancing nervously.

I leave the tile in the fountain and hop back out in the growing dark. I walk to the door of the gabled house. There's a moment I remember you can never build things the same way twice, and I wonder if I've got things figured out after all, if anything in the world can stay the same.

I knock anyway.

A tall man with a round potbelly comes out. His hair is thinning around his ears, just like Baba's, and his eyes are wide and brown with long lashes. At first I'm sure I've seen him somewhere before, he looks so familiar. But then he squints at me in the shadows and frowns, and I doubt myself.

"Yes? Who are you?" he asks in Spanish.

I try to say my name, but nothing comes out. In the pit of my stomach, something whispers that I'm wrong, and the fear turns my throat and lungs to stone.

I lift my chin and force a smile. The name comes. "Rawiya."

"Rawiya?" The man repeats it like I've said something that has jogged his memory. He bends toward me, and the last of the light catches him. He wears a thick knitted sweater with a shawl at the neck, like a sailor might wear to watch the sea. He hasn't shaved his beard in days. It's grown wild, spreading like wisteria up his cheeks, tangling in his sideburns, and curling down his neck into the collar of his sweater.

He looks toward the street and sees Zahra and Yusuf gripping the gate. Has he got Baba's eyes and nose, or is it only my imagination?

"I fixed your fountain." I forget to use my Spanish, but I stand my ground, licking salt from my lips. "Mama gave me the last tile."

The man says, "The tile?"

"She said it's hard to make something the same way twice." I raise my face. "Uncle Ma'mun?"

"Ya Allah!" he says. "Nour? You look so much like your baba." He wraps his arms around me. "Come in," he bellows to Zahra and Yusuf. He lumbers down the path toward the gate. "Hamdulillah! Come in. You made it all this way!"

"You knew we were coming?" I lope after him through the ferns.

Uncle Ma'mun lets Zahra and Yusuf in through the gate and hugs them both, lifting Zahra off her feet. "I will not have my family standing on my step like vagabonds," he says. "Come inside."

We go in. The sparrows hush in the courtyard with its cool stones and arched doors. Uncle Ma'mun leads us through a warm kitchen, past a raw wood table that looks like it was carved from driftwood. It's been smoothed by hands and years, polished with spilled oil. The soft wood is rippled with burls. Somewhere fish stew is cooking, giving off that warm, heady smell I remember from Sitt Shadid's kitchen—the smell of home.

The smell is so comforting and familiar that I stand rigid on the tile, rooted and overwhelmed. The sudden shock of safety makes me feel like I'm going to die from my heart hammering its relief into my chest.

Uncle Ma'mun shoos us through the house, and we pick up speed as we go. We jog upstairs, then down a hall lined with bedrooms. A single door stands cracked, a salt breeze clinging to the jamb. I see the curtains first, white linen and lace. Then curls of soft lavender paint themselves over my vision: I smell roses.

I swallow around a hard lump in my throat. A woman sits at the window, her back to us, watching the strait.

It comes back: Huda in the bed in the Damascus hospital, blood on the bandages. I draw closer. I swallow air, looking for the scent of death, but none comes. The sharp yellow of that salt smell is overpowering at first. Then, behind it, comes red and violet, the smell of pomegranates and flowers, the smell that got swallowed up in Manhattan by Mama's tears.

"Mama?"

The woman turns from the window. "Habibti!"

I throw myself to the window, grabbing Mama with both arms, tangling us in the curtain. She wraps her arms around me, rocking me against her ribs. I feel the band of her amber ring on the back of my neck. Her smell is everywhere: between my eyelashes, in the bristles of my short hair. It's the smell of Syria, as though I never left home.

"I read what was underneath," I say into her blouse. "I know what happened to us. I know the story by heart."

"You didn't need a map to tell you that," Mama says, her lips to the crown of my head. "You have the map of that inside you."

I can't hold my question in. I pull back. "Huppy?"

Behind me comes the strained husk of a voice: "Ya Nouri?"

And that shiver goes through me, the same one I felt in the funeral home when I saw it was Baba's body on the slab. That feeling that came first, before the sticky dread of death: the tingling feeling of blood rushing out of my scalp, joy like overwhelming terror. Like the land of the dead has doubled over to cough up the living.

I turn to face the voice. In the single bed, a girl is wrapped in a pale yellow blanket, the folds of it draped over her left shoulder. It's not her thin face I recognize first, her eyes older than I've ever seen them. It's the pattern of her scarf, long hidden under smears of dust.

The roses.

"Huppy!" I bound over to her, and Zahra shouts something behind me that isn't words. I toss myself down on the bed, pressing my cheek to Huda's scarf. I breathe in, and then I know where the purple scent of flowers came from. Huda is the reason I smelled roses.

Huda bends her arm around me, her left shoulder still under the blanket. She holds me to her chest.

"Hamdulillah," Mama says—thanks be to God. She hushes Zahra's questions. "We heard you were dead while we were still in the hospital. Ya Allah, when they rocketed the aid ferry, I thought—" Mama rises and sits at the end of the bed. The breeze lifts the sea through the window, twisting the curtains.

"Your mama and sister were in danger," Uncle Ma'mun says. "They crossed the desert with smugglers."

"By the time the surgery was over and we left the hospital," Mama says, "Algeria had closed its border with Libya. There was a man, a truck with other families. We were stopped at the Tunisian border and turned back. The second time, we crossed in the desert. We made it. Many didn't. They put sand in the food. To make us drink less water, they mixed it with gasoline." Mama rests her mouth in her hand and looks away. "But none of that matters now."

Uncle Ma'mun pulls a chair up to the bed. "I waited for months," he says, "hoping you would come."

"Your Uncle Ma'mun helps people who have nothing," Mama says. "He helps them find places to live, makes sure they have food for their families and help with their papers. But some people get angry. They think we are dangerous. We scare them."

"I didn't want to scare them," I say. I bury my face in Huda's hijab. "I just wanted to come home."

Uncle Ma'mun bows his head, his hands clasped in his lap. When he looks up, his eyes are round and wet as a pony's, the laugh still in them somewhere deep. He says, "You are."

I turn to hug Huda again and pull the blanket off her shoulder. But her left arm isn't there. Her arm is gone below her bicep, the end of it patched with bandages, her sleeve folded neatly up. If I concentrate, I can imagine the slender curve of her elbow and her smooth, thin-fingered hand.

Huda says, "The infection was moving toward my heart." She shifts in bed. Her biceps flexes to compensate under her folded sleeve. "They said it would be less painful, less dangerous. So many doctors had fled or been killed."

"The hospital was overwhelmed," Mama says, reaching for me. "Sometimes we didn't have electricity or medicine."

I push myself up on my knees, and even the sheets sting the blisters on my shins with their friction. I touch my fingers to the bone above Huda's bandages. Underneath are scars like mine, worse than mine. To lose the metal inside her, she had to give up a part of herself.

"The metal is gone," I say to her. "Isn't it?"

Huda pulls my head to her collarbone with her right arm, and her left shoulder curves around me as though the rest of her arm were still there.

"Things can't be like they were," she says, "but I'm still your Huppy."

Holding on to Huda, I can feel the spot where her ribs meet each other, near her heart. Her blood and mine thrum in the backs of our necks and our fingertips.

"I would have given mine up," I say. "I wouldn't mind having more scars, if you could've had less."

Huda strokes the knob of bone where my neck bends into my shoulders. "There are worse things in life than scars," she says. She lays her palm over the baby hairs matted to my skull. "Just because

I had to lose the bones the shrapnel cracked," she says, "doesn't mean that all my bones are broken."

My belly aches with blood, all the way up to my heart. "Mine either."

Beyond the peninsula, the wind jumps into the strait. It slips away past stucco and pine forest, tugging the salt from my words.

The Last Empty Space

*

The next day, Rawiya and Khaldun left Rawiya's mother's house in Benzú to check on al-Idrisi and tell him the good news. They returned along the coastal road and entered the city, arriving at his estate by midday.

They found him waiting for them in the garden. The fountain had been restored to its bubbling and mumbling, the water splashing on the ferns around the tiled basin.

They walked the grounds of the estate, stopping every so often so that al-Idrisi could catch his breath.

"We had wonderful adventures, didn't we?" al-Idrisi said. "We saw fantastical sights, things I had read about but never seen. Things I had never dreamed of seeing."

"We found treasures beyond imagining," Rawiya said. "We mapped the world, survived a war, and banished the tyranny of the roc from ash-Sham and the shores of the Maghreb for generations to come."

"From what the poets say," Khaldun said, "the death of the roc, the greatest of the eagles, was foretold hundreds of years ago. He has vanished from the earth now, leaving only the white eagles in his wake."

"The legend is complete," al-Idrisi said, "and at its end."

"What legend?" Rawiya asked.

"Vega. The star called Waqi, the great falling eagle." Al-Idrisi motioned at the blue heavens where the stars turned, invisible above them. "The great eagle fell. The legend of Vega is complete." He pulled his astrolabe from the pocket of his robe. "This is all that remains of the roc," he said, pointing to the shape of a bird on the rete, the symbol that indicated Vega. "But we who know the truth will pass on the legend to the generations after us, telling the story of his might and his power and his tyranny, and also the story of how tyranny met its end."

They came again to the fountain. Rawiya and Khaldun helped al-Idrisi sit at its edge. They looked out onto the white and yellow houses on the peninsula far below and, beyond that, the open palm of the sea.

"But what is the lesson?" Rawiya asked. "What is there to learn from all this—this brokenness, this chaos? We saw the wounded, magnificent world, its mountains, its rivers, its deserts. Is there any making sense of it?"

Al-Idrisi laughed and held the astrolabe out to Rawiya. The sun glinted off its engraved rete, the silver shifting like lace. Rawiya took it. Just as it had so many years ago, the fat disk warmed her hand.

"Must there be a lesson?" al-Idrisi said. "Perhaps the story simply goes on and on. Time rises and falls like an ever-breathing lung. The road comes and goes and suffering with it. But the generations of men, some kind and some cruel, go on and on beneath the stars."

* * *

SITT SHADID AGREES to walk us to the neck of the dock but no farther. She waves us on. "I will wait here, habibti," she tells me in Arabic, and settles into a bench under a palm tree. "Don't drag your feet. Your mama and uncle will have lunch ready before long."

Zahra, Huda, and I walk out onto the La Puntilla dock, past the red-roofed bunkers and the loose piles of steel beams and wire.

It's the second weekend of October, and the shearwater migration has begun. The air is full of brown and white feathers. They fill in the cracks between Ceuta's seven hills like the glue between the Pleiades' seven stars.

Somewhere on the hill near the harbor, Mama is in Uncle Ma'mun's kitchen painting maps again, and he is clearing out an upstairs bedroom for the two refugee women, Aisha and Fatima, who arrived early this morning. After kneeling in his midday prayers, Uncle Ma'mun will explain to them how to apply for asylum over cups of tea and bowls of lentils and burghul. The light will be coming through the curtains now, the late morning haze muffling the car horns.

I trot ahead past the old tire bumpers chained to the dock, out to the edge of the pier. Across the entrance to the harbor is the Alfau dock, reaching toward us like an arm.

I sit down at the edge of the dock, swinging my legs over the green water, and the sun glints off the pink ovals of my scars. Zahra and Huda sit down next to me. The sea moves like a living thing, scraping wood and concrete, a rainbow of voiceless mumbling.

"I wish Yusuf could see this," Zahra says, the salt tangling her curls.

I tap each of the wooden supports along the dock, one at a time. "I bet he asked you."

Zahra smiles and tucks a black curl behind her ear. "Mama said he asked her permission first. She told him it wasn't up to her."

"Are you going to marry him?" I ask. "After you finish school?"

Zahra looks out at the clouds, her hair brushing the soft scar on her jaw. "I think I already said yes inside," she says, "that first day in Ceuta, when I saw him coming down the hill." The words come out surprised, like they came from someone else's tongue.

Huda points with her right hand and says, "You can see the Spanish mainland from here."

Tarifa is a blue strip on the horizon, the ribs of low mountains.

How many miles of water are there between Europe and Africa? The green mirror of the sea twists my reflection with ripples. I think about how the water, like the earth, touches everything. A pebble dropped into the East River could make the Strait of Gibraltar ring with echoes.

I fidget with the green-and-purple half-stone in my pocket. Somewhere in the green, Abu Sayeed is still holding his flat little stone, the one he kept for his son. Did God ever speak to us through stones?

The concrete is warm beneath our thighs, the sun hot on our brown shoulders.

"Do you still have it?" Huda asks. "Mama's map of stories?"

"Sure," I say. "Of course I do."

Sailboats slice the water, tipped by the wind.

I swing my legs. "I wonder if all maps are stories."

"Or all stories are maps," Huda says.

I finger the half-stone in my pocket. "Maybe we're maps too. Our whole bodies."

Zahra leans back and stretches out her arms on the pier. "To what?"

I lean over the water, and my face appears. Ripples stretch my eyes and nose. By a trick of the light, I see Baba's face instead. "Ourselves?"

"Your wonderings are over my head." Zahra laughs and stretches. "Come on. Sitt Shadid is waiting."

"Coming." I pull the half-stone from my pocket. I don't listen for Baba's caramel and oak-brown voice. I open my hand and drop the stone into the sea. It sinks slow. It seems to pulse, like I had dropped in a heart.

We start back. A flock of shearwaters bursts over our heads toward the strait, the air humming with thousands of wings. Their white bellies pass over us, and for a second, all we hear are their joyful cries.

AT THE HOUSE, Zahra helps Mama dry her brushes. Rahila helps Umm Yusuf set out blue ceramic plates, and Yusuf and Sitt Shadid open the curtains to let the light in.

I pass through the kitchen on the way to my bedroom. Uncle Ma'mun is sitting at the table with Aisha and Fatima, scattered tufts of papers and half-full cups of sage tea between them. The women turn to smile at Huda and me. Aisha tucks two slender fingers into the handle of her peony-patterned teacup. A single button on Fatima's cardigan is mismatched, and I recognize the milk-white plastic of the unraveling button from Mama's blouse. Mama must have sewed it on for her this morning. Warmth fills up the little kitchen.

"Come and sit down," Uncle Ma'mun says. "Lunch is almost ready."

"We'll be right back." I twine my fingers into Huda's. "I want to show her something."

"Ya 'amo," Uncle Ma'mun calls out as we climb the stairs, laughing, "you are always running. Where are you going to in such a hurry?"

"Just a minute." I tug Huda to my room with me, pushing open my wooden door.

Up here, you can smell the sea and the pine forest. I take the burlap bag from its place in the corner and pull out the map, unrolling the canvas.

"See," I say to Huda. "I still have it. I would've hung it up, but I can't reach."

Huda smiles. The dust never really washed out of her hijab. The roses are faded, one of those things that have been loved into disrepair.

She says, "I can."

We choose an empty spot on the wall, above my bed. Huda holds the top left corner with her right hand while I tack the map in place. We hang it together, smoothing out the wrinkled corners.

I lie down on the bed with my legs up the wall, and Huda sits next to me. I stare at my knees that aren't so knobby anymore, the way my bony toes are long enough now to reach the bottom of the map.

Canvas peeks through at the corner from under a fleck of paint. The map's fabric is the same pink-gray color as Huda's roses.

That blank spot draws my eye again, the only one Mama didn't fill with color or words.

Huda follows my eye. She asks me, "What do you see?"

"What's missing." I grab a pen and uncap it. A breeze flutters the corners of the map, and white shearwater feathers balance themselves on the sill like tiny clouds. My pen hovers over the last empty space. Steadying my hand, I fill it in.

Author's Note

*

This book is a work of fiction. The characters of al-Idrisi, King Roger, and King William are based on real people—Caliph az-Zafir, mentioned briefly, was an actual Fatimid caliph in Cairo from 1149 to 1154 as well—but all the other characters are fictional, including all the characters in the contemporary timeline. Any resemblance to real people, living or dead, is purely coincidental. None of the characters or situations in the contemporary timeline are based on the lives or experiences of myself or my family.

Rawiya is a figment of my imagination, one of the windows through which I hoped to show readers an extraordinary historical time period. Al-Idrisi was a scholar and mapmaker, born in Ceuta around 1099, who collaborated with the Norman King Roger II in Palermo to create, in 1154, what is known as the Tabula Rogeriana, the most accurate world map ever made to that date, as well as *al-Kitab ar-Rujari* (*The Book of Roger*) and the silver planisphere. It is unclear how much of al-Idrisi's knowledge of the world was gathered through firsthand accounts of his own travels, as much of the information contained in *al-Kitab ar-Rujari* was based on the accounts of other travelers and merchants passing through Palermo, but al-Idrisi himself did travel widely, including a trip to Anatolia (in modern-day Turkey) when he was a teenager. From my research, it is unclear whether al-Idrisi ever married or had any children, as details about his personal life are scant; allusions to his family life made in the text are imaginative speculation on my part.

Al-Idrisi's Tabula Rogeriana was, indeed, oriented with south at the top, as was common for Arab mapmakers at that time. Al-Idrisi's maps were considered the most accurate in the world for many years. For three centuries, they were copied without alteration. *Al-Kitab ar-Rujari* or *Kitab Nuzhat al-Mushtaq fi Ikhtiraq al-Afaq* (typically loosely translated from the Arabic as *The Book of Pleasant Journeys into Faraway Lands*) has been translated in full into Latin and French, and excerpts have been translated into several other languages. The manuscript survives to this day in libraries across the world, though copies are rare and hard to come by. A digital copy of a 1592 Arabic manuscript without maps is available via the Yale University Library's Digital Collections (http://findit.library .yale.edu/catalog/digcoll:177851).

I am grateful to have had the opportunity to study analyses and excerpts of the *Kitab Nuzhat al-Mushtaq* translated into Spanish and Catalán via the work of Juan Piqueras Haba and Ghaleb Fansa ("Cartografía Islámica de Sharq Al-Andalus. Siglos X–XII. Al-Idrisi y Los Precursores," *Cuadernos de Geografía* 86, 2009, pp. 137–64; "Geografia dels països catalans segons el llibre de Roger d'Al-Sarif Al-Idrisi," *Cuadernos de Geografía* 87, 2010, pp. 65–88) as well as in descriptions included in *Palestine under the Moslems*, translated by Guy Le Strange, originally published in 1890 by A. P. Watt, London, and in *The History of Cartography: Volume Two, Book One*, cited below. After doing research in Ceuta, I also had the chance to study scholarly work on al-Idrisi's life, translations of excerpts of *Kitab Nuzhat al-Mushtaq* into Spanish, and descriptions of medieval Andalucía compiled by the Instituto de Estudios Ceutíes in a book entitled *El Mundo del Geógrafo Ceutí al Idrisi* (Ceuta, Spain, 2011). In addition, I am grateful to have had the opportunity to study Konrad Miller's 1927 restoration (and romanized transliteration) of al-Idrisi's Tabula Rogeriana, available from the Library of Congress

(Idrīsī and Konrad Miller, *Weltkarte des Idrisi vom Jahr 1154 n. Ch.*, *Charta Rogeriana*, Stuttgart: Konrad Miller, 1928. Retrieved from the Library of Congress, https://www.loc.gov/item/2007626789/). Miller's *Mappae Arabicae* (*Mappae Arabicae: Arabische Welt- und Länderkarten*, I.–III. Band, Stuttgart: 1926 & 1927) also proved very helpful in interpreting al-Idrisi's Tabula Rogeriana.

As for the silver planisphere, no one really knows what happened to it; some say it was melted down or disappeared after the coup against King William in 1160, which took place six years after King Roger's death. The novel's speculation as to its possible survival and whereabouts, including the hiding place on the island of Ustica, are just that, I'm afraid—purely imaginative speculation.

In telling the tale of Rawiya and al-Idrisi, I did my best to keep geographical locations and the years of historical events as accurate as possible, with as few deviations as necessary to accommodate the plot. Nur ad-Din did, in fact, take possession of Damascus in 1154 when his help was requested to repel the Crusader siege of Damascus during the Second Crusade, though the mythical roc, of course, had nothing to do with this. In actuality, the roc comes from *The Thousand and One Nights*, specifically the tale of Sinbad the Sailor, in which the giant serpents also make an appearance. The roc's conquest of Bilad ash-Sham and subsequent defeat are purely symbolic inventions of my own imagination, as is the legend of the roc's eye stone (though aspects of the stone itself have their basis in a real gemstone). This "legend" referred to in the text is loosely based on the tale of the fisherman and the jinni from *The Thousand and One Nights*. The inclusion of these elements of the *Thousand and One Nights* serve to anchor the tale of Rawiya and al-Idrisi firmly in the storytelling traditions of the Arab and Islamic world. I am sorry to report that there is no legend that relates the roc to the star Vega; this was a connection of my own making, owing to the old Arabic name for the star: an-Nasr al-Waqi, the Falling Eagle.

Early Arab and Islamic astronomy is a particular area of interest of mine, and I enjoyed researching it immensely. All the names and histories of the constellations mentioned are based in fact. For further reading, I highly suggest the following sources: "Bedouin Star-Lore in Sinai and the Negev," by Clinton Bailey, *Bulletin of the School of Oriental and African Studies*, University of London, vol. 37, no. 3 (1974), pp. 580–96 (http://www.jstor.org/stable/613801); *The History of Cartography, Volume Two, Book One: Cartography in the Traditional Islamic and South Asian Societies*, edited by J. B. Harley and David Woodward, University of Chicago Press (pdfs available here: http://www.press.uchicago.edu/books/HOC/HOC_V2_B1 /Volume2_Book1.html); and *An Eleventh-Century Egyptian Guide to the Universe: The Book of Curiosities*, edited with an annotated translation by Yossef Rapoport and Emilie Savage-Smith, Boston, MA: Brill, 2014. For further reading on the culinary traditions of the medieval Middle East and North Africa (including recipes), I suggest *Medieval Cuisine of the Islamic World: A Concise History with 174 Recipes*, California Studies in Food and Culture no. 18, by Lilia Zaouali and translated by M. B. DeBevoise, with a foreword by Charles Perry (Oakland, CA: University of California Press, 2007). The research of ArchAtlas at the Department of Archaeology at the University of Sheffield proved very helpful in making the locations of khans and caravanserais in twelfth-century Syria as historically accurate as possible (Cinzia Tavernari, "The CIERA program and activities: focus on the roads and wayside caravanserais in medieval Syria," ArchAtlas, Version 4.1, 2009, http://www.archatlas.org /workshop09/works09-tavernari.php).

The Imazighen (singular: Amazigh) are an ethnic group indigenous to North Africa. The term *Imazighen* encompasses several different communities, all of which have been marginalized to varying degrees by both Arabization and European colonialism, and their history is only alluded to in this novel. I strongly suggest that the reader seek out literature written by Amazigh authors who detail their own experiences in their own words. As a starting point, I recommend several sources, including *We Are Imazighen: The Development of Algerian Berber Identity in Twentieth-Century Literature and Culture* by Fazia Aïtel (Gainesville, FL: University Press of Florida, 2014) and the works of Assia Djebar, particularly *Fantasia: An Algerian Cavalcade*, translated by Dorothy S. Blair (Portsmouth, NH: Heinemann, 1993).

I need not remind the reader that the war in Syria and the Syrian refugee crisis are both very real and that refugees face horrific violence and injustice in their attempts to find safety. Refugee women are at particular risk of violence, especially sexual violence. A March 2017 study by Save the Children found that more than 70 percent of Syrian children showed signs of toxic stress or post–traumatic stress disorder after their country had been wracked with war for nearly six years (A. McDonald, M. Buswell, S. Khush, M. Brophy, "Invisible Wounds: The Impact of Six Years of War on Syria's Children"). Over the course of this conflict, childhoods have been cut short; dreams and promising careers have been shattered; families have been broken. I hope that this book serves as a starting point for education and empathy and that readers will seek out additional resources, particularly those written by Syrians in their own words.

Acknowledgments

*

This book would not exist were it not for the help of a great many people, to each of whom it would be impossible for me to express the full depth of my gratitude:

Trish Todd, this book is so much stronger because of you, and I am honored to have you as my editor. Thank you for polishing the salt from the raw stone and making this book the best it could be. To the whole incredible team at Simon & Schuster, particularly Susan Moldow, David Falk, Tara Parsons, Cherlynne Li, Kaitlin Olson, Kelsey Manning, Martha Schwartz, and Peg Haller, thank you for your passion for this book and for shepherding it into the world. Thank you for making my mission your mission.

Michelle Brower, my literary agent extraordinaire: Thank you for your insight and for seeing what this book was trying to be from the beginning. Thank you for tirelessly championing my work, for believing in me, and for making my dreams come true. Thank you also to Chelsey Heller, Esmond Harmsworth, the whole team at Aevitas Creative Management, and all my international co-agents for working to bring this book to readers around the world. I am deeply grateful for your efforts.

Beth Phelan, thank you for creating the #DVPit Twitter pitching contest and for constantly uplifting the voices of marginalized writers. I am also endlessly grateful to Amy Rosenbaum for finding me via

#DVPit and referring me to Michelle, an act of generosity I will never forget. Thank you to my friends in the #DVSquad for sharing in this journey. I can't wait to hold all your books in my hands.

To my Voices of Our Nations Arts Foundation (VONA) family: Tina Zafreen Alam, Cinelle Barnes, Arla Shephard Bull, Jai Dulani, Sarah González, John Hyunwook Joo, Devi S. Laskar, Soniya Munshi, and Nour Naas. Thank you for supporting me, uplifting me, and for holding space for me and for my words. Thank you to Tina, Arla, John, and Devi for reading sections of this book and providing invaluable feedback. Thank you, Elmaz Abinader, for your encouragement, for the absolutely vital work that you do, and for bringing our Political Content Workshop family together. Love you, Poetical Content!

Thank you to the Radius of Arab American Writers (RAWI), especially Randa Jarrar, Hayan Charara, Susan Muaddi Darraj, and the staff of *Mizna*, particularly Lana Barkawi, for encouraging me when I was an emerging writer, for believing in my work, and for welcoming me into a community of writers where I know that I belong.

Thank you to the libraries that have been places of inspiration and refuge throughout my life. Thank you to the teachers who encouraged me when I was a young, aspiring writer. Thank you to the editors who published my short stories and championed my work along the way.

Thank you to my grandmother Zeynab. Thank you to my family and friends for loving, supporting, and believing in me. You mean more to me than I can say, no matter how many miles there are between us. May we celebrate peace together one day, insha'Allah.

About the Author

*

Zeyn Joukhadar is a Syrian American author and a member of the Radius of Arab American Writers (RAWI) and of American Mensa. Joukhadar's writing has appeared in *Salon*, the *Paris Review*, the *Kenyon Review*, the *Saturday Evening Post*, and elsewhere and has been nominated for a Pushcart Prize and the Best of the Net. Joukhadar is a 2017–2020 Montalvo Arts Center Lucas Artists Program Literary Arts Fellow and a 2019 artist in residence at the Arab American National Museum.

The
Map *of* Salt
and Stars

———— ✳ ————

Zeyn Joukhadar

Introduction

*

The Map of Salt and Stars is the story of Nour, a Syrian American girl reeling from the recent loss of her beloved Baba (father) to cancer. After returning to Syria before the war breaks out, Nour and her family must flee across the Middle East and North Africa in a desperate and dangerous search for safety. Nour's journey intertwines with the story of Rawiya and the legendary mapmaker al-Idrisi who made the same journey nine hundred years before in their quest to map the world. This rich, moving, compelling, and lyrical debut novel is the first to bring the headlines about the Syrian crisis to life, placing our current moment in the sweep of history.

Topics and Questions for Discussion

*

1. What can you surmise from the novel about Baba's connection to each of his daughters and how the girls come to depend on those bonds after the bombing in Syria?

2. How do the two different timelines influence the plot? Was this an effective way to tell the story? What demands does it place upon you, and what are its pleasures? Did it help you to feel closer to the characters? Why or why not?

3. What effect does Baba's death have on Noor's mother and her relationship with her daughters?

4. What effect does Abu Sayeed's arrival have on Nour and her family? Compare and contrast Abu Sayeed's relationship with Mama, Zahra, and Nour. Discuss the role of family and community in the lives of the characters. Provide examples of the different ways the author defines family in the novel.

5. How is *The Map of Salt and Stars* like others novels you have read about refugees, and how is it different? How much did you know about the Syrian refuge crisis before reading the novel? How does the novel challenge your perception of the Syrian refugee crisis?

6. How do the characters rely on their religion throughout the novel?

7. What meaning does the title of the novel hold for the characters? Why do you think the author chose this and what does it mean to you?

8. Child narrators in adult fiction are often used to question things that adults might take for granted. Did having Nour as the narrator for *The Map of Salt and Stars* change the way you viewed the events of the novel? Compare and contrast the benefits and disadvantages of having a young narrator.

9. Evaluate the importance of the constellations and how the stars help to advance the story in both timelines. Discuss the symbolism of birds.

10. What is the significance of the stone and why does Nour discard it?

11. Khaldun says, "The words of others can overwhelm and drown out your own. So, you see, you must keep careful track of the borders of your stories, where your voice ends and another's begins" (page 133). Discuss the power of stories and the importance of the stories to the characters. Provide examples of the characters protecting their voices. How do you stay true to yourself?

12. Nour says to Yusuf, "I thought you were like the other bad men" (page 223). Discuss the significance of Yusuf. Were you expecting a different outcome for his character? Explain your answers.

13. How do the characters react to the trauma of sexual violence? What are its lasting effects? Analyze the reasons Nour tells Yusuf and no one else about Huda's attack, and why Huda

chooses not to choose to disclose the attack immediately. What was your reaction to that scene?

14. Huda, Zahra, and Nour are very different. What makes them alike as sisters, and what sets them apart? How do they evolve over the course of the novel?

15. Compare and contrast the storylines of Rawiya and Nour. Discuss how Nour's superpower and Rawiya's being the roc slayer helped to save their families.

16. What is al-Idrisi's role in the story? Does knowing that this character is based on a real person affect the way you read the novel? What are some of the pleasures and drawbacks of reading historical novels? Discuss what might have happened to the planisphere "guarded forever, safe from selfish hands" (page 307).

Enhance Your Book Club

*

1. Are you a synesthete? Go to https://www.synesthesiatest.org/ to find out.

2. Create a map depicting places you traveled that had a major impact on your life when you were Nour's age. What did you learn from that time? How did you change after that experience?

3. Name your top five favorite books with a child narrator. What are the advantages and disadvantages of having a young narrator?

4. *The Map of Salt and Stars* for the most part is a very realistic coming-of-age story of a Syrian refugee, but there are several instances when the story reveals magical elements. Provide some examples of magical realism. How do these moments enhance the plot?

5. Visit the author's website, http://www.zeynjoukhadar.com, to learn more and to read his collection of short stories and essays.

A Conversation with
Zeyn Joukhadar

*

How do you think *The Map of Salt and Stars* can help readers to understand the Syrian refugee crisis?

I hope that this novel will serve as a starting point for readers to seek out accounts of the Syrian refugee crisis written by Syrians. It's important to me that readers understand that this novel was written by an author with a mostly Western perspective, an author born in the United States and not in Syria, an author who has not lived through the war in Syria or been a refugee. While I have more nuanced insight into the situation as a Syrian American than someone without a link to Syria, my insight is still incomplete; and because it is impossible for a writer to ever entirely discard their lens of nationality, race, gender, and other factors, it is impossible for my American upbringing not to leave traces on this novel. That said, I wrote this book primarily for people like me: people living in the Syrian diaspora, unable to return to their ancestral homeland, who are in deep pain and grieving the beloved people, places, and heritage that have been lost and that continue to be lost every day. What can we take with us? What can be salvaged? Where can we call home? These are the questions I primarily concerned myself with in writing this book. I do hope, however, that non-Syrian readers will also, by reading the fictional story of a single family, have increased empathy for refugees and feel more personally connected to and invested in the situation in Syria after reading this novel, and that this emotional, empathic connection will help spur readers to combat the antirefugee, anti-Arab, and Islamophobic rhetoric that is deeply wounding the communities of which I am a part.

Tell us more about the selection of the poems and the novel's structure. What inspired you to choose the poems that open each part? Who wrote the poems? Who is the "beloved" of the poems?
I wrote the poems. Each poem focuses on the themes and events of each of the book's five parts. Although I prefer to leave my work up to the reader's interpretation, I read the "beloved" of the poems in a couple of different ways. When I was writing the poems, I wrote them from the point of view of a character addressing Syria, but I think there are other valid interpretations, which I won't reveal here to keep from spoiling the ending.

Synesthesia alters perception, allowing people who have the condition to see the world differently. Which variation of synesthesia do you have and how does the condition influence your writing?
I have several types of synesthesia, including grapheme-color synesthesia (letters and numbers evoke colors); sound-color synesthesia; smell-color synesthesia; taste-color synesthesia; and a few other, rarer types. It's hard to say how it affects my writing because I will never know what it is like to not have it. For me, synesthesia makes everyday life an intensely colorful and sensory experience. Synesthesia links my senses together so that no experience is ever ordinary, and I suppose that shows in my writing.

You mention in the author's note that one of your areas of interest is early Arab and Islamic astronomy. Tell your readers more about that.
I've always been interested in the stars. The constellations and star names known in the West mostly come from Ptolemy's *Almagest* (which in turn drew on even earlier sources), but the Arabs named

these same stars and described their own constellations as well. Of these two traditions, I am far more interested in the star lore and knowledge of the natural world that my Arab ancestors possessed. I'm always interested in alternatives to Western traditional knowledge, and I think it's important for non-European peoples to draw on their own rich traditions—for example, the breadth and depth of scientific knowledge created during the Islamic Golden Age, which is rarely acknowledged in the West.

You worked as a biomedical research scientist before switching careers. What made you leave science to pursue a career in writing? What do you enjoy about both professions?
I was a writer long before I was a scientist—I started writing short novels at the age of nine—and I wrote throughout my education and my career as a scientist. My dream had always been to be a novelist. But I think my interest in science and my interest in writing stem from the same place, which is a desire to know why the world is the way it is. Scientific inquiry offers one set of explanations, and writing, by examining the emotional reality of the human condition, offers another.

One of your many interests is learning new languages. How many languages do you speak? Which is your favorite?
In addition to my native English, I'm proficient in Spanish and German, and I speak (and read) some Arabic as well. I taught myself Latin in high school, which has been very helpful for my writing. I can understand a fair bit of French and Italian, too, which I learned during my vocal training in high school and college. (I'm a classically trained lyric soprano.)

What does the title *The Map of Salt and Stars* mean to you?
Salt symbolizes several related themes in the book, including grief and healing from it, not only in terms of the sea's salt but also the way that salt occurs as an imperfection in precious stones. For me, this

symbolizes life's traumas that, on the one hand, can be "polished" from us (healed) by the love of family, community, belonging—but also, on the other hand, the losses and pains of life that we have no choice but to endure. In its own way, grief and healing make us the precious stones that we are. We can't always see this, just as we can't always see the value of a raw gemstone when it comes out of the earth. This does not mean that suffering is inherently good or even necessary, but because we cannot avoid suffering and trauma, it's important to remember that our traumas do not make us unlovable. They do not make us irreparably damaged. They do not make us worthless. There is life after trauma, and it can absolutely be filled with love and wonder.

This lesson, dear reader, is for you.

You signed with an agent through a #DVpit referral. What was that experience like? What advice would you give new writers?
#DVPit was exhilarating, and I'm so grateful for the work that Beth Phelan does to organize #DVPit for maginalized writers. I think it's a space that's very necessary and opens doors for a lot of talented writers. Many of the other authors I've met as a result of #DVPit have become friends whose work I deeply respect.

The experience of pitching was surreal. I had never participated in a pitching event before, and the day went fast. I signed with my agent, Michelle Brower, through a referral from #DVPit-participating agent Amy Rosenbaum, and I knew immediately that Michelle and I were on the same page about our visions for what we wanted the book to be. Michelle is very insightful and absolutely helped to push *The Map of Salt and Stars* to be the best version of itself that it could be. I'm so grateful to have her in my corner.

As for advice for new writers: read a lot. Read everything. Don't put too much pressure on your first novel; give yourself permission to play, and write it for you. Write the book you want to read that only you can write. I'm a firm believer in writing for yourself first, and this is especially true while you're honing your craft. You don't have to blow anyone's mind with your first effort. You just have to finish it. Part of what makes you a writer is the fact that there will always be another project. Eventually, try to find other writers whose work you respect to read and critique your work. But whatever you do, make sure you don't write just what you think others want to read. It took me a long time to start writing about people like me: Arab Americans, people with interfaith families, people living in diaspora, people struggling with trauma or feeling like they didn't belong. But it was only once I started writing from those difficult places that my work began to come alive. Don't let anyone tell you that people like you are not worthy of being the heroes of your stories.

Why did you decide to make Nour the narrator of *The Map of Salt and Stars*? What are her strengths as narrator?
I think young or child narrators allow us to see the absurdity, terror, or joy in certain situations much more clearly because they don't try to rationalize the world the way that adults do. They observe things and can hold contradictions without trying to explain them away. That was a quality I wanted in the narrator of *The Map of Salt and Stars*; I wanted a narrator who would not flinch or look away from the pain inherent in the story, so that readers would not be able to look away either, but I also wanted a narrator who would find beauty and joy in unexpected places. I think Nour does that very well.

You are also an award-winning author of short stories. What is the difference between writing a short story and writing a novel?
The most challenging and rewarding thing for me about writing short stories is that because of their length, every single word has to be in just the right place and has to do a minimum of double duty—better yet, it has to advance the plot, build character, create tone, and convey theme at the same time. To waste a single sentence in a short story can unravel it. I think of both short stories and novels as engines; they just have to be different sizes, because they power

completely different story vehicles. A short story engine is delicate where a novel engine must be robust. I do love that because short stories don't have to sustain themselves over many pages, you can create a much more delicate story milieu that would be impossible to sustain over three to four hundred pages.

The intersection between short stories and novels, for me, is in the fact that a short story has the same pieces as a novel, just writ smaller: you can have a complete three-act structure in a short story, and you certainly need to have a character arc, but you can gesture at parts of these structures that would need to be more fully developed in a novel. For this reason, I like to write each of my novels as a short story first, a kind of thumbnail sketch or bird's-eye view where I can see the novel's structure as a whole and make sure it's working before I expand it. I talked about this at more length in an essay I wrote for *Bird's Thumb* in 2017.

Which authors have influenced your writing the most?
My earliest influences were mostly fantasy novels like Tolkien's *The Hobbit* and Tamora Pierce's Song of the Lioness quartet. As I got older my writing was also influenced by the magical realism of Gabriel García Márquez (*One Hundred Years of Solitude* is tied for my favorite book of all time) and Jorge Luis Borges. Some of my favorite contemporary authors include Helen Oyeyemi, Roxane Gay, Rabih Alameddine (*The Hakawati* and *The Angel of History* are tied for my other two favorite books), Randa Jarrar, and Celeste Ng.

What's next for you?
Without saying too much, I'm working on a second standalone novel that discusses Syrian immigration to the United States over the last century, Islamophobia and anti-Arab sentiment in post-9/11 America, and the particular mythology of New York City. Served up, of course, with a healthy dose of magical realism.

Turn the page for an exclusive look at
Zeyn Joukhadar's new novel,

THE
THIRTY
NAMES
OF
NIGHT

available Fall 2020 from Atria Books

ONE / ██████

TONIGHT, FIVE YEARS TO the day since I lost you, forty-eight white-throated sparrows fall from the sky. Tomorrow, the papers will count and photograph them, arrange them on black garbage bags and speculate on the causes of the blight. But for now, here on the roof of Teta's apartment building, the sheen of evening rain on the tar paper slicks the soles of my sneakers, and velvet arrows drop one by one from the autumn migration sweeping over Boerum Hill.

The sparrows thud onto the houses around me, old three- and four-story brownstones, generation homes with sculpted stoops, a handful recently bought from the families who have owned them for decades and gutted for resale. Nothing has stayed the way it was since you died, not even the way we grieve you. Downstairs in Teta's apartment, I've drawn the curtains, tucked Teta's glasses back into their drawer so that even if she wakes, she won't look down on this street dashed with dying birds. Five years ago, when your absence stitched her mouth shut for weeks, I hid your collection of feathers, hid the preserved shells of robin's eggs, hid the specimens of bone. Each egg was its own shade of blue; I slipped them into a shoebox under my bed. When you were alive, the warmth of each shell held the thrill of possibility. I first learned to mix paint by matching the smooth turquoise of a heron's egg: first aqua, then celadon, then cooling the warmth of cadmium yellow with phthalo blue. When you died, Teta quoted Attar: *The self has passed away in the beloved.* Tonight, the sparrows' feathers are brushstrokes on the dark. This evening is its own witness, the birds' throats stars on the canvas of the night. They clap into cars and crash through skylights, thunk into steel trash cans with the lids off, slice through the branches of boxed-in gingkoes. Gravity snaps shut their wings. The evening's fog smears the city to blinding. Migrating birds, you used to say, the city's light can kill.

A sparrow's beak strikes my hand and gashes my palm. I clutch the wound, the meat of my thumb dark with my own blood. You taught me a long time ago to identify the species by the yellow patches around their eyes, their black whiskers, their white throats, and their ivory crowns. You were the one who taught me to imitate their calls—*Sam Peabody, Peabody, Peabody.* In your career as an ornithologist, you taught me two dozen East Coast birdcalls, things I thought you'd always be here to teach me. I reach down to scoop the sparrow from the rooftop with my bloodied hands. He weighs almost nothing. There is so much of you—and, therefore, of myself—that I will never know.

Tomorrow, when the ghost of you enters my window with the smell of rain, I will tell you how, since you died, the birds have never left me. The sparrows are the most recent of a long chain of moments into which the birds, like you, have intruded: the red-tailed hawks perched on the fire escape above Sahadi's awning, or the female barred owl that alights on Borough Hall when I emerge from the subway. For all my prayers the night you died, the divine was nowhere to be found. The forty-eight white-throated sparrows that plummet from the sky are my only companions in grief tonight, the omen that keeps me from leaning out into the air.

My gynecologist is using purple gloves again. They are the only color in this all-white examination room. I set my feet in the stirrups with my knees together, only separating my thighs when he taps my foot. The paper gown crinkles. The white noise of my blood thrums in my ears. There is no rainbow-colored ceiling tile with dolphins here like the one at Teta's dentist. Last spring, I got my teeth cleaned while she had a root canal just so I could hold her hand.

I clench and unclench my sweaty fingers. The speculum is a rude column of ice. I focus on a pinprick of iodine staining the ceiling tile and force myself to imagine how it got there. I will myself out of my body the way I used to do when I was bleeding. The summer after you died, my periods were the heaviest they'd ever been. I spent the rainless evenings standing in fields at sunset, waiting to be raptured into the green flash of twilight, wishing there were another way to exist in the world than to be bodied. It had been less than a year since I'd closed my hand around those eggs in the nest, and still I wanted nothing more than to disappear into the weightless womb waiting inside each round, perfect eggshell, that place of possibility where a soul could hum unburdened and unbound. The man between my legs checks for the string of my IUD, and I am flooded with the urge to return my body and slip myself into a different softness: the stems of orchids, maybe; the line of sap running up the trunk of a maple; the fist of a fox's heart.

Instead I am jolted back to my body by the shiver of lube running down the crack of my ass. He pulls off his gloves and tells me to get dressed. There are never enough tissues, so I use the paper gown and ball it up in the trash. My gyno returns just as I tug my T-shirt over the shapewear compressing my chest.

"Everything looks good," he says, sitting down at the computer. He adjusts the pens in the pocket of his lab coat, though none of the doctors in this place write on paper anymore. "I can't find any reason for your pain."

"But I've been spotting and cramping ever since I got this thing."

By the look on his face, he doesn't take this seriously. He hands me a pharmaceutical pamphlet on the IUD, the kind with women laughing on the glossy front, shopping or hiking or holding their boyfriends' hands. He urges me to wait a few more months until things stabilize, then asks me if I'm using backup protection. I say yes, though I haven't had sex in years. For some reason, my first crush pops into my mind, the white girl in my high school biology class who loved acoustic guitar music and coconut rum. It's been so long since I've allowed myself to want anyone or anything.

"I thought this thing was supposed to stop my period." I pick at a hole that's starting on the knee of my jeans. "And my chest is sore. Didn't know that was a side effect."

"Sure, breast tenderness can happen in the beginning." The gyno looks at me like I am a puzzle he's lost a piece to. "It might make your periods heavier, too, but that should settle down after a few cycles." He asks me about my moods, but I can tell bleeding, cramping, and sore breasts aren't going to be enough to convince him to take the thing out. In his mind, a woman should be used to these things. There is no way to explain the eggshell or the fox's heart. My insufficient, unnameable suffering is my own problem.

I hop off the table. I say, "It's probably just that time of year again."

He softens. You went to him before I did, and you still hang between us in the waiting room when I come for my appointments. He asks me if I'm back to painting, trying to make small talk, but I don't know how to answer.

"You need to get inspired. Get your mind off things." He suggests an exhibit at the Met on Impressionist painters. I try not to roll my eyes. He pats me on the shoulder as I leave. On my way out, the receptionist calls me *miss*.

The sun is low when I step outside. It will be angling red through the window when I arrive home, and Teta will be dozing in her armchair. I can't stand the thought of another summer sunset in that silent apartment, so I take the 6 uptown to the Met. Now that I'm taking care of Teta, their pay-what-you-wish policy for New York residents makes it one of the few museums I can still afford. Maybe a change of scenery would be good, I tell myself.

The grandness of the Great Hall, with its columns and its vaulted ceilings, makes me hate the undignified way my sneakers squeak on the polished stone. I wander into the Impressionist exhibit, which turns out to be more than just Impressionists. *Representations of the Body: From Impressionism to the Avant Garde* is essentially a study of nudes, a departure from the plein air landscapes typically associated with the Impressionists. I pause in front of Degas's toilettes, Cézanne's bathers, Renoir's nudes. The women's bodies are not overly posed or idealized; at the time, this was a provocation. I look for Mary Cassatt, for Eva Gonzalès, for Berthe Morisot, but I don't find them. Gauguin is here, though, and the plaques beside his paintings of brown-skinned Tahitian women make no mention of his dehumanizing gaze, nor of the pubescent girls he had sex with in Tahiti. Matisse, too, is here, with his 1927 Orientalist fantasy, *Odalisque with Gray Trousers*: "I paint odalisques in order to paint the nude. Otherwise, how is the nude to be painted without being artificial?" In that moment, my body and the bodies of all the women I know are on the wall as sexualized ciphers for the desires of white men. I don't know why I am here in this place where I should feel belonging but am, instead, an outsider. I'm grateful that the Met has little contemporary art. I know all the names, know who will be at the Venice Biennale this year and who was featured in the contemporary art magazines, but I can't imagine my name listed among them. I'm not the only one, of course. The last time I saw one of my male classmates from art school, he consoled me about my artist's block by telling me how few of the girls we studied with were painting anymore. It is one thing to have a body; it is another thing to struggle under the menacing weight of its meaning.

I stop to wash my hands on the way out. The museum's bathroom is decorated with a print of a white woman posed over a clawfoot tub, her belly and breasts perfect pink globes. This is not Impressionism. She turns to regard the viewer at such a severe angle that it's as though the artist has painted, instead of a woman, a porcelain bowl for holding pears.

By the time I get off the subway in Boerum Hill, it's the golden hour. There are no signs of last night's sparrows, just hot pavement and sweating brick. I make the left onto Hoyt from Atlantic and pass the Hoyt Street Garden and the peach stucco of the Iglesia del Cristo Vivo with its yellow sign. At the intersection with Pacific, I nod to the crossing guard in front of the Hopkins Center. I'm one building down from Teta's apartment when I spot the owl feather, white against the green ivy that snakes over the brick posts on either side of Teta's stoop. The tangled down at the base of its hollow shaft and its brown striping give the owl away. The feather is a fat, weightless thing, the tip oiled with soot, the down still warm from the leaves.

Brooklyn simmers in September, when the urine-and-soot stink of the subways sifts up through the sidewalk vents and Atlantic is noisy with restaurant-goers who don't know that hummus is Arabic for chickpeas. While I fumble with my key chain, a white family pushes a stroller down the sidewalk, and the toddler inside reaches for the Swedish ivy bursting from Mrs. King's window boxes. Lately I've been wondering how long Teta will be able to stay in this building. It's the same story in every borough these days: the weekends bring the expensive strollers and the tiny dogs, the couples who comment on how much safer the neighborhood has gotten. Rent goes up and up and up. The family-owned bodegas keep on closing, replaced by artisanal cupcake shops and overpriced organic grocery stores whose customers hurry past the homeless and the flowers laid on street corners for Black boys shot by the cops. Some people go their whole lives in New York shutting their eyes to the fact that this city was built for the people who took this land from the Lenape. Sometimes I wonder why you never spoke of this—maybe you thought I was too young to understand, or you were just desperate to eke out an existence here. Now I am old enough to understand that we live on land that remembers. I hear the voices when I touch the brick or pavement, catch fragments of words exchanged hundreds of years before the island of Mannahatta was paved. I sometimes think about the Arabs and other immigrants who came here a century before my own family, hoping they wouldn't be devoured by the bottomless hunger of the very forces that drove them from their homelands, hoping they could survive in this place that was not built for them.

Teta's been baking: the stairwell is perfumed with walnuts and rose water. Inside the apartment, a fresh pan of bitlawah steams on the counter. If I'm honest, no matter how much I long for the apartment I had in Jackson Heights before Teta's back pain got worse and she needed someone to take care of her, I'd miss the smell of her house if I left it. It's just the two of us now, fielding the occasional call from Reem up in Boston. I can't blame my sister for not wanting to be reminded of what we've lost; the gears of memory lock their teeth every time I remember.

I slip off my shoes by the door, allowing the purls of Teta's Persian carpet to separate my bare toes. Asmahan gets up from the living room couch and stretches, then shakes the sleep from the ruff of fur around her neck. It wasn't long before that horrible day that Asmahan came to us, but Teta and I never stopped calling her your cat.

"Better let the bitlawah sit, habibti," Teta calls to me from her favorite armchair without looking up, "it's hot. Get us a cup of coffee, eh?" The afternoon light catches on the white brow feathers of the scarred old barred owl that sits on the sill watching Teta every evening. Teta meets its gaze, but I pretend not to see.

Asmahan follows me into the kitchen. On my way, I pick up the half-empty plastic cups on the coffee table. Asmahan loves to drink from unattended water glasses, so Teta indulges her by leaving cups of water around the house. Asmahan knocks one over now and then—thus the plastic. The way Teta spoils that cat.

In the kitchen, I retrieve the electric bill and the unpaid rent notice I tucked in the top drawer, fold them, and stuff them in my pocket before Teta sees. I get out the tiny cups you brought with you from Syria when you and Teta came over to the States years ago. The painted blossoms look almost new. I don't know how Teta keeps them so pristine, how she makes sure they don't get dropped or chipped in the cabinet by the plates or the forty mismatched jars of spices we've got knocking around in there. We always make our own spice mixtures, just like the women in our family have been doing for generations. Teta's got everything labeled neatly in Arabic, so those were the first few words I learned how to read. She has her own chai mixes, her own baharat, her own fresh za'atar. She makes them from memory, never measuring anything out, just estimating by the handful or the scoop or the pinch. The mothers and grandmothers of the other Arab kids I knew in school never wrote a recipe down, either; it was something you learned by heart. I'm sure Teta thought you would be around to teach me when I got older. Instead she had to teach me herself.

I fill the long-handled coffeepot with water and add the ground coffee, sugar, fresh-crushed cardamom. Out the window, impending rain hangs like dusk. Asmahan trots over to the kitchen table and hops up. Someone's staring at me from one of the chairs. I don't have to turn to know who it is.

"It's okay, Mom," I say without turning my head. "You don't have to get up."

But you do, and I know you're coming over to me even though I can't hear your footsteps. When I turn, you are gazing out the window with your hands on the countertop. You're always smiling, smiling at everything like there's still too much world to be experienced. I let the ring of electric coolness that surrounds you raise the black hairs on my arms, wishing, as I do every time, for some sign that you are real: a touch, a sound, a shadow. Instead the scent of fresh thyme fills my mouth as though you're holding a clipping under my nose, and I want to cry. You turn your head and smile at me. I smile back in the tired way the living have of appeasing the dead. How are you supposed to smile at a ghost without feeling lonely?

The coffee froths up, and you wait while I pour off the froth into our cups. You reach down and offer your hand for Asmahan to sniff. I almost put out three cups instead of two.

"You've been around more often," I say, turning my face as though I expect the scent of thyme to weaken. It doesn't. "Summer must be getting on."

You look at me—that stricken look. This is our agreement: we don't talk about the night of the fire, not even as its anniversary hurtles toward us like a planet and you continue your wordless visitations. Every year, the end of summer is the same. You'll come in the morning and sit in your favorite kitchen chair, the one you always used to sit in when Teta had us over for dinner. Teta can't cook like she used to, so I'll be in the kitchen, bringing her spices or making sure the onions don't burn. It's been four—damn, five years ago now—since we lost you, and nothing has tasted the same since. You'll watch me cook, watch me clean or read or make coffee for everyone but you. Sometimes you'll lean in close to my ear, and the earthen smell of thyme will offer up the names of things in Arabic to me, calling the coffee *ahweh* and the oil *zeit*, and in this strange and silent way we'll talk until it gets dark and you disappear.

The coffee froths up the second time. I shut off the gas range and pour it out into your tiny cups, gentle so as not to slosh them and disturb the grounds. I leave the coffeepot on the burner, avoiding our reflections in the window above the sink. You consider the long handle and the dark liquid in the pot like you want to join us.

"Yalla," I say, beckoning with my eyebrows toward the living room. It's no use: outside, dark has fallen. Teta coughs, and Asmahan trots toward her between my legs. When I look up, you're gone. In your place is that scent of fresh thyme, the kind you used to grow on the fire escape to make za'atar from memory.

I bring the coffee and a diamond of bitlawah to Teta in the living room, setting it on the table beside her armchair. She's fallen asleep with her favorite blanket folded on her lap, a lavender underscarf wrapped around her head like she always wears in the house, even though we don't get visitors anymore. She winces and opens her eyes, and I help her sit upright in her chair, arranging the pillows behind the small of her back and her shawl around her shoulders. It's been a few years since her multiple myeloma went into remission, but she never regained the bone density she lost, and her back is a knot of constant pain.

"Keef halik, Teta?"

"Alhamdulillah." She squeezes my hand. "Sit, sit. I never see you sleep anymore. Where you go all night?"

I kiss her papery forehead. "Let me get the heating pad."

When I come back, Teta's nodded off again with the coffee in her hand. I set it on the table, but my hand slips trying not to wake her, and it spills on my jeans. The cup clatters back onto its dish.

"Storm of the storms!" Teta exclaims while I curse under my breath and wipe myself with a napkin. She's been calling me that ever since I broke one of her teacups as a kid. She must have heard it on the news at some point, *storm of storms*, maybe. Somehow it journeyed through Arabic and was resurrected as *storm of the storms*, and now my clumsiness has its own nickname. Teta means it lovingly, but my face burns. I inspect the cup for chips.

When I slide the heating pad behind her, Teta furrows her brow at me. I bend forward, a force of habit, and hope my loose tee hides the fact that I'm using the shapewear she gave me to flatten my chest, rather than smooth the belly and hips Teta thinks I'm self-conscious of. I take a breath, and the cloth pulls across my ribs. This, too, is a border I am transgressing. Last week, I slashed the polyester at the rib cage to flatten the passengers on my chest that hide the surface of me. I have not told Teta this. I wouldn't know where to begin.

"Hope I didn't wake you banging around in the kitchen," I say before she can question me again. I sit down across from her on the sofa, a gorgeous old Damascene thing with a wooden frame and rolled arm pillows whose damask patterns have long since faded into gold and burgundy splotches, an heirloom from the bilad.

Teta holds my eyes for half a second before glancing away out the window. She laughs, shifting her back against the heating pad. "I sleep heavy these days."

There's no way she didn't hear me talking to you, but this is the response I expect. Though we both see you, we never admit it. You are first on the list of things we don't talk about, questions we don't ask, ghosts we don't count. I've never told her about the others, but I know she's seen you.

The envelopes in my pocket crinkle when I cross my ankle over my knee. This is the second thing we do not speak of: money. I'm Teta's only caretaker now, the one who pays the bills and the rent, and though Teta often tries to write out checks for birthdays or for food shopping, both our savings are dwindling. It's an ugly thing, but your social security only goes so far for two people in the city. Teta and I have reversed roles now; when you and my father were still together, she changed my diapers and babysat me until you both came home from work. She cooked meals for us, took me to the playground, quit her odd jobs when the family needed her. Now, long after your divorce, after your death, after my father has stopped even feigning promises of help, I've done the same. Though we both thank God for the Medicare that covers the bulk of Teta's medical bills, we are still paying off the cost of chemo and radiation a year later. I scold myself for it, but I've begun to hope Reem will start helping out now that she's finally taken a corporate job, though I know Teta's pride would never allow her to accept Reem's money. Here in this city whose lifeblood is the dollar, our solution to its weight is silence. It's not that Teta doesn't think about money—that's a privilege our family will never know—but to discuss her anxieties with me would be 'ayb. It would be a mark of shame; she'd feel like she'd failed me. The children and grandchildren of "real Americans," the ones who made it, shouldn't need to fear poverty. But Teta has found walls in this country that she never could have imagined.

I drain my demitasse and roll the warm ceramic between my hands. I'm sitting in that way you used to correct me for, legs spread like a boy, elbows on my knees, leaning forward so my hair drops in my eyes. I clear my throat and try to draw myself up, mussing my hair out of my face, but the movements are wrong. They are always wrong: my elephant feet, my way of closing cabinets with a bang, my bad posture. Do you see? I've memorized even your comments that used to drive me crazy.

"Mom would've been fifty-five this year." I glance up to meet Teta's eyes. "Wouldn't she?"

Teta sets the half-empty cup of coffee on the side table and folds her thick arms over the blanket in her lap. She shifts her weight forward and then back, rivulets of pain cabling her face until she settles into the heating pad. "It was beautiful, the day, until the rain."

The cup in my hands yields its heat to my palms. "Beautiful."

"When I was young," Teta says, and a smile sneaks onto her face, "we used to stay inside and play tawleh when came the rain. My father, Allah yarhamu, when he was alive, all the men in our town used to come to our family café to smoke arghile and talk politics. Immi kept the coffee hot all day. When it rained the men start to come, until we had the place full."

I want to ask her how my great-grandfather died, but it is one of the stories Teta has never told me, one of the many she keeps in her locked trunk of memories. His death, too, is on the list of things we don't discuss. "How old were you when he passed away?"

"Seventeen," she says, and then she drains her coffee and falls silent.

It's no use. The television drones from the corner, too low to be heard. "Tell me again about the bicycle woman." I look up from the sludge of coffee grounds at the bottom of my cup. "The one who flew."

Teta perks up in her chair. She's always preferred to tell fantastical stories rather than recount the past, and this is one of her favorites, a fail-safe. The first time she told it to me was after Jiddo died. In that first version, Teta spoke of a woman in her village in Syria who built a flying machine out of a bicycle and two sets of linen wings. She peddled hard to gain speed, then hit a ridge and became airborne for a quarter mile before crashing in a field outside the village. The story didn't bring me any comfort then, but it felt real, and I never quite believed the version she told after that, the one where the woman on the bicycle escaped gravity, never to be seen again. As a kid, it was more comforting to imagine this woman ending up somewhere warm and colorful, like San Francisco or Miami, but it was too easy an ending. Teta never said where the story came from. I knew better than to ask.

"It was my friend saw her go up into the air," Teta says when she's finished recounting the story. She's told it so many times I could probably relate it by heart. "No one else in the village thought she could do it. Immi kept me home that day, but I heard every detail. We were all of us amazed." She ends with the same bewildered shake of her head and a reminder to believe in the un-believable.

"They called her Majnouna," she says, wagging her finger.

"I know, Teta. The crazy woman." I take our cups and pat her hand. She is cold, has always been that way, and her circulation has gotten worse these past few months. This, too, the myeloma took from her. We don't get much sun in this western-facing apartment, and the nights are starting to turn cool. I've told Teta a thousand times to turn the heat on at night to keep her blood flowing, but she knows how much it costs. In the winter, it will be worse.

I smile to keep Teta from reading all this on my face. "If Asmahan starts drinking our coffee, Majnouna will be the least of our worries."

After I get up, Teta clears her throat and calls out to my back, "Fifty-four." When I turn to her, she directs her eyes to her hands. "November," she says, "she would be fifty-four."